MIRRORED SWORD

MIRRORED SWORD

PART ONE

ALLAN HANDS

THE DANCE

Published in 2021 by

Ross McPherson

Copyright © 2021 Ross McPherson

ISBN (paperback) 978-0-6451982-2-5

ISBN (ebook) 978-0-6451982-1-8

Project Assistance by Jeannette Banks

Cover Design and Illustration by Patrick Knowles Design

Interior Layout by designforwriters.com

For Judith

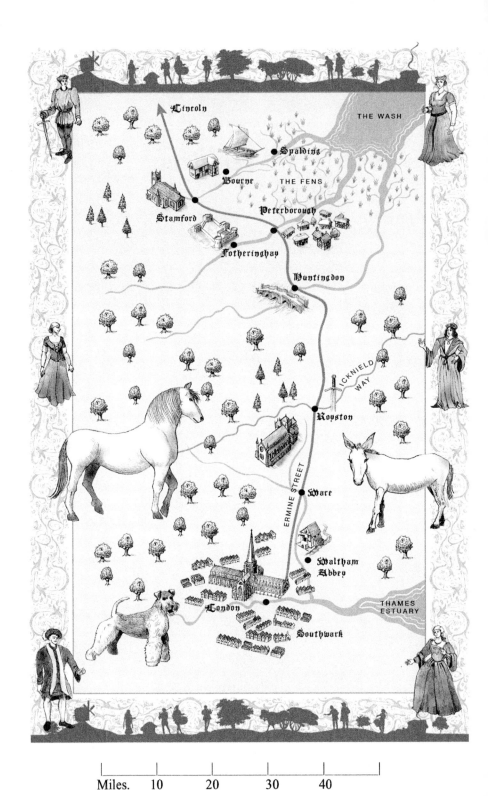

Lincoln

THE WASH

Spalding

Bourne

THE FENS

Stamford

Peterborough

Fotheringhay

Huntingdon

ICKNIELD WAY

Royston

ERMINE STREET

Ware

Waltham Abbey

London

THAMES ESTUARY

Southwark

Miles.   10   20   30   40

CONTENTS

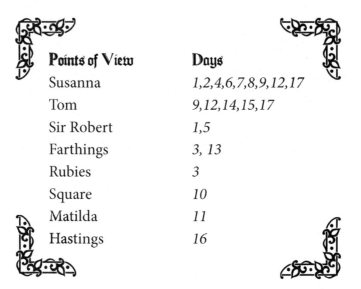

Points of View	Days
Susanna	*1,2,4,6,7,8,9,12,17*
Tom	*9,12,14,15,17*
Sir Robert	*1,5*
Farthings	*3, 13*
Rubies	*3*
Square	*10*
Matilda	*11*
Hastings	*16*

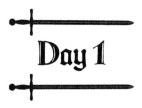

Day 1

Wednesday 7th of February 1470

Susanna Mandeville felt safe at her aunt's house in Bourne. Rebels preyed on travellers and isolated buildings but even a woman as beautiful as herself—a woman, moreover, devoted to the Yorkist king—could reasonably expect to get through the day unmolested, if she stayed in town, minding her own business.

Today was the best weather in months, a good chance for her to concentrate on the great business of her life, so she exchanged the smoke-blackened rafters and busy noise of the chimneyless house for the sunlight and quiet of the neighbouring orchard. Families used to live here once, but recurring bouts of plague had left it vacant and survivors had claimed it as their own. Aunt Marian's portion hosted plums, apples and pears, presently reduced to wintry trunks and leafless branches, bordered by the barren sticks of a hawthorn hedge.

"Try to keep still," Susanna urged the boy trembling before her.

"B-b-but I'm-m-m c-c-cold!"

He was about ten years old, wearing only a tunic. A greasy woollen coat lay at his feet and he was clutching a bundle of sticks.

"Think Summer," she urged him.

It was important to work quickly, while the paint was fresh on the bristles, and the world still fired her imagination with its mysterious impulses. High overhead, white clouds disappeared wisp by wisp, uncovering a background of wintry blue. Meanwhile the white background facing Susanna kept disappearing stroke by stroke of her quick brush, acquiring the first, dark suggestions of a tragic scene.

She had been planning something big throughout the winter, sketching with charcoal on wooden boards, drawing in ink on bleached paper, perforating a cardboard template for bagging with crushed charcoal, till at last the outline of her subject had emerged as delicate as a spider's web, ready for painting. The opportunity hadn't come cheap. The frame and backing were common limewood but the surface was the best plaster, painstakingly layered to produce a texture as smooth and glossy as silk. The whole thing weighed as much as a small child. Propped up on a chair, carried from the house with all her equipment, it weighed almost as much as an adult. The artist too needed a seat. Susanna made do with an upturned barrel, conveniently placed next to an apple tree, one of its gnarled branches stretched out like a helping hand. Her tray of paints hung balanced in the wooden fingers.

Now at last her masterpiece was coming to life in vivid colour, applied with quick dabs of her brush, and even the mundane task of breaking an egg thrilled her with immense possibilities, its yellow lustre begging to be dyed with the colours lurking in the phials set out alongside. She was painting a boy collecting firewood for a hillside altar: Isaac, the son of Abraham. God had commanded the father to sacrifice him in place of the usual lamb, but what was a test of faith for Abraham and for the Church was a test of skill for her. Only a great artist could bring everything to life with the right colours and the right brushwork, evoking the boy's sudden awareness that he, not one of the lambs, is destined for the knife. Moreover, there had to be something vital and brave in the way he looked out from the painting, or she could take no joy in his suffering. Here in the leafless orchard, where there was a powerful suggestion of tinder, and the imminent promise of Spring, it was above all the presence of a real boy that fired her inspiration.

He was Adam Galt the Younger. His parents and elder brother, another Adam, were common thieves and idlers, and no doubt he was destined to become one too. Aunt Marian had taken them under her wing out of charity, because the town was over-crowded with travellers stranded by the rebellion, and nobody else could find room for them. They should have felt grateful, but the parents had stubbornly refused to let Susanna use their son as her model, until finally she

2

had promised them a shilling. Something about him demanded to be painted: a look of innocent self-respect peering from a life already too big with betrayals.

His trembling with cold was a minor distraction. A worse distraction kept hanging about with a hairbrush, always looking for an opportunity to tame Susanna's wild locks, which the damned woman kept stroking in the abrupt manner of a cat licking a kitten.

"Put that stupid brush away," Susanna objected.

"You put yours away."

"Matilda, you are interrupting my work!"

"You are interrupting mine."

"And stop crowding me."

Matilda was supposed to stay out of sight but she kept edging forward for a better look at her own handiwork. The woman was obsessed with appearances, especially her own, highlighted now by a hooded cloak of scarlet, finished like felt, with an annoying lining that kept winking yellow. Susanna was interested in appearances too but only as a painter. The daughter of a wealthy merchant, she usually dressed like the daughter of a respectable peasant, and today was no exception, with a plain woollen cloak draped over an ankle-length smock.

"A woman should take pride in her looks," Matilda insisted for the thousandth time, though plain-faced herself and overly tall.

"You take enough in yours for both of us."

"Ask the boy what he thinks of your beauty, since he is so important to you. Ask him if he has ever seen a more beautiful creature. Ask!"

Susanna lowered her brush and gave Adam one of her appraising looks.

"When do I g-g-get our sh-shilling?" he asked.

"After the face is finished. Faces always come last."

"Faces come first!" Matilda objected. "Yet here you sit wasting yours on a mere boy."

Susanna rolled her eyes in search of patience. Her beauty was a topic that bored her. Her father had kept a letter by one of his would-be sons-in-law and often read it aloud just to embarrass her. It praised her mouth, "red and proud as a summer rose", her nose "petite as a wild lily half-hidden in snow", her eyes, "blue as the sky at mid-morning", her cheeks, "round as apples that ask to be bitten", and her hair, "the colour of copper." She was a picture. She was a picture without any effort at all. That was what bored her.

"Ouch!" she cried, her hair snagged in Matilda's brush. "By God, Matilda, do that once more and I will knock you down, you nuisance, I promise you that."

"You brought it on yourself," pleaded the maid. "The only men you are interested in are painted ones. A spinster in spite of your face and figure! Me twice a widow in spite of mine. Ha! Is it any wonder that I grow careless! Is it any wonder that your father has banished you here, as punishment for disobedience, your aunt so pious, we might as well be nuns in a convent!"

"My father has betrothed me to five men so far, and they have all regretted it," Susanna acknowledged while picking up a new brush. "If there is a sixth, I'll make him eat one of my paints—cinnabar, I think."

"Cinnab-b-b-bar?" asked Adam.

"Pleasing to the eye," she explained, "deadly to the taste."

"Then it is like you," Matilda opined. "For you are pleasing to the eye and deadly to anyone that dares say it."

"It is *my* beauty, and I will do with it as I please."

"It is more *mine* than yours. I see it all day, and you only ever see it in a mirror."

The maid thrust her brush at Susanna's hair again and again snagged it.

"That does it!" cried Susanna, jumping from the barrel with clenched fists.

Most people who had heard anything about Susanna Mandeville knew she was good with her fists, but few knew that she could paint, unless it was painting noses red. There were prostitutes in Southwark, where she had been raised, who swore she could hit harder than most men. Matilda had been with her for over a year but had yet to experience a thrashing. It was only luck that prevented her experiencing it now. A worse nuisance was approaching.

"Oh no," Susanna observed: "Watt."

Watt was one boy too many for Susanna at any time, let alone now. Aunt Marian had adopted him at birth. Nobody knew anything

4

about his real mother, except that she was fortunate to get free of him. Watt was always a disaster looking for somewhere to happen. A week ago, he had stolen some of Susanna's paints and had lost them in the vegetable patch. A goose had died the next day, undoubtedly poisoned. Boys like Watt were a good reason never to get married. Only five years old, he was now bringing along a dead rat, trailed on the end of a long string. Earlier this morning, he had been swinging it at Aunt Marian's enormous watchdog, Thunderbolt, currently tied up by the stable door for the boy's own protection. Thunderbolt could be vindictive.

"Matilda," said Susanna, thinking to kill two birds with one stone, "find something for Watt to do somewhere else, preferably before he gets here."

"I already gave him the string," Matilda reminded her.

"Adam, why don't you go play with Watt?" was Susanna's next option. "I have got all I need from you for now, and we can do the face later."

"I don't like Watt," Adam answered defiantly.

"I'll pay you another shilling," she pleaded.

"As if you are made of money!" scoffed Matilda.

Susanna's living allowance had been cancelled by her father—part of her punishment for rejecting another husband—and now she had no money left. Matilda had made good the loss with small sums from her own savings. It was a secret agreement between them: two pennies back for every penny lent, all to be settled by Christmas. Susanna already owed her four pounds, five shillings and fourpence, and that wasn't taking into account the two shillings now promised to Adam.

"Ding, ding, ding!" Watt gurgled on arrival.

He dangled his rat over a low branch of the apple tree, almost upsetting the paints balanced in the gnarled, wooden fingers. Susanna rested a steadying hand on them.

"Go away," she cautioned the boy, "before I lose my patience."

"Ding, ding, ding!" Watt insisted, making the rat rise and fall by tugging on the string.

"He thinks the tree is a bell," Matilda surmised, "and the rat is a clapper."

"Somebody is ringing a bell somewhere," Susanna realised.

A tinkling noise was coming from the hawthorn hedge. Strange noises were nothing unusual from that direction, the lane beyond the hedge being a shortcut for stranded travellers, passing between the abbey, where many of them had lodged, and the taverns and various alehouses where they drowned their sorrows. A gate in the hedge was resting on its side, the hinges having been stolen about a month ago—probably Adam's father—so it was prudent to keep a careful watch on that corner of the orchard, in case trouble entered unseen. Susanna soon spotted something unusual. A hawk half-hopped, half-fluttered along the hedge, a small leash and some bells attached to one leg. It was the kind of hawk that a baronet might wear on a fashionable glove, unleashing it to catch supper on the wing, or just for the pleasure of watching it fly. It had only to get its leash snagged in the hedge to add one more distraction to Susanna's already over-crowded morning. She tried to see the funny side of things.

"Oh look!" she said, pointing it out to everyone. "A jester has lost his cap-and-bells, and now it's looking for another head to put itself on. I wonder whose?"

"Yours!" said Matilda. "A beautiful spinster is a joke worthy of a jester."

"Jesser jesser jesser!" Watt squealed, always happy to discover a new word he could mispronounce.

"The word is *jester*," Susanna told him, before taking the string from his fingers and lifting the rat out of the branch. "A jester, Watt, is someone who amuses kings. Shall I tell you about kings? There are two. One is called Edward of York, who lives in a great big palace at Westminster—*he* is very handsome—and the other is a grubby lunatic called Henry of Lancaster. *He* lives in the Tower of London. Why are there two kings? A good question! It is because there are two kinds of people in England today: people who try to do great things, and other people, like maids and small boys, who try to stop them."

"When it comes to doing great things," Matilda objected, "twice a widow trumps a spinster by a hundred miles."

"Shall I tell you *my* idea of marriage?" Susanna scoffed. "It is when the heart is a mix of colours, all embracing a form that seems forever—but *I* get that from painting."

"A painting can't keep you warm at night," was Matilda's next tilt.

"Adam, I want to be alone with Matilda, so please take Watt and his rat somewhere else—or don't you want that extra shilling?"

She dropped the rat on the firewood that Adam was holding. Adam pondered it for a moment, wondering what to do. A shilling is a lot of money, so he soon dropped the firewood, put on his coat and dragged the rat off by the string, Watt following behind, laughing at the trouble he had caused.

"They will be tormenting Thunderbolt with it soon enough," Matilda surmised. "Men and boys are all the same creature, forever bent on their own destruction."

"Two of them married you," Susanna conceded.

"The first one fell under a waggon, and the second fell off a roof," Matilda affirmed. "But nobody is reckless or bold enough to marry you, Mistress. A man's eyes and other parts might wish he could, but then you speak, and his ears hate you."

It was for this impertinence that Susanna at last struck her across the face. She only did it with an open hand, not with the closed fist, but small mercies were wasted on Matilda. She burst into tears and ran back to the house. Susanna had never regretted striking anyone before and she wasn't inclined to regret it now. Still, she wished Matilda hadn't taken it so much like a cry-baby, because now she would have to say *sorry*. However, there was no hurry.

She sat on the barrel again and pondered her progress. Mostly it was still bare plaster, but already she could see great prospects of success. This painting was like a child. It was seeded in her life's experiences, and someday soon it would take on a life of its own, when many others would see it as she did, with a mixture of wonder and gratitude. Maybe then she would be given the respect she craved. Respect buys freedom. She could paint the way she wanted, if she were free, free to soar to the heights of human skill and imagination, gliding on the wings of confidence, and swooping to claim whatever prize caught her eye. Her present style of painting was technically accomplished but—it was important to be honest with oneself—a bit stiff. She had learned the English method, working step by step in tempera, with its studied air of unearthly beauty. She would much rather practise the new, more spontaneous style of painting in oils, because then she could capture the real world in its own colours, making dreams come true. Only the Dutch had mastered the new materials and routines, and she had often begged her father to let her live with his brother in Utrecht, a Dutch city where raw, English wool could be traded for expertly crafted wares. In Utrecht, she could learn the new style from some of its greatest exponents, and yes, she might even consent to marrying one of the city's burghers, provided it was someone with enough money and talent to indulge hers, and with too little skill in English to annoy her with a man's so-called *conversation*. Men could be so bovine! No Englishman had ever excited her marriage hopes, though maybe one had captured her heart.

The king of England.

Edward, the glorious fourth of that name, was the darling of the whole country, or that half that was Yorkist, and she had loved him, as many young women had done, from a distance, ever since he had burst on the public imagination almost ten years ago, the embodiment of male perfection. She had met him just once, when they had shared a brief dance during May Day celebrations in the Strand, two years ago. His impressive height, the gracefulness of his moves, his manly confidence, his pleasant and good-natured way with everyone—these she had often heard about, yet it had still come as a shock to find that it was all true. That dance had been the greatest moment of her life.

Her love for His Majesty was too pure and intense to be spoken of, and she had always kept it to herself, a jealously guarded secret. If her father ever came to know of it, he might think she was interested in men generally, and then he would never stop pushing fiancés at her. Others too must never know, or she could end up the butt of their jokes, especially back home in Southwark. Here in Bourne, she was her aunt's respected niece, but back home she was her father's torment and the terror of their neighbourhood: the Shrew of Southwark. Oh, how her enemies would laugh, if they thought she was just another mawkish female dreaming of impossibilities! And His Majesty *was* an impossibility, a man far beyond her reach. Or maybe not. There had been rumours lately that he was now the pampered and self-indulgent companion of liars, cheats and profligates. It was even rumoured that he had almost as many mistresses as he had female subjects. Surely this last accusation couldn't be true, or Susanna would have enjoyed more than just a dance with him. But if there was any truth in the gossip, there could only be one explanation: he had married the wrong woman. He was like a painting in the wrong hands.

Thinking about the king, and remembering the enchantment of their brief dance, Susanna began looking through her brushwork as if it no longer mattered. Painting isn't everything, is it? This was an unusual sensation. She resisted it and forced herself to dabble the brush in some fresh paint. The paint dried on the bristles before she could think what to do with it. She put the brush down. If only she could have that dance once more, that flirtation with majestic strength and grace, the touch of a man so winning, she could still feel his presence even here in a distant orchard two years later! So she got to her feet and closed her eyes, willing the moment back. It returned like music, a step to the left, a step to the right, forward and backward, in unison with the perfect man, to the accompaniment of pipes, tabors and bells.

Bells.

Opening her eyes, she observed the hawk, now perched in the apple tree just overhead. It looked sleek and muscular, eyes cold as winter, the prettiness of its bells refuted by the ugly talons. Its presence was disturbing but not frightening. It was wholly intent on a rat scurrying through the orchard: Watt's rat, following Adam at the end of a long string. The moment Adam stopped, the rat stopped too, crouching low in the grass. It was too much temptation for the predator. It pushed off the tree and glided like a bead on a string unerringly towards its target, arriving as quietly as death. Talons plunging into soft fur, it buried its prey and its own tinkling bells in the shadow of outstretched wings, excluding all hope of escape. There was something almost beautiful about its command of the moment, and Susanna was not alone admiring it. Watt emerged from behind a pear tree, gurgling for joy as he ran towards the hawk.

"Watt!" Susanna shouted, now running too.

The thing that happened next was so shocking, it was as if her portrait of Isaac had been lifted from the chair and smashed against the apple tree. She reached Watt too soon to protect him, the hawk

9

launching its outrage at her instead, buffeting her with the fury of a
storm, its claws branches enmeshed in her hair, sticks tearing at her
tresses, knives questing for the scalp, stabbing at her eyes, wings beating wildly, while Thunderbolt barked, somewhere women screamed
and, louder than anything else, bells, bells tolled like a town on fire,
until suddenly she seemed lifted off the ground, wrestling with the sky
itself, impossible to shake off. If *she* screamed, it was lost in the uproar,
thoughts reeling in the terrible grip of a moment that had latched onto
her with an artist's own passion for the ultimate sacrifice, even as she
fought against it, lest the pain bite deep and her beauty be marred
forever, never valued till now. This was no bird. This was a struggle
growing out of her, or turning into her, the whole world feathered in
human skin, strong of bone and mighty of muscle, legs greater than
hers, arms greater than hers, fingers as powerful as claws, all grabbing
at her as if they owned her or she owned them, slapping at her head,
flapping to get clear, yearning for freedom, for mastery of the future.
She could fly to Utrecht, if she were winged like this beast. She could
break all holds. She could do anything she wanted.

"Old still, Lahl Dingy!"

Was this the hawk talking? Was it herself emerging as someone or
something else? It was not her usual voice. It was not how they spoke
here in the Midlands or back home in London and Southwark. She
was thrust aside, meeting the ground with a jolt, springing her eyes
open. Something human towered over her, wings beating around
broad shoulders, almost an angel but for the green and brown garb,
coloured like the woods. The apparition had grey eyes, large with
concern, bright with curiosity, until stepping back, becoming suddenly
a grim-faced man with a hawk perched on a leather glove, the bird's
wintry gaze hooded, the bell silenced for now. He said nothing. There
was no explanation, no apology. He merely turned and headed for
the gap in the hawthorn hedge, where the gate used to be. Watt? He
was sitting nearby, crying his eyes out. Susanna grabbed him and held
him close, then she drew Adam in with a frantic wave and grabbed
hold of him too. Matilda arrived with a flurry of alarm, enfolding
them all in the yellow lining of her cloak. Aunt Marian burst from
the house.

"Ho Thunderbolt!" the good woman cried on reaching the stable, where a great tug released the knot from the dog's collar.

The animal was the size of a small horse, and bayed like the Devil, bounding after the stranger with six, seven, eight ferocious leaps, before suddenly stopping, taking up the dead rat and savagely shaking it from side to side. The man with the hawk sheathed a knife he had momentarily produced, then turned and vanished into the lane.

Sir Robert Welles staggered under the weight of the young deer draped across his shoulders, almost thankful not to have caught the large stag he had been hunting. Reaching the long table by the fireplace, he paused for a big breath, lowered his head then lifted the inert mass off his shoulders and down beside some waiting cups of wine, producing a *thud* that reverberated around the great hall. His companions cheered and piled a dozen or so lifeless birds next to his catch. It had been a good day's sport in the park attached to Grimsthorpe Castle, one of the bastions of the Welles clan, a few miles from Bourne. Its wooden palisades and stone towers dominated western Lincolnshire.

"Find me some Yorkists," Sir Robert rejoiced, "so I can add them to the pile!"

"They're getting to be as rare in these parts as unicorns," said his lieutenant, John Denby, adding a pheasant to the kill before accepting one of the cups the servants were handing out.

Sir Robert clapped him on the back. Denby was a man's man and the best company in the world. It was he who had felled the deer, thrusting it through with a lance when it had sprung between their startled horses, otherwise they might have returned to the palisades and towers with nothing to brag about.

"A toast to your father!" said Denby, personally handing Sir Robert a mighty chalice studded with gems, a family heirloom. "God bless Lord Welles!"

"God bless my father," Sir Robert concurred, raising the chalice as a prompt to all their companions. "Lord Welles, God bless him."

"Lord Welles, God bless him!" cried the assembly, some thirty strong, each man with an embossed silver cup gleaming at the end of his reach.

Lord Welles had gone to Westminster for talks with the king, escorted by a great cavalcade of retainers, about a week ago. If the talks had gone according to plan, Lincolnshire would end up his personal fiefdom, even if ostensibly ruled on the king's behalf. News of his success was expected any day now. It would be their crowning triumph after years of hard work, peeling supporters from the king's friends and grafting them onto their own cohort. Lord Welles was a bulldog for courage and persistence, and Sir Robert was devoted to him, yet it was good to be out from under his shadow for once, the first man in Lincolnshire, at least for now.

"God bless him," he repeated as he prepared to drink from the chalice.

"What a coincidence!" said a tall figure all in black, emerging from behind one of the pillars in the hall.

Bertram Kilsby.

Kilsby was an agent of the mighty earl of Warwick, an important ally in the fractured politics of the realm. *Ally?* The earl was nobody's ally. His only ambition in a conflict with the throne was to go on being the real power behind it, no matter whether a Yorkist or Lancastrian happened to perch there. Creatures like Kilsby were Warwick's eyes and ears, always sticking his nose where it didn't belong. He had been a guest of Lord Welles and Sir Robert for a month now, at Grimsthorpe Castle and other bastions of the Welles clan—wherever he could be kept under close watch by his hosts, while he kept watch for the earl's benefit, maybe in support of the rebels, maybe not.

"*Coincidence?*" asked Denby. "What are you driving at, Kilsby?"

"Yes, what are you driving at?" said Sir Robert, since the man in black seemed in no hurry to explain himself, casually strolling in and out between pillars, as if he owned the place.

"A messenger has just reached me from the earl," Kilsby said as he finally approached the trophy-laden table, "while you were out hunting. The man is still here for questioning. Shall I spare you the trouble? Lord Welles never met the king. The talks were bait for a trap. But fear not, Sir Robert! Or at least not yet. Your father got wind of the mischief and sprinted for the closest refuge, Westminster Abbey. His retinue has been stripped of all their heraldic trappings, weapons and horses, and set loose like beggars. So now you get the picture! Your father's safety is in God's hands, holed up in the abbey, minus friends and supporters, and here you are, mentioning him and God in the same breath! Uncanny co-incidence, wouldn't you say? God bless Lord Welles!"

Kilsby lifted his eyes in mock piety towards the rafters.

Sir Robert was stunned. So were his men. They all exchanged looks of dismay.

"Hellfire and fury!" Sir Robert thundered—what was the point of being left in charge if he didn't take charge now! "My father goes to the king for talks and *this* is the thanks he gets? We ride to Westminster! Send word to our cohort! Raise up the whole of Lincolnshire!"

"Now wait a moment," said Denby, resting a hand on Sir Robert's shoulder. "Let's not rush into anything just yet. We don't even know if Kilsby's report is true."

Kilsby responded to this with one of his supercilious looks. He was naturally suited to looking down on people, his green eyes being separated by a long nose, like an elegant stone mullion dividing lancet windows, so that the eyebrows had a lofty quality even when he wasn't being supercilious. It was a face Sir Robert wanted to admire but when a man looks *that* haughty, anyone below knows he is being scorned. Sir Robert rose to the challenge. He set his untasted chalice on the table, signifying an end to frivolity, then stroked his moustache. It was a wild collection of brown whiskers and Sir Robert was proud of it. A clean shave was customary, even the law for other Englishmen, but the son of Lord Welles could do as he damn well pleased, and a moustache proved it. His father was the only other Englishman sporting anything like it, and it was intolerable thinking of his whiskers being confined to Westminster Abbey.

"How do we even know your report is true, Kilsby?" he demanded to know.

"Question the messenger yourself, if you don't believe me," said Kilsby with a shrug, meanwhile helping himself to a cup of wine. "Better still, ask the earl. He's headed for Middleham Castle."

"That's a week's ride there and back," Denby confided in Sir Robert. "We'll hear from our own people before then."

"Your own people?" was Kilsby's response, eyes twinkling over the rim of his borrowed cup. "Do they know what the king is planning, let alone the earl, and do they have a counter-plan, these people of your own, Denby?"

"What are you talking about now?" said Denby.

"Yes, God damn it," said Sir Robert. "The king has a plan, and your earl too? Is that it? Let's hear them then."

"Of course, I can say nothing of the earl's plans," said Kilsby, after another sip of borrowed wine. "A man as brilliant as England's greatest nobleman has many friends, plans, contingencies, complexities that require the subtlest thought, the most careful co-ordination, information distributed when and as required, so that, in summary, only *he* ever knows all his own plans. You and I might know something of them once your rider returns from Middleham Castle. I can only tell you what the earl's messenger has told me about the king's plans."

"Then get on with it," Denby prompted him.

"This is a mighty hole," Kilsby said as he inserted a finger into the deer's punctured hide. "Your work, Sir Robert?"

"It might as well be," said the young knight, irritated more than ever by Kilsby's manner of not getting to the point straight away.

"The king is the creature of his wife's family," Kilsby continued, pausing for another drink of wine, "and his plans are theirs. They are still smarting over the deaths of her father and her brother in last year's rebellion, and they have begun preparations for amassing a large force. Officially, it will be to keep the peace here in Lincolnshire, as if they mean to broker an agreement between their people and yours. *Officially*, mind you. In fact, they mean to crush you rebels once and for all. By the time they are finished, your heads will be looking down from the gates of your own castle, though it will be no longer yours by then. A collection of heads, like so many trophies on the table here."

He waved a careless hand at the day's catch.

"Good God," said Sir Robert.

Grimsthorpe Castle, without his father, was a void, a question framed in timber and stone, and no amount of staring from the parapet, or following in his father's footsteps, had prepared Sir Robert for the kind of tricks being played now. It was fortunate that Lord Welles had left behind a good counsellor in Denby the Dasher, a man of action that knew the right time to pull back on the reins and when to dig in the spurs. Sir Robert looked to him now.

"It was the earl of Warwick got us into this trouble, starting with the rebellion last year," Denby reminded him. "Now he must show himself on our side or lose face with his allies everywhere—assuming that these reports are even true."

"That's right, Kilsby," said Sir Robert. "Your earl loses face if he doesn't help us now, if what you say is true."

"The earl loses face if you lose your heads?" Kilsby mused. "But speaking of reports! The messenger sent here by the earl must continue to France, so that our friends in exile will be ready to respond appropriately. You have ships in the fens. Let's place him in one of those."

This was a quick shift in business and Sir Robert wasn't surprised when Denby shook his head.

"The earl has ships of his own," he reminded Sir Robert. "This is just Kilsby's latest excuse for snooping in our affairs."

"The fens are the most direct route to France," Kilsby persisted. "There is no time for delays. Or shall I report to the earl, whom you now rely on for your heads, that you have been—how shall I put it—unhelpful?"

"Our people in the fens don't take kindly to outsiders," Denby insisted.

Sir Robert wasn't deaf to good advice but Denby could already claim credit for the deer, and it was bad policy to rely on anyone too much, so Sir Robert fingered his moustache again, like a man still considering the issue. He was still fingering it some moments later when one of the servants heralded the arrival of the abbot from Bourne Abbey, barely preventing the abbot announcing himself.

"I am in no mood for niceties!" he said as he advanced impatiently on Sir Robert. "I want something done. Your family has made itself the only power here in Lincolnshire, and I have come to you for help.

15

The rebellion has turned my abbey into an inn. It is coming apart at the seams. People have nowhere else to go. Where is your father? I want to speak with him."

Usually the abbot was a model of courtesy, and Sir Robert was too taken aback to say anything at first. Kilsby filled the void.

"It is the season for hiding in abbeys," he remarked with a laugh: "Lord Welles at the abbey in Westminster, and his enemies here at the abbey in Bourne."

The abbot stared at him.

"Who is this?" he asked Sir Robert. "Everywhere I look these days, it's another face, another name I am expected to know. My abbey is full of them. Yet *enemies*? Who says *my* abbey houses anyone's enemies? They are frightened travellers anxious to go home. But *Westminster Abbey*? Lord Welles has taken refuge at Westminster Abbey? Who says?"

"Bertram Kilsby," said Denby, passing the abbot a cup of wine. "He is merely a clerk that the earl of Warwick has yet to find a proper use for. Meanwhile we are making our own enquiries and, needless to say, we are still the power in Lincolnshire."

"I am no less a man than my father," Sir Robert affirmed, this being both a matter of pride and something of a joke, since he and his father were equally diminutive in stature, and big hearted in spite of it.

The abbot however was in no mood for pleasantries.

"This rebellion must end for everyone's sake," he said, flushing scarlet. "*I* am at the end of my wits. Only today there was a fresh outrage. One of your ruffians invaded the home of the spinster, Marian Kempe, a pious woman, and a great friend to me, the abbey, Bourne manor and the entire town. He set his hawk on her niece. A hawk! So, what is to be done about it?"

"*Ruffians?*" Sir Robert objected, now no longer in a mood for pleasantries either. "My men are all men of the best stamp, I'd have you know. But this Kempe spinster is a stranger to me—and who is her niece? Some whore by God or she wouldn't be spreading lies about any man that rides with Sir Robert Welles."

"Susanna Mandeville," the abbot revealed. "As chaste as a drift of snow, and almost a nun in her steadfast love of solitude! Her father is a merchant in the bishop of Winchester's manor in Southwark, almost a neighbour to his palace. These are not people you can take lightly."

"Chaste as a drift of snow," Kilsby queried, wandering around a nearby post, "from Southwark? I had heard it is all whores on that side of the Thames."

"Envy is tongued like the Devil," said the abbot, glaring. "Marian has ever been as beautiful as an angel, in body and in character, and her niece is cut from the same cloth. No ill must be spoken of those two women in my presence."

"But who was the fellow with the hawk?" said Denby. "Does *he* have a name?"

"Oh yes, everyone has a name," the abbot complained, "which is why I am always struggling to remember them all, and why it takes forever investigating damages, missing items and endless complaints. Like a common inn! But he never gave his name. He said little. According to the niece, his accent was so far north, it nearly had a kilt on it."

"Tom Roussell," said Denby, quick as a flash. "He is still out hunting."

"Tom Roussell," affirmed Sir Robert's other hunting companions, nodding to each other. "It must be Tom. He is a northerner, a Yorkshireman. Who else could it be?"

"Tom Roussell!" marvelled the abbot. "Isn't he——"

"The Beast of Ferrybridge!" said Sir Robert, eager to see the effect.

Roussell was the hardest of hard men, the foremost of all the heroes that the Lancastrian cause had ever summoned to its banners. He had once fought an entire county single-handed—and won. Most people in authority were familiar with his reputation, including the abbot, and he nearly choked on his wine.

"It was *him*? The man that flew the hawk at Marian's niece was the Beast of Ferrybridge? A man like that in our neighbourhood! I should have been warned."

"We don't like to brag," said Sir Robert, "so we have kept his visit here quiet, like a sword in its sheath, biding the hour when we strike terror into the hearts of our foes."

'When better than now," said Denby, "though scaring girls wasn't quite what we had in mind."

"They have been frightened enough already, even without knowing the man's name," mused the abbot. "But someone must apologise, if not the Beast himself, then someone on his behalf."

Kilsby circled around to the abbot and presented himself with an elegant bow.

"Roussell is more a colleague of mine than a friend of Sir Robert," he declared in all his dark impudence. "We are both indentured to the earl of Warwick. But my apologies for speaking out of turn a moment ago. Pray allow me to introduce myself properly. My name is Bertram Kilsby, a cousin—"

"A distant cousin," Denby interposed, "almost no cousin at all."

"—of the earl of Warwick," Kilsby persisted, "whom it is my pleasure to serve as a kind of roving steward. That is to say, I oversee the work of other stewards, helping out wherever I can: dusting off contracts, adding new clauses, investigating discrepancies—"

"Snooping," added Denby.

"The Beast of Ferrybridge helps with that?" the abbot wondered.

"He is a lamb when not a lion," Kilsby assured him. "We are heading to the fens tomorrow, on business for the earl, and I will personally see to it that Tom offers both the Kempe woman and her niece his humblest apologies."

"Tom saying *sorry* is something I'd like to see myself," Denby volunteered, "and a visit is just what our people in the fens will need, if Kilsby's reports are true, but there is no call for the earl's snoop to tag along."

"There can be no apologies then," said the man in black. "Tom goes nowhere in Lincolnshire without the earl's authority, which, for present purposes, is invested in me."

"But an apology is essential," pleaded the abbot. "Someone must apologise."

"Enough of all such wrangles!" said Sir Robert, actually glad of this chance to assert himself, since they all seemed to have forgotten who was in charge here. "There is no friendship without trust, and trust is what we must have. Tom Roussell is my guest and he will apologise tomorrow. Kilsby is also my guest and he may travel with Tom to the fens. Denby will go too, just to keep a watch on things. That's final."

"And what of all the people in my abbey?" said the abbot. "They'll never leave without a guarantee of safe passage. The county is swarming with bandits. These troubles cannot to be endured a day longer."

"These are difficult times for me too, damn it!" Sir Robert snapped. "I have responsibilities, not just here but—where?"

"Lincoln," Denby advised him. "Yet the abbot is a good friend. You should be able to visit him—tomorrow week?"

"Expect me at your abbey tomorrow week," Sir Robert advised the abbot. "If I like what I see, I'll arrange an escort out of Lincolnshire for all who require it. But why people want to leave, when things here are better now than they ever were under the Yorkists, is something that makes me wonder whose side those people are on."

Susanna was embarrassed at how little damage the hawk had actually done: a gash to the palm of her right hand, some punctures high on her forehead, and a few scratches on her scalp. The real hurt had been to her pride. She had needed rescuing from a bird hardly bigger than an alley cat, and her rescuer hadn't even thought her worth an apology. She was still wrinkling her nose at one of Aunt Marian's home remedies—a poultice that stank of crowfoot and vinegar—when the abbot arrived late in the afternoon, with news that the apology was on its way. This was the first time, in Susanna's recollection, that he had ever visited the house in all his Church regalia, a measure of the occasion's seriousness. The invasion of a respectable home, especially one belonging to a force like Marian, was not to be tolerated.

"It is intolerable!" he said, banging the floor with his crozier. "An attack on your household, Marian, is an attack on us all. It is an attack on the abbey itself. However, I have made enquiries and I have discovered the culprit."

"Yes?"

"He is indentured to the earl of Warwick, and he has been staying at Grimsthorpe Castle off and on for a month now. He will make his apologies tomorrow, sometime in the morning, I think."

"Name and details?"

"A man-at-arms from Yorkshire: Tom Roussell."

The abbot looked ready to say something else but pursed his lips instead. He was often more eyes than words in their company, and he finally left after kissing Marian's hand as devotedly as if she were the pope.

"*Sometime in the morning?*" Susanna mused after the door had closed on his visit. "That doesn't sound very sorry to me. Today would be sorrier."

"Tomorrow gives us more time. We must look our best."

"Look our best for a rebel?" Susanna scoffed, her pride disallowing any change to her usual routine. "You heard what the abbot said. Roussell is indentured to the earl of Warwick, and we all know that Warwick is *the* biggest trouble-maker in the kingdom. And Grimsthorpe Castle! A festering sore we all know is *the* seat of rebellion here in Lincolnshire. That Roussell creature is a traitor's lickspittle if he is in with that lot. I am not going to dress up for the likes of him."

"He is just an untutored Yorkshireman," her aunt conceded, "but he must be made to see how important you are, or he won't know how wrong he is."

"I must make myself look as bold as an alehouse sign, as a woman of consequence, or he won't know any better?"

"What about that beautiful blue gown I bought for you, when I presented you to Lady Margaret Beaufort? *That* will put him in his place."

Aunt Marian's piety was seasoned with lashings of worldly wisdom, otherwise Susanna could never have loved her so much. However, Marian didn't know everything. The blue gown had been ripped almost in half and Susanna had been keeping it from her notice for over two months. Lady Margaret Beaufort was one of the greatest women in England, and the damage had been done by Sir Henry Beaufort, her husband. Matilda knew most of the story, and Susanna confided in her next.

"I need you to do an errand for me," she whispered: they shared a tiny room partitioned from the hall by a screen of white swans, painted by Susanna herself during a previous stay. "Did you hear me or are you deaf?"

Matilda was sitting on the bed, face averted, arms folded. The slap across the face had not been forgiven in spite of everything else that had happened since.

"I'm sorry I slapped you," Susanna now volunteered.

"It hurt!"

"It was meant to. Now stop sulking and listen. I have to wear something suitable for tomorrow's apology."

"Apologies matter to you?"

"I am really, really sorry I slapped you."

"I don't believe you."

"Then lend me some forgiveness until Christmas, when we settle my other debts, and I'll apologise twice. This is important. That blue gown I asked you to keep hidden for me—"

"After Sir Henry ripped it."

"Hush! I told you it was an accident."

"Such accidents never happen to me."

"He said he was going to show me some paintings in Lady Margaret's solarium, he tripped on the stairs—"

"Grabbing your gown, just to steady himself."

"I don't want trouble between Lady Margaret and my aunt. We must pretend it never happened."

Matilda brightened for a moment.

"I have the perfect cloak for that gown. It's English wool, French design, all in lemon and white, with a draw-string at the collar."

"How will that improve things?"

"You want to hide the damage, don't you?"

"Your cloak won't hide it from *me*."

"Then how about I lend you one of my own gowns! A few nips and tucks are all it needs for a good fit."

"I don't want to look like you. We have to repair the blue one."

"It's beyond even my skills, but I know the right woman. She won't come cheap: an expert seamstress working late into the night, making invisible repairs—sixpence at least."

"A nice, round sum. That's always the way with you, isn't it! Anyway, I'll pay you back later. Tell the seamstress it's one of yours."

"The style is elegant enough to be one of mine. Your aunt has good taste."

"You'll have to come up with some excuse for leaving the house," Susanna reflected. "Marian is on the alert now and she is watching everyone and everything like a … like a …"

"Hawk?"

"And now I have thought of a good excuse! Watt's dog went missing. We can say you are out looking for it."

"It is hardly a real dog, nothing like Thunderbolt."

"Watt calls it *Dog*, and I wouldn't call Thunderbolt a real dog after today's episode."

"Why must your aunt always take in riff-raff? It is probably out killing the neighbours' chickens again."

"She wants Dog found and that's good enough for me. Now, hide the gown in your shawl, and off you go."

"I am charging you at the usual rate—two returned for every one borrowed—so the sixpence I am lending is another shilling. That's now four pounds, six shillings and fourpence, not including the money promised to Adam, all payable to me by Christmas."

"Yes, yes, off you go."

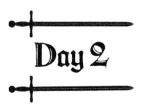

Day 2

Thursday 8th of February

Susanna was delighted when the gown was returned at dawn, the repairs invisible.

"Sixpence is a lot of money for something I can't even see," she quipped when Matilda held it out for inspection.

"It cost you a shilling," Matilda reminded her. "A shilling by Christmas."

Susanna slipped into the gown straight away, preparing for an apology that could come at any time. It fitted as good as new. She drew the fleecy lining of her best cloak tight around the shoulders then fixed a brooch to keep all secure. She pulled on a pair of blue gloves, taking care not to disturb the gashed palm, then donned her favourite slippers, half-hidden by the hem of the gown. Next, she wondered how to hide the punctures and scratches on her forehead. It was her entitlement, as an unmarried woman, not to burden her head with a stuffy bonnet. Instead, she concealed the inflamed marks under the encircling braids of her red hair, lightly enclosed in a gauze coif. Her own appearance out of the way, her next concern was how the household should look. Her aunt however had already begun the preparations.

"I have invited the abbot, his canons and all the heads of the local households," she said as Susanna helped her put away the swan-painted screen, creating more space for visitors. "Including my own household, my tenants and guests, that's more than a hundred people: a respectable gathering."

Not all these people however were respectable, certainly not Adam the Younger's family, the Galts. They were seldom allowed in the house and spent all but the worst nights in the stables with Friar Fryer, a mendicant Franciscan who had made himself their spiritual advisor, though he had long struggled with enough demons of his own. He was more lunatic than priest as far as Susanna could tell.

"Do we need the Galts and their friar?" she complained. "Adam the Younger, I don't mind, but the rest of them?"

"We can hide them in the crowd. This is their chance to learn how respectable people behave. You and I shall be seated at the centre, in the place of honour. Roussell must apologise to us first, then to Adam and Watt, and finally to the gathering as a whole. You must say nothing. You have only to nod or frown. I will do all the talking."

"As if I am utterly beyond his reach."

"It is not a battle but a surrender."

"And everyone else—how will they conduct themselves?" Susanna wondered. "I think silence would be best."

"They will have no need to speak, since we are all in agreement."

"A crowd's silence has weight."

"He must be made to feel alone."

"Small and insignificant," Susanna affirmed.

Aunt Marian asked Friar Fryer to conduct Mass in the hall for her household, her guests and her tenants, as preparation for the apology and because his skills as an ordained priest needed some brushing up. After the service, she gave everyone instructions about their different roles. The five largest of her tenant farmers were tasked with keeping watch outdoors for anyone resembling Roussell's description. When he came, they were to keep him waiting in the cold, while her gardener hurried to the abbey with news of his arrival. The abbot and his canons would carry the news around town, summoning the leading citizens. Under no circumstance was Roussell to be admitted into the house until all these local worthies were organised indoors. They would be ranged along two sides of the hall. Aunt Marian and Susanna would be seated, facing the door, with the regular guests, tenants and servants standing behind them. The five farmers would follow the culprit inside, thus enclosing him in a fortress of resolved men and women. Marian would speak for all, a point so important she stressed it several times.

There was nothing more to do then but wait. The farmers went outside to keep vigil. The household stayed inside, some attending to basic chores, others merely loitering. The morning dragged on towards noon and meanwhile the weather forgot that it was almost Spring. Dark clouds rolled in low, and gusting winds pelted sleet under the door and through cracks in the shutters, until swirling draughts snatched sparks and smoke from the central fireplace and chased them scurrying around the hall. Aunt Marian ordered the coals be extinguished and carried outside. The hall grew darker and ever colder, the household ever more restless, with only rushlights to see by. People disappeared from time to time, some to attend to chores, some to fetch another layer of clothes, others like the Galt father, for no apparent reason at all. The Galt mother fell asleep in Marian's seigneurial chair, and then Watt threw a handful of wet ash at Adam Galt the Elder. Adam Galt the Elder made him eat it. Watt ran around the hall with blackened mouth and blackened hands, shrieking like the wind, until Adam the Younger caught hold of him for Marian to buckle into a child's harness, tethered to a post. The Galt mother awoke with a cacophonous snort, as if a door had slammed shut in her throat, and then the real door opened and one of the farmers put his head in through a flurry of sleet:

"He's here!" he said. "A large party also—two dozen or more."

"Only Roussell comes in," Aunt Marian reminded him, "and we're not ready yet! Wait for the signal."

The head disappeared and the door closed, while the gardener left by the back door, heading for the abbey. Susanna took a deep breath to calm her nerves. She felt suddenly uncomfortable in the blue gown: the invisible repairs were to the fabric, not to her memories of being manhandled, firstly by Margaret Beaufort's husband, and yesterday by the rebel Yorkshireman. She tested the braids of her hair, making sure they stayed put, then finally she took her seat in the appointed place. Aunt Marian shooed the Galt mother out of the seigneurial chair, directing her to join the servants and guests at the back of the hall, but then it was discovered that the Galt father still hadn't returned, and Marian was directing one of the maids to find him, when Watt suddenly escaped from his harness. Friar Fryer caught him again and was still leading him back to it when the door opened with a great burst of wind-driven sleet, and in blew two strangers, looking enormous in billowing cloaks. One of them turned and forcefully closed the door with his shoulder, trapping the wind until it died like an animal caught by the neck.

"T day is windier than t devil's arse!" he said as he faced the hall again, brushing off the sleet still clinging to his coat.

Susanna recognised him immediately, as much by his northern accent as by his appearance, while the rushlights that had survived his arrival began to flicker and go out one by one, extinguished by a trapped draught of air.

"Language, Tom!" said his companion. "You're here to say sorry, remember."

Aunt Marian grabbed the only flame that soon remained and hurried around the hall, reigniting the rushlights.

"Who let you two in?" she objected as soon as she had restored enough light. "I haven't even sat down yet!"

"John Denby of Horncastle," said Roussell's companion, a taller man than the Yorkshireman and quite good looking. "Friends call me *Denby the Dasher*. I was hoping for a blazing fire."

"Get out," Aunt Marian told him.

"I am here to see him apologise."

"We don't need your help," she insisted.

"It is freezing outside," he pleaded.

"Throw t rogue aht," said Roussell, laughing as he lent his friend a push towards the door.

Denby replied to Roussell with a smile and an even bigger push back, to which Roussell responded with a two-handed shove that sent Denby tottering sideways. Denby answered with a half-hearted push, and then Roussell sent him careering across the room so that he crashed into a wall stud. There followed some high-spirited wrestling which, between two strong men, alarmed the household just as much as if two stags had got indoors and locked antlers. One of the maids whimpered and another burst into tears. Susanna removed one of her gloves and forced her nails into yesterday's wound, drawing courage from self-inflicted pain. Meanwhile Aunt Marian stood her ground at the margins of the tussle.

"Stop this at once!" she cried.

They did stop.

"Tis is fault," said Roussell, smiling broadly in the flickering light she was still nursing in their vicinity. "T rogue as bin makin jokes abaht me ever sin yestudee."

"He is lying," said Denby, meanwhile reorganizing his cloak, twisted awkwardly around his neck, "this *Beast of Ferrybridge*! No manners at all."

Alarmed murmurs broke out as the nickname caught fire and spread from mouth to mouth: *Beast of Ferrybridge*. Susanna had never heard it before and she resolved that it would mean nothing to her now. Her aunt wasn't put off by it either.

"We have no time for this blather," she decreed, pushing Denby towards the door. "Get out!"

"Aht into t wind n reeain, Denby t Dasher!" Roussell laughed. "Tha av done thy dash naw."

Marian's courage was inspirational. Susanna sprang from her chair and, just as her aunt slammed the door on Denby, slapped Roussell across the face. The effect on the household was immediate. The maid stopped whimpering. The other maid stopped crying. Watt, still out of his harness, sat on the floor as a precaution. Order had been restored.

"I have bolted the door!" Aunt Marian declared. "Now we shall all wait in silence for the abbot and our other honoured guests."

This sounded like a prompt for Susanna to return to her place. She half moved back to her chair before deciding to study Roussell up close, so then she grabbed a nearby rushlight and used it to ignite a proper candle. It was cheap tallow—Aunt Marian kept the beeswax candles under lock and key—but its stench of burning grease suited Susanna's mood. She returned to Roussell and thrust the light in his face. He was maybe forty years old, give or take a dozen years, his features chiselled or else blunted by whatever savagery breeds rebels in the north. His grey eyes were bright and sharp but as unflinching as slate. She kept her nerve while he studied her in return, and then she edged gradually from his gaze, circling round to bring the rest of him to light. His brown, shoulder-length hair was drenched with rain, adding to the beads of moisture glistening on his coat, accumulating on the scabbard of his sword, finally dripping from the scabbard's bronze tip. The sword, big enough to fell a tree, was sheathed behind his back in outlandish fashion. A proper gentleman would have worn a more ceremonial blade, hung from the belt or, better still, he would have left it outside. This monstrous thing was tied to a tartan sash, looped over his shoulder, which she followed round to the front once more, the chequered cloth ending in a brass ring attached to his belt buckle. The coat was of greasy wool, better suited to weatherproofing than to looking respectable. It hung open below the hips, revealing green hose and high boots, all ending in a pair of gleaming spurs. He was dressed for action, not for an apology.

When their eyes met again, he was lifting a hand, maybe to reach for the sword hilt at his shoulder, maybe to repay her slap—the stony face gave nothing away. She stood her ground. If life in Southwark had taught her anything, it was that most men can be faced down, if a woman relies on her own boldness. Roussell scratched his head and next rubbed his chin, muttering something. It was then that she noticed a red smear across his cheek, gleaming for all to see in the light of the candle she held up to him.

"That's blood," Aunt Marian observed, stepping closer.

"Wow, blood!" said Adam the Younger, peering from between their vacant chairs. "She sure hits hard!"

"Fetch the crowfoot and vinegar," Marian told one of the servants.

"No!" Susanna pleaded. "He deserves no such attention."

"He is our guest," Marian reminded her.

"Tit for tat," Susanna insisted, "so let him bleed."

Roussell began fingering his cheek, testing the wound. It disappeared after a light rub. He inspected his fingertips. There was no sign of blood there either, as far as Susanna could make out, and then an important fact dawned on her: a mere slap to the cheek doesn't draw blood. It must have come from her wounded palm, now clamped on the candle. It was an awkward discovery but she decided to brazen it out.

"It's my own blood!" she confessed to the entire hall, swapping the candle to the other hand so as to display her wounded palm. "He shed it yesterday, so he can wear it today, like the savage he is."

"Ah'm neya savage," he protested. "It were t awk a drew thy blood, not Ah."

"Didn't you hear my aunt, or don't you understand plain English?" she retorted. "You were told to wait in silence."

"She told tha tooa, dint she?"

"The creature doesn't understand plain English," Susanna advised their audience, "even after I have spelt it out for him."

"Susanna …" Aunt Marian interposed.

"Sorry, Aunt, but why should *I* keep silent! *I* have nothing to be ashamed of. *He* is supposed to be apologising, yet he bursts in here with his foul language and his insolence, dressed like this, as if he had better things to do than say he's sorry, and just look at the way he stands, like a lump of idiotic wood, no dignity, no grace, utterly devoid of self-awareness! If a tree stood in this lumpish manner, I wouldn't mind. A tree knows no better."

This complaint seemed to register with him. He tried to stand more self-consciously. She circled him again, looking for signs that he really meant to co-operate. He watched her out of the corner of his eye, as if wondering what she might do next.

"What have you to say for yourself?" she said as she came around to face him once more, since there were many questions she was burning to ask. "You are permitted to speak."

"T awk attacked tha, Ah dint," he insisted.

"Maybe the hawk should apologise!" she scoffed.

"Ah doubt she will."

"*She?*"

"Male awk is smaller."

"What a shame *we* aren't hawks."

"Ah would be i trouble then," he conceded.

"You are in trouble now."

His eyes betrayed a glimmer of smugness.

"'Awks dooant attack fowk," he declared, "unless provoked."

"Oh so it is all my fault!" she scoffed. "The poor, little hawk, with its poor, little beak, and its poor, little claws: I provoked her. Yes, I always go out into my aunt's orchard hoping to provoke passing hawks. But that innocent bird of yours was about to attack the innocent little boy here, and I just happened to get in the way first."

The visitor looked to where she pointed: Watt picking his nose.

"Then Ah'm sorry fert lad's sake," he said, his gaze returning to Susanna, "yet tha could allus try thankin me for comin t elp tha."

"Oh thank you for your help," she scoffed next, "especially the way you threw me around like a, a—what do they train hawks with?"

The question was addressed to the household, not to Roussell. A drawling northern rebel was the last person she would ever turn to for the right word.

"A dead rat," Adam the Younger offered.

"A lure," Roussell said to correct him. "We train awks wi lures."

"I didn't ask for your help!" she snapped.

"Tha dint ask for it yestudee either, but tha are welcome to t all t sem."

There were two sides to Susanna's nature and this man was an irritant to both. As Marian's niece, she expected to be treated with courtesy. As the girl from Southwark, she was ready to fight, bite and scratch for every inch of territory she deemed hers. This man had brought those two sides into collision. He had burst into her aunt's orchard as if it were a lane in Southwark, and he had tossed her around as if she were a common slut, yet here he now stood, trying to be civil and even apologetic, when she would much rather just fetch him a box on the ear. But how typical of a Lancastrian rebel, causing disagreement and confusion! Her contempt for him hardened and he appeared to sense it.

"Let me expleeain mesen," he pleaded. "Ah were aht untin wi Sir Robert Welles n is party, not far from eear, n some o t men were awkin a pigeons. One o t birds dint return, so Ah went lookin for a. Ah saw tha tanglin wi awk as Ah were passin, n Ah thought t elp tha aht, so Ah took a from tha. Were a t wrong thin ta doa?"

"Your English is dreadful," was her considered reply, "but your behaviour is worse. Invading someone else's property, the way you did yesterday, and leaving without explanations or apologies, after flying your hawk at me—that was the act of a barbarian."

"Tha weren't dressed then t way tha are naw."

"A creature like you only knows true merit when it hits you on the head with a mace," she snapped, brandishing her fist in his face.

"Aye a's true enough."

"Your friend called you *Beast of Ferrybridge*. No doubt you deserve some such title."

"Ah were raised i Wharfedale, i service t Lord Clifford. My parents taught me t be courteous. E trained me t be loyal and t speak English t way London speaks it. Ah'm not t savage tha think Ah am."

"He speaks English like a Londoner!" she repeated for the amusement of their audience. "And Loyal! As if a Lancastrian rebel knows what it means to be loyal."

"Susanna," said Aunt Marian, "this is not the time—"

"When better to confront these rebels than now, with one of them here to answer for them all!" Susanna couldn't stop herself saying. "He and his fellow traitors have yet to pay for last year's rebellion, and already they are at it again."

"Ah thought Ah were summoned ecar ta say sorry fer yestudee, but now Ah mun say sorry fert rebellion as well?"

"You serve the earl of Warwick. You have been staying at Grimsthorpe Castle, a stronghold of Lord Welles. Traitors all! Have the decency to admit it."

"*Traitors?* Whoa av we betrayed?"

"His Majesty, King Edward."

"T pretender? E locked true king int Tower."

"*My* king has earned the right to loyalty. *Yours* hasn't."

"Sa then loyalty is payment? Is t alreight t stab old friends int back, if others are mooar deservin? Should we get rid o our fathers n adopt new ones, ont sem principle, whenever t suits?"

"The idea has some merit," she conceded, thinking it would serve her own father right, "if I understood you correctly."

"So let's stretch t argument aht a wee bit," he offered. "Is it alreight for dog t find imself a new master? Ah only ask cos a dog followed me yestudee n Ah think it came fra ecar. A middlin-size, black n tan dog, enjoys is own compenny, but friendly-like."

"That would be Dog," Marian interposed. "He's a pet."

"E's a great dog n Ah'll tell tha wha as impressed me abaht im. Abaht a mile from ecar, we were, when e caught scent o fox, flushed it from cover n chased it daahn a well—then jumps in after t. E were draggin t aht again when Ah arrived ont spot. Ah av nivva seen owt like it. Nem thy price and Ah'll buy thy champion hunter reight gladly. If not, e's ahtside and thine t tek back."

"Keep him," Susanna scoffed. "The previous owner was a poacher. He was hung last year from the gibbet by the town pond: more a rebel's kind of dog than ours."

Meanwhile there was an insistent banging and shouting at the door, getting louder all the time. It was the sound of a large company demanding to be let in: just the kind of noise a mob of rebels might make.

"They're gettin reight impatient," Roussell observed. "Ah av made my apologies naw, n they'll be makin thersen a ome, if Ah doan't get movin soon."

"I have invited half the town to witness a formal apology," Marian countered. "You are staying here until they have heard it. Your friends can go somewhere else, but Dog is welcome."

Marian went to the door and boldly opened it, determined to fetch Watt's pet. Her movement was immediately checked by a gust of wind and a volley of sleet, followed by a large group of men, clamouring to come in out of the cold. Not even Marian was an obstacle to such a press of people, with a storm at their backs, and she was forced to retreat until Roussell hollered to them to stop. He waved his hands, urging them back outside, then followed on their heels, closing the door behind him. Meanwhile Susanna's candle and all the rushlights had been extinguished, leaving the hall in complete darkness.

"He left," Susanna called out to Marian, "without apologising!"

"Everyone keep still!" said Marian.

A spark was soon struck from a tinder box, a glowing charcloth becoming a flame in her hands, which she then divided with a maid, reigniting rushlights around the hall, one by one. She was replacing a rushlight, affixed to a post, when an apparition, dressed in black from head to toe, stepped suddenly from behind it. The maid screamed and Marian took a step back.

"What the devil!" she protested. "Who are you?"

"The earl of Warwick," came the reply, with a slight bow. "That is to say, I am his humble servant."

"That would make me the Lord God Almighty," Marian scoffed. "Get out with the rest of them!"

She waved her arms at him but he was as unresponsive as his black hose, black doublet, black cloak, black bonnet, black shoes and black gloves, one of which clutched a rope, tied to a black and tan terrier: Dog. The tail wagged.

"I am looking for a miracle," said the apparition: "a woman from Southwark, chaste as a drift of snow. Have you seen it?"

"I'll take that!" Marian offered instead, reaching for the rope.

"You must be Marian Kempe," he observed while keeping the rope out of her reach. "My sympathies—it was the abbot's wish. But where is your niece?"

"My niece? What is she to you?"

"It almost snows today, as if to confirm a miracle, with Spring almost upon us," he continued, stepping around Marian as if she were a mere post. "Yet what is snow! Water that turns to ice for a time then mud at last, wouldn't you say?"

The extinguished candle dropped from Susanna's fingers. She made no effort to retrieve it, hardly able to take her eyes off the intruder, he seemed so much like a ghost. She felt with her heel for something, anything to sit on, groping with a hand stretched out behind, until she came to grips with the reassuring solidity of wood. It was Marian's seigneurial chair and yet it felt barely able to support the full weight of Susanna's bewilderment and horror.

"Explain yourself!" Marian demanded of the apparition.

"I am returning a dog," came the response. "Woof, woof."

This elicited a welcome from one person at least.

"Dog, Dog, Dog!" said Watt, getting to his feet.

The boy waddled towards the pet he had never shown much interest in until now. The man in black barred his advance with the upraised sole of his shoe then pushed with the heel against the boy's forehead, forcing him to sit on the floor again.

"The dog is for the woman," he explained.

"Here!" said Susanna. "I'm here."

He followed the voice as if following a smell, looking for her.

"Ah there you are," he soon observed. "But how hard it is to see anything in this light, after staring into a gale half the morning!"

"Say what you came to say and leave!" she commanded him.

33

"No sooner in than she wants him out again," he observed with a smirk. "My friends won't be staying long, not even for me, and business calls me away, but still, the heart may linger for a few beats, *ca-thump*, *ca-thump*, *ca-thump*, might it not? But what is it about beauty that every man thinks he owns it?" he continued, drawing ever closer. "As if the moon should rise or sink for his pleasure alone. Do such thoughts seem strange?"

"They do to me," said Marian.

"Who wants your opinion!" he scolded, turning on her for a moment. "Though I see the resemblance. But what of that? Shall people notice you in her presence, just because there is a shadow of her beauty in that old face! You lack her fire, you lack the purity of her being, her youth."

"I didn't quite catch your name," said Marian. "Who *are* you?"

"He's leaving," Susanna assured her, being anxious to keep matters under her own control.

"And if I refuse," he wanted to know, "who will throw me out?"

"You think *I* won't?" Susanna dared to say.

He was tall and strong but her speed and strength had surprised him once, and this time she had Marian's household to help her, if that was needed. Nevertheless, he closed on her, dragging the dog along with him, till he was able to stoop over her, breathing heavily and dripping rain into her lap while he tied the rope around the leg of the chair.

"Be careful," she warned him, her skin rigid with revulsion.

He straightened gradually and inhaled loudly, as if drawing her presence in through his nostrils.

"Such a leash you have put on me! But duty calls. Even beauty like yours may not subvert reason long enough to detain me a moment more, Sweet Thing."

That said, he stepped back, bowed his head, strode to the door, flung it open and walked out into the teeth of the gale. Marian struggled to shut the door behind him, even with the help of the friar and two of her maids, and meanwhile Susanna hurried to the storeroom at the rear of the hall, desperate to bury herself in its confined space, anywhere to get away from the memories pursuing her. It was pitch black inside. She felt her way past the usual items, her face brushing against strings of onions, clutches of dried fish, and a dangling chicken, while her feet stumbled on sacks of flour and a fragrant basket of herbs, until she finally reached the back wall, where she stood and waited for her composure to return. She was still waiting when Aunt Marian appeared, sheltering a rushlight in one hand.

"What in Heaven's name, Susanna! Who——"

"Has he left?"

"They all have but——"

"Kilsby! Bertram Kilsby."

"*Your* Kilsby?"

"Not mine, the Devil's!"

"But ... I thought he was dead."

"Kilsby?" said Matilda, behind Marian's shoulder.

It was a question best ignored. Kilsby was a private nightmare and Susanna had long resolved to keep him a secret, shared only with her father, her brother, her aunt and too many others already.

Day 3

Friday 9th of February

Rubies was a nickname that Sir Thomas Burgh took pride in, being proof of his greatest passion in life: gemstones. He wore them on his fingers, his ears and his clothes, from his hat down to his shoes. Extravagant? Yes of course, but he had earned these miracles of colour through his administrative talents, his readiness for work, and his loyalty to King Edward, whom he had served in various capacities, most recently as Constable of Lincoln Castle. The rebels had chased him out of Lincolnshire, however, and the king had been keeping him busy ever since with small errands around Westminster. The humiliation was hard to bear yet some moments still shone as brightly as gems

"It's one of the best things I have ever done," the Westminster jeweller said of his latest masterpiece, a blue garter with lettering in gold thread, encrusted with amethysts and sapphires. The king had sent Rubies to collect it. "The colours are modelled on the skin of an African snake," the jeweller explained, "which my apprentice is keeping warm against his skin. Will you be returning the snake to the Tower?"

Rubies glimpsed something big squirming and bulging inside the apprentice's jacket, and shook his head. The garter, which he fondled on the way out, was all the distraction he could manage for now, its velvet, its gold and its gems snaking over his fingers in a mesmerising display of exquisite colours. Nothing could better represent the spirit of the Yorkist regime than this marvel! The deposed monarch, Henry of Lancaster, had been a gloomy, priest-ridden, insignificant, little man, an embarrassment to the kingdom and to the court. He

was *still* an embarrassment, a lunatic locked in the Tower with His
Majesty's monkeys, lions, peacocks, snakes and the rest of the royal
menagerie. The animals made amusing captives, but Henry was a
lingering excuse for treason. He would have been put to death long
ago, if King Edward had listened to friends like Rubies.

"What does my apprentice do with the snake?" the jeweller called
from the door of his workshop. "It's getting restless."

The jeweller's shop was a small link in a great chain of buildings
making up the city of Westminster, where labourers, tradesmen, merchants, scholars, magistrates, nobles, foreign dignitaries and court
functionaries had been busy long before dawn, carting loads, carrying
messages, keeping schedules, rehearsing routines, discussing agendas,
formulating policies and, no doubt, spreading gossip, as virulent as the
Plague. A man down on his luck never escapes the suspicion that he has
deserved his downfall. Only a hundred yards from the jeweller's shop,
a group of musicians stood practising tunes around a marble fountain,
the halting twang of their lutes and the fitful hum of their recorders as
playful as the plash of water, spilling into the basin from the yawning
mouths of lions. Or was there a note of mockery in their performance,
aimed at the once mighty Constable of Lincoln Castle, now a mere
errand boy? A little further on, a raucous team of stevedores passed
by with a load of wood from the quay, posts stacked together as hap-
hazardly as the obscenities they kept mouthing. Were these coarse men
behaving according to their low station in life, or were they trying to
be insolent—and to whom? Meanwhile, in a nearby courtyard, two
pages exchanged blows with wooden swords, and a pair of laundry
maids giggled behind sheets, stretched on tenterhooks. Were the girls
giggling at the boys or at the Constable of Lincoln Castle? A bevy of
lawyers collided with each other in their haste to reach the Great Hall,
then stood in the middle of the street disputing each other's right of
way. Did they grow suddenly quiet because Rubies was passing, or
were they pondering some deep point of legal protocol? A little further on, an acrobat trained in the open air, performing somersaults
on a juggler's shoulders, the multi-coloured balls and particoloured
legs soaring so high, they seemed to challenge even the pigeons for
mastery of the sky. Higher still rose Westminster Abbey, peering over

the surrounding roofs, pigeons, particoloured legs and multi-coloured balls like a dark cloud. Rubies' nemesis, Lord Welles, had taken refuge there about a week ago.

"You belong in the Tower of London," Rubies told the cathedral's coronet of spires. "You belong with the monkeys, the snakes and the lunatic ex-king—*your* king, you Lancastrian has-been!"

Lord Welles had come to Westminster for peace talks. It was a worrying prospect for Rubies and his friends, since the present king always sidestepped trouble when he could, and a rebellion led by Welles could easily be made to look like a private feud provoked by Rubies. Fortunately, some well-placed rumours had scared the rebel lord into taking refuge at the abbey, and there he had stayed, fearing for his life. It was better lodgings than he had deserved but it was only temporary. The king had now scheduled a hearing in the Star Chamber in a week's time. Welles might yet get an opportunity to present his side of the story.

The royal city's hustle and bustle reached a crescendo in the square outside the Great Hall where, infuriated by yet another glimpse of the abbey ("More a damnable inn for trouble-makers than a place of worship!" Rubies shouted at it), he nearly collided with two processions converging across his path: a troop of palace guards shouldering billhooks one way, and a line of cooks' apprentices carrying pots and trays the other. Halting just in time, he waited a few moments for the human curtain to open, then had an uninterrupted walk the rest of the way to the Hall.

Rubies never tired of Westminster's Great Hall. No matter how often he came here, or in what circumstances, it always felt like the first time. It was an architectural wonder, as befitted a cornerstone of England's national life. Vast hammer beams supported the ceiling yet seemed to hang miraculously in mid-air, ribbed and arched like the roof of a gigantic mouth. To enter here was to feel like Jonah, getting swallowed whole by a whale, the floor of Purbeck marble as grey as a gigantic tongue, wriggling with crowds. Do whales have teeth? Market stalls lining the aisles worked like teeth, grinding large coins to smaller denominations, converting small denominations to trinkets, as clerks, lawyers, litigants, officers of state and all kinds of passers-by haggled

over all kinds of goods—quills, paper, sealing wax, cases to store documents in, cloaks to keep out the cold, meals to keep in the warmth,
ale to satisfy a thirst, claret to settle the nerves—all within easy reach
of the Chancery, squirrelled away in an alcove, and the courts of the
King's Bench and Common Pleas, looming large on a dais at the end
of the promenade. Above all this busy confusion stood centuries of
kings carved in uncompromising stone, staring forbiddingly from ped-
estals distributed around the walls. There could be no rebellion here.

Beyond the Great Hall, within earshot of the choristers hymning
upstairs in the Chapel of St Stephens, and the choristers chanting
downstairs in the Chapel of Mary Undercroft, lay White Hall, where
the king often banqueted with his friends. Here Rubies had spent many
of his happiest hours, a successful man in the company of successful
men, where the merry sounds of minstrels blended with the angelic
voices of the nearby chapels, turning Heaven into Earth and Earth
into Heaven. Here he had often got drunk, and from here he now
took the public stairs to the Painted Chamber, feeling as if he might be
drunk still, half giddy with remembered pleasures, half sick with the
thought that it could all end in disgrace a week from now, if Lord Welles
presented a convincing case in front of the king and his Councillors.

The Painted Chamber was the final promenade separating His
Majesty from the court. It was the perfect place for a handsome, young
king to receive visits. Italian frescoes depicted a semi-naked crowd of
biblical heroes and Roman demigods, whose perfect bodies foreshad-
owed His Majesty's own glorious physique, even while their bare skin
contrasted starkly with the extravagant vestments of the crowd gathered there now: court dignitaries, nobles and magnates, their presence
inflated by silk, fur, felt and brilliantly dyed wool. Here, rose-like in the
intense scarlet of her gown and in the odour of her imported perfume,
ranged a plump, shortish woman, pinpointed by a tall, conical hat: the
king's sister-in-law, Anne Woodville, drifting from a polite exchange
of opinions here to a studied comment there, all the while gradually
making for the ornate screen that marked off the inner sanctum, the
king's bedchamber. Rubies timed his movements to coincide with hers
so that they might arrive at the screen together. He identified with the
gentry, same as she did, and he owed everything to the king's favours,

just as she did. Both of them represented the new face of England, and yet she seemed not to notice him this morning, as if he might already be one of the old faces, good only for running errands. He had never much liked her either, he remembered.

Several other guests had already gathered by the screen, waiting to be summoned into the bedchamber. None of them looked important enough to get in ahead of the queen's sister and the Constable of Lincoln Castle, or former Constable, and Rubies barely found time to study them. Only one caught his eye, at least for a lingering moment, a middle-aged man he had never seen before, though he knew the type well enough: somebody overawed by the occasion, with bulging eyes (a comical match for his potbelly) and stiff limbs (as awkward as the cut of his unimpressive clothes). He must be a merchant with a doomed petition—successful petitioners had no need of interviews with His Majesty—and it occurred to Rubies that he himself might end up waiting like this man someday, if Lord Welles ever presented his case in the Star Chamber.

The screen door opened just long enough to admit Anne Wood-ville first and Rubies second, before closing again like a reassuring embrace.

"Viscountess Anne Woodville, and—Sir Thomas Burgh!"

The announcement barely caused a ripple in the crowd of other friends, standing and lounging in attendance at the king's bedside. Among the most conspicuous, by reason of his mellifluous voice, which wound through the surrounding chatter like the velvet garter Rubies carried wrapped around his fingers, was John Tiptoft—*Read-a-lot* to his friends, *Book* to his enemies, and just plain *earl of Worcester* to everyone else—otherwise not easy to locate this morning. He was seated in a corner of the room with a leg thrown over the arm of a chair, reading Latin poetry as unselfconsciously as a dog licks its balls. Most conspicuous of all, nearer the enormous bed, stood the king's best friend and right-hand man, the Lord Chamberlain, William Hastings, looking his usual, amused and authoritative self. The half-dressed figure of His Majesty lay a little further off, glimpsed through half-drawn curtains, a giant of a man propping himself up on royal pillows while conversing privately with a naked woman. This was Elizabeth Shore, the wife of a London goldsmith, the latest in a long line of royal mistresses. Her nakedness was barely covered by a creased, satin sheet, as a bee is barely hidden by the petals of a flower.

Rubies overheard Anne Woodville quickly suck in her breath, her eyes as sharp as her conical hat. His Majesty's sexual indiscretions were too many to be kept secret, and managing them was her responsibility. Mistresses were inevitable, and they could even be a welcome relief for the queen, but his trysts were supposed to be discreet. This was hardly discreet, especially on a Friday morning, which the Church reserves for abstinence and introspection. Completing Anne's obvious humiliation was the spectacle of her own husband, Viscount Bourchier, sauntering past just then with his head draped in a woman's shimmering underwear.

"What oyster have I found here?" said the great woman, plucking the garment from his face.

"Oh are you here?" he replied, blinking.

"Whose?" she insisted, waving the silky fabric at him as if dusting a vase.

"Mine!" the bee volunteered, sitting up now with the bed sheet folded around her.

"Shall my husband continue wearing it for you, or would you like it back?"

"Let your husband wear it!" said His Majesty with a merry guffaw. "Hereafter I shall call him *Silk*, in recognition of his new fashion in bonnets."

Rubies laughed with the king's other friends and so did the newly dubbed Silk, though it annoyed the queen's sister, who made a point of dropping her husband's new namesake on the floor. She would certainly report this incident to the queen. The king loved his partners in pleasure even more wholeheartedly than the queen bore grudges, so it paid to laugh, if it wasn't overdone. Rubies stopped when the others did.

"How is the queen this morning?" Lord Hastings enquired—diplomacy was a prerequisite in his line of work as Lord Chamberlain.

"Her Majesty has the toothache," the viscountess announced, as if sharing her pain. "She will take Mass in her own apartment today."

"I shall worship here!" said Edward, inserting a hand between his mistress's thighs.

His enthusiasm for a new mistress sometimes got the better of him but this was a bit much even for his friends. Read-a-lot's Latin faltered. Lord Hastings coughed.

"Hasn't His Majesty more important business?" the viscountess protested in the pointed manner of a needle prying out a splinter.

"None to compete with this beautiful creature," said the king, clasping Shore's agenda to his powerful, twenty-eight-year-old physique. "What business shall I transact with my Darling Elizabeth? *Elizabeth?* Elizabeth is my wife's name. Our first business must be to give you a new name."

"How about *The Goldsmith's Wife?*" said the viscountess.

"Heaven forbid," said Edward.

"How about *Jane?*" said Shore. "It's easy to remember."

"Jane Shore!" the king affirmed. "My wife can't object to that. My beautiful Jane Shore!"

"The queen could object to many things but often chooses not to," the viscountess reminded everyone.

"But enough of this sloth!" said the Lord Chamberlain—he was confident enough in his status as the king's best friend and chief advisor even to lord it over the king himself sometimes. "Your Majesty really must attend to the proper business of the day. Business is the foundation of all our pleasures."

"A wise fool," the viscountess observed—she was confident enough in her status as the queen's sister even to lord it over the Lord Chamberlain sometimes. "But since business is now in hand, rather than just pleasure, I am here with an important request from Her Majesty: she implores you to fetch home our youngest brother."

"Where did I send him?" the king wondered.

Here Rubies saw a chance to be helpful both to the king and to the queen's sister.

"You sent him north with his eldest brother," he called out, "to oversee the military readiness of the Midlands."

"God help him if the rebels catch him!" said the viscountess. "We have already lost one brother that way, as well as our father."

"Naturally you are anxious for his safety," the king conceded, since the other two had been beheaded by rebels in last year's troubles, "yet a boy must learn to be a man sometime."

"He has learned to be a man before he has finished being a boy," came another voice, mellifluous even in English: Read-a-lot, his volume of Latin poems now silent on his lap. "Send him home, Your Majesty, for everyone's sake."

The queen's family, unpopular with most of England, had powerful supporters among the king's closest friends, and Read-a-lot was one of them, maybe because he was even more unpopular than they were. The king however had always valued the bookish earl for the very thing that had made him unloved by everyone else: a biting intellect.

"*For everyone's sake?*" the king wondered.

"Edward Woodville is such a lecher at fifteen," Read-a-lot explained, "that no virgins will be left in the Midlands by the time he is sixteen, unless he comes home now."

"Yes and who bears the blame for that!" said the viscountess with a censorious glance at the Lord Chamberlain, not however excluding the king himself. "Those who lead by example should be careful about the example they set."

"He shall come home!" the king decreed. "There are no virgins left here in the south, are there, Hastings?"

"How curious you should ask!" said the Lord Chamberlain. "It has some relevance to our first item for the day."

"Tell me more."

"I have scheduled a petitioner to see you this morning: John Mandeville, a Southwark merchant—*Farthings* to his friends."

"He imports wine for the court," Edward recalled, being genuinely interested in trade, both as a king and as a trader himself.

"He smuggles it from France," said the viscountess, still in a fault-finding mood, "and the French are our enemies, if you recall."

"The French have allied themselves to the Lancastrian rebels," His Majesty conceded, "but that's no reason to treat their wine like an enemy too."

The bedchamber erupted in applause.

"Strictly speaking, Farthings imports Spanish olives," Lord Hastings continued, "but the London guild of wine merchants is now threatening to stop and search his shipments. He requests that you warn them off."

The king began to look concerned.

"I don't want trouble with London."

"Farthings operates from the bishop of Winchester's manor," Hastings continued. "The bishop doesn't want trouble either, so our friend is getting desperate. However, I agree with your reservations, and the petition should be rejected. Farthings is a versatile man and can make money out of something else. Meanwhile we can get all the wine we need by plundering French ports."

"So ..." the king said by way of encouragement, because Hastings would not have introduced this topic without some larger relevance.

"Mandeville has a daughter, said to be among the most beautiful women in all England—and still a virgin!"

"Susanna!" the king recalled, sitting up. "I danced with her once. It was a May Day. She was a mummer, playing Maid Marian. I will never forget that face, or her figure. How did she get away?"

"She is known to have the manners of a brawling shrew, Your Majesty," the viscountess explained, "and her marriage prospects are zero. Your friends have a duty to shield you from such indiscretions."

"God shield me from my friends!" the king cried. "Where is she now?"

"Bourne," said the Lord Chamberlain. "I recently received a letter from there, sent by a reliable source, who heard it from another reliable source, a guest of Margaret Beaufort at a dinner in her manor house. Apparently, Sir Henry Beaufort groped the girl while he thought nobody was looking. Tore her gown. Not a word of it reached his wife. Margaret Beaufort is in the dark still."

"That sounds like discretion to me," His Majesty enthused.

"But—" protested the queen's sister.

"Show her father in," he insisted. "It's time we renewed this acquaintance."

The door opened and John Farthings Mandeville, merchant of Southwark, was announced. It was the very merchant that Rubies had noticed looking out of place earlier, and he looked even more out of place here. The Lord Chamberlain handed the merchant's petition to the king, and the king made a great show of reading it, pausing once to finger his chin and once to fondle Shore's knee.

"I'll consider this further when I have more time," he soon informed Farthings, before placing the petition on the bed sheet. "But you are a loyal friend of ours, Farthings, and I would like to show you our gratitude in some way. What can we manage for him, my Lord Chamberlain?"

"Well, there is a banquet and dance at Baynard Castle on the second day in March, some two weeks from now," said Hastings. "It will be an opportunity to get together with our Italian money—Italian *friends*, I should say."

"Wonderful!" said the king. "A lively bunch, those Italians. Bring your family with you, Mandeville. You have a daughter?"

"Yes, Your Majesty," Farthings answered after a nervous, almost terrified genuflection, "but she is in Lincolnshire."

"Two weeks is plenty of time to fetch her home," said Hastings.

"I once travelled to Lincolnshire and back with an entire army," added the king, "in little more than a week."

"But the rebellion!" Farthings reminded them after a deep bow. "Is it safe?"

"Good God, Mandeville," said Hastings. "It is not every day a man and his daughter are given an introduction to the court and its Italian money. But if it is a problem for you …"

"I will bring her home in time for the dance!" Farthings promised, almost prostrating himself at the foot of the bed. "There may be difficulties. Nevertheless, I will manage it."

"Good man!"

Farthings was shown out.

"Speaking of Lincolnshire and its rebels, the Constable of Lincoln Castle should have finished his errand by now," said the king, beckoning him with a wave.

Was His Majesty mocking Rubies or showing him a kindness? It was hard to tell. Rubies stepped forward, bowed and handed over the garter. Edward buckled it around Jane Shore's calf amid wolf whistles from his courtiers.

"Honi soit qui mal y pense!" he said, pointing to the gold lettering as he read it out aloud: "Shame on him who thinks ill!"

Farthings Mandeville had travelled to Westminster by the river Thames and he returned home to Southwark the same way, disembarking from his hired boat at the Liberty Manor wharf. Deep in thought, he was surprised by the bevy of prostitutes that usually waited there, though it was nothing unusual for them to be friendly.

"How is the *princess?*" one enquired. "Homesick yet?"

"How is Bourne?" asked another. "Sick of her yet?"

"And the *saint?*" asked a third. "Will he ever get to Heaven?"

"He is always homesick for that place," said a fourth. "His death can't come soon enough."

The princess and the saint usually came and went by a more respectable wharf just a little downstream, outside the church of St Mary Overie. Whores can forgive almost anything but never a cold shoulder, and obviously the saint must have treated them to yet another one just this morning.

"How about a kiss?" a fifth wanted to know, because Farthings always respected a prostitute's right to work, even if his two children didn't.

Red and *Square* were their nicknames in more polite company, because red was the colour of Susanna's hair, and because his son liked everything to be just right. The neighbourly whores were politely known as *Winchester Geese*, and the bishop of Winchester was their landlord, as he was for Farthings. Farthing always paid his rent promptly but it was the extra little things he did for his landlord that really mattered. Cheaper premises weren't hard to find, but a history of mutual favours with a powerful man is the work of a lifetime.

A history of mutual favours, however, can be like trading in anything else—it creates expectations, and expectations can lead to disappointments—and there had been a mysterious cooling in the bishop's attitude towards him lately. Was the bishop still smarting over the failure of a joint venture, twelve years ago? They had set up a scriptorium in the loft of the house Farthings rented, turning out illuminated prayer books, portraits of saints and other devotional stuff that the bishop planned selling in the diocese. Farthings had even talked him into sharing the cost of a glass window, big enough to provide their artist good light in all weathers, but sales had never been good, then the artist had died, and finally Farthings had turned the scriptorium into a private solarium for himself and his family, so that he could concentrate on the carpentry side of his business. That decision had rankled with the bishop and he had retaliated with a hike in the rent. Was that punishment no longer considered enough or was there some new disappointment?

The latest favour done for the bishop was some work at the nearby church of St Mary Overie, repairing the nave roof after its collapse last year. Many people had said the collapse was God's comment on the country's woes. It was at least His addition to them, and yet every misfortune is an opportunity for someone to make friends or money. Farthings had contracted to repair it for little more than the cost of labour and materials, both of which he could provide at bargain prices. The London guilds always struggled to control free spirits this side of the river. However, there had been a problem with the quality of the new timber, leading to some unavoidable delays, and maybe the bishop was miffed about that.

These were difficult days for everyone, especially in trade. When not pointing the finger at the Germans and French, always warring with England, most merchants whispered against the Lancastrians and Yorkists, always warring with each other, and yet a free spirit makes the most of his chances, and Farthings had found an opening for himself in the wine trade, smuggling the bishop's and His Majesty's favourite French wines into England. It was a joint venture with his brother, married into an influential family in Utrecht, a Dutch principality always open for business, but now the London vintners had got wind of it, and they were demanding to inspect his barrels of Spanish olives, even after the king's own customs officers had approved them. The arrogance of the vintners was a threat to law and order, a threat to free trade, and a threat to the bishop's and His Majesty's supply of French wines, yet all that the bishop had done to help was suggest he petition the king, and all that His Majesty had offered him today was an invitation to Baynard Castle for a banquet and dances. The petition's fate seemed to hang on his acceptance—or rather, *hers*.

Would Susanna co-operate? She had danced with His Majesty once before, and he had seemed to take a fancy to her at the time, though nothing had come of it. Why the renewal of interest now? There had been a naked woman in the king's bed this morning. Was that a signal of his plans for Susanna, or just a careless oversight? His Majesty was wasting his time if he had any designs on Red. She had always admired the king, considered simply as a king, but she had never admired men, considered simply as men. She was a determined spinster and a formidable shrew. Finding her a husband had long been Farthings' worst nightmare. Punishments and threats had never worked with her so far. Pleading and begging had had no effect either. She was the most contrary, ungovernable female it was any man's misfortune to have for a daughter, but Farthings was never one to give in easily. She had behaved beautifully for the king the last time they had danced. Why not again? Maybe this time it would result in some material benefit, if not in the wine business then something else, financed by the king's Italian money. At the very least, she could win Farthings the favourable notice of important people at court, maybe even a worthy son-in-law. The king had opened a door for him. Now he just had to get Susanna through it.

There was much to gain but there was also much to lose. What if she went to Baynard Castle, eager to meet her king, and he behaved like any ordinary man? *Ordinary?* According to popular rumour, his sexual appetites were king-sized. The woman in his bed this morning was proof of that. If he was expecting Susanna to be just as obliging, he was in for a rude shock. Anyone foolish enough to take liberties with her always got rewarded with the sharp lash of her tongue, sometimes with actual violence: a kick in the shins or even a punch in the face. The *princess* was capable of anything. Things could hardly be more awkward if His Majesty had designs on Square. The Mandeville fortunes were already teetering on the brink of ruin. Now Susanna was in a position to give them the final push. It was with mixed feelings therefore that Farthings made his way home from the wharf.

Home was a converted warehouse in a gated lane, shared with some of Southwark's other respectable or semi-respectable homes and businesses, set well back from the waterfront brothels, the church and the bishop's palace. The warehouse was actually quite ancient and had once stood at the end of a navigable inlet. Improvements to the land, and renovations to the building, had since given it the high-and-dry look of a significant house. Inside was a cavernous workshop-cum-hall, separated from the living quarters by a brick façade as lofty as a castle wall. A sign out front indicated that this was the residence and workshop of a merchant-carpenter, but everything else pointed to someone destined for even bigger things someday, if Susanna didn't ruin everything first.

By now, work had already been set aside for lunch, and the usual trestle tables had been set up for servants and labourers. It was a humble meal, this being Friday, when the Church expects abstinence. Humility also suited the financial situation. Nevertheless, privileged members of the household always sat at a permanent table, elevated on a dais. Everyone knew the routine. All rose respectfully when Farthings appeared, and only sat again after he did. Hushed anticipation awaited any news, reprimands or orders he might hand out.

"I have come to you straight from the king's bedchamber," he announced. "He and I have had a friendly chat."

"*The king's bedchamber!*" came the admiring echo from all the staff as he helped himself to a cup of plain ale. "*A friendly chat!*"

"He was actually in bed," he added, just to evoke something of the friendly atmosphere, "and a woman was with him. She wasn't the queen."

"*In bed! Not the queen!*"

"I am trusting all of you with this information, just as His Majesty trusted me with it. We are not merely his loyal subjects now. We are his friends."

Most of the staff hadn't been paid in weeks. The promise of pay was all that kept them working, and that promise was beginning to wear thin. Good news was important.

"Your Spanish olives are safe now?" asked a little man on Farthing's right.

This was Spicer, or *Spicer the Mouse*, as Susanna was wont to call him. He was the head carpenter and latest, failed candidate for son-in-law. Farthings had always paid him like a journeyman but his skills were those of a master craftsman, so of course keeping him happy was a commercial imperative. Susanna had scorned him in spite of that.

"The king is still considering my petition," Farthings answered respectfully, "but he would never have invited me into his bedchamber if he had meant to turn me down."

"And the woman?" Spicer wanted to know next, for he was as lonely as any underpaid mouse of a man can get.

"I have seen her about town before now, Spicer, but never like that: thighs smooth as ivory. It was the London goldsmith's wife, Elizabeth Shore."

"A lucky man then," said Spicer, licking porridge from a spoon.

"*Lucky*? It was hard work and thrift that have earned me that privilege, not luck."

"I meant the king."

"The king? Yes, of course! Bedding a creature like Elizabeth Shore is something that you or I might consider the answer to our wildest dreams, but for a handsome king like Edward it is just another stroke of good luck. So, you have put your finger on it once again, Spicer. As deft with words as you are with timber: the Spicer touch."

"If I were king," Spicer mused dreamily, "I would have a dozen such woman at my beck and call."

"How are you managing with Noah and his Ark?" Farthings added, for the best way to keep Spicer from brooding on his need for a wife was to keep him thinking about the thing he had most talent for, which was work and more work. The bishop had asked for some wooden replicas of the biblical scene, to be ready by the Ides of March, in time for the annual commemoration of the Flood, and this project had priority even over repairs to the church roof.

"The animals and the Ark are done," Spicer reminded him. "Noah and his family are still to come. They will be ready in time."

The news that Farthings had delivered so far was all good and the results were promising: Spicer looked happier than usual and so did the other staff. The rest of the news was going to be more difficult. Susanna had made herself enemies with almost everyone, including their own household. He was tempted to keep her imminent return secret, yet he knew from experience that bad news is like water in a lead pipe. If it isn't kept flowing, it will find its own way out somewhere, making an even worse mess than if it had been allowed to move freely. Lies, on the other hand, are like any other stuff a man trades in—their value increases as they grow rarer. He was wondering how to break, bend or polish the bad news, without actually lying, when his son leaned towards him with an expression that Farthings had long since come to despise, as if the fool were choking on something.

"His Majesty … was in bed …" he said, struggling to get the words out.

"In bed and in fine form," Farthings said for him. "This anxious look on your face, I could understand, if he were sick or dying. A sick or dying king would be a concern for us all."

"… with another man's wife?" Square at last managed to get out.

"Yes, another man's wife! A king does as he pleases, Square. That is what makes him a king. It is yourself you should be worrying about, for if anything is likely to bring a man into public contempt, it is your habit of always looking at things as if there might be something wrong with them, after I just told you we had a friendly chat."

Farthings was not a pious man but he was sure that there must be a God somewhere, exactly like the one that always frowns from the Bible, punishing pleasure with guilt, because only a jealous and vindictive God could have cursed him with a son like Square, so horribly like his sister, yet so horribly unlike her too! Both of them imagined themselves somehow superior to others, but whereas she used fists as the ultimate weapons, he used Scripture. Southwark fitted Farthings like a glove. It fitted Square like a hair shirt.

"There was no attempt to hide her?"

"It would not have been such an honour for me if His Majesty had tried hiding her," Farthings reasoned with him. "We don't hide things from our friends, Square. Perhaps that is why you have none—except for your sister. You and she are the same frog. So, I have some good news for you: she is coming home."

This was greeted with an alarmed murmur all around the hall. Only Old Will and Cook looked unperturbed, because Old Will was too old and Cook was a woman too even-tempered to expect trouble. The rest of the staff were hopeful males and they had all felt the rebuke of Susanna's tongue or hands at some time or other. Spicer the Mouse took the news worst of all.

"So soon?" he wondered, almost knocking over his tankard of ale. "But I'll never marry her—not after the way she treated me!"

"She won't ever make fun of you again," Farthings assured him. "I value you as a man, Spicer, not just as a carpenter. Isn't that why I banished her to her aunt's house in Bourne?"

"I would never have accepted your offer of her hand in marriage if I had known she would act towards her own fiancé like that," Spicer went on. "She is cruel, cruel with her tongue, and even crueller with her hands."

"It's lucky you were small enough to crawl into places she couldn't reach," Farthings offered sympathetically. "But she has been gone more than six months now, and it's time to give her a chance with someone else. In fact, I should tell you some more good news." He paused for a big draught of ale, because he was taking a big risk, yet there seemed no alternative. "The king has invited Susanna and me to Baynard Castle, the second day in March. I made some inquiries before I left the palace, and it seems it will be an afternoon of banqueting, with dances between courses as the main entertainment. The best and greatest names in London, many of the country's greatest magnates, and a horde of Italian worthies will be our fellow guests. It is a great honour for me, for Susanna and for this household. The king would never have invited us unless he means to dance with her himself."

Spicer's and the staff's earlier alarm now began to waver in a cross-wind of wonderment. They might yet tolerate her return, with a bit of delicate handling, but Square was the weakest link in the Mandeville chain and he just couldn't help opening his pious mouth again.

"Is this wise?" he wondered. "After you saw the goldsmith's wife! Just yesterday, I overheard one of the chantry priests at St Mary's calling the court another Sodom and Gomorrah, and several others have said—"

"There you go again!" Farthings protested. "Always the prude. Always inspecting every cloud for signs of thunder. As if the court could be any worse than Southwark! His Majesty honours us by this invitation and we must make the most of it."

"She could decline the invitation," was Square's next reservation. "She might even refuse to come home. She is great friends with Aunt Marian."

"If she refuses to come home, it will be because I banished her there. Disobedience is her way of punishing me back. So, we must keep news of the king's invitation quiet, until I find the right time to share it with her. Till then, we can say that I am sending her to stay with her uncle in Utrecht. She has always wanted to go to Utrecht. She'll come back for that. Those Dutchmen are mad-keen painters."

"You are ordering us all to tell lies?" Square wondered.

"I am ordering everyone to embellish the truth. It is but plastering over a hole. You are a carpenter, aren't you? Then don't make such a fuss."

"No, I won't have it!" cried Spicer, jumping to his feet. "She can't come back here."

"It's only for a short time," Farthings pleaded, "and it's the king's wish, Spicer, not mine. Besides, I really will send her to Utrecht someday."

"When?"

"You are getting a bit personal, aren't you?"

"If she's coming back here, I'm going!"

"The king's wishes come first."

"The king be damned!" Spicer cried, not at all like a mouse now.

"He could be damned if Square is right about Sodom and Gomorrah, but so long as he is the king—*our* king—he must be obeyed. Susanna is coming home, and that's all there is to it."

"I am about to leave. Yes, I'm going."

"What about Noah and the Ark? The bishop looks forward to a grand display."

"I don't care about Noah. I don't care about the Ark. I don't care about the bishop, and I don't care about you. I'm leaving!"

Spicer jumped from the dais, vanished into the kitchen, where his personal gear was stored in a box bed, then emerged clutching a meagre basket, and left.

"Well that's gratitude for you," Farthings complained. "After all I have done for that man."

His departure was a savage blow. A craftsman with Spicer's high level of skill and low expectation of pay can't be replaced at the drop of a hat. However, it was important not to let the remaining staff detect any weakness, so Farthings merely shrugged and helped himself to some smoked cod. Any other day but Fishy Friday, he would have consoled himself with some beef.

"He will be difficult to replace," Square observed like the fool he was.

"Anyone can be replaced!" Farthings snapped. "Anyone but you and your sister. I'm stuck with you two whether I like it or not. But let's not be put off by Spicer's want of nerve. Susanna is coming home. You must make the travel arrangements, Lister. Lister? Did you hear me?"

Lister was another privileged member of the household, seated at the high table. He was the Mandeville sergeant-at-arms. An impoverished veteran of the wars in France, he was always up for a bit of rough stuff when and as required, and yet now he began to look frail.

"All the way to Bourne and back?" he wondered. "By the second day in March, while all Lincolnshire is up to its ears in rebellion? It can't be done."

"The king can manage it with an entire army in little more than a week. He told me so himself."

"I'm not the king. An army would help."

"It was you and Square that took her to Bourne last time," Farthings reminded him, "and yet you got back in just under two weeks, didn't you?"

"Last year's rebellion had already ended by then, and this year's hadn't started. It's more dangerous now."

"Take some of our men with you. That's protection enough."

"They're busy with the church nave," Lister reminded him.

"Then you must hire men from somewhere else—men who can handle themselves. But not above three pounds for the lot. Money is tight just now."

"It will cost you more than three pounds," Lister objected. "Good men don't come cheap."

"With you, the Terror of France, leading them? They'll be good enough at half that price."

"It's a long ride to Lincolnshire," Lister complained, shifting uneasily on his chair. "I'm not up to it just now."

"You and your piles! I don't know why I employ you."

"Good men don't come cheap," he said again.

"I would fetch her myself, if I could," Farthings reasoned with him, "but some important payments are due by the ides, and I have to watch my olives. You must go, Lister. I insist."

"Well if I must go," said Lister, pausing to drain his tankard, "I'm not coming back."

He stepped down from the dais, collected his belongings from the kitchen quarters he shared with Spicer, and departed.

"She isn't even home yet and already she is causing trouble." Farthings complained. "So that leaves you, Square. Are you man enough to ride all the way to Lincolnshire and return with your sister, within two weeks, without Lister's help? She can always protect you on the way back, if there is any fighting to be done."

Pacifism was one of the Christian duties Square had always taken to absurd lengths, even in disputes where he happened to be in the right, and Susanna had been protecting him from bullies ever since she had grown to half his size. Oddly enough, though, he had a taste for bloodthirsty literature: tales of knightly adventures, whose chivalrous heroes do nothing but ride about all day, slaying wicked varlets, vanquishing dragons and rescuing damsels in distress. In fact, the only times Square ever experienced anything like camaraderie were Friday nights, when fellow fans and authors of his favourite drivel gathered to share stories, usually at the Tabard Inn. Sometimes he came home with memorabilia, such as the wooden cup he was drinking from this morning, painted with the likeness of King Arthur, wielding his magical sword, Excalibur. It gave Farthings an idea.

"It's Friday," he recalled. "Maybe you can find someone at the Tabard to go with you—good men who can fight a bit, and who are ready to ride at short notice. You should ask."

"The king was in bed with another man's wife," Square repeated, as if this this might still be a serious obstacle.

"The king is a sinner, My Boy, and he will pay for it someday, but that must be in God's own time, not ours. Meanwhile, don't underestimate your sister. His Majesty will turn saint before she turns whore."

Square became more than usually thoughtful, then nodded and smiled. Farthing had expected more of a battle than this, but a merchant never mistrusts his luck in a crisis, and they were running out of time.

"When do you want me to leave?"

"That's the spirit! Tomorrow. I can't afford more than three pounds. That includes hired hands and travel expenses, so you must borrow horses, stay with friends—that sort of thing. Charity costs nothing."

"Tomorrow leaves little time for borrowing horses," Square demurred, "but the age of chivalry isn't dead yet and I know just the right man: England's foremost knight, Sir Thomas Malory! He has turned the history of Camelot into an epic story, *The Death of Arthur*. We have been hearing him read excerpts every Friday night for the past month."

"Does he come cheap?"

"Rescuing damsels in distress is its own reward for men like that."

"Is he good with a sword?"

"A true knight ever advances the cause of peace, but should that fail, *then forth he draws his mighty blade, like lightning from the throne of Heaven, and deals upon his foe stern blows of hardened steel.*"

Square demonstrated the action in miniature, wielding his kitchen knife against an imaginary foe.

"Bring your sister back in time for the dance and I'll never laugh at chivalry again."

Day 4

T ursday 15t of February

Susanna sat with bowed head, listening with the rest of the household to Aunt Marian's morning prayer, all on benches by the outside fireplace. Attendance was compulsory. This was the time Marian instructed everyone in their jobs for the day. Even the Galts were required to attend, though there were few jobs they could be trusted with.

"We are fast approaching another special day in the life of our Church, Dear Lord," said Marian in tones that would do justice to a Mother Superior, one eye closed in prayer, the other watching her little flock: Watt's feud with Adam Galt the Elder had persisted for a week now and was threatening to get out of hand again. "Soon it will be Septuagesima Sunday, a time when pious households begin Lent early. Help us remember, in our heart of hearts, that Lent is the season when we practise abstinence and self-reflection, commemorating how Thy Son Jesus triumphed over the Devil after wandering the desert forty days and forty nights. We earnestly pray that we also triumph over the devils that tempt us, today as much as ever, the more so as we are but imperfect servants of Thy will and need all the help we can get."

"Amen," Susanna said with the rest of the household.

"And Lord!" Aunt Marian continued, loud enough to command even Watt's attention, since he was preparing to throw sticks and gravel at Adam the Elder, who was getting ready to retaliate with a similar handful. "We think today especially of our visitors, not just the Galts and Friar Fryer, but all our other friends stranded in the township, especially in the abbey, which is straining under the burden of so many in such great need. May the Holy Spirit move among us today, inspiring Sir Robert Welles to grant everyone's sincerest wish: safe passage from Lincolnshire for all who desire it, in a true spirit of peace and forgiveness."

"Amen," said Susanna and the others again.

The prayer now out of the way, the threatened exchange between Watt and Adam the Elder materialised in a spray that enveloped the little congregation. An uneasy truce followed, Friar Fryer counselling the Elder in earnest whispers, while Marian took firm hold of Watt's hand.

"Tasks for today," she resumed, Watt struggling to break free. "I shall be going to the abbey this morning, lending my own voice to the voices of the abbot, the visitors and the whole township, pleading with Sir Robert. Meanwhile Friar Fryer—you will stay here and supervise the Galts. The indoor fireplace needs a good sweep, the lanterns must be polished, a hen plucked. Watt had best come with me. There was something else I meant to say, something else to do with Watt, I think."

"Dog has run away again," the friar reminded her.

"Yes, Watt's Dog has gone missing yet again, so everyone please keep an eye out for it. Matilda! You will oversee the laundry, including items from the abbey. They cannot cope with the extra load, and the abbot has sent us some habits for washing. Meanwhile, since Sir Robert is in the neighbourhood, Susanna and I will have an opportunity to complain to him about the apology we received last week, or didn't receive—Susanna?"

Susanna was shaking her head, signalling her reluctance to speak with Sir Robert. The last thing she wanted was another 'apology', in case Kilsby mistook it for another excuse to come calling. Putting her scruples into words, or not putting them into words, required some thought.

"Maybe Sir Robert already has enough to think about for one day," she came out with.

"A generous thought!" said Marian. "The public good must ever come first. We can always complain another time, and meanwhile this household is well protected. My tenant farmers will be here again this morning, keeping watch, and the whole town is on alert, ready to punish trespass. Susanna, you will be in charge here till I get back."

A few more instructions followed and then the household disbanded, Aunt Marian and Watt to the abbey, everyone else to their various chores. Susanna ensured nobody was idle then withdrew to her private quarters behind the swan-screen, intent on a chore of her own: the portrait of Isaac. A week had passed since she had started it in the orchard and she had now finished everything but the face, still just an oval of white plaster. Faces give portraits their whole life, meaning and character, and the inspiration for it had deserted her. If only she could paint in oils, instead of quick-drying tempera! Then she could push the paint around until something useful happened.

"All I can see is *him*," she grumbled.

Kilsby's smirking and haughty looks had haunted her for a week now, his green eyes especially. Usually she found green eyes madly attractive, but his were the colour of pondweed, steeped in a cold world all their own, and it was hard to focus on anyone else's eyes, with those rank pools always hovering in her mind. Isaac's eyes were supposed to be as blue and brave as a cloudless sky, modelled on those of Adam Galt the Younger. If Aunt Marian's prayers were answered, and all the stranded travellers left Bourne, the Galt family would probably head home too, taking Adam with them, and then Susanna would be an artist not just without inspiration, but even without a model to work from. She wouldn't mind leaving Lincolnshire herself in that case, now that Kilsby was in the neighbourhood, and yet nowhere on the road would be safe for her if *he* got to hear about it, especially if he had made common cause with the rebels.

In Southwark, whenever inspiration failed her, she could always stimulate her creative energies with outings across the river, losing herself in the hustle and bustle of Cheapside, or in the grandeur of St Paul's. Some real colour and movement, a breath of excitement, the distractions of real life—that's all the artist in her ever needed to get fired up about her work.

"I should have gone with Marian," she told Isaac's blank face. "But what if Kilsby is there? He has something to do with Sir Robert Welles, or he wouldn't have come here with Roussell and that bunch of trouble-makers from Grimsthorpe Castle. Best I keep myself out of notice. Or is that cowardice? Is that why I can't see your face, Isaac? Only the brave know how the brave look."

She was still pondering the situation when music began wafting around her screen of swans: a solitary pipe playing a haunting melody, *Divinum Mysterium*. It was a popular hymn, heard almost everywhere—in taverns as well as churches, in streets and fields, morning, noon and night—but never till now in Marian's strictly regulated domain. Susanna turned Isaac's portrait to the wall and went to investigate.

The Galts, supervised by Friar Fryer, should have been at least half way through their chores by now—polishing lanterns, sweeping the hearth, and plucking a chicken—but there was no sign of him. The Galt mother had fallen asleep with a neglected lantern nursed on her lap, its little door hanging open like a baby's mouth, vainly awaiting the next spoonful. The Galt father sat by the hearth, looking dejectedly at an undisturbed pile of ash. Fourteen years old, Adam the Elder lay stretched out on the floor, using the chicken as a pillow, meanwhile keeping a solitary feather hovering above his pouting lips with little puffs of barely exhaled breath. Only Adam the Younger was keeping busy. He sat in sunlight by the rear door, playing on a humble pipe, his fingers somehow finding the right stops and releasing them at exactly the right instant, with a dexterity that belied his tender years. A born musician! His parents and brother sometimes used his talent to pay for their gambling and drinking habits but there was nothing mercenary about the impulse animating him now.

Was it his innocent delight in music, eyes closed so he could savour it without distraction, or was it the sunshine making a halo of his hair, that gave him a peculiarly biblical look at this moment? Susanna approached quietly, hoping even now for inspiration, and maybe she would have found it too, had not something else, glimpsed through the doorway, grabbed all her attention next.

A tall, overly well-dressed maid stood by the outside fireplace, a wooden paddle in hand, stirring a vat of steaming water—Matilda washing clothes—but that wasn't what caught Susanna's eye. Nor was she distracted by the five men seated around the vat, enjoying the warmth of the fire, and the heat of Matilda's gossip: Marian's tenant farmers. It wasn't the gigantic watchdog, padding about the yard like a horse at pasture: Thunderbolt. It wasn't the orchard and its trees, festooned with the black habits of Augustinian canons: Matilda had used the bare branches as clothes props.

It was Friar Fryer.

He was wandering through the orchard stark naked, fingering the fabric of each habit he came to. Mystified and disgusted, Susanna, decided to investigate. She stepped around Adam and signalled to Matilda to accompany her. Matilda, who had fished out an Augustinian stocking on the end of her paddle, just to emphasise whatever saucy point she had been making for her audience of farmers, now carried it like a banner, dripping with scandal, while she marched alongside Susanna, agog at the scene awaiting them. The friar's only covering was a thick matt of ginger hair, spreading from his chest down to his tiny penis, thence across his buttocks.

"Friar Fryer!" said Susanna, surprising him as he was examining a black habit, almost as wet as Matilda's stocking. "What do you think you are doing out here, like that!"

"I am looking for the driest one," he explained.

"Your own is dry," she reminded him, pointing to his grey, Franciscan habit, hanging from a pear tree.

"The abbot doesn't want me in the abbey, so I am going as one of his canons."

"That will amuse him!"

The friar had a history of problems with the abbot, rooted in the rivalry of their religious orders, but the Galts and the rebellion had made things worse. The Galts were serfs indentured to Ware Manor, which was also home to the friar, and he had followed them to Lincolnshire after they had stolen a silver plate from the manor house there, worth an artisan's entire wages for a year. It was a hanging offence at that price but farms were short of labourers and the friar had persuaded them that they would be pardoned by the manorial court if they returned before the next session. They had got only as far as Bourne when the rebellion had erupted, stranding them with their precious silver. At first, they had sheltered in the abbey, but a beadle from Ware happened to be stranded there too, and he and the friar had exchanged blows in an argument over the plate. Shortly after that, the Galts had been caught stealing wine from under the sacrist's nose, and then the abbot had discovered the friar hearing their confessions in the refectory. The Augustinians could forgive almost anything, but not an unauthorised confession in their own abbey, so the friar had been cast out and the Galts had left with him. Aunt Marian had taken them under her wing as an act of mercy.

"The abbot is a fool," said the friar, finally choosing a black habit that dripped less than the others.

"Nobody is *that* big a fool."

"People see what they expect to see," he insisted after pulling the habit over his shoulders. "He won't recognise me in black."

"In what part of the Bible did you learn this trick, Friar: The Book of Galts?"

"God loves even thieves," he affirmed, meanwhile squeezing some drops out of his hem. "How do I look?"

"Like a thief. Now explain yourself."

"I have no choice," he said with a defiant shrug. "One of the farmers just told me the bad news: Sir Robert Welles has refused everyone safe passage. Yet there is still some hope for private appeals, if they are addressed to his men. I will appeal on behalf of the Galts. They must return to Ware before their repentance wears off."

"Why would the rebels listen to *you?*"

"I shall take the Galts with me."

"Disguised as Augustinians?"

"No need for that. The abbot's grievance is with *me*. Once the rebels see them as they truly are—a family of serfs—they'll know they are no threat to their rebellion."

"A threat to their silver maybe."

"They won't deny my appeal. I have prayed to the Lord. The Lord will give my voice wings."

"In that case, Friar, let your voice fly to the abbey by itself. You have responsibilities here and so do the Galts. Now get back to the house and finish your chores! Or shall I warn my aunt and the abbot about your sneaking ways?"

She supported her authority by folding her arms and giving him one of her aunt's most withering looks. It was a useful weapon in respectable company and Susanna had got quite good at it—it was less trouble than boxing people on the ear—but it was wasted on this man, because he never looked directly at anyone, not even when conversing.

"You don't frighten me," he told the ground at her feet. "You aren't the kind that snitches."

The Augustinian imposter hurried back to the house and soon reappeared with the Galts, heading for the abbey. Matilda shouldered her paddle and stocking in disgust.

"The only naked man I have seen since we left Southwark, and his bum looks like a pair of hedgehogs!" she complained.

"Bourne was alright till we met some of the neighbours."

"We should appeal to the rebels ourselves. I have to get out of here, before your aunt's early Lent drives me crazy. It's always Lent with her, always abstinence and more abstinence. Abstinence is the only thing she indulges in to excess."

"We could go to the abbey disguised," Susanna thought to add.

"*Disguised?*"

"Like each other. I can dress up for once and you can dress down. Nobody will recognise us. It might even be fun, don't you think?"

"Maybe for you, dressed up like me."

"We'll call me the daughter of some knight from somewhere or other, and you can be a proper maid for once. Why not! You have been nagging me about going home ever since we left Southwark."

"You never listened till now. But why disguised?"

Susanna wondered if she should tell Matilda about her problems with Bertram Kilsby and why a disguise would be helpful, but quickly decided to keep her secret quiet.

"Oh come on Matilda!" she pleaded instead. "I'll give you another shilling." Matilda held out her hand for immediate payment. "Alright, you'll have to lend it to me first."

"Then that's another *two* shillings owed me by Christmas, amounting now to a grand total of four pounds, eight shillings and fourpence."

"That's getting to be a lot of money," Susanna couldn't help notic-ing, meanwhile trying not to look too scandalised. "What makes you think I'll ever get it out of my father?"

"I wouldn't risk it for anyone else," was Matilda's nobly reply. "You need the money, and I'm happy to help."

"Plus you hope to make a big profit," Susanna reminded her.

They returned indoors and searched through each other's clothes for something suitable. Susanna was of middling height and Matilda unusually long in the legs, a difference in sizes that limited their options. Susanna, in a hurry, settled on Matilda's most luxurious robe, a fantas-tic, all-white creation whose deep hood and abundant folds looked even more abundant and luxurious on someone a little too short for them. Matilda, on the other hand, simply couldn't bring herself to choose from a limited wardrobe, and Susanna ended up choosing for her: a green gown under a grey, hooded cloak. It was a pretty combination on Susanna, but it exposed Matilda's calves.

"The higher the hem, the lower the woman," she complained. "I look like a drudge."

"You can hide yourself in the crowd," Susanna assured her.

They left the farmers minding the house and hurried to the abbey church. Some disappointed people were already leaving by then, and Aunt Marian was consoling them amid gravestones, while Watt kept tugging on her arm, trying to get free. Susanna avoided the woman's keen gaze, leading Matilda round to the porch. Once inside, she paused at the stoup as if to bless herself, but actually to reconnoitre. Most of the faces were glum but none were Kilsby's, as far as she could tell in such a crowded space. Many travellers had still not lost hope, gathering in knots around members of the Welles' entourage, pleading for special permission to leave the county. Conspicuous among these hopefuls, at least to Susanna's knowing eye, was an Augustinian canon that looked ridiculously like Friar Fryer, trying his winged voice on some pimply pageboy. Meanwhile the Galts were drifting through the distracted congregation like experienced thieves, lurking here, lingering there. Susanna resisted the impulse to warn everyone. Her priority was to get herself out of Lincolnshire, and that meant finding someone to address her appeal to, preferably someone better than the friar's page.

She had never set eyes on Sir Robert Welles before now, but she knew from reports that he looked distinctly un-English, thanks to a moustache. There was no facial hair in the church, as far as she could see from her end of the nave, but there was someone resembling a nobleman's son, looking proud and aloof at the far end, where he was leaning against the chancel screen as casually as if he owned it. He was very short but wore a tall beaver hat, otherwise Susanna would not have glimpsed him through openings in the crowd, and his shoulders were swathed in a sable-lined cloak, whose high collar enveloped his mouth.

Collar? No, it was a moustache.

"This way!" she urged Matilda.

"Oh my blessed stars!" gasped Matilda, steadying herself against a pillar. "A god."

She was looking at someone in the aisle on the right: a barrel-chested figure a bit under average height, dressed in the manner of a respectable craftsman, yet with the face of a masterful angel, as if newly carved from stone.

"Forget him," Susanna ordered her.

"The love of my life? He doesn't even know it yet."

The outrageous flirt threw back her hood then followed her heart to the right, determined on conquest. Susanna pressed on regardless along the aisle on the left, obliquely advancing on Sir Robert, all the while wondering how best to phrase her appeal for safe passage. The nearer she drew, the less like a nobleman he seemed. Too much of his height was taken up by his very tall hat, and the face looked like a boy's, apart from the moustache. Whiskers on the Virgin Mother would have looked less improbable. He wore a short sword that was obviously too big for him, the scabbard harnessed at an abrupt angle, otherwise the tip would have rested on the ground. He borrowed some dignity and power from his costly garments, sprinkled with exquisite gold and silver trinkets, yet he lacked what every self-respecting nobleman never goes anywhere without: a close ring of bodyguards. They must have scattered with the rest of his entourage, listening on his behalf to appeals from desperate travellers. He wasn't utterly alone. He was in animated conversation with somebody even less visible than himself, seated low on the steps of the ornate pulpit. Susanna feared it might be Kilsby—all she could see at first was black shoes and black stockings—but after positioning herself for a better look, she found it was the abbot, now dressed like a regular Augustinian, with his habit hitched above his knees. She almost withdrew back along the nave, in case he saw through her disguise, but then she noticed that only Sir Robert talked, while the abbot seemed absorbed in gloomy thoughts all his own. She buried her face deeper in Matilda's hood, as an extra precaution, then inched ever closer, hoping to overhear whatever the rebel leader could be saying that was so uninteresting to the abbot.

"The seas …" said Sir Robert, barely audible through the hubbub of the crowd, "damned expensive … bloody foreigners … that's what causes it … the kingdom is not properly ruled, by God, or … Yes? What do _you_ want?"

The little man was staring at her.

"I am looking for Sir Robert Welles," she decided to say, meanwhile putting the pulpit's ornate breastwork between herself and the abbot. "I require safe passage out of the county. Maybe you could point him out to me."

"Sir Robert's men have ears," said Sir Robert, still leaning against the chancel screen, as if nothing anybody said could ever move him. "Talk to one of them."

"Don't _you_ have ears?"

"_I_ am busy."

"You don't look it."

He ignored this, but silence was as good as a nod for Susanna's purpose, and she continued loitering next to him. This was the man that was terrorising the whole county, and threatening her king. He had a nerve coming here.

"I wonder how Sir Robert can sleep at night," she confided in him, "considering the nuisance his rebels have made of themselves."

"Sir Robert sleeps the sleep of the righteous, being confident in his cause," he answered proudly.

"He must be sleeping still, or he would be easier to find."

"A woman's babble. Be off home with you."

"I would be off home with me gladly if Sir Robert and his rebels hadn't made the roads so dangerous," she retorted. "Why else would I have come here to ask for safe passage!"

"It is the false king that has made the roads dangerous," he protested, parting company with the screen at last, as if ready for an argument. "It is Sir Robert that has made them safe."

"Not even Sir Robert believes that."

"You know him well, do you?"

"Well enough to know why he keeps himself hidden!" she declared hotly.

"*Hidden?*" he protested.

"He is ashamed of himself."

"*I* am Sir Robert Welles!" he shouted, flushing such a bright shade of red, even his moustache seemed to catch fire.

"You took your time admitting it."

"I expect people to know it!"

This sounded unusually loud and there was a good reason why: the surrounding hubbub had now been replaced by silence, everyone in the church having noticed the confrontation developing by the pulpit. It was an awkward moment, more for him than for her, since she was still in disguise. Suddenly confronted with a large audience, he fingered his moustache a few times then swaggered along the nave, his sword scraping along the ground even in spite of the jaunty angle, while he worked himself up to something big.

"I am keeping hidden, am I?" he complained, glaring up at the faces in the congregation. "Sir Robert Welles, the power in Lincolnshire, is hiding in this abbey, is he? Ashamed of himself, is he? Sir Robert Welles, whose ancestors ruled Lincolnshire since even before the dykes were built! A fine thing to be mocked by some female, here in an abbey that now looks to him for its protection."

"A traitor has no cause to boast," Susanna countered from beside the pulpit still, because this man lacked the presence to keep her quiet, especially now that he was already defending himself.

Some of his men moved as if to silence her on his behalf but his anger proved too quick for them.

"*Traitor?*" he objected, his moustache almost jumping off his face as he returned along the nave. "Didn't I just say my family has been here since before the dykes? It is Edward Plantagenet, that passes himself off as king, that is the traitor, being the friend of upstarts like Rubies Burgh, the Constable of Lincoln Castle, and creatures like you, whoever you are that dares get above herself in this way!"

His willingness to engage in debate only encouraged her further.

"His Majesty won the throne by his own efforts," she said on behalf of her king. "*You* were knighted by your father, I suppose."

He stared at her in amazement then stared at the congregation. Only his men looked sympathetic and maybe that was what emboldened him to laugh out loud.

"By God, she must be pretty!" he said. "The Yorkist king has an eye for a wench, so maybe she has come here piping hot from Westminster."

"His loyal subject," she answered with a dignified bow of her hooded head, because she wasn't in Southwark now, otherwise she would have answered his lewd accusation with a fistful of riverside mud, shoved into his hairy face. "But what excuse is there for a nobleman's disloyalty to his king? I suppose it's your family connections! Yes, you are all relatives of one another, you nobles, and maybe that is why you think you can make and unmake kings to please yourselves. Meanwhile everyone else must pay for it with nothing but endless inconvenience."

There was a murmur of sympathy all though the church. She was regarded as a trouble-maker back home in Southwark. She felt like a leader here. Sir Robert looked ready to lose his temper again, but fingered his moustache instead.

"Yes, we nobles are all related to each other," he confessed, "or there would be no telling us from riff-raff like you. Someone has sent you here in all your boldness, meaning to defy me in my own domain, and maybe it is Sir Thomas *Rubies* Burgh, for it is he that hides himself, not I. His ancestors were mucking out stables while mine were galloping at jousts! But if Rubies were a pretty girl, I wouldn't mind him so much, so let's see who you are. Put off that hood and show yourself, My Lady Mystery."

The congregation shared his curiosity, its murmurs rising to an inquisitive pitch, but one voice louder than all the rest was in no doubt about her identity.

"Daddy, it really is Susanna Mandeville! I am sure it is. If that is Matilda over there, dressed like her, this must be Susanna over here, dressed like Matilda. I know her manner and voice anywhere, dressed up or down. No other woman stands up for herself like this."

Susanna knew that flattering voice well enough. It belonged to her cousin Cecily Norton. Till now, if she gave Cecily any thought at all, it was under the assumption that she was still at home in London.

"Susanna?" the abbot enquired as he lifted himself off the pulpit steps, for he had overheard Cecily too. "Why so it is! Sir Robert, this is Susanna Mandeville, the girl we spoke of last week."

"The drift of snow?" Sir Robert wondered.

Kilsby had described her in those same words only a week ago. There was no use hiding in a hood any longer, so she threw it back over her shoulders. Astonishing people with her beauty could be gratifying sometimes, and this was one of them. The congregation erupted in murmurs of admiration. Sir Robert leaned against the abbot, quite taken aback. Beauty is a beggar's bowl, however, since it leaves benefactors to give as much or as little as they choose, so she gritted her teeth and took three, four steps towards the upstart nobleman, wishing she could astonish him with her fists instead.

"*Drift of snow?*" she objected. "I am a merchant's daughter, hot-blooded and sure of my rights. It is my right to be treated with respect."

"You have a strange way of showing it," he pleaded.

"I am angry, and why shouldn't I be! Last week, you sent your men to apologise for a savage and unprovoked attack by a hawk. Well, I wasn't satisfied with the apology I got. They were insolent and rude: Tom Roussell and Bertram Kilsby."

"They are the earl of Warwick's men, not mine."

Mention of the earl added more fuel to her fire.

"The earl of Warwick!" she hooted in scorn. "The king's false friend one year, his worst enemy the next. And now his men are your guests at Grimsthorpe Castle. I wonder why!"

"Damn me if my business is any of yours," said Sir Robert, resting a hand on the hilt of his sword. "You are on thin ice now, My Lovely."

There had been a time once when a proud aristocrat would have cut down an insubordinate commoner even in a church, irrespective of gender or age, and Sir Robert was a scion of those days. Susanna, a scion of Southwark, knew when to rely on her wits.

"But this argument between us is pointless," she declared, taking three, four steps out of his reach, nearer the door. "And what of these other people here? All they want is safe passage out of Lincolnshire. Please allow them the freedom to go about their business. You must give these people safe passage, if you have any sense of honour left in you."

There was a large murmur of assent throughout the church.

"Does anyone else here want to tell me my business?" Sir Robert growled, as he glared again at the congregation.

"Yes I have something to say!" came a voice from the far end. "Did I hear you mention the earl of Warwick?"

"Who is talking now!" Sir Robert protested.

A stout man came forward in a crimson bonnet and stopped to bow.

"I am Walter Wheaton, a beadle of Ware, which is a manor in the possession of the earl of Warwick," he announced. "If I could have safe passage——"

"Safe passage?" the diminutive knight objected. "I have already said No to that petition when it was put to me by the abbot on behalf of all. Is everyone here deaf? And now, when my father is stuck in Westminster Abbey, by the treachery of a false king, that I should be expected to let a lot of strangers gad about the countryside for their own amusement and convenience, against my own inclinations, at a time like this, as if I hadn't enough to do! It's unreasonable. Address your appeals to my men, not to me, or keep your silence, all of you, if you have any sense."

"But your Lordship!" the beadle persisted. "I was between Spalding and Ware, on business for the earl, when I happened upon a set of thieves with a silver plate they stole from his manor, hiding out here in the abbey. I crave safe passage, your Lordship! So that I may haul those felons to the manor, to be tried by their betters."

"Liar!" intruded yet another voice, this one belonging to an Augustinian canon in a friar's sandals. "I was returning with the Galts to Ware even before you showed up! They are entitled to a pardon. I know because I told them so."

"Friar Fryer!" the abbot protested, rising up the pulpit steps in a white-knuckled fury, the better to damn the interloper. "Out of my abbey before I have you flogged! Sir Robert, this is what I have been talking about! This man was caught hearing confessions in the refectory. A Franciscan friar, now disguised as one of my canons! Yet this is typical of the troubles I am having. How can I manage these disturbances, all these people lodging here! It is not in the nature of things and does not reflect well on *any* of us"

"We all have our problems," Sir Robert reminded him huffily. "My ancestral rights are abused every day by upstarts like Rubies Burgh and this—this red-haired creature in a white gown—because the false king named Edward cares more for imposters like Rubies Burgh than for his own nobles."

The church was in an uproar as travellers, townsmen and Welles' retainers began arguing with each other over whose rights were getting abused the most. Susanna cursed her bad luck: Kilsby was certain to hear about this fiasco. She pulled her hood over her head once more and made a quick retreat.

"Susanna! Susanna!" Cecily called out to her, following from the porch as far as the abbey gate. "It's me, Cecily Norton! Don't you recognise your own cousin?"

"After you got *me* recognised?" she protested, not stopping even to look around. "Stay away!"

Day 5

Friday 16th of February

Sir Robert stood warming himself by a flaming brazier at the top of his favourite tower, gazing from Grimsthorpe Castle into the gathering gloom southwards—the countryside had just emerged through lifting rain and it was about to disappear into the darkness of evening—when the clatter of hooves drew his attention to the courtyard below.

"Up here for some sport!" he called down from the parapet.

"Is it better than a hot bath?" someone called back.

Denby had returned with the Beast of Ferrybridge and Bertram Kilsby from their week-long excursion to the fens. Sir Robert was eager to hear a report and he had some news to give in return—five items of news in fact. He counted the items on his fingers while waiting for the others to make their way upstairs.

"They'll want to hear about my visit to Lincoln, so that's *one*," he advised himself, marking the item with his thumb. "The news from Westminster is item *two*, and *three* is news from the earl of Warwick," he added, holding out his index and middle finger. "*Four* is the local news, and *five* should arrive any moment now. It's a nice coincidence, them showing up in time for it."

Denby arrived at the top of the stairs looking tired and sullen, the day's ride having left him soaked with rain and spattered with mud. The legendary Beast looked just as muddy but even more tired and sullen. Kilsby arrived cheerfully aloof as always. His black clothes concealed all traces of mud, as if he had flown rather than ridden.

"Keep your eyes out there," Sir Robert urged them all as he pointed to the south. "It will be a good omen if we see it in this weather."

Denby joined Sir Robert at the brazier and spread his hands close to the fire. He stamped his feet, as if to summon warmth from the cold stones, and sighed wearily.

"What are we looking for?"

"Obviously a beacon of some kind," said Kilsby, now loitering where the fire and the fading light of afternoon cast the fewest gleams, beside the open door of the stairwell. "What else could we possibly see in the distance this late in the day, Denby?"

"*Obviously a beacon*," mimicked Denby, as if tasting a lemon.

"How was your journey?" asked Sir Robert, feeling mischievous: it was already clear that they had not enjoyed each other's company, and it would enhance his authority if he could reconcile them when need arose.

"Foul and filthy for the most part."

"Journeys often reach a kind of crossroads," was Kilsby's verdict, still haunting the shadows, "a point where nothing turns out well or ill—at least not to our certain knowledge—and then every man has a choice: he can relax into indifference, or he can set his eyes on the greatest destination possible for flesh and blood, which is the proper regulation of his thoughts and feelings, so that he is neither the dupe of his hopes, nor the prisoner of his disappointments. Only then is he truly himself, a man worthy of success."

"I didn't understand a word of that," said Sir Robert.

"He found the journey a waste of his time," Denby said for him, "but he is like an eel and never gets straight to the point. It comes from always snooping for his earl."

"The *earl's eel*!" snorted Sir Robert, the undignified title amusing him immensely. "But how did Tom find the journey?"

The Beast of Ferrybridge was standing with his back to everyone, elbows propped on the parapet, staring into the gathering darkness, and he remained that way despite Sir Robert's prompting. When a rebel leader meets with that sort of insouciance, he knows he is being treated to less respect than he deserves, because a man can be weary from his travels and still be polite, and he can face people and still look south—Denby had managed it, and so had Kilsby. However, a legend is entitled to some leeway, especially if he is a friend, and Sir Robert tried teasing him a bit, just to open him up some.

"The earl's eel, eh Tom?" he prompted him. "You and Kilsby are colleagues, and maybe you feel the same way about things."

Still no response.

"He has more important matters than Kilsby on his mind," Denby explained.

"He doesn't share *your* opinion of me," Kilsby said in his own defence. "He chooses to serve the earl and therefore he chooses to be my colleague."

"*Chooses!*" scoffed Denby. "Tom was forced into that indenture."

The earl of Warwick's association with the Beast of Ferrybridge was an unfortunate but intriguing part of the legend. The earl had captured him with some other Lancastrian die-hards six years ago, after turning the royal cannons on their last refuge, Bamburgh Castle. The earl in those days was the Yorkist king's greatest supporter, and everyone had expected the Lancastrian hero to die a prisoner. He had astonished everyone just a few months later, walking free after signing up to the earl's service! Most doubts about his reasons seemed to have been answered last year, when Warwick had sided with the rebels, trapping the surprised king between their forces and his own. It had been the king's turn then to be Warwick's prisoner, and the captain in charge of the men escorting him to the place of confinement happened to be—it was impossible to imagine a more fitting turn of events—the Beast of Ferrybridge! That was at Middleham Castle, the same place where Tom himself had been incarcerated. The irony had added a new lustre to the Beast's legend, and yet his service to the earl was still something of an embarrassment to his friends, especially now that the king too had been released from captivity, when nobody knew which way the earl would jump next.

"How do you mean Tom *was forced* into that indenture?" Kilsby wanted to know. "The earl released him from captivity on condition that he never again take sides against him. The king was released from captivity last year on the same condition. The confinement of either man does not diminish the operation of free will in respect of the choices he made. I also have strong inducements to serve the earl, in part financial and in part natural, the earl and I being consanguineous on my mother's side. Does that mean I too serve him against my will?"

"Didn't understand a word of that either," said Sir Robert with a chuckle. "But what happened on your trip? I am as much in the dark as ever."

"There were few surprises," said Denby. "The fenmen don't trust the earl and they don't like Kilsby. It's his manner."

"What's wrong with Kilsby's manner?" Sir Robert couldn't help asking, even though he knew the answer already.

"He enjoys his own company more than he enjoys the good cheer of honest men," said Denby.

"Tom was nobody's boon companion either," Kilsby countered, "yet that didn't stop the fenmen crowding round to see him, wherever we went."

"He has good reasons to be moody just now, and his friends have every reason to love him in spite of it."

"The fenmen might have welcomed me too, Denby, if your attitude hadn't suggested otherwise," Kilsby objected, now beginning to look irritated at last. "Whether people enjoy my company or not is immaterial of course—to me, that is, for I am not ignorant of my own worth—but your petty suspicions have interfered with important plans, with the result, in this particular instance, that the earl's courier to France is still waiting for a ship. Who knows what the consequences of that failure might be!"

"As if people can't smell a rat without me pointing it out to them," Denby grumbled.

"But what's eating Tom?" Sir Robert couldn't help wondering.

He still hadn't moved an inch from the parapet. It was nothing unusual for people to return from the fens utterly changed from the people that had ventured in, and maybe this was just the latest example. A flooded wilderness, a vast and dreary expanse where land, sea, rivers and sky lose themselves in each other's bewildering embrace, the Lincolnshire fens could drive any man to despair, especially if he strayed from its few well-worn paths. Sir Robert himself never went that way if he could help it.

"He has been given some bad news," Denby now revealed.

"Then let's hear it," said Sir Robert, happy to help out the best he could. "What are friends for if not to share and share alike, the bad as well as the good! Tell me your news first, Tom, and then I'll tell you mine."

Still there was no response.

"Well, *I* am not shy of sharing news," Sir Robert persisted. "So then, here is my first item of news! *One*: I got back from the Lincoln visit the day before yesterday. Everyone there is red hot to ride in our support the moment the king dares take the field against us."

"You mean *if*," Denby cautioned him.

"I mean *when*. That's *two*, my second item of news: our people started returning from Westminster three days ago, stripped of everything but a few rags. Everyone confirmed Kilsby's report: my father has taken refuge at Westminster Abbey. It is a war to the death now, or we are traitors to our own cause."

This was received in thoughtful silence, interrupted only by a hiss of some raindrops on the fire. Sir Robert chaffed his hands merrily, interpreting the silence and the hiss as timely omens of better things to come. He was in command of the situation.

"We must plan carefully," Denby cautioned him.

"The plans are already made. *Three*: my third item of news! Our rider to the earl returned just this morning. He says the earl has pledged me his support, and with a cracking, great oath too. Warwick even called on his own ancestors as witnesses to his good faith. He will fight with us against the king or languish in Hell for all eternity."

"Not a word of it in writing," Denby surmised.

"Only fools put their plans in writing," said Kilsby, meanwhile advancing to the brazier, where he removed his gloves and warmed his hands next to Sir Robert's. "So, what are Warwick's plans? Did he say?"

"Go back to your earl and ask him yourself," Denby objected.

Denby knew better than a weather vane where the wind sits in troubled times but he was clearly in a huff now, and this was Sir Robert's chance to exert his authority.

"Put a bridle and bit on all your fuss and bother, Denby," he told him. "We're all in this together. The plans are good ones! The earl has made me the keystone to everything. I am to rally all our friends at Lincoln on Shrove Tuesday, eighteen days from now. That is after I issue pamphlets throughout the county, styling myself *Great Captain of the People*. Damn me if that is not a good name for me. Meantime, word of my defiance will reach the king, who must then march against us earlier than he had hoped, and with fewer preparations. The earl will march north too, as if to support him but …"

He left the climax hanging in the air.

"He will declare himself on your side at the last moment?" Kilsby surmised.

"The king will be walking into a trap," Sir Robert affirmed.

"But that's how the earl outfoxed him last year," Denby objected.

"It worked well then too."

"Nobody is stupid enough to fall for it twice."

"Everyone will think we're not stupid enough to try it twice," Sir Robert countered.

Denby stepped away from the brazier shaking his head.

"This is madness," he said. "All we have is the earl's unwritten promise of support, and a request that you organise some kind of army—out of what? Out of whatever rabble turns up on Shrove Tuesday. *We* could be the ones walking into a trap."

"*Rabble?*" wondered Sir Robert. "Didn't you hear what I just told you about all the support for me in Lincoln?"

"Yes, and I just told you about our trip to the fens," Denby pleaded. "There is no enthusiasm for an alliance with Warwick, none that we met with. He captured the king last year and released him again! Our friends haven't forgotten. Nobody will join us in this battle, not now—nobody but a few ruffians and villains whose services we can well do without."

"What of the exiles in France?" said Kilsby, now wandering along the parapet, tightly clutching both gloves in one hand: "The former queen, her son and heir to the throne, and all their most loyal followers: are they mere ruffians and villains? Now we see the full extent of your folly, Denby, when you prevented the earl's courier taking ship for France. Invaluable support may have been lost!"

"The exiles are going to rescue us?" Denby scoffed, wandering in the opposite direction. "You mean a handful of old men and some boys! And who knows but this is all some plot by Warwick and the king to lure them to the scaffold! If the Lancastrian queen and her son die, the cause dies with them."

"Who knows but that the French themselves might flock to your banner, if the earl's courier reaches them!" Kilsby countered, turning again to Sir Robert.

"Yes and which side will true Englishmen fight on then?" Denby almost laughed.

Sir Robert was in an awkward spot. Both Denby and Kilsby were making good sense. Denby was a man's man but Kilby was Warwick's, and Warwick was vital to their chances of success, if he could be trusted. Choosing sides was a difficult business. Tom Roussell was still standing with his back to everyone, still leaning on the parapet, staring at the darkness, and maybe he was keeping some good advice to himself.

"What do *you* think, Tom?" Sir Robert asked him. "You are very quiet."

Now at last the Beast detached himself from the parapet, taking a few strides one way, a few strides the other, before pausing and turning to face Sir Robert.

"Ah'll not be joinin tha fert comin battle, so dooant rely on me for owt," he said at last. "Ah'm sorry, Sir Robert, but a is ow t is."

Sir Robert almost burned his hands on the brazier. He had never got used to Tom's northern accent and maybe he had misheard him. The Beast of Ferrybridge wouldn't be in the rebel camp? The mere idea of going into battle against England's king, without support from England's greatest warrior, was enough to make a strong man go weak at the knees. Sir Robert pulled himself together.

"What are you saying?"

Tom pleaded for privacy with a wave of his hand, then turned back to the darkness.

"It is the bad news I mentioned earlier," Denby said for him. "It concerns his baby brother."

"He has a brother?"

"Peter, five years his junior," Denby revealed. "He is meant to be in Paris studying at the university there. Most of Tom's wages from the earl have been going to his education. Now he has snuck back into England, disguised as an Italian. He has been in London some months already, without a word to Tom. Tom learned about it just a few days ago from an old friend of ours in the fens, Midge Mason."

"But why did nobody tell *me* about this?" Kilsby complained, looking injured for once.

"And what does it all mean?" Sir Robert wondered.

"It means Tom wants to be in London more than anywhere else right now," Denby explained, "so he can find his brother and send him back to Paris. But that was before you told us your own news, Sir Robert. Now we need Tom here."

"Neya, not eear," Tom growled, turning round to face them all again. "Ah'm goin t London."

"But—" Denby tried reasoning with him.

"London!" Tom insisted.

Sir Robert could feel his mind reeling as it groped for the consequences of these revelations. Meanwhile a burst of wings sent roosting pigeons scattering into the gloom, spooked by Kilsby slapping his gloves against the palm of one hand. He soon halted by the brazier, pulling his gloves back on as tidily as if he had found an answer to something.

"Once again, Denby displays a grasp of strategy so weak, he risks helping the wrong side," he boldly declared. "London is self-evidently the only place for Tom right now."

"How do you work that out?" Sir Robert marvelled.

"Let me answer with another question: why would a Lancastrian sympathiser sneak into England from France, disguised as an Italian, headed for London? He has been sent, obviously."

"Sent?" Sir Robert wondered. "By our people in France?"

"To rally supporters for the cause," Kilsby affirmed, "almost certainly as part of some greater plot against the Yorkist government."

"T lahl dingy is neya threat t Yorkist rule—a danger onny ta imself!" Tom protested, waving his arms about in a fury.

"Tom's brother couldn't find is own arse in the dark, not even if his hands were guided to the spot," Denby added. "He is a dreamer and a scholar."

"Would the exiles and our friends in the French court have sent him to London without proper training, without a list of contacts, and no clear strategy?" Kilsby persisted. "Sir Robert, this is an opportunity too good to miss! A plan has already suggested itself to my mind, which I think you, Tom and the earl of Warwick will all support."

"Let's hear it then," said Sir Robert, impressed by Kilsby's sudden manner of getting straight to the point.

"Tom wants to join his brother in London. Alright, if that's where his heart lies, where better! Imagine them together—the Beast of Ferrybridge, backed by the earl's resources, and his brother, trained by the French in the art of secret warfare—both gathering to themselves a covert army of Lancastrians, ready to take London by storm. The king won't know which way to turn. Rebellion here in Lincolnshire, rebellion there in London, the earl of Warwick snapping at the royal heels, and Sir Robert Welles, Great Captain of the People, poised to drive the dagger home, whichever way the king turns!"

Kilsby thrust a gloved finger into the coals of the brazier, sending a flurry of sparks into the gathering night. He was a mesmerising speaker, now that he was no longer playing games.

"That sounds like good thinking to me," observed Sir Robert. "What about you, Tom?"

Tom rested a friendly hand on his shoulder.

"Ah wish Peter ad stayed i Paris, n Ah wish thy father ad stayed eear i Lincolnshire, but wha's done is done and there's nowt can change a. A man's neares an deares mun allus come fust. So Ah'm goan t London, Sir Robert, an' nowt anybody seays can stop me."

Sir Robert grabbed Tom's hand and squeezed it.

"Your duty calls you to London," he affirmed, "my duty keeps me here: a brother needs your help, a father needs mine. Loyalty to our own kind is what this rebellion is all about, damn it, or I am not Sir Robert Welles."

"Ah'll return an elp tha if Ah can, whenever Ah can."

"No you won't," Denby dared to say. "The Beast of Ferrybridge, isolated in London on the eve of another rebellion—the king would be mad to let you come back here. Your brother will be the death of you. It's suicide."

"Quit worryin. T earl o Warwick is still t real power i Englan n Ah'm indentured ta im. Meanwhile dooan't underestimate yoursen,

Denby t Dasher! Ah av nivva known a finer warrior. Tha can get Sir Robert's Shrove Tuesday army into fightin shape as well as Ah can, an mayhap better."

Denby tried not to laugh.

"I need more than praise, Tom. I need good men, good supplies, good horses."

"Ah'll leave tha my own followin," Tom offered, "all but my archer. We'll tek a mule n a couple o nags. That's enough t get im and me t London."

A chilly mist drifted over the tower as they all considered matters in silence. Sir Robert wondered if he should feel quite so confident about the chances of victory as he did before. However, optimism had always been the biggest thing about him and he chose to embrace it now.

"Now here is a coincidence!" he announced. "All this talk about men and horses reminds me of my next bit of news. *Four*: we confiscated a nice courser just this afternoon. Some other horses came with it; not bad some of them. The rest are just half-starved hobbies, and the riders aren't much better: mostly drunkards and trouble-makers out of London. Hardly sober enough to draw breath let alone draw a sword, by God."

"We'll be lucky if our Shrove Tuesday army is any better," said Denby.

"They're all in the cell downstairs," Sir Robert continued. "One of them is an author, Sir Thomas Malory. The man writes about King Arthur, chivalry and all that sort of thing, and the courser is his. But this is the bit that will interest you, Tom: he came with the brother of that girl, the abbot's drift of snow, the one that tangled with your hawk a week ago. He's come to Lincolnshire to fetch her back home. She tangled with me just yesterday. Almost started a riot in the abbey, the hussy."

"T wildcat Yorkist," Tom recalled.

"I have half a mind to put her over my knee and spank her."

Sir Robert demonstrated his style by lifting a leg and slapping his knee. Tom rubbed his chin like a man deep in thought.

"Ah advise aginst it."

"But look!" Sir Robert urged everyone, meanwhile pointing to a faint, red glow far to the south, its light blunted and scattered by the intervening mist and rain. "*Five*: My fifth and final item of news. It's a manor belonging to the king himself. I have given orders for his people to be spared, our cause being merciful and just, but the buildings are to be torched, as the signal of our defiance. The omens are good, if we can see it even on such a sodden night as this."

"There is no turning back now," Denby conceded.

Day 6

Saturday 17th of February

Susanna sat indoors, shrouded in the smoke of a dying fire, a mug of ale in hand. Thunderbolt, her aunt's gigantic watchdog, lay asleep at her feet, hogging the fireplace's remaining warmth, his nose almost in it. His usual place was by the stables but Susanna had brought him into the house as a last line of defence, in case someone tried breaking through the bolted doors and shuttered windows. As a watchdog, he left a lot to be desired—he had recently defended her from the Beast of Ferrybridge by savaging a dead rat, and now he looked as alert as a piece of furniture—but any protection is better than none.

It was a wintry day, the world outside veiled by rain. Everyone had gone to the abbey to farewell the Hallelujah Coffin, commemorating the last Hallelujahs to be heard in church until the end of Lent, some two months away. Gone were Marian and her servants. Gone were the farmers who had been keeping guard for days. Even Matilda had gone, lured to the mock funeral by an overpowering itch for the masterful angel she had first seen two days ago. Gone were the Galts, probably fleecing the congregation even now, and gone was Friar Fryer, though not to the abbey. He was somewhere in the woods outside town, giving the last rites to one of the hermits in the local leper colony. Susanna had volunteered to mind Marian's house in everyone's absence, being anxious to keep herself out of public notice. Solitude hadn't eased her troubled mind however. She was alone with her fears.

She wished she could talk with someone, but a good confidante is hard to find even when there are people about. Matilda and Aunt

Marian were good listeners—too good, if you weren't careful: secrets, like fish, are prone to taking bait. Susanna's cousin, Cecily Norton, on the other hand, though usually a safe listener, made for boring company, on account of her simplicity. She had been staying with her father at the abbey's manor, a little outside town, yet nobody in Marian's household had known that she was in the neighbourhood until the fiasco in the church, two days ago. Susanna wasn't inclined to renew the acquaintance. She still hadn't forgiven her for betraying her identity to Sir Robert and everyone else in the abbey church.

Thunderbolt? The fact that someone is only a dog was never a good reason to stop talking, but this one's manners were confronting, and a good set of ears doesn't always make for good company. No, there was only one pair of ears born to hear Susanna out in the sympathetic manner of a true confidante: Lady Lorna Blakeney. Lady Lorna's powers of empathy were surprising yet immediately obvious to anyone who met her, making her one of the most popular characters in Southwark, where she had led the Easter parade four years in a row. Only Jesus ever rode her, and only on that day, yet the Mandeville's landlord, the bishop of Winchester, always kept a stall for her in his own stables, free of charge. Marian's stables were a hovel compared with his, but they were close to the house, and Lady Lorna was happy to be anywhere near Susanna. Even so, Susanna couldn't bring herself to venture even that far outside the door just now. She sat in the gloom feeling lonelier than the friar's lepers and hermits. Even the fire seemed to be deserting her, fading little by little. Smoke hung about in listless clouds, looking for louvres to escape through and, just to round off her misery, the ale was old and tasted off.

Solitude rarely bothered Susanna. It was like blank paper and bare plaster, a vacancy that she could fill with life whenever inspiration took hold. This solitude wasn't like that. It filled her, not with life but with a vacancy that felt like death, evoking no end of dark thoughts.

"If there is a knock at the door," she told the sleeping Thunderbolt, "keep quiet: it could be Cecily. We'll just pretend nobody is home. But what if it's Kilsby? Watt's Dog is still missing. If that creep shows up here with Dog on a rope once more, or even if it is only some friends of his, like the Beast of Ferrybridge, get ready to bark up a storm. But no, you will just lie there, I suppose. Best I lock you in with them and set fire to the house, you lazy oaf."

Just then there came a loud **bang-bang-bang**. Susanna jumped to her feet, ale spilling over the top of her mug, hissing on hot coals. Silence ensued. She waited and wondered. Then it started again, more urgent than before, as if someone might actually be trying to break down the door. Thunderbolt should have been on his feet by this time, barking in defence of his castle. Susanna prodded him politely with her foot and still he slept. She dared not kick him a second time. He was a *very* big dog.

"Open up!" came a voice Susanna recognised.

Just to make sure, she peered through a crack in one of the shutters, and glimpsed an elaborate cloak and gown, sheltering under the eaves.

"You'll never guess who I saw just now!" Matilda gasped as she hurried into the room, hardly waiting for the door to be unlocked.

"If this is about the latest love of your life—"

"You'll never guess!" she insisted, her face an uneasy mixture of wonder, alarm and anticipation, all served up in a dripping hood. "He's headed this way."

"Kilsby!" Susanna hated to think, but Matilda was still in the dark about that creep, so Susanna prodded her memory by adding: "the stranger all in black. He brought Dog back last week."

"What about him?"

"Nothing, but maybe you saw his friend, the Beast of Ferrybridge?"

"Your brother!"

This was not what Susanna had expected at all.

"Square—here in Bourne?"

"With a party of armed men!" Matilda added, pulling back shutters in readiness for the expected arrival. "Like he was a man on a mission. I knew him in spite of that. Old Will is with him. Naturally, Square couldn't bring one of your father's handsome young carpenters. It had to be his faithful old drudge, eighty at least. The others I never saw before, all young but looking miserable in the rain, which is not to say they won't dry out to something respectable. One is all in armour. I couldn't see his face but something about the way he leans in the saddle doesn't inspire hope. They were riding through the town square when

85

I saw them. That was between the tinker's stall and the *Ensign's Rest*, so they can't be far behind me now. They must have come to take us back home, do you think?"

"Home!"

The word was like an answer to Susanna's prayers. Southwark, in spite of all its problems, or because of them, was more than just her home: it was her fortress. Nobody could match her knowledge of all its lanes and corners, garden walls and hedgerows, innumerable nooks and crannies for hiding and lurking, where it was always so easy to turn flight to ambush and ambush to headlong pursuit, as she had done so many times in her skirmishes with Square's bullies, and with the riverside whores, the Winchester Geese. Kilsby was in big trouble if he ever tried anything there. But why was she being fetched back home this early? It was only seven months since Square and Lister had brought her here. Her persecution of Spicer the Mouse should have earned her a longer banishment than this.

"What is Papa up to?" she wondered, returning to her chair.

"Say nothing to your brother about the money you owe me," Matilda whispered, though only Thunderbolt was near enough to overhear, and he was still asleep. "If your father ever finds out——"

"He must have come up with another fiancé."

"——he'll say it's *usury*, and you know what the Church says about usury: a crime against God! But we only ever exchange gifts, two of yours for every one of mine. That's hardly a crime like lending at interest."

"Who has he found this time? Some buffoon, no doubt."

"You know how jealous your father is about money. He'll banish you here forever, if he finds out, and then you'll have neither a maid nor a banker. How will you manage then?"

"I'm not going home," she decided while clamping her hands on the chair.

"*Not?*" Matilda marvelled. "In what sense?"

"I'm staying here."

"You can't mean that!" Matilda pleaded, crouching low by the chair like a heron about to ambush a frog. "You are desperate to go home, or you would never have gone to the abbey yesterday as me. We must get you out of here before we both go mad. I miss Southwark. I miss London. I miss anywhere but here. I would stay for the angel in the abbey, if he noticed me. What chance of that! I stopped being noticed by handsome men the day I started noticing them."

"Oh I don't know what to do!" Susanna confessed, anxiously getting out of her chair. "I don't want to stay here, but I don't want to go home either. I won't be fetched this way every time Papa finds some new nincompoop for a son-in-law."

There was soon a loud knock at the door. Susanna opened it herself. Square entered, a sheepish smile in a mass of sodden fur. He shed a puddle at her feet while they embraced. If there was anyone in the world that she was always happy to see, even if he dripped rain on her slippers, it was this. If there was anyone in the world she would never trust with her safety, even if he loved her, it was this. She had been his protector even in childhood, though two years his junior and half his size, and now they were adults, nothing had changed. He was a naive, good-natured soul and she loved him dearly, yet they hadn't finished embracing before she was already glancing out the door to see who had come with him.

"Where's our aunt?" he asked cheerily.

"They're all at church."

"Tomorrow is Septuagesima Sunday!" he recalled, clapping a hand on his forgetful forehead. "She'll be with the Hallelujah Coffin. But why are you here? You love the fun and games of the Hallelujah Coffin as much as I do."

"But who is this?"

A knight in shining armour had followed him to the door. The details of an ornately engraved helmet and intricately designed breastplate were highlighted by the rain still dripping off the polished metal.

"Let me introduce you," said Square, encouraging the stranger to come further in. "Sir Thomas Malory—my sister, Susanna!"

The knight bowed stiffly then slowly removed his helmet, revealing a coarse-featured, middle-aged face with large, haunted eyes, and a bald dome partially covered with swept-up locks of silver hair.

"What is he to us?" asked Susanna, not liking the look of him.

"He is England's foremost authority on knightly chivalry!" Square enthused. "We have come to take you home, Susanna, if you are willing."

"This fellow has been hired for our protection?" she wondered, relieved that he wasn't her newest fiancé, yet not at all relieved that he had been hired for their protection.

"Fear not, sweet damsel!" Sir Thomas assured her, the locks uncoiling from the top of his head like albino eels, licking at his breastplate. "I have been entrusted with this errand, an errand that is sacred to me, returning a damsel to her father's bosom, and I shall not fail. Whatever perils lie in our way, you shall be snug again in your own bed within a week, or I am no true knight."

"Take care not to trip over the dog," Susanna warned him, Thunderbolt being stretched out nearby. "In fact, I don't want you in my aunt's house, Sir Knight. Wait outside."

"My sister could be feeling unwell," Square pleaded on her behalf, as he so often did whenever she spoke without ceremony, which was usually the case with anyone she instinctively disliked.

"I'll conduct my men to our lodgings," Sir Thomas gallantly offered. "Which are …"

"They can stay in the stables for now," Susanna advised Square. "Some other guests of our aunt are already lodged there: a friar and his charges, called the *Galts*. And Lady Lorna. Your knight and his men had best be careful with *her* or they will get no end of trouble from me."

"*Lady Lorna Blakeney*," Square informed the knight. "My sister's pet donkey, all as white as innocence itself. Susanna takes her everywhere."

"A damsel with a white ass!" Sir Thomas beamed. "It shall be sacred in my eyes. Beauteous ladies in distress do often go about on white asses."

"No damsels are in distress for very long when Sir Thomas is around," gushed Square, so besotted with his knight in shining armour that Susanna could hardly stop herself kicking both of them in the shins, for it was as clear as the knight's bald pate that his chivalry was more show than substance.

"Show Square's knight to the stables," Susanna told Matilda. "His horses can be put in the orchard till we work out what to do next."

"But you must have dinner with us, Sir Thomas," Square pleaded. "You have yet to give me a full account of King Arthur and his sword, Excalibur, even though you have been promising it ever since we set out from the Tabard Inn."

"Tomorrow night!" Sir Thomas assured him, before draping his dome once more in silver eels, then trapping them in the helmet he restored to his head. "All shall be revealed then! But tonight must be spent in manly fellowship with my comrades-in-arms, dining on whatever goodly fare is dispatched from your aunt's kitchen, which shall not be too long, I trust."

He returned to his men, five lightly armed riders looking dismal on sodden ponies.

"Where did you find that lot?" Susanna asked as the little troop moved off down the side of the house under Matilda's direction.

Square explained that he had found the knight at the Tabard Inn. Drafts of his story, *The Death of Arthur*, had been circulating among the Friday night patrons, he said, and the author was much in demand there as a dinner companion. Square didn't know where Sir Thomas had recruited his men, only that it must have been somewhere in London. Susanna loaded the fire with more wood then fetched two mugs of Marian's freshest cider, the fizzy fragrance tickling the nose before it tickled the tongue. She pulled up a chair and waited to hear the reason why she was being fetched home. Her brother smiled into his mug, he gazed at the crackling fire, and he said nothing. Maybe he was tired after the journey, yet she could read him like a stained-glass window, a transparent story, and it was already clear to her that his silence was deliberate. Something was troubling him, he was meant to keep it quiet and their father must be behind it.

"So how much is Papa paying for the escort?" she asked, just to get him talking.

"Three pounds," he said after a sip of cider. "Sir Thomas does chivalrous deeds for the pleasure of it, but his men never stir themselves without pay."

"Three pounds is cheap for a knight and five men."

"Our horses cost almost as much. Nobody can spare mounts just now, and nobody will hire them out for the ride to Lincolnshire, except for a pledge equal to the purchase price. I paid two pounds for ours. Yours is a fine chestnut mare, called *Mary of Reading*. You know it is a good horse when it has a name. I was told there is none better for a sometime rider."

"*You* paid for the horses? Why didn't Papa pay for them?"

"He is short of money just now."

"That's always his excuse for everything!" she protested. "But why didn't he send Lister and some of the carpenters? That would have saved him three pounds."

"He is having problems with staff," Square explained after another sip. "Spicer quit the moment he knew you were coming back."

"Spicer the Mouse!" she rejoiced. "Another would-be husband bites the dust."

"Lister has gone too. Bourne was too long a ride for him after the last time."

"*Lister with the Blisters* quit too?" she wondered. "So, Papa really is having problems. What's the reason—apart from me?"

"The London vintners. They have been stopping his shipments of olives."

"Because he has been smuggling French wine. You know it as well as I do. We've both smelt the shipments on his breath."

"*Honour thy father*, Susanna! The Bible wouldn't say it if God didn't mean it."

"Then *you* honour him with your words, Square, and let my ears do the rest."

This kind of conversation was a familiar ritual, and it was attended by a familiar gesture, Square lifting his right hand, then lowering it, lifting and lowering it, again and again. He happened to be holding a mug in that hand just now, but his favourite tool, as a carpenter, was the pump drill, its spindle driven by strings tangling and untangling, timed to the pressure of his fingers. It was only good for drilling through soft wood, but he often enacted its vacillating movements anytime he was working his way through a hard decision, usually when trying to reconcile his principles, as a pious Christian, with the murky realities of his life, as the son of a Southwark merchant.

"We don't have all day," she urged him.

"You are being sent to Utrecht to live with our uncle," he explained after finally resting the mug on his knee.

"Utrecht!"

Usually this was a magical word for Susanna, evoking visions of great painters working in the new, Dutch fashion, oils. The older, English fashion was associated with a pure, heavenly light, quite adequate for picturing saints in sacred texts, or adorning respectable homes with quaint scenes, but nothing like real flesh and blood. The Dutch were masters of flesh and blood. Utrecht was Dutch. If she could stay with her uncle, she could learn to paint the Dutch way. It was a dream come true, *if* it was true.

"Utrecht is the bait," she surmised. "What is he up to?"

Square lifted his mug then lowered it, lifted and lowered it again and again without touching a drop, slowly working through his dilemma.

"He has petitioned the king about his olives," he said at last, "and he was invited to Westminster to discuss it, just before I set out."

"He actually met the king?" she marvelled.

She felt a sudden flutter of excitement, as if approaching His Majesty with a petition all her own. A vision of his genial, manly face floated before her, his winning lips framing the answer to her desires.

"He met the king, yes," Square replied, eyes widening with something like horror, "and that wasn't all. Prepare yourself for a shock: the king was in bed with another man's wife! He made no attempt to hide her."

Susanna struggled to conceal her jealousy, even while sharing her brother's sense of horror. Square was too innocent to be entrusted with the secrets of a nature as passionate as hers.

"Who is she?"

"Elizabeth Shore, the London goldsmith's wife. She was naked, Susanna. The king of England in bed with a naked woman! The wickedness of it."

"She should be whipped!" Susanna conceded. "But what else do we know? What does she look like?"

"*Thighs smooth as ivory.* That's what our father said."

Susanna clenched one of her fists until she winced. Her palms still bore the scars from the hawk's beak and talons, and now new blood once again oozed from the scab. She rubbed the blood against her mug of cider, smearing it thinly enough to make it vanish.

"So how did their meeting go?" she asked as soon as she felt calm enough.

"If you can call it that," he answered thoughtfully: "a meeting of animals, brazen in their lust for each other."

"Papa's meeting with the king!" she snapped. "Really, Square, can't you be a little less obsessed with the Ten Commandments sometimes? You said Papa petitioned him."

"The petition is still being considered, but that isn't all that they discussed, Susanna. I am not breaking any vow of silence if I tell you this much: the king has invited him to some kind of banquet, at Baynard Castle, on the second day in March. It will include dances. His Majesty means to dance with a few of his guests, as part of the entertainment."

This astonished her.

"Was I invited?" she dared to hope, because the second day in March was more than a week off—just enough time to get herself to Baynard Castle.

Square didn't answer, instead playing with his imaginary pump drill. It was all the answer she needed. She jumped out of her chair in her excitement, spilling cider this time, the liquid hissing in the fire as it evaporated in a moment of boundless joy. His Majesty had kept her waiting two years for their second dance and yet she had always known the day would come sooner or later. Thunderbolt was in the way of her happy progress, so she gave him a sharp prod with her foot. The enormous hound stirred, rose reluctantly and retreated to a corner, leaving her free to pace happily around the flames, exulting in her good fortune. A vision of glorious opportunities swirled like sparks around her.

"You are pleased?" Square wondered.

She had almost forgotten he was there.

"Pleased? I have danced with His Majesty once before, I think."

"You rarely talk about it."

"It was just a dance. I honour him as our king, that's all."

She sat down again, the better to hide her true feelings.

"So, what is your decision?" Square surprised her by saying.

"Decision?" she wondered.

"About … you know."

He pressed the hint with a shamefaced look, as if had conspired in something sinful. Of course, *he* would feel like that, after betraying their father's secret, and no doubt the king's invitation to dance was, to a pious way of thinking, a sinful proposition, best rejected. For her however, it was a dream come true. Not dancing with His Majesty was utterly inconceivable. And yet, now that Square had raised the possibility, the thought resonated in her mind like the sound of a stone dropped into a deep well. There was more to this than she could fathom just yet. A few things were clear to her: the dance must be important to her father, or he would never have sent for her, and he had no idea how important the dance was to her, or he wouldn't have bothered dangling Utrecht as bait. She was in a powerful position, and a vulnerable one too. Much depended on her choices, if she could just work out what to do, when and how. Meanwhile she had to get home as soon as possible.

"Listen Square!" she said, resting a grateful hand on her brother's shoulder. "You did the right thing. I know it is never easy for you, disobeying Papa, especially when he wants you to keep a secret, but you didn't actually disobey him, did you! You chose your words very carefully, and Papa still has to break the news to me himself."

"But if he asks me whether or not I told you—"

"You didn't! Anyway, *I* won't say anything, and you know Papa: he thinks he owns you."

"But if he does ask—"

"Then be your usual self: a bit slow coming forward with the truth. And yet what am I saying!" she suddenly remembered. "It's too dangerous to go home."

"No woman is safe with that lecher on the throne," Square affirmed before angrily stamping one foot. "Monarchy is a sacred trust, Susanna, and how any Englishman can remain loyal to that man when—"

"I was thinking more about the journey," she explained. "Your knight and his hired louts don't inspire much confidence."

"Sometimes, Susanna, I wonder if you and I really understand each other at all."

"Give me a good reason to trust them."

"They don't look much in the rain," he conceded, "and, now that you have put me to the test, I can't say his men have always behaved like proper Christians. Maybe reports have reached you?"

"Surprise me."

"His men have been drunk most of the time, ever since we left Southwark, and foul-mouthed as savages. But here is the wisdom of it: he gave them that freedom for a reason, which is to see how far he can trust them. He told me so himself. He is experienced in these things. It is often our friends, more than our enemies, that we must be on our guard against, he says, because there is more treachery in the world today than chivalry. Tonight, he will school them in the old code of knightly discipline, and tomorrow they will be as courteous and chivalrous as himself, you may be sure of that. Mind you, they are pretty sober already. We spent yesterday and most of this morning at Grimsthorpe Castle."

"The rebel stronghold!" Susanna marvelled. "What were you doing there?"

"Not much. They put us in a dungeon."

"A dungeon!" she protested. "You belong in a church, Square, not a dungeon. What possible reason could they have for locking *you* up?"

"They mistrust strangers," he responded with a shrug. "I told them I don't like the present king any more than they do, and then I told them our only reason for coming was to fetch you home. They wouldn't listen. They were only interested in our horses, I think—Sir Thomas's horse especially. It is a magnificent animal, every inch like the proud and muscular courser one hears so much about in stories of knightly adventures. But in the end, Sir Thomas was let out to speak with the man in charge, Sir Robert Welles, and soon after that they released the rest of us, horses and all."

"What brought that about?"

"They are both knights, Susanna."

"You are saying it was chivalry?"

"Come with me to the Tabard on Friday nights and maybe then you'll understand. Knights are brothers-in-arms first and foremost, and only enemies when it can't be helped. But here is something else that might surprise you: Sir Robert gave Sir Thomas a written warrant for our safe passage."

"A warrant for safe passage! Let me see it."

"Sir Thomas has it."

"You are supposed to be the one in charge."

"I'm not a knight."

"You are merchant's son, Square. That makes you somebody important."

"A Southwark merchant's son," he reminded her.

"Papa has friends. But what's in the warrant? Do you know?"

"Sir Thomas showed it to me and I have it in memory. It is brief but to the point: *Show the bearer of this pass, Sir Thomas Malory, the courtesy and co-operation that you owe any friend of mine—signed Sir Robert Welles, this 17th day of February, valid until Tuesday.*"

"That is a warrant for almost anything," Susanna noted.

"Sir Thomas brings out the best in everyone," he explained. "Inspiring faith is his true mission but, if miscreants won't be persuaded to do what is right, *then forth he draws his mighty sword, like lightning from the throne of Heaven, and deals upon his foe stern blows of hardened steel.*"

Square enacted something of the heroic swordsmanship he imagined while quoting whatever nonsense he had read somewhere. People often dismissed him as a dreamer or a fool, but Susanna knew that he was gifted with a powerful faith in high ideals. If he could paint, his work would sell.

"Well Square, here is something you won't read in any of your stories of knightly adventures: you and Sir Thomas haven't been the only guests staying at Grimsthorpe Castle. Kilsby was staying there too, though not in the dungeon, I hasten to add. He and Sir Robert are like friends, both stooges of the earl of Warwick!"

"Kilsby?" Square wondered. "*Your* Kilsby?"

"The Devil himself."

It was Square's turn to jump from his chair, almost dousing the fire with all the cider that escaped his mug. He strode around the steam while he tried to get his mind around an impossibility.

"But …" was all he managed to get out.

"He is supposed to be dead," Susanna conceded. "Obviously he isn't. He visited this house just a few days ago, simpering and sneering under this very roof, almost on the same spot where you are standing even now."

Square hurriedly resumed his seat.

"Kilsby here in this house!" he gasped. "But how?"

"Evil finds a way."

"Then you must come home with me, Susanna—for your own safety."

"What makes you think I would be safer with you? Kilsby is in with the rebels, and they own the roads in Lincolnshire. A whole bunch of rebels came with him to this house about a week ago. One of them turned out to be a notorious trouble-maker, called *Beast of Ferrybridge*. Ever heard of *him*? He doesn't breathe the same air we do, not with a name like that. But I am not afraid of him. If you stand up to these bullies, Square, they soon back down. Still, we have to be careful, that's all."

"But I have a warrant for safe passage."

"Your story-teller has it."

"You still don't trust Sir Thomas?"

"No but then maybe I don't have to," she said, because she was determined to go home and a new thought suddenly became clear to her. "There are lots of travellers stranded in Bourne, many of them at the abbey—good men and women, desperate to get out of Lincolnshire. Cecily Norton and her father are among them."

"The Nortons are here?"

"We shall have no lack of honest companions tomorrow, many more than your gallant knight and his men can poke their swords at. A warrant for safe passage *and* safety in numbers! That's stacking the odds in our favour."

Day 7

Septuagesima Sunday

Susanna was awake before dawn but took care not to seem too eager to be on her way home, in case it hurt Aunt Marian's feelings. It was the best possible time to be going. Lent, the season of gloom and abstinence, always started in pious households on this Sunday, two weeks sooner than Southwark.

"Hellfire and Damnation here I come!" Matilda rejoiced as she began sorting out clothes.

"Southwark and London," Susanna insisted. "Don't talk them down."

"It is what your aunt calls them."

"My aunt means well."

"She pities us for going, I pity her for staying. A fully-rounded woman craves more than dry wafers, dry scripture and dry old men. There are no sausages here for breakfast. No sausages at noon. No sausages at night. Just dry wafers, dry scripture and dry, old men."

Matilda's smutty talk rarely bothered Susanna, if it didn't go on too long. It was like listening to old people and their ailments: it was good to know what she was missing out on.

"I am going to miss the peace and quiet," she reflected: "That was until Sir Robert and his friends showed up."

"What about the angel in the abbey!" Matilda recalled. "He is sure to be coming too. His name is John Smith, a blacksmith from Waltham Abbey, just a hop, skip and jump from Southwark. John Smith can hammer his steel on my anvil any time he pleases."

"I hope he hammers some sense into your head while he is at it."

Susanna and Matilda always had different priorities when dressing, never more so than now with a long ride ahead of them. Whereas Matilda struggled to choose between exotic appearance and practical comfort, then packed away all the clothes she finally rejected, Susanna dressed her painting gear first then got dressed into whatever came to hand. A leather cover, laced up like a jacket, kept the weather off her portrait of Isaac, already shielded from bumps by its wooden frame. The paints were stored in phials, wrapped individually in a wooden box to avoid breakages. Brushes, parchments and paper were enclosed in a satchel, together with charcoal, quills and ink. All this was carefully placed in a pair of wicker panniers for carrying out to the stables. Only one item of clothing seemed essential: a hooded riding mantle to cover her legs and whatever else Susanna wore or barely wore. Old Will, her father's ancient servant, helped carry the panniers outside, when he wasn't leaning on them for support.

Susanna's pet donkey greeted Susanna every morning with a shake of her head, a wiggle of her ears, a swish of her tail and a stamp of her hoof. This morning, the shake, wiggle, swish and stamp were more pronounced, the clever girl already anticipating a big change in routine. Though unused to carrying loads, except during Easter parades, she was good natured, and happily submitted to the panniers draped over her back.

"You will not be riding the mule, Dear Lady?" Sir Thomas asked.

"*Donkey*," Susanna quickly objected—she had heard these rumours before. "Appearances can be deceptive, Sir Knight."

"The white ass that your brother mentioned yesterday evening!" he recalled. "A most becoming mount for such a damsel as yourself, if I may be permitted an observation so bold."

He was standing by the stable door while two of his men fitted him into his fancy armour, each piece tied to his arming doublet as carefully as men with hangovers can manage in the light of a new day. Their singing last night had been florid, until Aunt Marian had silenced them all by banging on the stable wall. Almost as florid was the cuirass they were now shutting him into, engraved with arabesques.

"Nobody rides Lady Lorna, Dear Knight," Susanna advised him. "Do you mistake me for one of your characters, or for one of your readers?"

"I would be honoured either way."

"My brother reads your rubbish, I don't."

In fact, she had never learned to read. Farthings had paid only for Square's schooling.

"Where is the good pilgrim?"

"He has gone to the abbey to recruit some companions. Our safety won't be entirely in your hands, I am glad to say."

She left him to ponder her contempt, and returned indoors to see about some snacks for the road. Meanwhile news of a knight in shining armour, bearing a warrant for safe passage, had raced like a *Hallelujah* throughout the abbey, its manor and all about town. A hundred travellers soon assembled in the street outside Aunt Marian's house, eager to depart.

"I can't take all these people," said Sir Thomas when he discovered them waiting for him. "The warrant wasn't made out with such a multitude in mind."

"They are desperate to leave," Square pleaded.

"I can take women and children, maybe the sick and very old—the weak are entitled to the protection of a Christian knight—but most of these people are able-bodied men."

"What's wrong with able-bodied men?" Susanna wondered.

"A question I have often asked *you*," Matilda whispered in her ear, "and yet you are a spinster still."

"The warrant doesn't allow for so many," Sir Thomas insisted, "and chivalry doesn't require it. Am I a shield for cowards to hide behind?"

"But extra swords—" Square persisted.

"Are useless in unskilled hands," said the knight. "The bigger the cabbage, the more grubs it attracts. I refuse to lead them."

Susanna knew what he meant, thanks to her experiences as a painter. There comes a moment in every picture when more is less, every additional colour only making things worse, yet Sir Thomas and his men were already a bad picture on their own and no addition could possibly make things worse. His usefulness was thanks only to the warrant he carried, which he might yet use to his own advantage, unless those he protected could protect themselves, if not from the rebels, at least from him. So, she dug in her heels and told Square not to leave town without the bigger cabbage. Sir Thomas was equally intransigent. The impasse lasted until noon. By then the richest and proudest of the travellers—more than half the assembly—had swallowed their disappointment and drifted back to their lodgings, and Sir Thomas seemed reasonably satisfied with the remainder. Friar Fryer and the Galts were fairly typical of the group that was left: not poor (thanks to the silver plate bulging under the friar's habit), nor utterly helpless (the Galts had spent a lifetime helping themselves to other people's things), and quite able to discourage treachery through weight of numbers. Sir Thomas tried some final improvements.

"That man over there doesn't need a knight's protection."

"The blacksmith is with me," said Matilda.

"What about that proud fellow there?" he asked, indicating Cecily's father, a merchant who traded in fabrics, and who was a captain in the Bishopsgate militia one Saturday every month: just the sort of man they needed.

"He is with me," said Susanna.

"What about those two?"

Sir Thomas pointed out a short, thick man in a crimson bonnet, and a tall, thin man in a blue cap. One was Friar Fryer's arch-enemy—the beadle from Ware, Walter Wheaton—and the other introduced himself as a butler from Boston, named Felix Baxter. Both of them drew out their swords and flourished them in a style they must have thought manly, as if to persuade the knight of their usefulness.

"They can come," he concluded.

"Then you are ready to lead us, Sir Thomas?" Square asked his hero.

"They are, with few exceptions, as needy a group as I have ever seen," he replied. "It would be unchivalrous to ignore your pleas a moment longer."

By this time, Susanna was desperate to be gone already. The prospect of a dance with His Majesty was all the more alluring after the tedium of a wasted morning. She yearned for a life of movement, action and purpose. Aunt Marian urged caution, prudence, more planning and more delay, a departure some time tomorrow or, better still, after Lent. She shared Susanna's mistrust of the gallant knight and his men, but not her faith in the rest of the travelling party. Susanna tried reassuring her.

"They are tougher than they look," she insisted. "They have been stubborn enough to last all morning, and it's only a few miles to the next county. We don't need an entire army."

"But the knight and his men—"

"We outnumber them eight to one."

"At least wait till I send for my farmers. They can escort you to the border."

A messenger was dispatched in haste, bidding her farmers to come quickly. Meanwhile a few more travellers lost heart and returned to the abbey, since it was already getting late in the day. Susanna decided further delay could only make matters worse, and the farmers could always join them on the road, so she finally gave Square the much-awaited nod. Square then nodded to his knight in shining armour, and the little procession set off. The knight, at the head of the column, looked surprisingly gallant on his magnificent mount, a muscular courser champing at the bit. Square rode immediately behind him, dressed in his favourite garb, the white habit of a Carthusian monk, dyed green. His hired horse looked half-exhausted already. Alongside Square rode Cecily's father, handsomely mounted on a grey gelding that snorted with pleasure, after a morning spent breakfasting on expensive oats. They were followed by a couple of the knight's men on bad-tempered hobbies, then Cecily on a meek pony, a servant leading it while she sat side-saddle, having little more to do than look pretty. Susanna came next in line, not an experienced horsewoman but quite comfortable astride Mary of Reading, a mare that was everything Square had promised and more: gentle, forgiving and sure-footed, she seemed to be sharing the ride with Susanna rather than being ridden by her. Next came the ever-reliable family servant, Old Will, saddled on a hired mount and leading a sturdy pack horse, its broad back loaded up with a tower of possessions, mostly Matilda's wardrobe. Lady Lorna Blakeney ambled along behind the baggage, linked to it by rope yet happy to follow Susanna anywhere, even if some way behind.

Looking further back, Susanna glimpsed Matilda high astride a bony nag, happily conversing with her blacksmith, mounted on a mule—if you could call it *conversing* where Matilda did all the talking, and the blacksmith just minded where he was going. Then came Friar Fryer and the Galts, all on foot, closely followed by the beadle from Ware on a dispirited donkey, and the butler from Boston, stylishly astride a horse that needed only a second eye and both its ears to appear quite respectable.

"Walter Wheaton, a beadle from Ware, and Felix Baxter, a butler from Boston," Susanna said to herself, trying out their names for her own amusement, because they sounded rather absurd together. "Walter Wheaton and Felix Baxter, the beadle from Ware and the butler from Boston. Wheaton the beadle, Baxter the butler, Wheaton from Ware and Baxter from Boston."

Others in the party were just a faceless blur, a score of minor craftsmen, apprentices and itinerant vendors, together with some wives and servants, nobody, apart from Cecily's father, ranking higher than a merchant's daughter. Susanna felt herself to be in command. Meanwhile Aunt Marian and Watt followed them a little way from town, Marian waving, Watt throwing stones. Susanna returned the wave, Adam the Elder the stones. Low clouds threatened rain, occasional raindrops as big as blackberries darkening Susanna's sleeves. Marian's farmers failed to materialise. Maybe they didn't receive the message in time or maybe they took a different road, or maybe they were the suspicious-looking riders that one of the knight's men reported glimpsing in nearby woods, causing Sir Thomas to halt the entire party until the danger passed. By then, he had removed his helmet, more like a traveller enjoying the cool of the afternoon than a knight expecting trouble, and meanwhile the clouds scattered and lifted, even as the sun sank lower, winking through trees. The prospect of shelter for the night began to seem doubtful, and then a plume of smoke was glimpsed trailing the clouds ever higher: maybe a big fireplace somewhere nearby. Sir Thomas followed the smoke through leafless woods and it finally brought them to a cluster of buildings—a manor house, a hamlet of some dozen cottages, and an enormous barn—all set amid a handsome expanse of fields and pastures, dotted with coppices and shapely groves. However, nobody rode out to ask them their business, and nobody waited for them to arrive. There was no welcome. There were no people. The hamlet turned out to be a ransacked pile of rubble, the manor house a smouldering ruin. Only the barn was intact. Sir Thomas halted outside it.

"Guests of the king himself!" he declared, signifying His Majesty's personal emblem, a white rose, painted above the open doorway. "As staunch and capacious as the best inn one could hope to find this late in the day!"

It was indeed capacious, its magnificent proportions putting Susanna in mind of her king's heroic physique. It could have accommodated not just their own party but Southwark's Easter parade, spectators and all. At any other time, under any other circumstances, she would have welcomed spending the night here, but the anxious faces of the other travellers, and the ruinous state of the other buildings, were bad omens for a good night's rest, and that was even without the evil cawing of a raven, perched on the gable overhead. Other ravens roosted noiselessly amid the leafless branches of a nearby oak. More conspicuous than ravens were the two naked men hanging from branches by their necks. Each man's hand had been amputated at the wrist and shoved into the other's mouth. It was as if the tree had flowered cannibals. Susanna wasn't squeamish—she had lived all her life just across the river from London, its bridge perennially festooned with the heads of traitors—but this manor was obviously rebel territory now, and the gruesome execution was a clear warning: *Yorkists Keep Out.*

Only Sir Thomas dismounted.

"The rebels have been busy," he acknowledged with a glance at the oak, "but look!" he added, unhooking a lantern from inside the doorpost and holding it up for display. "They have left us some lanterns for when it gets dark. How is that for hospitality!"

It was hardly reassurance and even Mary of Reading was nervous, stepping back from the doorway without any prompting from Susanna. Not everyone however is blessed with a good horse's common sense.

"I was born to sleep anywhere," said the beadle from Ware with a great yawn, sliding off the back of his dejected mount.

"That goes for me too," said the butler from Boston, dismounting with an elegant flick of his cloak.

Nobody else followed their example.

"I am carrying a warrant for safe passage, signed by the rebel leader," Sir Thomas reminded everyone, whereupon he pulled off a gauntlet and rested one foot on the beam of a plough, propped against the barn. He unbuckled a greave, inserted some fingers inside and finally produced a slip of paper, which he waved in demonstration: the warrant. "You have nothing to fear with me here."

"What's the next town?" Susanna wondered.

"Stamford, if we can find it," said Cecily's father.

"I am all for riding on," said Matilda's blacksmith after a glance at the oak.

"I'm all for joining you," said Matilda.

"Well, this is as far as *I* go today," Sir Thomas insisted, slipping the warrant back into his greave.

His intransigence persuaded more of the travellers to dismount and that settled the argument in his favour. Susanna was one of the last out of the saddle, and by then the Galts were already in the barn, claiming the best spot for themselves. The raven on the gable took wing, spooked by the shutters of a loft window opening underneath it. The two Adams waved to Susanna, advertising their good luck.

"Mark that window!" Sir Thomas instructed his men, whereupon one of them aimed at the boys with a loaded crossbow, prompting them to close the shutters in a hurry. "All mounts to be tied to the rope here!" Sir Thomas announced next, signifying a rope that his men had stretched from the trunk of the oak tree to the beam of the abandoned plough. "All weapons and valuables in a pile by the door as you pass in. Hurry up! Nobody likes wasting time."

Sir Thomas restored his helmet to his head, and his men circled the group with weapons at the ready. Even the beadle and the butler now began to look anxious. The first to dismount, they were already clutching their belongings when one of the knight's men pushed them out front, where Sir Thomas stood ready to receive them in the doorway.

"I have nothing of value," pleaded the butler, loosening the drawstring on a pair of canvas panniers, as invitation for the knight to look inside.

"What about the satchel over your shoulder?"

"Just old manuscripts by some ancient author."

"I'm an author," Sir Thomas assured him, grabbing the satchel and peering inside. "Pamphlets on alchemy, it looks like, and — what do we have here? Four … six, seven, eight gold crowns. A profit already! Drop your sword and get in."

The butler unbuckled his sword and left it by the door. Sir Thomas turned his attention next to the Ware beadle, whose meagre belongings included a pile of clothes, a tinderbox, a pocket knife and a pot of pickled herrings, none of which interested the author of knightly adventures. Fruit often lurks in the top branches, however, and it was there he struck gold.

"A handsome bonnet," he observed, plucking it from the beadle's head so as to look inside, "with three angels and five groats in the lining! They're safe with me."

"The friar has a silver plate stashed inside his habit, worth twenty times as much," the beadle pleaded. "Why not take that instead?"

"All in good time!"

Susanna glanced around at her fellow travellers, wondering which of them would submit to robbery, which would rally to their mutual defence, and which would take to their heels. Meanwhile Square stepped forward.

"Is this another test of your men's character, Sir Thomas?" he enquired. "Why are you treating us in this high-handed manner?"

"Well Mandeville," came the droll reply, "I'll give you a choice. You can hear what this is all about, or I can tell you the story of young Arthur and the sword Excalibur. I did promise you the story, didn't I? So how does it go? There was this boy, Arthur, and he found a great sword called Excalibur, which was buried up to its hilt in a stone. Whoever could pull it out, would be king of England. *Fuck that!* cried the boy. *I'll put the stone on the throne and rule England in its place!* Hand over your valuables."

His men brandished their swords hideously, blades flashing like their grinning teeth, as they prepared themselves for mayhem. Square looked agog. Most of the other travellers crowded together like sheep. Susanna wasn't even shocked, merely furious with herself for not having heeded her own and her aunt's worst fears. Meanwhile two of the travellers drew swords: Cecily's father, who did it with a stylish flourish, and Matilda's blacksmith, cutting at the air as if wielding a hammer.

"Are you both mad?" protested the Ware beadle, meekly unbuckling his own sword and dropping it by the bonnet. "Do you want to get us all killed?"

His cowardice was infectious. A pile of discarded weapons and valuables quickly mushroomed at the knight's feet. But the blacksmith and the captain of the Bishopsgate militia remained defiant, drifting nearer each other for mutual support.

"Tut, tut," said Sir Thomas. "You are but two against six. I might even sit back and watch."

Boldness was their only hope now, and Susanna, pulled on the sword that hung useless by her brother's side. It was actually their father's sword, the steel pitted with impurities and rusted in the scabbard, and it complained loudly as it emerged in her hands.

"Make that three!" she said.

She had never before wielded such a weapon but she soon settled on a likely posture, the blade resting on one shoulder, ready to parry or slash. More troublesome than her inexperience with swords was the inconvenience of her riding mantle, the long hem dragging and threatening to trip her up. Disrobing in front of armed bandits didn't seem like a good idea, however, and she pulled the hood closer around her ears, the better to keep her good looks out of the false knight's hopes.

"Dear Lady!" Sir Thomas wondered with a grin. "Shall I lower my visor?"

"Even a Winchester Goose could knock you over, you pile of pans."

"No damsel in distress then," he said as he drew out his sword.

"We are bred tough in Southwark," she affirmed.

"Another story teller!" he scoffed. "But what of your brother—how tough is he?"

Square was tough in a pious way. He trusted in militant angels as a defence against demons, and he believed in gallant knights as a defence against wicked varlets, but he had long been accustomed to turning the other cheek when faced with bullies. The only personal weapon he had real faith in was the power of faith itself.

"This is all my own fault," he lamented as he took another step towards his latest tormentor. "Take my life, fool that I am, and spare these others, Sir Thomas."

"How can I refuse!"

The knight signalled to two of his men. One of them forced Square to his knees while the second rested a knife against his throat, awaiting the signal to cut deep. Cecily almost fainted in her father's arms, forcing him to drop his sword. Matilda screamed and clung to the blacksmith for protection. He smartly thrust her aside, the better to defend himself. Susanna hardly knew what to do. Relying on Sir Thomas for mercy was a desperate hope, but fighting could only make matters worse. Her father's sword fell from her fingers. The blacksmith held out a few moments longer, brandishing his sword as if he meant to heat it in the guts of the first wretch that dared come within reach, until finally he accepted the situation with a despairing shake of the head, tossing the blade onto the pile of other weapons. One of the loitering villains quickly thrust Matilda into his arms, encumbering him while they put a noose over his head. Next they wrapped the trailing end of the rope around his wrists, high up his back, the noose tightening every time his hands dropped. Matilda supported him as best she could, and meanwhile Cecily's father supported Cecily the best he could. Susanna clenched her fists, desperate to paint the scene other than it was.

"Have mercy on these others, Sir Thomas," Square continued to plead. "I offer you myself, to be killed or robbed just as you will, if only you will spare these others."

"He trades me a penny for a pound!" laughed the knight. "Maybe he thinks I am as mad as himself."

"I add my appeal to his," said Friar Fryer, kneeling beside Square. "Be merciful to these others if you ever hope for mercy from God."

'A choir of buffoons," the knight scoffed. "What can I sing them in reply? Something about a rogue with one leg. How does it go? *There was an old man of York, a devil used for his pitchfork* …"

He danced an obscene jig to accompany his own lyrics, his armour clinking as merrily as discs on a tambourine, but the bizarre spectacle only lasted a few moments, because a greater spectacle drew everyone's attention westwards. The sun had now sunk low on the horizon, and two figures were emerging from its radiance, part human, part animal, part elemental, all melting into each other one moment, blazing apart the next.

"Behold!" said Square. "The archangels, Michael and Gabriel, are coming to rescue us!"

"Hallelujah!" cried Friar Fryer, face bright with hope.

Cecily, still half-conscious in her father's arms, now fainted utterly, and he was forced to kneel with her, as if praying with Square and the friar. The blacksmith was the next to drop to his knees, not in prayer either but because the noose was gradually choking the life out of him. Matilda knelt with him, struggling to keep his hands up high. Other travellers fell to their knees also, in hope or bewilderment, maybe in wonder. Susanna prayed the same way she had always painted, standing. Meanwhile she shielded her eyes with one hand, watching between fingers as the vision paused in a sudden burst of intensifying light, some forty or fifty paces away. An instant later, the light disappeared like a snail into its shell, hidden in a thin banner of cloud. The archangels Michael and Gabriel shrank to two men, tying the reins of their horses to a coppiced hazel bush, a baggage mule browsing the grass nearby.

"It's just some interlopers," Sir Thomas observed. "This changes nothing."

The interlopers took a dozen or so steps towards the barn then halted. One of them was a knight, dressed all in steel. The visor was down and he stood casually resting his sword on his shoulder, much as Susanna had done with her father's sword. The other man was shortish and bandy-legged, very broad in the shoulders, the chest inflated even further by a padded jacket. He carried a crossbow and wore a kettle hat mounted by two little horns, curved like an ironic comment on the shape of his legs.

"Identify yourselves" said Sir Thomas. "Who are you? What do you want?"

A reply seemed to come from the man in armour but it was difficult to hear, the voice muffled by his visor. His archer interpreted for him.

"He says he is Life if you do as you are told, Death if you don't."

"*Life* or *Death!*" jeered Sir Thomas. "Is that why he doesn't talk for himself?"

"He never wastes words on the likes of you," was the archer's next response. "He has me do it for him."

The new knight's brooding silence dwarfed the verbosity and showiness of Sir Thomas, it seemed to Susanna. This was no mere interloper or mirage but a force to be reckoned with, and even Sir Thomas seemed to acknowledge it.

"I have here a warrant for safe passage, written by my good friend, Sir Robert Welles," he said, tapping his greave with the edge of his sword. "Don't do anything you'll regret."

Life or Death seemed to laugh.

"Does it have a sharp edge?" said the archer on his behalf.

"These people are my hostages," Sir Thomas then confessed. "If you're here about them, let's talk."

"One!" said the knight from the Sun, his own voice now as clear as a bell.

There was a loud *twunk* from the crossbow, a *fwss* past Susanna's ear, and a muffled *kaflump* from somewhere behind her. The thug who, only moments ago, had pointed his crossbow at the two Adams, now lay in her evening shadow, prostrate like a felled tree, his skull a shattered mess, his weapon trembling in convulsed fingers. Death unshouldered his sword and stood guard in front of his bandy-legged archer, while the crossbow was reloaded. Meanwhile Sir Thomas weighed the loss of a single companion without any obvious emotion.

"I admire your nerve," he told the new knight. "How about we go halves? I'll even let you have first pick."

Death muttered another indistinct response.

"*My* horse?" the story-teller protested in reply. "Are you from Grimsthorpe Castle? Is this some kind of joke?" Death laughed again as if it could be some kind of joke. "There are ample prizes here for those who share," Sir Thomas persisted. "I have already collected more than five pounds in gold, plus weapons, horses and the rest. There is at least fifty pounds up for grabs."

The new knight muttered something else incoherent.

"A true knight!" scoffed Sir Thomas.

"A true knight!" affirmed Square, clasping his hands together for joy.

Square had been wrong about the archangels, Michael and Gabriel, and Susanna wasn't entirely convinced that he was right this time. Something about Death seemed as disconcerting as his name, and she kept her face buried in her hood for her own protection, in case a woman's good looks brought him too much to life.

"How about my three pounds?" said Sir Thomas, fixing Square with a morose eye. "Give me my three pounds and we'll call it quits."

This sounded like an admission of defeat. Susanna was too emboldened or too outraged to give Square time to reply. She snatched up their father's sword once more and stepped between them.

"Three pounds, you Chamber Pot Knight?" she protested, angling the blade for a poke under the raised visor. "How about three stabs in your disgusting face!"

"You can't treat an honest knight like this," he pleaded, eyes swivelling rapidly back and forth between her and Death. "I have broken no laws."

"Not yet, you haven't," she conceded, "but I am working up to it."

"I have friends around here," he warned her: "important men, established connections—"

"Two!" cried Death.

There was another *twunk* and another of Sir Thomas's men dropped dead, or stood dead, this one's throat skewered to the barn door, where he quivered in his final death throes like a slaughtered hare. The knight's three remaining men jumped onto their horses and scattered as fast as their mounts could carry them, one off behind the barn, one into a line of trees, and the other along a paddock.

"I am surrounded by cowards," complained Sir Thomas.

Death approached him for a closer look, and meanwhile his archer pulled out a knife and rushed over to the blacksmith, severing the rope still binding his wrists. Matilda lifted the noose.

"What's going on and ... who are you?" Smith asked between gasps for air.

"Who's asking?" said the archer.

"John Smith, blacksmith of Waltham Abbey!" Matilda said for him.

"Do you have brains, Smith?" said the archer.

"I think so," said Smith.

"Brains and good looks! Lucky man."

The archer re-joined Death, now inspecting Sir Thomas's weapons and armour as casually as a customer browsing a market stall, and yet his sword remained up, his visor down, as if he could be Death still. The travellers began to gather around him warily, Susanna among them.

"Fancy armour!" observed the archer, tracing Sir Thomas's arabesques with the stubs of some missing fingers. "It's a poor fit though. The helmet too. My guess is they're stolen. Which bits do you want, Squire?"

Death pointed at Sir Thomas's ornate helmet and cuirass. His own helmet and cuirass were plain, dull in lustre and spotted with dints, and Susanna could readily understand a wish to replace them with something better. However, Death also indicated an interest in his captive's sword, though it was smaller than his own, and he showed no interest at all in the feet, even though Sir Thomas wore steel plates over both shoes, whereas Death only had steel on one foot, the other being encased in humble brown leather

"Alright, alright, I know when I am beaten!" said the false knight.

Sir Thomas dropped his blade and his gauntlets, then held out his arms. The archer made a quick search for small weapons, confiscated a dagger first, a knife next, then liberated the ornate helmet before gradually extracting the cuirass from the pieces around it. It reminded Susanna of an oyster being prised open. Sir Thomas was then free to go or, rather, Death silently ordered him to leave, pointing the way out with his great sword. A blue doublet barely concealed the man's thinness, and his bald scalp flushed crimson in the last rays of the setting sun, as the disgraced author walked off along the same road they had all come by. Then Death mounted Malory's horse, trying out its gait in the nearby pasture, while the bandy-legged archer packed the confiscated armour with their own baggage, strapped to their mule. Only then did Susanna remember something important.

"The warrant!" she told the archer, tugging on his sleeve to direct his gaze along the road out. "The other knight still has it. It was written by the rebel leader and it gives him anything he asks for. We have to get it back!"

"It'll keep till tonight," the archer responded with a shrug, meanwhile tightening the mule's baggage straps.

"He'll be back?" Susanna wondered.

"Does porridge stick to a spoon?"

"You are setting a trap for him," she guessed.

"Robin Hood stole from the rich to give to the poor. My Squire steals from men poor in courage and gives to their betters. It will be a wild night tonight."

Death trotted in a wide circle, standing in the stirrups as he cut the air with his massive sword, testing Malory's horse for its response. Soon he tested the response of the travellers, shouting something while pointing his blade at the barn. Susanna hardly understood a syllable yet his meaning was clear enough. Everyone moved quickly, gathering up their weapons and their valuables, fetching their mounts and almost falling over each other in their haste to get themselves and their belongings into the barn. Susanna brought in Lady Lorna and Mary of Reading. Smith lifted the dead man from the door, laid him next to the one with the shattered skull, then returned the bolts to the archer. Old Will took the lantern down from the doorpost, lit it from his tinderbox and soon brought to light Malory's other *lanterns*, actually a collection of greasy rags and some torches, piled in one corner. The new knight and his archer added one of their own horses and the two dead men's mounts to the herd indoors, then slowly rode off into the gathering gloom.

"We're the bait," said Susanna as she watched them leave. "Can we trust them?"

"Chivalry still lives!" Square assured her. "But did you see his feet, Susanna? He was wearing only one sabaton."

Square could name all the bits of a knight's armour but her painterly eye hadn't missed the relevant details.

"*Sabatons* are coverings for the boots," she guessed. "He must have lost one."

"True knights don't lose things, Susanna. The missing sabaton reminds him of something in his life, some great loss or sorrow, which it is his mission to set right. He has dedicated himself to that mission, body and soul, and he won't wear that sabaton again till he is victorious. A true knight! We shall sleep safely tonight."

"He didn't say much," she reflected, "nothing I heard clearly."

"His actions speak for him," said the blacksmith, closing the doors on the darkness outside, even as Old Will lit a great, flaring torch inside.

Day 8

Mon∂ay 19tħ of February

Susanna woke to Matilda's snores in one ear and Cecily's drowsy murmurs in the other. Extricating herself from their embraces—her warmest blankets—she lurched to her feet and tried remembering where she was. Her usual lodgings as a traveller were inns, monastic hospices and the homes of family friends, but the smell of horses was overpowering.

"The king's barn," she recalled.

Most of the travellers had slept up in the loft, out of the way of hooves, but the ladder was too steep for Cecily, any ladder was too steep for Matilda, and Isaac was too heavy to carry up, so Susanna had spent all night with her cousin, her maid and her painting in a stall on the ground floor, with Isaac resting on her box of paints, amid a fortress of other belongings. The Galts, who had been ingenious and desperate enough to steal the iron hinges from Marian's back gate, would love to get their fingers on the gold leaf stored in a painter's phials.

Susanna shook a leg, numb after a night of pressure from Matilda's thigh, then opened the stall gate and stepped out into a cavernous space, patrolled by horses, mules and two donkeys. Lady Lorna's white hide stood out like a beacon. The shake of her head, the wiggle of her ears, the swish of her tail and the stamp of a hoof demanded the usual attention, so Susanna spent some moments fondling her nose. An open door was the only source of light, and she shut one eye against it, looking to see who else was awake. Old Will was one of some dozen people wandering about, saddling and grooming animals. She exchanged greetings with him before noticing a shortish, barrel-chested man with a handsome face, standing with a rope across the doorway, keeping the horses in: Matilda's blacksmith. Fleeting shadows, glimpsed through the doorway, indicated something might be worth investigating outside. Susanna acknowledged Smith's smile with a nod before stepping around him.

A handful of her fellow travellers were loitering not far from the barn, some with eyes closed, some peering through steaming breath at the rising sun, glimmering in the nearby woods. Cecily's father was among them, asleep on his feet. He and Smith had taken turns keeping watch last night. A little further off was a man easily recognised by his horned helmet and bandy legs: yesterday's archer. He was up to something. Six horses had been roped end to end, and he seemed to be making panniers for them out of a pile of clothes—tying off loose ends and knotting together sleeves and legs—then stuffing them with bits of armour and weapons taken from another pile at his feet. More intriguing still was the oak where two naked men had been hanging yesterday. This morning it had sprouted five more men, draped over branches, this time partly clothed. A Southwark girl isn't easily shocked by death but Susanna couldn't help feeling perturbed by the gruesome arrangement. The archer noticed.

"It saves burying them," he explained, meanwhile lifting a pair of roughly made panniers onto one of the horses.

"Who are they?"

"Apart from the original two? Three of their murderers maybe, plus the two we killed yesterday afternoon."

"But all the armour?"

"We spared anyone that surrendered their gear."

"Malory?"

"That one got clean away. Knights usually do."

"And your own knight—where is *he*?"

"Trying out Malory's horse. Here he comes now."

Death rode into view, cantering around the barn. He was still in full armour, the visor now up as he hurried by. He was an expert horseman, lending power and grace to what was already a muscular and graceful animal. A black and tan dog hared after him, barking merrily. Susanna recognised it immediately.

"That's Dog," she observed with a start.

"*Wakefield.*"

"What?"

"*His* name for it."

This revelation was even more shocking than the extra bodies in the tree, because it hinted at the knight's identity, and yet it was hard to get past the word *Wakefield*, because it was only a decade ago that the Yorkists were nearly annihilated at a place of that name, and Susanna could still remember the widespread panic and dismay inspired by survivors galloping breathless through London and Southwark: *The Duke of York is dead! Nothing can stop the Lancastrians now! Their fanatical queen, the wild French woman, Margaret of Anjou—she is drunk on blood and thirsting for more!* Then a rumour had got started that the duke's young son and heir, Edward Plantagenet, had left the schoolroom to rescue England and to avenge his father. It had sounded like a fairy tale until the handsome prince actually appeared, leading a small band of supporters into London, gathering more as he rode northwards, inspiring everyone with faith in his courage, until finally, unbelievably, he unleashed himself on the mad queen's minions at Towton, where it was the turn of the Lancastrians to suffer annihilating defeat—justice for the slaughter suffered at the Battle of Wakefield.

"So your knight is …"

"A squire still. Knighthoods are a luxury. Anyway, he swore fealty to Lord Clifford, and Clifford died at Towton. Ever since then, he has served where he must, but always in loyalty to the old ways."

"Then this man is …"

"The Beast of Ferrybridge: Tom Roussell."

Susanna retreated back indoors. Recollections of the Beast and Kilsby in her aunt's house clawed at her like wild hawks. She tried fighting them off with arguments but nothing made sense. She stumbled back to the stall and prodded her bed mates awake, desperate for some companionship.

"Oh Susanna!" said Cecily, sitting up on her mattress of loose straw and spare clothes. "I dreamed we had all died yesterday, yet here we all are, safe and sound!"

"Where's Smith?" said Matilda.

These two were not ideal confidantes, and Susann hid her agitation, content for now to keep busy in their company.

"Let's get moving."

They helped groom and dress each other for the day ahead, then loaded Isaac and the box of paints into Lady Lorna's panniers, ready for a quick departure. Cecily soon went outside to be with her father, and Matilda joined the blacksmith for some more one-sided flirting. Susanna pocketed her phial of gold leaf, left Lady Lorna and the panniers in the care of Old Will then hurried up the ladder, stepping over and around stubborn sleepers, barely visible by the light of the loft window. The shutters had been pulled back, and the Galts were framed in the morning air, grabbing food out of each other's hands, no doubt stolen from someone else. Finally she found what she was looking for: Square. He was asleep in the gloom furthest from the window. She jumped beside him, relieved to have someone she could confide in at last.

"Guess who I just saw!" she said, prodding him awake.

"What, who?" he muttered, rubbing the sleep out of his eyes. "Susanna?"

"Do you remember what I told you about the Beast of Ferrybridge, Kilsby's friend?"

"The one with the hawk."

"I have just seen him! He's riding around outside as bold as daylight, as if he owns the place."

"*That* man here?" he wondered, sitting up. "And Kilsby?"

"Good question! I haven't seen him yet, but he might be lurking somewhere nearby."

Square mirrored her alarm for a brief moment, until the light of some other thought began to spread across his features.

"But the Knight of the Lost Sabaton—is *he* here?"

"*Knight of the Lost Sabaton?*"

"It's my name for him. He is missing one."

"The knight yesterday? This isn't a story, Square."

"It feels like one."

"Yes," she conceded, "especially the way he showed up just in time to save us from Malory!"

"If there is a damsel in distress, an honest pilgrim in need of help, or a dragon in need of slaying, a true knight will always show up just in the nick of time, in my experience."

"Like it was planned. Maybe it *was* planned."

"You've seen him," he guessed. "Then there is nothing to fear."

"You think not?"

"He rode from the Sun, Susanna. It was a sign from God. A knight like that—not even Kilsby's Beast of Ferrybridge is a match for him." Square was still dressed in his green Carthusian habit, now stuffed with spare clothes as padding against the cold night. She pulled some of the stuffing out from the hood, so that he looked more human. "What's the matter, Susanna?" he wondered. "You still seem troubled. Have faith. Our true knight will protect us."

"I don't know how to tell you this, Square," she replied as she thrust some rolled-up hose into his hands. "Your Knight of the Lost Sabaton *is* the Beast of Ferrybridge."

"What?"

"Your new knight in shining armour is even worse than your last one."

He stared at her. She squeezed his hand for comfort. He lifted her hand then lowered it, lifted and lowered it again and again—his usual routine with the pump drill—while he worked through the problem that she had presented him with.

"The knight who saved us yesterday is Kilsby's friend?"

"Yes, both of them chums with Sir Robert Welles, all stooges of the earl of Warwick. Traitors all! But people in Bourne say Tom Roussell – that's *your* new knight and *Kilsby's* Beast of Ferrybridge – they say he is the most bloodthirsty Lancastrian that ever lived. And he was never a real knight. His archer was telling me just now. He has dedicated his life to some dead nobleman and he won't kneel for anyone else. A rebel through and through!"

"He apologised for the hawk, didn't he? You said he returned to Aunt Marian's house to apologise."

"You are making excuses for him?" she marvelled. "Roussell only apologised because Marian complained to the abbot."

Square pumped her hand a little longer.

"His association with Kilsby doesn't do him credit," he came out with next, "but people can't always be judged by the company they keep, can they? Our Lord Jesus himself was the friend of sinners."

"Are you preaching at me?" she objected, snatching back her hand. "You know how I hate you preaching. But listen while I tell you this! You remember the oak? There are extra bodies hanging in it. *He* put them there—your new knight! Who does something like that? Even thieves and murderers deserve a proper burial, Square. Yet he has stripped them of almost everything: their horses, their weapons, armour, clothes. He's keeping it all as booty, and his archer is collecting it even now."

"It is hard to understand," came the reply, Square nodding sympathetically, "but chivalry actually does allow knights to take trophies from vanquished rivals."

"How many knights keep bits of armour and weapons stuffed inside men's shirts and stockings?" she scoffed.

"Sometimes first thoughts are best," he persisted, "and I just can't believe I was wrong about him yesterday. Once you weigh all the evidence—"

"Evidence? I'll give you evidence! Think about it. Sir Robert Welles locked you up, then suddenly he changed his mind and gave Sir Thomas Malory a warrant for safe passage. Doesn't that strike you as odd? Then Malory brings us here to the king's manor, which has been ransacked and torched by rebels not all that long ago, and suddenly the Beast shows up just at the right time to earn our gratitude. Hardly a coincidence! Don't you see? Something is going on, Square. Even you must see that."

"You think the earl of Warwick might be involved?"

"No," she decided after a moment's thought. "The king invited me to a dance at Baynard Castle but that's no reason for the earl to bother with us. Kilsby must be involved. I am certain of that."

"How can you be certain?"

"It's like when I'm sketching for a painting, and the hand knows what the eye can't see. It's a feeling, but I know it's right. The details will come later."

"He came from the Sun, Susanna. The Knight of the Lost Sabaton rode from the Sun. It was a sign of God's grace."

"It was late and the Sun was setting. But is it any wonder that you imagine these things, my poor Square, after everything Sir Thomas Malory put you through!"

She picked a straw from his tangled hair and kissed him on the forehead, all the while wishing that she could talk with their father instead. Farthings understood the world better than anyone, better even than Aunt Marian. He would have made a good confidante at a time like this. Nevertheless, Susanna had no better friend than her brother, and it was always good to share with him. Their little talk had at least settled her nerves, and a few moments of quiet reflection began to make some things clearer to her. The Beast's arrival yesterday had taken Malory by surprise, and men had actually died, so it can't have been a mere pretence. In that case, Square was partly right: the Beast of Ferrybridge really had rescued them from danger. However, he was Kilsby's colleague, and there could yet be even greater dangers ahead of them. This much was undeniable: Tom Roussell was a hero of the Lancastrian cause, and she was a Yorkist. She owed him nothing.

"The Knight of the lost Sabaton hasn't failed us so far," Square pleaded as they got to their feet. "Give him more time, Susanna."

"More time to fail us?" she wondered. "And yet what choice do we have!"

They joined the other travellers, gathering on the ground floor, some with the haggard look of people who haven't slept well, some with a bemused expression, still wondering at yesterday's events. Some were busily getting their mounts ready, and some were breakfasting on whatever food and drink they had brought with them. Cecily and her father had packed bread, pickled eel, dried pears and ale, but it had gone missing in the night. Susanna decided not to mention names, but she commiserated with father and daughter and invited them to share the snacks she had made under Aunt Marian's watch. It was a Lenten breakfast—tasteless biscuits, washed down with a tasteless cider—but it was pleasant enough outside, with the sun peering at them over the woods, the wall of the barn snug against their backs. Susanna was upending the last drops of cider from her cup when the new love of Matilda's life, Smith, happened to ride by on his mule, leading the Beast's mule on a rope. Susanna glimpsed Malory's fancy armour peeping from under canvas. The blacksmith signalled for people to follow him, and everyone soon assembled at the doorway, where he halted for an announcement.

"Listen here and let's keep this short!" he shouted, voice ringing like an iron hoop under the blows of a hammer, loud enough to be heard by everyone indoors and outdoors. "I'm John Smith from Waltham Abbey, as maybe you already know. Tom Roussell—that's the knight that's been helping us—he has left me in charge. He's gone off scouting for us and says he'll re-join us outside Stamford. That's a town just a few miles off. So, let's get mounted, Everyone! It's time we got moving."

His news was received with murmurs of surprise and disapproval. Everyone felt they were entitled to hear Roussell speak for himself. The beadle from Ware was loudest of all.

"Hold on!" he said, "The knight left you in charge of his mule, not us. I've been a beadle ten years. I should be the one giving orders."

"We saw your leadership style yesterday," objected Matilda.

"A man must prove he can lead in hard times," the beadle affirmed, his chest puffed out. "Now here's a test for the blacksmith: someone stole my herrings last night and I know *who*. The Galts! Anyone can smell it on their breath. What is the blacksmith going to do about it, I want to know!"

"*Herrings?*" came a protest from overhead: Friar Fryer leaning from the loft window, the Galts clustered around him. "You ungrateful fool! There are people here who have lost everything!"

He pointed at the oak tree, a sobering comparison.

"String the Galts up with them, I say!" said the beadle.

There wasn't much support for this.

"Shouldn't we bury those men before we leave?" Square wondered.

There was some support for this. One of the ravens roosting around the bodies raised its voice against, and then the butler from Boston said they could all end up food for the birds if they didn't get moving soon. The beadle piped up again, reminding everyone that the dead men had meant to rob and murder them all. Cecily's father said they should at least stop long enough to bury the original two. Then the bandy-legged archer entered the controversy, though he was leading a long baggage train of horses that tugged each other and stumbled as they went, like a demented caterpillar, bristling with swords, polearms and staves.

"Bury them with what?" he scoffed.

Even Susanna couldn't deny that this was a good argument: nobody had a hoe, basket or any other proper digging tools.

"Why not take the bodies with us?" Square thought to ask next. "We could pay for their funerals from the sale of their horses and gear."

"We have no time for that," the archer grumbled. "Lead off, Smith, or we'll be here all day."

"Ho, Goodman Archer!" scolded Matilda. "Who are you to give orders, when your master left Smith in charge, not you!"

"*Andrew Barton*, Goodwife Chatterbox, but you may call me *Easy*, a good name for the easy-going man you see before you now, otherwise I might take offence at your tone."

"*Bandy-Andy* suites him better," Susanna decided to say, because he had no right to lord it over her maid, "on account of his bandy legs."

"A very easy name to remember!" Matilda affirmed. "So just you keep quiet, Bandy-Andy, and leave a man's man to rule the roost, for we are beholden to John Smith more than we are beholden to you. He earned our respect long before you showed up."

"Enough blather!" said the blacksmith. "Time to get moving."

Most of the roads in England were in bad need of repair and the road into Stamford was no exception. Crown law required a good clearing either side of the king's highways and yet bushes and trees brushed against the travellers like hands searching for valuables. Everywhere was a likely shelter for cut-throats. Susanna was dreading another encounter with the Beast when suddenly he appeared, as Smith had said he would, outside the town.

"There is a picture for you!" said Square, bringing his horse to a halt to admire the view.

Susanna could think of no reply. The Beast was waiting for them on a grassy rise, in bright sunshine. The muscular look of his armour, and his easy mastery of a powerful horse, made him seem every inch a true knight, comfortable in steel and comfortable in the saddle because accustomed to bend everything to his will. Churches, rising above the level of the town walls, crowned him with their steeples, and a dog, crouching by the horse's hooves, was just the sort of touch an artist might have added, nicely softening the general air of manly strength and lordly pride. However, with men, as with portraits, there is an ideal distance, and blemishes began emerging the nearer Susanna and the others approached. He was now wearing a tabard decorated with the earl of Warwick's coat of arms: a rampant bear chained to a tree. His visor was up and his face reminded her of the face that she had slapped in her aunt's house. This was no true knight. This was the stooge of a traitorous earl, on a horse looted from Malory and with a dog stolen from Watt.

"'Ear is as far as chivalry mun tek tha," he announced to the travellers as soon as they were all within earshot. "Ah plan t reach Peterborough afowa sunset, eddin for London. Come wi me or dooan't, a thy own risk."

"What takes a Lancastrian to London?" Susanna couldn't help asking, emboldened by the proximity of a friendly town.

"A orse," came the smirking reply.

"You took that horse off Malory," she reminded him. "How do we know that you are any more trustworthy than he turned out to be?"

"Tha dooan't."

His high-and-mighty insolence irritated her, being a stark reminder of his boorish behaviour in her aunt's house, and she urged Mary of Reading forward till the mare stood alongside Malory's mount, the better to confront the rebel hero.

"This fellow is the Beast of Ferrybridge, a notorious Lancastrian!" she advised her fellow travellers, because everyone had a right to know, and then she waited for the anxious murmurs to subside before continuing. "You all saw the ruinous state of the king's manor. I am not saying he torched it himself, but maybe he knows who did, and don't we deserve to be told how he happened to show up in time to rescue us yesterday? He couldn't have seen anything from the road. He must have been following us, or lurking about there already. Let us hear how he responds to our concerns before we consent to go another yard in his company. Otherwise he must answer to the authorities in the town there."

She was only doing her duty as His Majesty's loyal subject and yet nobody seemed eager to back her up so far. The Beast even laughed.

"Sir Thomas is such a pleeain rogue, all a were missin t make it pleeainer still were **Rogue** printed i gold letters on is elmet! But sin tha were blinded by whateva blinds a daft lass, Ah followed tha a a scaht's distance, knowin tha ad need o rescuin afowa long. But *thanks* is all t reward Ah ask."

"Here now!" said the beadle from Ware, nudging his donkey forward. "What happened to your archer friend?"

Bandy-Andy and his baggage train were supposed to be following in the rear but there was no sign of them now.

"Ah towd im ta sell those orses a Oakham, t other en o dis rowud," came the Beast's reply. "We'll get a good price for em theear."

"So *thanks* is not your only reward," Susanna noted.

"What about *our* share?" the beadle added. "We were all in the same danger as you."

"And some were in more danger than most!" said Felix Baxter, the butler from Boston, urging his horse forward to stand alongside the beadle's donkey. "I was the first to be robbed, so I should have first choice of Malory's stuff. His horse is worth a fortune, and his helmet and cuirass looked like Burgundian gear, the best in the market."

"You have a right to nothing, for you did nothing!" cried John Smith, urging his mule forward to confront the beadle and butler.

"Says you, the Yorky knight's lickspittle!" the beadle snarled.

"Says John Smith, the Hammer-fist of Waltham Abbey!" said the blacksmith, rising in his stirrups. "Ask for me there and they'll tell you, or ask for me here, and I'll show you—with *this!*"

He brandished a cudgel-sized collection of knuckles under the beadle's nose.

"We'll av neya fights unless Ah start em," said the Beast, "so all o tha pipe dahn n folla me!"

Stamford, like Roussell, was best seen from a distance. Susanna was not a complete stranger to it, having stopped there once before. The town walls had been damaged by Lancastrian forces after their victory at Wakefield, and expensive repairs were still waiting all these years later. The old gatehouse was just a derelict arch, blocked for now by a wagon. Men with billhooks, bows and crossbows loitered behind it.

"Who comes there?" the commander of the watch demanded to know.

"Just some travellers puttin Lincolnshire's troubles behin em," said the Beast.

He approached the wagon and handed over a document. The commander of the watch unrolled it and began reading aloud.

"*Tom Roussell … on business for the earl of Warwick.* Tom Roussell. Tom Roussell? The earl of Warwick? By God—the Beast of Ferrybridge!"

A trumpet sounded. The billhooks, bows and crossbows at the gate became agitated. Others quickly joined them, swarming like bees. Archers appeared on what remained of the parapet, taking precarious aim from behind crumbling masonry.

"What's ta fuss abaht?" said the Beast.

"You passed this way in '61," said the commander. "You think we have forgotten?"

"T whole Lancastrian army passed this weeay i '61," the Beast reminded him. "Many are naw t king's friends. T earl o Warwick tooa, last tahhm Ah eard. Open up, or tha'll av earl imself ta answer ta."

"Wait a moment."

There was a delay while the matter was referred to someone else.

"You can enter free, for the earl's sake," said the commander at last, "but it's a penny for each of your companions, and it serves them right for keeping such doubtful company!"

This was robbery—travellers with no wagons and nothing to sell ordinarily passed through walled towns for nothing, or a farthing at most, and even that was steep if it was payment for repairs to the town defences, damaged in '61—but the insulting notion that they had anything to do with a notorious Lancastrian was what ruffled Susanna's feathers the most.

"We're not *his* companions," she protested, urging her mare forward. "We just happen to be travelling the same way, that's all. I am His Majesty's loyal subject. A penny is outrageous. I refuse to pay it." This lured the commander out from behind the wagon, swaggering with a hand on the hilt of his sword, as if even a penny might no longer be enough. Now was not a good time for defiance, Susanna then decided, being desperate to get home in time for the dance. "My brother is carrying a letter of commendation from the bishop of Winchester," she recalled, because they never left London without it. "We just want to stop here briefly for some refreshments," she pleaded, "and then we will be on our way. Do we have to pay so much?"

"Maybe a penny is a bit steep" the commander confessed, resting a hand on Mary of Reading's nose while peering up into the shadows of Susanna's hood.

"How kind you are," she replied, barely hiding the revulsion she always felt for men as impertinent as this one, their fingers as sticky as frogs in search of a pond, their eyes as watchful as owls.

"I am not always rude to pretty girls" he explained as he moved nearer her stirrup, his mouth as dark as a dirty secret, missing most of the teeth. "We're all a bit on edge here lately, on account of a lot of trouble we've been having, and not all of it from rebels. Two Derbyshire households passed this way, Yorkists through and through, but feuding and racing each other to Westminster—broken windows, brawls and a stabbing. Two days of it! They even smashed a Hallelujah Coffin. Worse than a whole army of rebels! But they've gone now, and everything is back to peace and good order. Will you be staying long?"

"I have to get to London quickly. Which is the best way?"

"The Peterborough road every other year but you would be wise to avoid it now," he said, fondling her bridle. "There have been rebels and brigands hanging about there for a week. Try the king's stronghold at Fotheringhay due south. It's a quieter road, or it used to be: the Derbyshire households went that way this morning, the ones I told you about. Some other travellers taking that road are mustering by St Mary's at town's end, ready to leave at Sext, if they can find enough fellows. That's the church where the Hallelujah Coffin got smashed. We're burying it this morning."

"We found some dead men at a royal manor a couple of miles off," she told him, since he kept clinging to the bridle and obviously needed something to busy his hands with. "One of the king's manors. They could do with some burying too."

"They'll have to bury themselves. We have enough to do."

The wagon was rolled aside and the travellers were assessed for toll on the basis of whatever business they were bringing with them. Since none had any business in Stamford, they were all allowed through for free. Square was questioned longer than everyone else, his resemblance to a green monk making him a curiosity, but the letter from their landlord smoothed things over, and that got him through eventually. Their fellow travellers disbanded about town, buying or begging necessities for the journey south, and Susanna and her little household headed for a tavern at town's end, where Cecily's father said there was always a good meal to be had. The way there was an illustration of England's problems and also its resilience. Ruined walls, charred stones, derelict buildings and vacant allotments memorialised visits of the Plague and the '61 Lancastrians. Newly broken doors and a dead horse, its bowels trampled into the mud of the main street, gave witness to the recent feuding between the Derbyshire households. The town was prosperous in spite of all that, its shops and stalls doing a brisk trade with locals and travellers alike. This far from Aunt Marian's abstemious example, Square bought jugs of ale, a pork pie and beef sausages for himself, Susanna, Matilda and Old Will, while they all rested at a tavern with Cecily, her father and their three servants, waiting for Sext. They then moved on to St Mary's, near the bridge over the Welland. Several parties of travellers had already assembled there, all eyeing each other with a view to combining for their mutual protection, including nuisances like the Galts, the beadle from Ware, the butler from Boston and—worst of all—the Beast. Most of the travellers kept milling around him, the armour and rampant bear marking out a powerful figure.

"Him again," Susanna moaned. "He told us he was going by Peterborough."

"Maybe he is afraid of the rebels there," said Cecily.

"No Cecily, he is a rebel himself: the most notorious of them all! That is why we were almost fined a penny, just for travelling with him. What if he keeps following us and we end up getting tolled too much in every town we come to!"

"You'll talk us through somehow, Susanna," Cecily gushed. "Nobody can resist *you*."

Her cousin's flattery wasn't always insufferable and sometimes it was even quite pleasant to have her around. Meanwhile the townsmen were flocking to the church. They seemed too festive for Mass, and the gate commander's words were still fresh in memory.

"It must be the Hallelujah Coffin," said Square.

The annual ritual of the Hallelujah Coffin was one of Square's favourite festivals and even Susanna usually relished the fun, with parishes everywhere collecting toys and mementos inside mock coffins, for burial on the eve of Septuagesima Sunday, to be dug up again on Easter Sunday, when happy *Hallelujahs* are heard and even saints are said to laugh. This parish was late getting started thanks to some Derbyshire vandals, and thus Square and Susanna, who had also missed out this year, joined the congregation, standing in the nave doorway, looking in.

"It reminds me of our own church," Square said above the voices of the mock choir.

The roof of their Southwark church had collapsed last year as an act of God, and it was still propped up with their father's scaffolding, undergoing repairs. There was scaffolding here too but the damage was a decade old and rebels had been the cause of it.

"The '61 Lancastrians have a lot to answer for," said Susanna, eyeing the wounds with a sense of personal injury. "The Beast should be tolled a pound for every Lancastrian that came this way."

"At least he didn't smash the Hallelujah Coffin," was Square's view of things.

"He calls the dog *Wakefield*. He is still proud of what the Lancastrians did."

"Loyalty to an old cause is proof of a stout heart."

"He didn't get a name like *Beast of Ferrybridge* for nothing, Square."

"Knights often have terrifying names."

"He was never a knight. He just dresses in steel."

"Knighthood isn't a virtue. It is the reward for virtue, and not every hero gets rewarded."

"His Majesty's emblem is a white rose."

"The white rose of York, yes, but the royal coat-of-arms has lions on it. Is the king therefore a beast? Another man's wife in his bed is what makes our king a beast."

"I would rather call her one. But keep quiet and let's enjoy the spectacle."

They were still standing by the door when the congregation emerged with the make-believe coffin, boy choristers singing *Hallelujah dulce carmen*, gingerbread crosses waved in the air, home-made censers wafting fragrant smoke, fake holy water spattering the bystanders as the playful procession slowly advanced outdoors. Square received the holy water as if it were real, rejoicing in his sorrow, because drunken pranksters from Derbyshire had not destroyed a wonderful occasion, only postponed it. Susanna rejoiced for his sake, because the world had never yet crushed the goodness out of him. On the road outside, however, things once more went horribly wrong for the town. The notorious rebel from '61 had remounted Malory's horse, maybe to get a better look over the heads of the crowd, and somebody in the congregation recognised him:

"The Beast of Ferrybridge! That's him! The Beast of Ferrybridge!"

The congregation jostled each other in their fright. One of the choristers stumbled. A marzipan crucifix, perched on the lid of the coffin, fell to the road and smashed into small pieces. It was soon followed by the coffin itself, spilling the parish's little mementos along the ground, all the bright trinkets and toys the neighbourhood had treasured over years, memorials of happy days, scattering as far as the proud hooves of the terrifying Lancastrian. The Beast's reaction was disgraceful, of course. He curled his lip in disdain, slammed his visor shut in furious contempt for ordinary people's little misfortunes, then pricked Malory's horse onwards, ambling across the bridge out of town, as if owing nobody any apologies for anything. The other travellers followed in haste, less afraid of him than they were of possible brigands, lying in wait for lonely wayfarers. Susanna and Square stayed back to offer the townsmen help and sympathy, until the risk of travelling alone loomed too large even for them. At last they made a rushed departure and somehow, while Susanna was getting into the saddle, without anybody to lend a helping hand—Matilda had already hurried away in pursuit of her blacksmith—the hem of the riding mantle got caught up under one knee, baring her leg shamelessly in front of the already scandalised town.

"A Hallelujah Coffin smashed to pieces!" she protested while Square trotted beside her, hooves clattering over the bridge. "And now I must

ride after the man responsible, with my legs bared like a Winchester
Goose!"

"It was an accident, Susanna."

"It was an omen, Square. His name is Death."

Susanna approached Fotheringhay Castle as if it were a picture just
now painting itself. It was His Majesty's ancestral stronghold, and every
stone seemed aware of that fact. She had passed this way only once
before, Peterborough being the usual route to and from Bourne, but
everything here still looked as fresh and bold as the first time she had
seen it. The centrepiece was a massive stone tower emerging from the
midst of several roofs, the roofs peeping above a series of mighty walls,
as if no amount of masonry could quite accommodate a great king, all
softened however in a mellow afternoon light, the light now floating
in a faint shower of rain, as if the castle might be the man himself,
standing behind a silk curtain that emphasised rather than concealed
his hardness. She stopped to admire the scene and meanwhile most of
her fellow-travellers pricked their mounts onwards, racing each other
to get the best of Fotheringhay's accommodation.

The road to the castle threaded through a village, dominated by
a magnificent church and a mysterious inn. Susanna, an avid student
of the king's personal history, had heard reports of an ambitious plan
to turn the church into a virtual cathedral, with the construction of
a cloister to support a large college of priests, daily chanting orisons
for him, his family and ancestors. One end was already masked in
scaffolding, and voices from the church were raised in glorious song
even now, confirming the knowledge she treasured in her heart: His
Majesty was a man of action. Meanwhile travellers were milling
around the church's handsome gatehouse, unable to get in—the
hospice was already full up—and some travellers could be seen going
about the village, knocking on cottage doors, hallooing from garden
gates, negotiating bed and board. The inn was virtually empty when
Susanna and others peered into the courtyard. The innkeeper was
baffling.

"No room here!" he said as he bustled past with an armful of pans. "This inn is for losers. The castle inn is for winners. Try there."

He wouldn't stop for explanations so they moved on to the castle in the hope that they might be winners. It commanded a bend in the river Nene, whose waters were channelled to make a large moat, almost like a second river, crossed by a long bridge. Access to the bridge was temporarily blocked by a wooden barricade. The other end was closed too, the gatehouse grinning defiantly through a heavy, iron grille. A large crowd had gathered on both sides of the moat, some standing by the water, others looking down from the castle walls. Colours waved on both sides. Square said something chivalrous must be afoot and his hopes were quickly vindicated by spectators eager to tell him all they knew.

"We must stay on our horses," he reported back to Susanna, "or we won't see over all these heads."

"What are we going to see?"

"A trial by battle! The people on this side of the moat are the Vernons, and those on the inside are the Greys. The Vernons and Greys are the two Derbyshire households we were told about at Stamford, remember."

"Who killed the horse and smashed the coffin!" Cecily recalled with horror.

She and her father were part of the group that had stayed with Susanna and Square, or maybe they had stayed with the Beast, because he was hanging about too, staring at His Majesty's magnificent castle from Malory's magnificent horse, as if he hoped to mount a challenge himself.

"Even here the two families can't govern themselves," Square continued, "so they have been kept apart until the battle decides which side may lodge at the castle inn. The other side must withdraw to the inn in the village."

"The inn for losers," Susanna recalled.

"The Greys got here first but that was only a race. The Vernons expect to win the battle, but the prize both families covet most of all is the queen's youngest brother, Edward Woodville. He has been lodged in the castle for days, awaiting an escort to Westminster. The winners will have the honour of conducting him home."

This didn't sound like an honour to Susanna. The queen's family had an evil reputation for making their personal fortunes out of England's misfortunes, and for gilding their ill-gotten gains by marrying into some of the greatest titles in the land. The best place for the whole tribe was the bottom of the moat, in Susanna's humble opinion, and she was sure that the Vernons and Greys thought so too, even if they contended for the dubious honour of bringing one home.

"The Vernon champion is a Burgundian nobleman, long known as the greatest swordsman in all Christendom," Square added. "The Grey champion is an Englishman. He calls himself the *Red Knight* but he was never knighted. His father is only a park warden. People this side say he is certain to lose. We can't ask the Greys what they think—"

"Because they are in the castle!" said Cecily.

"Well spotted, Cecily," said Susanna, trying not to sound too disdainful: her cousin's mind, like her appearance, never rose much above the cute.

"The Englishman is going to cut off the Burgundian's head," came a voice between Susanna's stirrup and Square's.

It was Adam the Younger, squirming in pleasurable anticipation of a battle he couldn't possibly see on foot, unless he squeezed to the front of the crowd. The other Galts were already in the thick of things, obviously intent on their usual sport.

"Nobody is going to get killed, I hope," said Cecily. "I have seen too much bloodshed already."

"It's all for show," Square assured her. "The two combatants will carry shields and use only wooden swords. A referee will make sure they obey the rules, and then victory will be awarded on points. That fine fellow with a trumpet up on the gatehouse parapet—he will give them the signal when to start and when to stop. It is sure to be as chivalrous as any contest we see at a Smithfield tournament."

Susanna was almost inclined to let Adam sit with her on Mary of Reading, or with Isaac on Lady Lorna, or he wouldn't see any of the entertainment, but then she noticed a large treadmill by the moat, just like the Thames cranes she had seen at work all her life. Piles of building materials had been unloaded from barges and stacked nearby, one a neat mound of dressed stones, assembled in a series of steps, finally reaching the right height for an audience.

"Let's sit like royalty!" she told her closest companions: "our very own stand."

They were all a bit saddle-sore and gladly left their mounts with their servants. Susanna stayed to fondle Lady Lorna's ears a few moments, unlaced Isaac's jacket, so that his plaster could breathe, then raced Adam the Younger for the highest step, where both stopped just in time to avoid a sharp drop on the other side. She laughed with him as they sat together, and meanwhile she threw back her hood, rejoicing in the freedom she always felt whenever people were busy gazing somewhere else. Cecily and Square positioned themselves rather timidly on a lower step. It wasn't long before a trumpet sounded from the gatehouse and then a herald announced the names of the combatants, the rules of the contest and the prizes, all as Square had foretold. The Vernons' champion emerged from the village end of the bridge, a green tabard over his armour, emblazoned with the grinning head of a ferocious boar. The Red Knight emerged from the castle a little later, his tabard depicting a red hand on a white background.

"The boar's head is the Vernon emblem, promising bravery and hospitality," Square explained. "Those blue and white banners up on the parapet are the Grey colours. The red hand must be special to their champion."

"But what does it mean—a red hand?" Susanna wondered.

"A hand promises justice," Square explained, "and red is for valour."

"Mayhap red as summa ta doa wi magic."

Susanna could hardly believe her ears. The voice had come almost like a whisper from close behind her, where nobody could be sitting, since hers was the highest step and there was a drop of some six feet as sheer as a wall. Turning her head, she found that the Beast had sneaked Malory's horse alongside. Her seat was higher than his saddle, putting her head on a level with his, and he had removed his helmet, now resting beside her.

"Who do *you* want!" she objected.

"Or t could be summa t doa wi alchemy," he added, ignoring her protest for the moment. "Ah'm just watchin, sem as tha."

"Then watch somewhere else."

His face looked harder than the stone she was sitting on but cracked into a smile while he seemed to contemplate another response.

"Av tha eard o *Red Tincture?*" he came out with next.

"You mean cinnabar?" she marvelled. "What's that to you?"

"Tincture is what my father uses in his vats," Cecily volunteered from the next step down—she hardly understood the Beast's history and his connections or she would never have turned around to encourage him like this.

"Neya, not cinnabar nor dyer's stuff either. It's summa alchemists meeake. Lord Grey is an alchemist, so mayhap is Red Knight is li some kin of Red Tincture i armour, or new speriment i fightin."

"*Speriment?*" asked Adam.

"*Experiment* is the English word he was trying to say," Susanna explained for the boy. "It means an effort to do something new. It's like me painting you as Isaac."

"N appen *alchemist* is another word tha ant eard afowa," the interloper added. "It's someone whoa thinks everythin can be turned intoa summa else. Red Tincture elps im bring t abaht someweays. Most o em ope ta make thersen rich turnin things intoa gold, but Ah say it's neya better than magic, li pullin coins aht o thin air."

"My parents do that," Adam volunteered.

"That's called *stealing,*" Susanna reminded him while trying not to laugh.

"Lord Grey as purchased a royal license ta doa t speriments, so a least t king is makin gold art o is nonsense," continued the Lancastrian, as if anyone could be bothered listening to him. "Ah av nivva eard o t Red Knight afowa naw. It will take summa li alchemy to turn im into t winner today. T Burgundian as nivva lost."

Adam and Cecily rewarded him with smiles and appreciative nods over their shoulders, but Susanna wasn't so easily fooled.

"The people of Stamford dropped their Hallelujah Coffin, thanks to you," she recalled. "Are you proud of yourself?"

"Ah'm t bleame for a?"

"*You* frightened them!"

"Fear allus belongs within, not fra ahtside."

"You understand fear," she guessed. "It helps you prey on your victims."

"It elps keep me alive."

He smiled his defiance and she ended the conversation by pulling her hood back over her head. There was little time for more conversation anyway, a trumpet sounding once again, summoning the two combatants to meet in the middle of the bridge. The referee briefly separated them with a herald's staff and spoke to them privately, before finally stepping back as a signal for the fight to begin. A roar went up on both sides of the moat. The battle looked disappointing at first, blows traded without points being awarded, until suddenly the Burgundian's sword flew through the air and landed in the water, where it floated in mockery of the passions aroused on all sides. The referee signalled victory for the Red Knight but somehow the battle continued.

"What is the Red Knight doing to the Green one?" Cecily wondered.

"He is picking him up," Susanna observed.

"And throwing him into the water!" Adam enthused. "Wow he's strong!"

The Burgundian disappeared with a great splash and didn't resurface.

"Is that allowed?" Susanna wondered.

There was stunned silence on both sides of the moat. Soon naked Vernons began plunging into the water, frantically searching for their lost champion. Jeers floated down from the walls, the Greys enjoying their victory in comfort and safety. It was provocation the Vernons could stomach no longer. The barricade was swept aside and they poured onto the bridge, brandishing swords, battle axes and pikes. Nobody emerged from the other side, the gate still barred shut by order of the referee, determined to keep the families apart. The trumpet kept blaring from the gatehouse parapet but nobody was listening.

The Red Knight stood alone against a multitude. He cast off his shield and wooden foil, wrested a real sword from the hand of the first Vernon that came his way and promptly cut off his head with it. He carved the next man almost in two and skewered a third. The rest of the fighting was too quick and too crowded with combatants for Susanna to see what was happening but it ended in still more Vernons dying and the rest taking to their heels. The Red Knight owned the bridge. The gate finally opened and his friends mobbed him for joy.

Susanna instinctively glanced at the Beast, to see his reaction, but he had gone. There was no time to think about this, however, as heavy rain began falling, and Cecily chose this moment to swoon, overwhelmed by the sight of so much carnage on the bridge. She slid down the steps, prostrate and bumping from one to the next, in a gradual movement that ended with her on her back in a gathering puddle of mud. She didn't look to be hurt, but she was tearful when her eyes opened on the rain, and Susanna experienced a wave of compassion that made assistance the most important thing she could do. She was still at her cousin's side, lending comfort and encouragement, when the barricade, originally intended to keep the Vernons off the bridge, became the planks carrying their corpses and body parts to the nearby church. The surviving Vernons followed in a struggle with mud that seemed to spring as much from their bewilderment and grief as from the rain that continued tumbling from a dark sky. It was a picture that Susanna hoped never to paint but which struck her as compelling. Meanwhile the rain washed the bridge clean of bloodshed, making it easier to cross for any non-Vernons who still hoped to find accommodation inside the castle walls.

All weapons, including Square's sword, were surrendered at the gatehouse in exchange for tokens, to be returned in the morning, and then the commander of the gatehouse explained the layout of the outer bailey and its choice of shelters. It was shaped like a crescent moon, and his gatehouse lay near one end. An inner gatehouse, set in the middle, provided access to the castle proper, including the towering keep and the royal apartments. Only the most privileged guests ever found themselves inside that gate—today, the queen's brother, Edward Woodville. The inn for winners was located between the two gatehouses, and today it was reserved for the Greys and their celebrations. Common travellers usually stayed in some wooden cabins pitched against the bailey wall but these had already been claimed by families fleeing the troubles in Lincolnshire. There were some farm buildings at the other end of the moon, including stables and a barn, and all the travellers from Bourne and Stamford

were directed to stay there. Fortunately, however, the gate commander's wife took a sympathetic interest in Cecily, providing her
with a private space to get cleaned and changed, even presenting
her with a pomander to restore her spirits. She soon revealed that
there were spare beds in the bailey kitchen, located near the inn for
winners—enough beds for the patient and any three companions
she cared to nominate.

"Daddy and Susanna!" Cecily stipulated, already beginning to
feel much better. "And good old Square. We four! Or Matilda."

"I'm with John Smith," Matilda let her know. "If I can find him!"

Matilda went off to the farming end of the bailey in search of
Smith. Susanna led Cecily into the kitchen in search of warmth.
The fireplace was bigger than any Susanna had ever seen till now,
monstrous flames savaging various implements of iron. Here, kept
at a safe distance in an alcove, were four camp beds, covered in fresh
blankets already warm with the kitchen's heat. The guests were soon
treated to a hot supper, courtesy of the gatehouse commander and
his wife, who joined them on their beds with jugs of spiced ale. Meat
burned as the cooks and their apprentices forgot themselves, lost
in admiration of the guests, until Susanna hooded herself, leaving
them only her plump but pretty cousin to stare at.

Conversation turned to the tragedy they had all witnessed. The
commander marvelled at the Red Knight's extraordinary power and
skill but deplored the deaths as unnecessary. He was sure the king
would be furious once he learned of the scandal, and he quietly
blamed Lord Grey for inciting the Red Knight's rampage. His wife
too was convinced that something like justice would prevail. Later,
after his wife retired, the commander wandered outside with Square
and Cecily's father to discuss the proper management of a gatehouse
and bailey. Meanwhile Susanna and Cecily got to talking about men.

"If men were not so violent, I would think better of them than I
do now," Cecily observed meekly. "But all I have seen of them since
we left Bourne, is daggers at throats, and bodies dangling from oaks,
and now a drowning, and blood, blood, blood, till I am sick of them.
I am beginning to understand why you hate men so much."

"I don't hate *all* men," Susanna objected. "Only husbands."

"You are like a man yourself. That is what I have heard my friends say."

This was shocking gossip.

"I am a woman like any other," she protested.

"You are bolder than most women."

"I stand up for myself."

"Yet many people say you are the most beautiful woman they ever saw."

"People say all kinds of stupid things."

"But isn't there any man you feel you must love or you will die?"

"Actually, there is one man," Susanna revealed, because a love as great as hers is always bursting to get out.

"Who?" Cecily wondered, taking the pomander from her nose and resting it expectantly on her lap.

"The king."

"Oh pooh. What is he to us?"

"England and its future."

"I once over-heard Daddy saying he is unfaithful to his queen."

"The Ah-Ha woman."

"*Ah-Ha?*"

This was a term of Susanna's own making and she was happy to explain it.

"*Ah-Ha* is the name I have bestowed on the whole Woodville clan, and that includes her brother in the castle here. It's because there are two sides to those people. The queen's father was an Englishman of little better status than you or I, which makes people go *Ha!* Because the king might as well have married you or me, if nobility means so little. Their mother though was Jaquetta of Luxembourg, descended from the emperor Charlemagne, which makes people go *Ah!* As if the Woodvilles might be nobles after all. The Ah-Has are neither common nor noble, but a family of grasping, greedy, self-serving upstarts, hated by everyone. It's time you knew."

Cecily considered the matter in silence for a while.

"Daddy is always hiding ugly things from me," she confessed. "I'm glad you told me. But don't you ever feel you need a man to hold you?"

"No," said Susanna, taking another sip of ale.

"Sometimes I think I want to be a spinster like you, just to grow old in peace and quiet and never feel the way I do when I see a handsome face, all as if I am on fire. But if men cut off each other's head day after day, I would have no cause to fall in love with any of them."

"You could do worse than marry a headless man."

"They should all just chop each other up and then you and I can go on happily talking to each other, in the manner of grown women, without ever stopping to think or care what men are up to, the way some silly women do."

Susanna silently reminded herself that she hated most women almost as much as she hated men, just before Matilda burst into the kitchen.

"He's gone!" she cried, snatching a jug of ale from Susanna's fingers, and draining it at one gulp. "Smith!" she explained after dropping onto Cecily's bed, like a woman who has come to the end of her hopes. "There isn't a corner of the castle I haven't searched. They must have gone together. Just when a man begins to be interesting, he ups and disappears. The same old story!"

"*They?*" Susanna wondered.

"Smith and Square's knight in shining armour."

"The Beast of Ferrybridge has gone?

"He took a liking to my blacksmith from the first, and now they have gone off together, or I would have found some trace of either one by now."

"But where have they gone?" Cecily wondered.

"As far from here as a Lancastrian coward can get!" Susanna concluded, feeling angry, vindicated and disappointed all at the same time. "This is His Majesty's ancestral home. Naturally a notorious rebel didn't dare venture inside."

"Cowards," Matilda affirmed. "All men are cowards. Yet I would have rewarded the blacksmith for his courage at the king's burnt-out manor, if he had stayed. But let him go. Love is an alehouse dream."

She inverted the borrowed jug and shook out a few remaining drops as if they were tears.

"I am sure I could never be so brave as you are, Matilda," Cecily reflected as she clutched the pomander to her nose. "If ever there was a man who could break my heart, I would keep him under lock and key for the rest of his life."

"Find me a lock and key that will do the job!"

Matilda returned Susanna's jug then headed off for her lodgings at the rural end of the bailey. Not long afterwards, a group of men entered the kitchen, reeking of wine yet looking important. Susanna guessed they must be from the inn for winners, here to say something about the evening meal. However, they ignored the deep bows of the cooks and their apprentices, all the while gazing around in search of something or someone important enough to be of special interest to people like themselves. Soon they spotted Susanna and Cecily.

"Mmm, the women from Bourne, huh," one of them observed.

His fine robes indicated nobility, so Susanna and her cousin rose from their beds, bowing at his approach.

"Swa you are the ones all the talk is about huh, from Bourne eh?"

"From Southwark originally," Susanna replied with another bow. "My cousin is from London."

"Smah, there is a report that Tom Roussell, hmmph, is pavelling with your trarty—mmm, travelling with your party. Heading for London. What say you, eh?"

"You are looking for Tom Roussell?" Susanna queried.

"Hmm the Feast of Berrybridge … Berrybridge Feast … Beast of Ferrybridge."

"I don't understand."

"Uh Lord Grey of Codnor, hmmph. Is he, fwt, travelling with you to London, hmmm?"

"*You* are Lord Grey?"

"Hmph are you deaf fwa?"

The Beast had described Lord Grey as an alchemist—one of those men that turn everything into something else, preferably gold—and Susanna now wondered if the nobleman's speech had been affected by his experiments. He looked to be between thirty and forty and there was nothing remarkable about his appearance, except his magnificent clothes, appropriate to his rank, and his staring eyes, bulging disconcertingly whenever he had trouble pronouncing a word. She wondered if she should feel sorry for him or if he was merely drunk.

"Tom Roussell was travelling with us," she explained. "We don't like his politics though."

"Hmrwa where is he now fwt?"

"We haven't seen him since this afternoon's fight on the bridge."

"Mrwa did you see him at a manor two days ago ha, outside Stamford?"

"A royal manor, yes."

"Torched by rebels hmmm? Other travellers in your party saw him there what say you."

"He arrived after we did, and it was already torched by then."

Lord Grey was alarming even on his own but doubly so in the company of a youth that kept pouting and winking over his shoulder, sometimes at Susanna, sometimes at Cecily. The youth now paused to whisper something in the noble alchemist's ear.

"Mmm, this is Edward Woodville, the queen's broungest yother, hmmph," Grey then revealed. "Queen's youngest brother, what have you. There is a bath for you, hmmm, up in the castle keep, if you are ready for something hot fwt."

Susanna bowed to the royal brother-in-law, as etiquette required, all the while feeling aghast at the coincidence: she had just now been laughing at the Ah-Ha Woodvilles, and here suddenly she was faced with the youngest of the brood. But was it really a coincidence? It was rumoured that the Woodvilles had insinuated themselves into the king's affairs so thoroughly that nothing was his own anymore—apparently not even a bailey kitchen! This one was perhaps the strangest Ah-Ha of them all. His complexion, framed between black ringlets, was arrestingly pale, his eyes dark and lustrous, and he kept turning this way and that, angling for a better look at Susanna, or angling for her to get a better look at him, with a sudden glance downwards, next a slow, appraising look upwards, then an insolent leer of his cocked head, shifting to a smirk of his smouldering profile. Susanna guessed he must be anywhere between twelve and sixteen, an age that suited his reticence better than it suited his lewd and knowing looks.

"No baths thanks," she pleaded, pulling her hood even further over her face. "My cousin and I have an affliction, spread by sharing."

"Hush Susanna!" whispered Cecily. "You're embarrassing me."

Edward Woodville murmured something more in Lord Grey's ear. Once again Lord Grey did the talking.

"Swah, you must have heard about the rebellion, huh? Mmm we are heading for London tomorrow. You will come with us for your own safety, eh? My Right Kned will, er, protect you. Kned Right. Red Knight. Hrwa, Tom Roussell is no match for my Red Knight, if it comes to a fight, what say you. Come with us tomorrow. Mmm I insist ha."

Grey's manner and the Woodville boy's smirks were highly disturbing but the offer of protection could hardly be refused, coming as it did from a lord and the king's own brother-in-law. Susanna nodded her reluctant assent. The men left and she exchanged bewildered looks with her cousin.

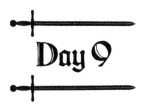

Day 9

Tuesday 20th of February

Susanna was dancing on a village green with the king of England when suddenly she realised that she was in fact a parsnip and he was a carrot, and that they were dancing in a ring with other parsnips and carrots, because the village green was a cauldron of soup, and the cook stirring them was Lord Grey, who could turn anything into something else. He could even turn himself into something else, because he exploded like a flock of startled sparrows, immediately regathering and settling into the likeness of Tom Roussel, the Beast of Ferrybridge, *hmmm uh Feast of Berrybridge, Berrrybridge Feast fwt*, who snatched her from the soup, *Old still, Lahl Dingy*, bit into the palm of her hand and became *Woof, woof*—Bertram Kilsby.

She woke gasping for air.

Kitchen apprentices were busy preparing for a new day, fetching wood and carrying pots, cleaning grates and greasing pans, dicing roots and punching dough, all in the restless glow of a new fire, while Square, Cecily and Cecily's father lay gently snoring on adjacent beds, squirrelled away in the alcove. Susanna rose and went out to breathe the fresh air of a new morning, then shivered in the realisation that it was freezing. Stars peeped through gaps in the clouds and gradually faded in the gathering dawn. A hobbled herd of horses and mules browsed the bailey, and so did one donkey, whose white coat loomed large in the twilight, greeting Susanna with a shake of the head, a wiggle of the ears, a swish of the tail and a stamp of one hoof. They exchanged warmth while Susanna took in the rest of her surroundings.

The inn where Lord Grey and his confederates had caroused much of the night stood dark now and utterly quiet, and from there Susanna's gaze followed the curve of the inner moat, a glimmering path of water that led her thoughts to the inner gatehouse. Her eye leapt over it, drawn into the royal sanctuary by the towering keep, lifted to that eminence as if by some lordly act of pride, the final bastion. A window at the very top winked at her: a glass casement. Only glass would wink at this hour, catching the light of a new day as it turned on its hinges. She could imagine someone like herself at that very window, looking at the girl far below, shivering in the light of a new day.

Leaving Lady Lorna to continue browsing weeds, she returned to the kitchen and shared steaming possets with her three companions, then walked with Square to the nearby church for some site-seeing. This was his favourite time for worship: dawn congregations were so small, he said, that it was possible to feel almost alone with the Creator. It was His Majesty's church and that was reason enough for her. Today, however, wasn't the best time for tourists. Vernons had gathered by the rood screen, full of grief and sorrowful prayer for their dead kinsmen, laid out in the nearby inn for losers. Nevertheless, monks chanted the usual hymns—sorrow and grief are nothing new in the history of the Church—and the arcades offered scope for privacy, Square kneeling in prayer by a small altar, Susanna standing by a tall pillar, her cheek pressed against the stone as she entered into the life of His Majesty's building.

By the time they returned to the outer bailey, Lord Grey and his household were loitering outside the inn, huddled in sickly companionship while jaded servants mustered and saddled their mounts for them. Round at the farming end, an orchard lifted its naked arms above grubbing pigs and scratching hens, while travellers, who had spent an uncomfortable night lodged in the stables and barn, tried keeping themselves warm with preparations for another day. Some looked worn out already. Matilda had exhausted herself brooding too much over her vanished blacksmith. The Ware beadle and Boston butler, pale with resentment, muttered complaints about the vanished Beast and Malory's vanished horse and armour. The Galts were sick after eating something that had disagreed with them, and Adam the Younger looked particularly ill—too ill for another day's journey on foot. Friar Fryer borrowed some cloaks to wrap the boy in, and Susanna readily agreed to let the patient ride Lady Lorna. Only Jesus had ever ridden her till now, but Lady Lorna didn't mind, even though she was already loaded with the panniers, carrying Isaac and the painting gear.

"You look as pale as each other," Susanna confided in the boy after inspecting the portrait. "Try not to bump one another."

"I still haven't got my two shillings," Adam reminded her then coughed.

"I only promised you one."

"Two!" he insisted. "One to be painted and one to play with Watt."

"Two," she recalled. "You'll get the money when you look more like yourself and less like Isaac."

Old Will was tightening the last straps on the Mandeville horses, and Cecily was already hanging about on her pony, when Square bustled up to Susanna with some surprising news:

"I just saw Sir Thomas Malory!"

He nodded at the latrines, located high on the bailey parapet, overhanging the river. A balding head, draped in white locks, could be seen barely peeping over a wooden screen.

"Is he hiding from us?" Susanna wondered.

"It's mutual," said Square. "I looked right through him, as if he weren't there."

"He came from London," Susanna recalled. "He must be heading back."

"We should report him to the authorities!" said Matilda, shrugging off her lovesick melancholy long enough to shudder with disgust. "He tried to rob and murder us."

"No!" Susanna hastened to say, because she was desperate to get home. "His men are dead, he didn't get paid, and we were helped by the Beast of Ferrybridge, who stole his horse and armour. *We* could be the ones ending up behind bars."

"Lord Grey might help us," was Cecily's suggestion.

"In return for what?" Susanna scoffed. "Sometimes the cure is worse than the disease. But now I have an idea! Leave Sir Thomas to me. I'll fix him."

Edward Ah-Ha Woodville emerged from the inner gatehouse, looking sleek and pampered astride a handsome gelding. He and his followers joined the Grey household at the outer gatehouse, all busy reclaiming their weapons, when a messenger reminded Susanna and Cecily that they were now expected to join their retinue. Cecily and her father welcomed the arrangement as protection against rebels and brigands. Susanna acquiesced reluctantly, since it was no protection against Edward Woodville. Finally, a fanfare of trumpets announced everyone's departure, the Red Knight leading the way across the bridge, the site of his grisly triumph yesterday. Lord Grey rode out in the midst of his household, banners and pennants fluttering proudly above a hundred servants and retainers, all looking as queasy and grey-faced as himself. Edward Woodville, no less pale this morning, continued loitering by the gate until Susanna and Cecily drew near, when he rolled his eyes and pursed his lips to indicate his lewd ambitions. They reigned in their horses, an invitation for him to precede them across the moat, and meanwhile Susanna thought up a name for him.

"*Edward the Bedward,*" she confided in her cousin. "It suits him, don't you think?"

"His eyes are as naughty as puppets."

"That isn't all of him that has a life of its own, I am thinking."

"I'm glad you are with me, Susanna."

"We must give him the slip before it gets dark."

Meanwhile a more pressing task required attention.

"Gate Commander!" Susanna called to their host from the previous night, his friendly face overseeing the return of weapons. "There is a bald man here in the bailey, with a few straggling locks of white hair. I have heard that he is carrying some kind of warrant signed by Sir Robert Welles, the Lincolnshire rebel. You should look into it!" The news was received by the commander with a look of surprise, followed by a nod of thanks. "Hopefully our gallant knight will end up a guest of His Majesty for a very long time," Susanna confided in Cecily as they rode out together.

"Do you think he still has the warrant?"

"Does porridge stick to a spoon?"

The weather had started fine but the road to London often bore evidence of chronic rain, at best a crust of drying mud, otherwise a quagmire, requiring frequent diversions across fields and paddocks and sometimes through woods. It began raining again by mid-morning and continued well into the afternoon, at last fading into high clouds and drizzle at Huntingdon, the next major town on the road south. This was another place struggling to recover from incursions of the Plague and the '61 Lancastrians, memorialised here and there in ruins and neglected yards. Most desolate of all was a circuit of low hills at the edge of town, enclosing the crumbling remnants of a tower: the ramparts and motte of a castle captured and destroyed hundreds of years ago. Obviously civil war was nothing new, and neither was a problem with accommodation. Edward the Bedward and Lord Grey had no difficulty, wealthy doors opening for them as obediently as bowing servants. An invitation to join them reached Susanna and Cecily the moment they entered the town square. They declined and were preparing to move into the first available lodgings they could find—an overcrowded hospice in the local priory—when Friar Fryer gave them a bit of cautionary advice.

"I am not meant to speak against my fellows in Christ, but that priory is an inn for sinners, and some of the brothers are worse than their guests."

Maybe he was exaggerating the dangers—his piety was at least as extreme as Square's—but with Edward the Bedward and his cronies in town, it was best not to chance it. Susanna asked him if he knew anywhere better.

"Try the inns at Godmanchester, just across the river. The God-manchester town watch can be difficult at this hour, so you might not get through, but you could try the old castle instead. The priory cantor lives there on his own, a saintly hermit overseeing a few cells for travellers as prayerful as himself. But Adam the Younger needs somewhere warm tonight and it's an alehouse for us. You could end up joining us, if you don't mind sleeping at a table."

Leaving Adam with the friar—the ride had already done him some good—Susanna's littlehousehold and Cecily's headed towards the river Ouse, in hopes of finding an inn on the other side. Huntingdon and Godmanchester were joined by a bridge, or were divided by it, a closed gate at the far end being patrolled by the Godmanchester watch. Town rivalries, and suspicions fuelled by the latest rebellion, were not something mere travellers could easily argue their way around this late in the day, though Square and Cecily's father tried. The pleas continued and the gate remained locked while Susanna, Cecily and the rest of their little troop loitered on the bridge, acquainting themselves with its peculiar construction. Its opposite sides were opposite even in their design, and there was also a quirky, little bend in it.

"Susanna, what a strange bridge this is!" Cecily observed, still seated side-saddle on her pony, a servant leading her back and forth.

"Yes," Susanna conceded, for she had already learned the bridge's history from previous visits. "This bridge is what happens when two towns won't speak with each other. The people of Huntingdon started building from one end, the people of Godmanchester from the other, and they never discussed their plans, and that's how everything finally met at a funny angle."

"There are squares at that end," added Cecily, pointing to a squared pedestrian bay, "and triangles at this end. It reminds me of men and women. They are different shapes, but they all come together somehow in spite of everything."

"Or don't come together," said Matilda, still feeling sorry for herself, "because the triangles are cowards."

The Godmanchester watch remained intransigent, and the travellers refused to pay the exorbitant toll demanded of them, finally turning in desperation to the derelict castle and its saintly hermit. The original earth ramparts, facing the river, were all that remained of the outer wall, now fenced with hedges and the occasional tree. The ancient bailey survived as a town common and as a small huddle of sombre buildings, traversed by a causeway leading up to the derelict motte. The hermit almost seemed to be waiting for them, warming a pot of stew in a rough kitchen next to the causeway. It turned out to be dinner for prisoners in the nearby county gaol, as well as for other guests, already lodged in rude shelters, each a monkish cell with a tattered curtain for a door. The weary travellers loitered there for a while, debating what to do next, and the hermit kept them even longer with a scandalous account of the priory, its history being one of mismanagement and depravity. It was too much for Cecily's dainty ears and, bored with the gossip, Susanna agreed to take her for a short walk. They soon ventured onto the riverside rampart, while the setting sun broke through the far edge of the clouds, casting a glow across the landscape. Susanna lost herself in admiration of the view, distant hills illuminated by dying light, like islands in a darkening sea. Across the water, a peasant woman collected reeds, inspiring Susanna to imagine her as the spirit of the countryside, eternal yet still devoted to the moment. The bridge caught her eye next, and she remembered what Cecily and Matilda had said. It was as if the sexual urge had turned to stone, captured in a form that didn't quite satisfy anyone. Was it a symbol for marriage perhaps, merely an awkward union, or a victory over differences? Perhaps it was something more romantic: stone gradually accepting human idiosyncrasies, the curve of a muscle, the thrust of a hip, overpowered by a need for something other?

"That bridge over there," she remarked carelessly over her shoulder, when she heard footsteps coming up behind her; "you were quite right about it. It really is like men and women, meeting in the middle somehow. A kiss immortalised in stone. Does that sound funny? Coming from me, I suppose it must. So now you must be wondering if this really is Susanna talking or somebody else."

She prepared a wry face for Cecily but, on turning around, found a man standing over her, as commanding as a king. He enfolded her in his arms as if he had a right to her, or she stepped into his arms as if she thought so too, just as some light rain began falling, when they kissed.

Tom Roussell had been dead to feelings of love for years but he had observed Susanna Mandeville in the evening shadows and he kissed her now because it would have been a wasted opportunity not to. Was it a mere co-incidence, finding her here? The bridge funnelled travellers into Huntingdon from many miles around, and the old castle was a well-known landmark. It was here he had agreed to rendezvous with his archer, once the confiscated horses and other booty had been offloaded—all but Malory's fancy stuff, which Tom was hoping to sell for a good price nearer London. The archer had already come and gone, and he was now somewhere about town, buying a flagon of beer, because they had been expecting a tedious night, and it had seemed like a good idea to get drunk while waiting for sleep to claim them amid the ruins of a forgotten past. Tom hadn't been expecting anything like Susanna Mandeville to come along, yet women once had a way of coming along whenever he had most need of them. Maybe it was destiny. Maybe it was a fighting man's luck. Maybe it was folly. Whatever, she was just another woman he must soon forget, though memories often come at their own prompting, like the rain.

The last time he had kissed a woman was six years ago, an encounter so vivid, he is reliving it even now. Her name is Alice, she is his betrothed, and yet she yields to him today only because he surprised her while she was picking gorse flowers in the ancient quarry near their Wharfedale homes. Their marriage had been arranged even before they were born, as a way to settle differences between their two families, competing for the best riverside meadow. Tom would rather fight Alice's family than marry into it, confident in his power to take and hold whatever he wants. On the other hand, Alice is pretty and her prettiness has surprised him in the quarry today just as much as his passion has surprised her. They seem to have surprised each other even here at Huntingdon, Susanna Mandeville turning into Alice, Tom suddenly casting off six long years.

It isn't just her ripeness that works on him. His blood is already up, hot in anticipation of looming adventures, the thrilling promise of action in a glorious cause. It had seemed glorious then, six years ago. How hard to sustain a kiss with memories bursting through the mind in a shower of fragments, entire months and years reduced to mere grains of gunpowder! Lancastrian fortunes had revived like a flame erupting from ash and charcoal, the north already wrested back from Yorkist hands, the summer promising victories in the south. It had been a time to stand up for manhood, and thus he had led his betrothed from the quarry into the nearby woods, questing for something brighter still, something sweeter and more intense. It had been among wildflowers, not far from a brook whispering behind a shelving bank, that they had lain together as if married already, conceiving a child.

Those pleasures are long gone. There was a bitter awakening, the Lancastrian army succumbing to defeats at Hedgeley Moor and then at Hexham. The proud remnant of the rebel cause retreated into Bamburgh Castle, where they somehow managed to hold on a few more months, until finally blasted into submission by the earl of Warwick's three great cannons, named as if they were cities, *Dijon*, *Newcastle* and *London*. The castle surrendered en masse, and Tom ended up behind bars at Warwick's stronghold, Middleham Castle, too dangerous to be released, too useful to be killed.

Seven months were spent staring into the darkness of a vanishing life, wasting away at the earl's pleasure, when Tom got word that Alice was in danger and needed his help. About the same time, a clerk at Middleham Castle, Bertram Kilsby, came up with a set of terms that any proud Lancastrian could put his name to. It merely obliged Tom never to fight against the earl, yet it also offered him an option to serve as marshal in that very castle where he had been imprisoned. The money was good, the work was easy, and the earl might not always be a Yorkist. Tom was his own man still and so he signed.

His release came too late for Alice. He arrived home in the chill of winter to find his betrothed and their son in an unblessed grave. Her family had come up with a ready story: she had succumbed to a melancholy fit of madness, suffocating the unbaptised infant with a pillow before throwing herself down some stairs. Others told a different story: a forced betrothal to someone else and her refusal to marry. Tom later confronted her brutal uncle in a cattle stall, killing him along with three others who had been thatching it. According to their kinsmen, this was murder. According to Tom, it was justice. According to Bertram Kilsby, such scruples didn't matter. The earl of Warwick was more powerful than the king's laws in that part of the world.

Susanna Mandeville has Alice's mouth. It opens like a flower and intoxicates him like fermented honey. Yet there is something else happening here, a mood taking shape in her kiss, a growing carelessness that is more like someone else he remembers, someone before Alice.

The years keep melting away in the rain while other memories haunt him.

The heaviest blow to Lancastrian fortunes weren't dealt by *Dijon, Newcastle* and *London* at Bamburgh Castle six years ago, but by Edward Plantagenet at the Battle of Towton, almost a decade ago. The imposter wasn't king then, just a rising star, a youthful giant thrust into action by the death of his father, the duke of York. Tom was a rising star too, having made himself into a legend in fierce skirmishing at Ferrybridge, by the river Aire. News of Tom's heroics had spread through Lancastrian ranks like a trumpet blast, and he had been on loan to some commanders, as inspiration for their young recruits, when reports arrived that his own commander—his great mentor and idol, Lord Clifford—had perished not far from Ferrybridge, along with his elite bodyguard, the Flower of Craven, so of course finding and killing Edward Plantagenet had struck Tom as the proper way to avenge his comrades and their lord. He came close in the fighting around Towton several times, the Yorkist star looming large in the mist and rain. Time and again Tom hewed a path towards him, determined to cut him down to size, yet they were like arrows on different trajectories and somehow Tom always came short. Meanwhile the towering Yorkist kept hurling himself into the action at just the right times and places, turning the Lancastrian world topsy-turvy. Almost thirty thousand Lancastrians perished that day and the rest fled. Tom fled too, following other fugitives across a tributary stream of the Wharfe, swollen with blood, and gorged with the bodies of brothers-in-arms, dead or dying. There was no way out but to tread them down like marsh weeds.

It wasn't long after that that he met Annie.

He doesn't remember her last name, or even if she has one. Names don't matter with girls like this. Her friends know her simply as *Church Ale Annie* because she sells ale at a church in Londesborough, in the East Riding, where he has taken refuge. This girl drinks more than she sells. She is pretty in spite of her habits and willing enough to let him take her, having been trained by the local priest. Tom shares her with the priest on alternate days, Sunday being a day of rest. Her careless lips breathe forgetfulness into him, and he has more need of that than anything else. Annie would never shed tears over a lover and neither will Susanna Mandeville, if there is any truth in a kiss. The initial passion has already faded, her lips merely glad to be wanted. Yet there is something else going on here now, a tension that is part indifference, part lust.

Who came before Church Ale Annie?

If only he could lose himself in Susanna Mandeville, maybe he could forget! The past seems as present as the river Ouse, flowing only yards away. She was a dark-haired woman with eyes as lustrous as starlight. It was only for one night but, strangely enough, it happened here at Huntingdon Castle: perfunctory sex amid the relics of the past. The glorious victory at Wakefield was not far behind him, the misery of defeat at Towton not far ahead—how close they came to each other, those two frauds, complete victory and utter defeat! The Lancastrians this time were marching on London, and Edward Plantagenet was hardly more than a schoolboy, when the order went around to take and burn everything in their way. It came from the Lancastrian queen, Margaret of Anjou. It is not the role of an eighteen-years-old warrior to dispute orders, so Tom ransacked gold from a cellar, hired the best whore in town and brought her up here, out of harm's way and in the way of pleasure. In the streets below, comrades are taking any woman they can get their hands on. He can't understand them. Why run amok like animals when they can live like kings, paying for their pleasures handsomely in the knowledge that there is more gold in other cellars and towns yet to come! It is good to be alive.

Susanna Mandeville merely accepts his desires, like the dark-haired woman between victory and defeat. Yet there is also a longing in her lips, a need that is more than perfunctory, a satisfaction that knows itself to be wrong. There was someone else long before he had ever seen Huntingdon Castle. There were two women, in fact, often on the same day but never in the same bed.

He had started service at Skipton Castle as a page, rehearsing the arts of chivalry and the science of war at just twelve years of age. By the time he was sixteen, he still wasn't much versed in social refinements but his body had already become a muscular battering-ram, able to ride all day and fight on foot at the end of it, encased in steel as smooth and supple as silk. The castle almoner was an elderly man with a young wife. Tom was the morsel she begged for. The almoner didn't mind, having enough to do just keeping up with the real beggars at the gate, so they soon set up the first tryst and it became a regular feature in the week's schedule. Meanwhile Tom's eldest brother was sinking into the habits of a glutton and drunkard, leaving a pretty wife at a loose end day after day. *Ebbtide* was the name most people gave George, because his interest in most things was of an ebbing kind. By the time Tom was sixteen, Ebbtide George was already slobbering in his cups at breakfast, weeping in his cups at lunch and in bed dead drunk asleep in the afternoon. His wife soon became another regular part of Tom's training, the castle being only some ten miles from the farm: an easy ride for a good stallion and a fit youth. It was a tidy arrangement, and often he serviced Ebbtide's wife and the almoner's wife with just a brisk ride in between.

The kissing is becoming hard and loveless because it comes from the teeth and the bones, being a need like other needs, rooted deep in the nature of a man and woman, nothing to be proud of. Yet it keeps changing, moment by moment. Susanna Mandeville's lips are as cold as the rain. There is something else going on here, something that isn't in human nature at all. He yearns to run but she clings like rain.

The Roussell family home was within view of the Wharfe River and their neighbour was a witch. All the children in the parish had been warned about her, a ripple in the water before her victims lost their footing, or had it pulled out from under them. A river is hard to avoid, however, and Tom used to walk along it on his way to and from the chapel school at Bolton Abbey. He was twelve when he finally met her, and that was thanks to Peter, his youngest brother. Peter was the family's only prodigy at that time, being amazingly smart. Tom was no slouch when it came to academic studies either but Peter, then only six, was already more advanced in reading and arithmetic. He was the smartest little boy the monks at Bolton had ever taught and yet, judged by the standards of other boys, he was an idiot. Even a six-year-old can shy a stone at something nearby and stand a reasonable chance of hitting it, but not Peter. He was more likely to hit himself in the head. Peter couldn't walk without tripping over his own feet. He was all brains.

There was no sinister ripple in the water on the day that Peter fell in, or Tom would have pulled him away from the bank. There were ripples everywhere, turbulent water receding after heavy rains, and Tom had found a cowbell at the edge. It was attached to a dead cow, the cow attached to the remnants of a shed, swept downstream during flooding. Untying the bell from the submerged timber and carcass, posts and legs, should have been a simple matter, and Tom had almost managed it when Peter toddled alongside and immediately fell in. He sank like a rock. Jumping in after him was Tom's first taste of real courage, not so much because the witch terrified him at that time, but because he couldn't swim. The cold punched him in the chest, and he was thrust by the powerful current into the tangle somewhere below the bell, pinned there with his little brother longer than anyone can hold breath. It was then that he saw her, a weird creature breathing water the way others breathe air, the locks of her hair waving calmly, as if there could be no current where she floated, only peace and quiet.

"Come to me!" she is saying.

She stretched out a hand, a hand no bigger than his own, but he could tell it had a force even a grown man can never match, because she is beautiful and insistent, her skin radiant with an inner light that captivates any poor wretch that looks on her. He struggled to pull back. He struggled in vain. He was doomed, along with his brother, until something broke the surface above them, a flash of light reaching in to snatch Peter first, as expertly as a heron grabs a fish, almost at the same instant as another flash took hold of Tom. They were both lifted up out of the water and hurled onto the bank, gasping for air.

"I got you! By God I got you both!"

It was the grandson of a runaway serf. He had been raised in faraway Cambridgeshire, recently returning to Wharfedale to claim the promise of freedom. He was hardly older than Tom yet training for the longbow had already given him a man's strength, and he had just happened to be wading back and forth across shallows, building strength in thighs and hips, when he had glimpsed them falling in. All

Tom lost to the river that day was his left shoe. It was a good trade, and he had commemorated it ever since by never wearing a full covering on the left foot, always cutting the toe out of his stockings and, later, doing without one sabaton. Later still, he hired a silversmith to set a clutch of river pebbles into a pendent, always worn around his neck as a lucky charm. The best memento of all however was a lifelong friend, almost a brother—Andrew Easy Barton—now one of England's finest archers. The worst memento was an overpowering fear of deep water. Tom had been wary of it before and he had been terrified of it ever since.

The witch wasn't just in the Wharfe River, as people in the valley supposed. Tom had learned from hard experience that she could be anywhere he went, wherever there was deep water, because he was hers forever, even if he had managed to buy her off for a time at the cost of a shoe. She haunted rivers the way she haunted dreams, not every night and not every river, but according to her own mysterious impulses. She had been in the river at Ferrybridge the day he had made a name for himself. Would he have made a name for himself without her? It had happened while he was scouting enemy positions. A large troop of Yorkists, appearing out of the mist, surprised him on the wrong side of the river, because the dilapidated bridge there was slippery with ice, and he could see a tell-tale ripple of water underneath it. Crossing and drowning looked no different, so he turned to face a merely human foe, fighting each man as he arrived, fighting on a growing fortress of bodies, until only one menace remained: that ripple of water still lurking under the bridge.

The rain cascades down his face and water overwhelms him at last: she yields to pressure and draws him ever deeper into her own darkness. He thrusts her away like a drowning man coming to the surface, and gasps for air.

Susanna had kissed him once, at a dance two years ago. That was in a house on the Strand. Rain is falling here by the river Ouse, yet she is kissing him again, memories flickering on the insides of her eyelids, collapsing months, even years, into moments.

Meeting him had come as a complete surprise. It was May Day and she had gone to the house as Maid Marian in a play about Robin Hood, the only woman in a troupe of mummers organised by the Bishop of Winchester, collecting donations for an almshouse. Farthings was the wicked sheriff, Square was Friar Tuck, and Robin Hood was a dreary lawyer attached to the bishop's palace. Susanna was only supposed to make masks for the troupe but the original heroine, a boy, had come down with a fever, and a replacement couldn't be found in a hurry. Respectable women don't flaunt themselves on stage but who would ever know that this particular Maid Marian really was a woman, if she stayed in disguise! Susanna put herself forward and the other mummers yielded to persuasion. It was a rare opportunity to see inside some of London's greatest houses, and she hoped to admire their art collections without interruptions from admiring men.

The May Day festival was celebrated in different ways at the different houses they visited. In the last of them, the principal entertainment was a new craze, Italian dancing. The mummers interrupted it only briefly and were allowed to linger after their performance, as a colourful addition to the scenery. Farthings occupied the time making himself known to potential clients. Square found an illuminated Bible in the household chapel, and studied it reverently, hardly daring to turn a page. Meanwhile Susanna discovered a portrait by a Dutch master, not painted in tempera, which she was used to, but in the new medium: oils.

It was love at first sight. A powerful man stood chained to a marble pillar, only a loincloth separating him from the stone's nakedness. He was blind, yet he lacked nothing in the way of male attractions. The colours glowed with a depth and warmth she had never thought possible till then. Occasionally guests pestered her with attempts at conversation. Mostly they were men attracted to her on account of a rumour, started by the wicked sheriff, that Maid Marian was in fact the greatest beauty in England—Farthings could never let slip an opportunity to match her with eligible bachelors—but she rebuffed them all and the mask made it even easier than usual. She just wanted to be alone with a real man for once, even if he happened to be a painting.

An impertinent tap on the shoulder at last ended her happiness. Conversation she could ignore; an uninvited touch was too much. Acid gathered on her tongue as she prepared to face down the culprit but, turning, she was immediately struck dumb by a towering figure, topped by a handsome face and a winning smile. She hardly recognised the man that had surprised her here at Huntingdon, but she recognised him then: His Majesty! She had not expected to see him here and neither had anyone else. Nobody had invited him. He had invited himself. She would have bowed but he took her hand to prevent it.

"Dance?" he said.

"I ... I ..." she stammered: she had never learned dancing in the Italian style.

"I'll show you how."

He led her by the hand to a space in the hall where other couples were waiting for the music to begin. Most of them were Italians. Italians were always introducing new routines that made Englishmen look clumsy, in the arts, in business and in fashion. These ones were bankers but they had met their match in His Majesty. He had borrowed their steps but could return the loan with interest, out-dancing the bankers themselves. It was that same spirit of rivalry, that same quest for personal excellence, that same love of adventure that had made him the master of England. And now it had made him hers—for as long as she could hold him close.

He was a great teacher: cheerful, patient, encouraging, eager to please and easily pleased. She was dancing with a dream, until the music stopped, when a gang of counsellors and courtiers descended on him, determined to fetch him away on business somewhere. He stayed just long enough to ask a favour.

"May I kiss you?"

It was every English woman's fantasy, so she lifted her mask as if it were the lid of her paint box, revealing a world of promise, the promise realised in a kiss. It was a moment without boundaries, it seemed, yet it had become a boundary between her life before and her life ever since. His counsellors and courtiers swept him away and she had not encountered him again, until now on Huntingdon Hill.

Is it His Majesty? Of course, it can't be, not here, but this is no time to reject the moment, now while her lips are joined to his, even as memories crowd her mind like sketches on blank paper, when the hand knows what it is doing and the mind just seems to watch. Art is nothing, love is nothing, life is nothing if not self-forgetfulness. She had learned that lesson from the first man ever to win her heart.

Who was he?

The artist's hands move quickly, bringing form and colour to paper, plaster and wood, sometimes peopling murals with heroes, sometimes illuminating payer books with saints, or else enlivening portraits with characters drawn from daily life. He was a character himself, a young man old before his time, able to conjure up an imaginary world with a mere bit of charcoal, or a dab of paint: a great drunkard, one of those neglected talents Farthings was so good at getting his claws into, paying them a fraction of their real worth. The loft in the Mandeville house was the scriptorium where he worked, slept and drank and where she daily visited him, a small girl watching mesmerised as his otherwise unsteady fingers discovered grace and power through paint and wild imaginings. He hardly noticed her even when she filled his mug with the wine he craved. Sometimes she found him carelessly asleep amid his work, when she would drape a blanket over his shoulders and bestow a kiss on his forehead, surrounded by the tenderness of his extraordinary vision.

He died a broken man: the world is not a painting. Her father closed the scriptorium in the loft but not the one in her heart. She had learned to see a new kind of humanity, not people crushed by life, but the living, breathing images of people at one with their imaginary feelings, devotions and business, forever captured by the deft hand and the watchful eye of the singular artist. She loved them more than she could ever love even the finest examples of real flesh and blood, until she glimpsed flesh and blood stamped with the look of a true hero.

Who was that true hero? Who else but Edward Plantagenet, on the eve of his coronation!

She was just thirteen. He was fresh from his victory at Towton, a handsome prince riding through London in all his regalia, smiling on the crowds like a summer's day, crowds so colourful, they seemed like vast fields of flowers opening to him for joy, her joy the greatest of all. A passing face in the crowd, she must have seemed to him then, if he saw her at all; a vision of manly grace and power that would never fade, he seemed to her.

Disappointment drenches the soul the way rain drenches clothes, crying out to be discarded in a moment of abandonment. She isn't kissing her prince. All the more reason to prolong the kiss! She was sixteen when she discovered his weakness. A town crier broke the astonishing news. He had married, not a princess, as a king should, but a woman like any other, a creature from among the English gentry: Elizabeth Woodville. It had been a secret marriage, announced after the event, like an admission of guilt. Susanna had never dreamed such a marriage was possible and she received news of it like a slap in the face. Soon she was hearing about other women, a series of names mentioned in town gossip: his lovers and mistresses. She hated them all and she almost hated him, almost hated herself. Her only hope for happiness was revenge, turning all her feelings to lifeless dust, marrying someone she despised, her marriage a perfunctory routine: William Walden.

Disappointment leaves a woman naked and vulnerable at last, nowhere to hide from herself. William was the son of a London perfumer, his mother a distant cousin of the earl of Warwick, a connection as faint as the blue veins in that woman's lean hands. Farthings considered William a good match. Susanna considered him pretty in a bland kind of way, not very bold and not very clever. *Witless William* was her secret name for him. He was just the sort of husband a wife could rely on to obey her. There were times she even thought it might be fun marrying into a house that always smelt nice, the ground floor of the Walden residence being a shop crowded with samples of fuming pots and pomanders and rosaries of orris root, with hair powders and tooth powders and sweet-smelling gloves, arranged temptingly to catch the eye as well as nose of the browsing customer.

It was upstairs in the Walden home, while helping him open a window, that she experienced her first kiss as a woman, Witless pretending to be a man. She submitted to his lips without hope or certainty, since Witless was already too hopeful and uncertain all by himself. It is turning out that way now with this false king on Huntingdon Hill, the kiss becoming perfunctory, her partner a mere intruder. Yet His Majesty and Witless aren't the whole story. Who comes next? Who is loitering in the kisses between Witless William and His Majesty?

She had been visiting her prospective mother-in-law as a mark of good faith when a handsome young man suddenly manifested himself in an enchanting manner, rising from the shop floor to the family apartment with a series of light-footed leaps, completed with a mischievous smile. He was Witless's cousin on the mother's side, another lowly shoot on the earl of Warwick's family tree, but with a big future, evident in his smile at the top of the stairs. He was working for the earl as an itinerant clerk and he had recently arrived in London to help organise some books. Or was he on leave? His entire life might be a holiday, his manner so playful, even climbing a set of stairs was entertainment. Susanna met him several more times at the Walden home and one morning he surprised her, coming on her as she reclined alone on a couch, while her fiancé and his parents were busy with customers downstairs.

"Can anyone mistake William for a man?" he asked her in that sensuous, lilting voice he wove around anyone whose company he cultivated, as she made room for him on the couch, snug amid cushions, overlooked by the very window where she had exchanged a kiss with his cousin. "I would sooner call him a fragrance. A man must be bold when it is required, don't you think? Not William. A pot of polite odours that never can be bold, not even to please a wife. It is not his integrity or his decency I am questioning, you understand—you see through one so easily—though I might question the value of such things in general, for people must get on in this world, or else be put upon by others, wouldn't you say? William for example exists only for the convenience of others, I think is what I am driving at—a soap-monger, a supplier of pomanders, a purveyor of perfumes, a human pot for fumigating closed rooms, your betrothed; your husband, I might say, if you will allow me to share your joke with you, for I am sure you cannot (indeed, what woman could?) endure the thought of William Walden daily hanging about the house in any other capacity than a mere joke, a diffuse presence. Have I touched your sense of humour now? Have you ever treated William to such a smile? So beautiful a smile, I am glad you have made it all my own."

Here was a mysterious wit, packaged in a fine, slender yet strong figure, handsome in a measured, structured kind of way, but with a hint of devil-may-care pride that suggested anything is possible: a man barely struggling to keep his ambitions in hand. She felt drawn to him immediately, and he drew her to himself as easily as putting on a coat. She accepts his kiss even now, because she is a woman and a painter and he is self-evidently a man with a regal sort of manner, yet she resists too, because there is something not quite decent in their predicament, a promiscuous confusion, wanting but not wanting, resisting but not resisting, glad to be wanted for now, if not wanted too much.

The next time she saw him was at St Paul's cathedral, where people often went just to experience the energy, bustle and colour of London all in one place. There was no larger building in the world. It towered over the city like humanity's greatest boast—too big even for God, some said, because you can't keep the Devil out once you let the whole city in, the arcades crowded with vendors selling everything you could want, if you knew under which window to look. Paintings and illustrated books could be found under the window of St Sebastian, patron saint of survivors, his arrow-riddled body still breathing in living hues of rigid glass. London's artists bought the tools of their trade there, and stopped to discuss new trends and techniques in his agonised but colourful shadow. Susanna went at least once every week. It was there that she chanced to meet Bertram Kilsby a few days after their secret kiss.

"It is incredible that you and I have not met here before," he declared while she fingered the bristles of a new brush, "both of us being in love with St Paul's! And yet I suppose its sheer size makes strangers of us all—strangers even to our own selves, is how I might put it. It exalts our minds yet dwarfs our bodies, wouldn't you say? Or, since there is a dark side even to cathedrals, I could even say it dwarfs our capacity for reason, while exalting our physical nature, so that one feels like a vast shell, wherein we are all lost and utterly alone, without ever really being alone. But that is what I like about it. I admire the grandeur, and I especially enjoy the roof."

It was to the roof they then went, to experience the grandeur. A guided tour cost at least a halfpenny but Kilsby needed no guides. They followed on the heels of some Baltic tourists, climbing up long, winding stairwells where conversation reverberated like a hubbub of fading memories, and then they hid in a passage till the tourists returned downstairs. The doors had been left unlocked, and they had the roof all to themselves, if anything could be all to oneself when a great city is spread out below, streets seething with people, reduced to the size of ants but with voices here and there recognizably human, words crisp as bells amid the blurred noise of thousands of men, women and children walking, running, riding, touting, knocking, sawing, hammering, and whatever else people do amid the lowing of cattle, the whinnying of horses, dogs barking, pigs squealing, cranes dropping their loads with a crash, or lifting them with a groan of straining timbers and a rattle of tightening winches, London painting itself in miniatures of sound as well as colour, an illuminated text too great for any tongue to interpret. Meanwhile the Thames threaded down from Westminster, a silver cord marking the page where the exhausted mind must at last stop, overwhelmed by the effort at understanding.

Susanna pointed out the Mandeville house across the river, using the bishop's palace for reference. Kilsby replied by pointing out the rented apartment where he was staying, leaning with her over a water spout, but the view was too difficult, too far below to make out. He described it and she agreed to go see it.

The distance down from the roof of St Paul's to its nave door was much greater than the distance from that door to Kilsby's fifth floor apartment, and they seemed to arrive in no time at all, most of the way being downhill. The stairwell, though open to the sky, was as cramped as a chimney, and the room seem more cramped still, even after Kilsby threw open the shutters next to his bed. London buildings crowded out her view of London, except where gaps between them allowed glimpses of other buildings and, if you looked very carefully, you could just descry the rigging of a distant ship, its masts and yardarms as reclusive as a cobweb. Kilsby invited her to join him on the bed, so that he might point out some apartments whose occupants he knew by ill report. She complied so as not to cause offence but soon grew weary of the rumours and the view, instead noticing a religious icon hanging on the wall: an image of Saint Sebastian, painted on a wooden tablet.

He took it down to give her a better look. The saint's pose was identical to the one in the St Paul's window, showing the martyr stuck full of arrows, but the brushwork was poorly executed and, more disappointing still, iron nails had been stuck into it, as if mocking the merely painted shafts.

"It is almost a sculpture," she decided.

"Quite a coincidence, don't you think? Sebastian overlooks my bed, and he overlooks the stall where you buy your paints. It must be Fate, wouldn't you say?"

"Why did you do it?"

"The nails? Life without cruelty is—what?"

She began to realise there might be something odd about Kilsby's wit and he soon proved it by not letting her get off the bed. She struck him with an open hand and he struck her back with a closed fist. She immediately retaliated with her best punch, striking him even harder than he had hit her, a swift right to the point of his chin, so that his head turned sharply. He fell off the bed and she made a dash for one of two doors, but it was the wrong one. It didn't open onto the stairwell, as she had expected, but onto the next apartment. A half-naked woman lay on the bed, her face frozen in a look of horror because a knife had been stuck in her chest.

"My neighbour did that," Kilsby explained as he came up behind her, "but he has agreed to let me have his apartment, if I get rid of the body for him. Two apartments for the price of one! How could I say No?"

Susanna tried edging around him but he smashed the wooden Sebastian over her head then dragged her back to his own bed and raped her.

"Not a word to anyone, Susanna-Sweet-Thing," he urged while lightly tracing her face with an iron nail, "or I will be disposing of your body next."

He released her and she kept their secret until she got home. It all blurted out in her father's arms. Farthings dashed off to the bishop's palace, demanding justice for himself and for his daughter. The bishop urged caution. Going public about Susanna's rape would only increase her humiliation, nor was there any need to prosecute the villain for rape if they could arrest him for murder instead. The alderman in that ward was notified and the rooms were searched. No dead woman could be found. Farthings spoke a few days later with Witless and his parents. By that time, Kilsby had already told them a story of his own, emphasising her loose morals. They said her marriage to Witless was now impossible. They were quite sympathetic and agreed to keep her indiscretion quiet for the sake of her future chances, yet they were relieved to have discovered her unsuitability before the banns were published.

It was like being raped and released again.

She gasps for air and pushes him away—or does he push her away? It is all confusion, pain and grief, here in the rain at home, in London and in Huntingdon, alone with her drunken artist in the loft, Witless on the couch upstairs, the woman murdered in bed, surprised by Saint Sebastian, surprised by Kilsby, surprised by His Majesty, surprised by the Beast. She breaks free from their lingering hands and runs.

"Susanna!" cried Square when she hurried past him and the others in their party. "What's wrong!"

"The Devil!" she sobbed, bounding from the bailey as fast as her legs could go.

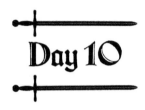

Day 10

Weðnesðay 21st of February

Square Mandeville almost blushed at his own boldness. He and his fellow travellers had been brought south to the Royston priory to be questioned about last night's devilry at Huntingdon, but the prior was a busy man—the town straddled the intersection of a Roman and prehistoric highway, two counties and five parishes—and they had been told to wait for him in the priory chapter house. They had all seated themselves on a semi-circular bench of sandstone, facing one another like monks awaiting interrogation on some disciplinary matter, but Square had helped himself to the prior's own chair, a throne-like edifice with a heraldic shield carved into the stone above his head. He had always dreamed of being a great servant of the Church, and the vacant chair had been too much temptation.

There was never a good time for spiritual pride but this was perhaps the worst. It was the eve of the feast of St Peter's Chair, commemorating the time when St Peter became the first ever Pope, an occasion for humility even for those really in authority. Last night's encounter with the Devil demanded extra humility. Were the Devil actually to appear now and offer him the chair, Square wasn't sure how he would respond. However, there was somewhere else in Royston that would tempt him even more: Arthur's Chapel.

What the Holy Grail was to King Arthur and his knights, Arthur's Chapel was to Square and his fellow fans of knightly adventure-stories. According to some patrons of the Tabard Inn, the chapel was a state of heavenly grace that could only be entered through prayer. Others said it was a real chapel, dedicated to the worship of God according to rituals once practised at Camelot. It was even said to house King Arthur's very own sword, Excalibur, sheathed once again in the stone from which the young Arthur had drawn it. However, nobody at the Tabard Inn had ever seen Arthur's Chapel let alone entered it. It was often rumoured to be in a secret location in Glastonbury or Winchester, but some reports even mentioned Royston. Finding it would be a rare privilege, like finding the Grail itself.

Square closed his eyes in silent prayer, beseeching God's forgiveness for spiritual pride. To be the discoverer of Arthur's Chapel, and to be the prior of Royston, worthy of the chair where he now sat, were dreams far beyond the reach of a journeyman carpenter from Southwark. Meanwhile he couldn't help thinking about last night. What had Susanna actually seen?

The Devil.

Nobody else had seen anything unusual but Susana's terror had been convincing and everyone had fled after her, in case she really had stumbled on the Prince of Darkness, Lucifer. The Huntingdon town watch had intercepted them in the main street, alarmed by their alarm. Susanna couldn't describe what she had seen and the others couldn't either, but the watch had been sympathetic. Mysterious visions were nothing new in Huntingdon, they had said, notably a headless man patrolling a vanished wall above the motte. Had Susanna seen *him*? Her lips were sealed tight, as tight as the sacristy door in their church at Southwark after the roof had collapsed, pressured shut by the weight of debris against it. Even Square could get nothing out of her. Meanwhile news of the Devil's visit had raced throughout Huntingdon, and Susanna and her fellow travellers had been welcomed into the homes of some leading burgesses, eager to hear more. Susanna and Square had ended up lodging with a grocer, who knew all the local gossip about strange sightings. Her silence was a common reaction, he said. Some people were so terrified by happenings in Huntingdon, they never spoke again.

The mystery had deepened still further this morning with reports that there had been another visitor at the castle last night: Tom Roussell. The monk there had been cooking him a stew when Susanna and the others had arrived, but Roussell had vanished as if into thin air at about the same time they had taken fright. Many people were asking if it was Roussell that had scared Susanna, rather than the Devil, and some trouble-makers were even saying that Roussell could in fact be the Devil himself. Whether or not someone is the Devil, only the Church can decide, and that could take a long time. A public disturbance however is a matter for the Crown, especially if it involves a notorious rebel, and Lord Grey had put himself in command of the investigation on behalf of the king. He had quizzed witnesses and organised a search. No trace of Roussell could be found, yet one of his associates was soon discovered in neighbouring Godmanchester, loitering by a baker's stall: John Smith, the blacksmith. He had travelled with Roussell from Fotheringhay Castle, yet he could shed no light on last night's mystery. Smith was certain of one thing only: Tom Roussell couldn't possibly be the Devil.

Square was of the same opinion as Smith. The Knight of the Lost Sabaton was too much a hero to be the Prince of Darkness, and only one devil had ever terrified Susanna till now: Bertram Kilsby. He was supposed to be dead but that hadn't stopped him appearing in their aunt's house two weeks ago. Square couldn't help wondering if she had seen *him* last night. The mere thought of that monster could reduce her to agonised silence, and Square had thought he recognised some symptoms today. She kept glaring and glancing over her shoulder, fists clenched as she stood or sat restlessly, and sometimes her body went rigid, as if expecting something, anything to happen at any moment, yet even Kilsby had never terrified her into such a long period of silence as this, so that that absolutely nobody knew what the matter was—not even Square himself! Truly something mysterious was afoot.

Square was soon roused from his reflections by the entry of a priory servant with a lighted taper, the little flame spreading like a cough from lamp to lamp, mounted on the walls above the heads of the witnesses. The sudden illumination put Square's spiritual pride in a garish light, so he vacated the prior's chair and sat on the bench with the others. There followed a noise of movement outside, Lord Grey arriving with some attendants. He seemed in no hurry to come in and remained standing by the door. Square supposed he must be waiting for the prior, yet the next worthy to appear turned out to be even more important. It was the king's right-hand man, the Lord Chamberlain himself, Lord Hastings! Square had seen him sometimes parading around London in the king's company for all the world to admire, but never this close. He could even overhear every word that the two peers exchanged in the gathering gloom outside.

"Mmph Lord Hastings huh!" said Grey, giving a deeper bow than he received. "Smwa I didn't know you were in town eh."

"Just arrived—off to Bedford tomorrow. The council there is getting nervous about Lincolnshire. But what brings *you* to Royston?"

"Hmm escorting the queen's brother to Westminster."

"I thought the Vernons were asked to do that."

"Pff."

"So where is the Woodville cupid now?"

"Hmmm, with the local apothecary's wife huh."

"She has the salve for his itch," Hastings laughed. "But what's this I hear about the Beast of Ferrybridge at Huntingdon? Something about him being the Devil? All Royston is abuzz with it. You took charge of the matter, I was told."

"Hmmph, rumours of him sneaking to London, and strange appearances and disappearances, hmmm. I questioned some witnesses but, swa, I can't get sense from them, what have you, fwt, so I brought them here for quizzing by the prior."

"Why the prior?"

"Hrmm, he's a churchman and Pustice of the Jeace, hrmm er Jeace of the Pustice ..."

"A Justice of the Peace," Hastings said for him.

"... authorised in civic and miritual spatters ... sparitual mitters ..."

Lord Grey seemed to be choking on something. Square had already discovered, during questioning at Huntingdon, that the nobleman suffered some kind of affliction that disordered his speech and distorted his face. Never comfortable witnessing a fellow Christian's embarrassment, he now averted his gaze and studied his own feet until Lord Grey finally came up with the right words:

"... spiritual matters hmra."

"A good choice then," Hastings conceded. "Where is he now?"

"Hmmm Arthur's Chapel."

"Playing Arthur himself I expect. Half England is besotted with tales of chivalry! But I think Roussell is more our concern than his, so let's get on with it."

The two lords entered the chapter house and all the witnesses rose and bowed. Grey introduced the Lord Chamberlain to them, the Lord Chamberlain helped himself to the prior's chair, and then Grey sat on the bench beside him. The travellers resumed their places, Square last of all, his mind still in a whirl at their mention of Arthur's Chapel. It must be an actual chapel somewhere nearby! He sat beside Lord Grey, agog to learn more.

"What's all this I hear about Tom Roussell and strange happenings at Huntingdon?" Hastings enquired of the group. "Don't be shy. Anyone?"

All eyes turned to Susanna, being the main witness. She was wearing her drabbest cloak, her face buried deep in a hood. If this was anything like one of her usual moods, it would be wise to leave her alone. Square thought it was time to put himself forward, so once again he got to his feet and bowed.

"We are travellers that set out from Bourne four days ago, Your Lordship," he volunteered. "My name is Square Mandeville, a journeyman carpenter of Southwark. I hope nobody minds me speaking first."

"Continue," said Lord Hastings.

"I heard you talking about Arthur's Chapel just now. Is it private or can anyone visit?"

It was a question he couldn't help asking but it annoyed Lord Grey.

"Psh don't question this man hmmm," he told Lord Hastings. "Pfwa his talk is all gallant knights and wicked varlets ha, and not a word of sense, pfwa."

"If it's Arthur's Chapel he wants, he has come to the right place," was the Lord Chamberlain's response. "So, my good fellow," he added, turning again to Square, "visits are by appointment only. I could arrange it for you. I have been there myself and it is well worth a look."

"My Lord!" said Square, almost prostrating himself before the prior's chair.

"But first tell us about Roussell. What mischief has he been up to? He has long devoted himself to rebel causes, and no doubt he has devoted himself to the Devil as well. It's time he was punished."

Square began to understand where all this was leading. Hastings was tempting him to bear false witness against Roussell, but Square could never accuse of devilry the man that had rescued him from Sir Thomas Malory. Still, Arthur's Chapel would be a dream come true, if only he could set eyes on it. The temptation was a real dilemma. He began working through it as if it were timber, requiring the back-and-forth pressure of a pump drill.

"You are wondering whether or not you should testify," Hastings observed. "That's no surprise. Roussell has an evil reputation—the Beast of Ferrybridge—and he serves one of the proudest men in the kingdom: the earl of Warwick. Nobody wants to cross men like those, if it can be helped. So, listen all of you, because this concerns everyone! I represent the king, whose power exceeds both Warwick's and Roussell's together, just as mine exceeds all yours. You will enjoy His Majesty's protection and my gratitude, if you co-operate with this inquiry. You may incur our displeasure, if you don't."

It was Square's civic duty to co-operate with His Majesty's government of course, but Farthings had discovered the king in bed with the goldsmith's wife, and adultery is one of the sins condemned by the Ten Commandments, so maybe it was Square's pious duty not to co-operate. Then again, a Christian shouldn't rush to judgement, and maybe the Lord Chamberlain was no more responsible for the king's wickedness than Square was responsible for the sins of Southwark, or Roussell was responsible for the crimes of some rebels. A little more drilling helped Square through his dilemma. He had already been rehearsing an account of his travels as entertainment for his fellow patrons at the Tabard, and Roussell's heroism loomed large in the story. Maybe the Lord Chamberlain could be won over to the truth that way.

"I didn't see Roussell last night," Square began, "but I can tell you what I saw two days before then, at a royal manor near Stamford—the smoking ruins of a manor, I should say. It was there that I first saw him."

"A royal manor near Stamford!" said Lord Hastings, now perched on the edge of the prior's chair. "I have heard reports of rebels torching and looting one near there. Was Roussell involved in that?"

"The villain in this story isn't Roussell, Your Lordship, but one that calls himself *Sir Thomas Malory*," Square cautioned him, "as cunning a rogue, as false a knight as ever pretended to stand up for chivalry! Maybe you have heard the name before. He makes himself out to be the author of a new history of King Arthur. We have been reading drafts at the Tabard Inn for weeks, and I saw no cause to doubt him. Whether or not he is the real author, others must decide, yet he is more likely to be a fiend from hell than is our hero, the dauntless Knight of the Lost Sabaton, for that is how I think of Tom Roussell, if I may make so bold as to dub him such."

"Mmm, as I said huh," muttered Lord Grey, shaking his head.

"How can I describe things to you so that you may see them with your own eyes?" Square persisted. "Imagine yourself travelling from Bourne with these good people here, when shadows begin to lengthen towards day's end, and now the false Sir Thomas lures us towards a column of smoke, perhaps a signpost to our lodgings for the night—or so we thought. What fools we were! For now we are prey to the false knight's minions, an evil crew intent on rapine and murder, while ruins lie smouldering this side and that—a knife is placed against this very throat, as God is my witness! For devils like Malory laugh at life as madly as they laugh at God. Imagine then the steel across your skin when, as by a miracle, like an angel of mercy—a mighty angel wielding the sword of righteousness—Roussell, in a great burst of light, appears as if from nowhere, in time to bring about our salvation!"

Square relived the moment for the Lord Chamberlain, imagining the Knight of the Lost Sabaton as he had first seen him, a wall-mounted lamp now serving as the sun, low on the horizon. He put up a hand to shield his eyes from the remembered glare.

"*A great burst of light?*" echoed the Lord Chamberlain. "*As if from nowhere?* That sounds like devilry to me."

"You misunderstand," Square pleaded. "True knights serve God and sometimes shine with Heaven's own radiance, if we but have the eyes to see it."

"Maybe Roussell was trying to plunder the manor, and the other knight was trying to stop him," Hastings suggested to Lord Grey. "We should find this Malory."

"Malory is a very devil for deception and treachery," Square cautioned him, "or I would never have hired him to be our guide and protector."

"Maybe we are better judges of character than you are," said Hastings, motioning him to sit down.

"And Arthur's Chapel?"

"Visits are by appointment only."

Square had hoped to defend his Knight of the Lost Sabaton from base slanders, and his failure now seemed to have cost him a visit to Arthur's Chapel. However, he was used to failure, and always accepted whatever punishment came his way, so he resumed his seat without protest. Meanwhile the tall, thin butler from Boston got to his feet, removed his hat and bowed before the prior's chair.

"My name is Felix Baxter, a butler from Boston, Your Lordship. I too was at the king's manor and maybe I can be more useful to you than was the last witness."

"Yes, let's hear more about the manor," said Hastings. "We can return to last night's devilry later."

The butler's head, being higher than the level of the nearest wall lamps, cast shadows on the vaulted ceiling. Square had the strangest feeling that the shadows had actually emerged from his head, in the manner of bats escaping Southwark's main drain at the close of day.

"None of us can say for certain if Sir Thomas Malory is a villain or not," declared the butler. "Some people here will say that he took things from us, and they aren't liars, but Malory said it was to keep our things safe, and maybe he just meant to keep them safe from Roussell, because the only property that ended up getting stolen from the manor that day was Malory's, and it was Roussell that took it—a horse as fine as any I ever saw, and some Burgundian armour, engraved all as fine as if it were a silver chalice. I don't know if there is a reward for its return, but there should be for this information, if Roussell gets locked up for it."

"And don't forget his archer!" volunteered the beadle from Ware, taking off his crimson bonnet as he jumped to his feet, which set many lamps winking around the room. "He took away a dozen horses and a great pile of armour for sale at Oakham. We're entitled to some of that too, if anyone is."

The blacksmith leapt to his feet.

"Ingrates!" he cried. "You two are entitled to get your heads knocked together."

He might have done it too if he hadn't paused to bow at the prior's chair, which gave the noblemen's servants time to keep the beadle and butler safely out of his reach.

"Hmmph, Roussell's friend, a blacksmith," Lord Grey explained to Lord Hastings. "Pfwa he disappeared with him at Fotheringhay the day before the trouble at Huntingdon, and we only found him this morning uh."

"Let's hear what the blacksmith has to say for himself," said Hastings while the butler and beadle were ushered back to their seats.

"Your Lordship, my name is John Smith, from Waltham Abbey," came the answer with another bow. "I got angry just now for good reason. Roussell saved us all from a gang of cut-throats, as Square just tried telling you, though you would never know it, if you believe this rascal butler and good-for-nothing beadle. The armour and horses that Roussell took away with him—they were taken from thieves by right of battle, as a reward for helping us, is how I see it."

The Lord Chamberlain smiled.

"Are you a lawyer, Blacksmith?" he said, picking at the ermine cuff of his ample sleeve, as if he had discovered a loose thread. "All property taken from thieves must be surrendered to the authorities, in this case the Crown. So, even if the knight and his men stole it first, and Roussell merely confiscated it, that's no different to stealing it again. He took someone else's property when it should have been surrendered to the king instead."

"Lawyers might say anything," Smith conceded. "But most witnesses here will say the king should be thankful to Roussell, instead of angry, since we were sheltering in his barn and Roussel was protecting us from a gang of murdering thieves. So maybe a lawyer can make something out of that too."

It isn't every day that a blacksmith stands up to a Lord Chamberlain, and his defiance caused an audible intake of breath all around the chapter house. Hastings and Grey exchanged looks, before Hastings turned back to Smith with a forbidding frown.

"Lord Grey says you disappeared with Roussell at Fotheringhay," he reminded him. "That makes you his accomplice."

"It was nothing like disappearing, Your Lordship," the blacksmith pleaded. "The archer—that's Roussell's servant—he went off to Oakham to sell the horses, so then Roussell asked me to serve him in his place till he got back. It was just for a short while, so I agreed. He paid me fourpence for it when we got to Huntingdon and that's where we parted company. My uncle is a baker in Godmanchester, across the river there, and I stayed with him last night. What Roussell was doing at that time, I don't know, but it can't have been wrong. A man like that makes trouble for villains, not for honest folks, if my opinion counts for anything."

"Am *I* a villain?" was the Lord Chamberlain's arch response. "Is the king? We must be, if your opinion counts for anything."

"I never said that."

"You implied it."

"I'm no lawyer," Smith conceded with an embarrassed scratch of his head.

"You have the manner of stalwart and reliable fellow," Hastings granted him, "but that carries more weight in a tavern than in a court of law. Now return to your seat and think more carefully about the kind of opinions you should be airing in public."

The blacksmith looked reluctant to sit down, as if he might have more to say on the topic, or maybe he was wary of Matilda. She had been sticking close to him ever since he had resurfaced in Godmanchester, and she had even sat beside him here in the chapter house. Now she was patting his place on the bench, smiling her encouragement for him to re-join her. He hesitated. The servants, who had ushered the beadle and butler back to their seats, then ushered him back to his, whereupon Matilda promptly rested a hand on his knee. He shooed the fingers away and they returned as shamelessly as flies. Square was scandalised. He had never considered her a suitable maid for Susanna but she had been their father's choice, and a father's decisions must be respected somehow.

"Let's get back to what happened last night at Huntingdon," said Lord Hastings. "Can anyone here shed light on Roussell's behaviour and why it frightened everyone?"

Again all eyes turned to Susanna and still she was unresponsive.

"I can shed light," volunteered the beadle.

"He wasn't even there," the blacksmith complained.

"Let him speak!" Hastings insisted.

"Thank you, Your Lordship. I am Walter Wheaton, the beadle from Ware, as I meant to tell you before now, and what I saw last night was no earthly vision. Whether or not it was what others saw, I don't know. Is there a reward and shall I go on? Ware is one of the Earl of Warwick's manors, and I am his loyal servant, but Tom Roussell might try getting me in trouble with him, if I speak out. But if you force me to speak, I will."

"You are speaking at my insistence," Hastings assured him. "Continue."

"And there is a reward?"

"If you deserve it."

"It's true I wasn't at the castle last night, as the blacksmith said just now. I was at the Huntingdon priory, but that's no hindrance. I could see the castle from there as clearly as I now see Your Lordship's face, and while I was looking up that way, out of nowhere suddenly he rises up, up, big enough for me to see from the priory, for he must have grown to enormous size with all the evil that was in him, like a cloud floating above the castle, or I wouldn't have believed it myself, and yet not like any cloud I ever saw till then, but a mist spreading as it rose, before my very eyes, larger than life, yet in his own shape, or I wouldn't have known it was him—Roussell, I mean. Shall I go on?"

Hastings nodded.

"And after him rose the Devil, or maybe it was Roussell, summoning himself back to Hell, like one that had escaped. It was a fearsome struggle, I beheld then, Your Lordship, fought between two devils a hundred times your size or mine, groaning and roaring over Huntingdon, each with Roussell's face and Roussell's body. And I hardly believed my own eyes, as maybe you can't believe my words, but I will swear to it even in church and, to cut a long story short, they struggled in the sky a while then disappeared back into the castle, the Devil and his minion—Roussell, I mean."

"Told like the lying beadle you are!" Smith protested, jumping to his feet again. "If anyone asks me, common man though I be, what I think of Tom Roussell, I will tell the truth, that he is a man like any other, only better, for if anyone is up to mischief, it is you, you lying beadle!"

"Watch yourself, Blacksmith," said Lord Hastings. "You will be sleeping in a cell tonight if there is any more of this bluster."

"Then lock me up with him!" cried Matilda, jumping to her feet also. "For he acts the way he looks, and he looks the way he is, all as bold and brave as his handsome face. Yes, I love him! Why shouldn't I admit it?"

There was a wild look in her eye, and an uncharacteristic slovenliness in her attire—the headdress was crooked and her cloak was half falling off one shoulder—as if a powerful experience had given her a terrible shaking.

"Maybe *you* saw something last night," Hastings suggested to her.

"*Me?*" she laughed. "All I wanted to see was *him*, my blacksmith, but he wasn't there last night, so I saw nothing. I felt nothing. I was nothing. But now that he has returned, I see only him, I think only him, I breathe only him, I live only for him, and I will always be there for him—if he will have me. Love tells no lies."

"I have only known this woman a few days," the blacksmith pleaded as he sat down.

Matilda sat beside him again.

"*I* should like to say something, though I am only a common girl, not worthy of the notice of great men," Cecily announced in a hushed voice, earnestly rising. "My name is Cecily Norton, and my father, sitting here beside me, is the London mercer, James Norton. We were at the castle last night too. I can vouch for what Matilda said just now, for she was heart-broken when Smith disappeared. She is truly in love with him, and I think it would be a good thing if he found some way to love her in return. That is all I have to say."

She resumed her seat.

"Did *you* see Tom Roussell last night?" Hastings prompted her. "Anything devilish or strange?"

"I didn't *see* anything," Cecily replied thoughtfully, "but I *felt* as if something devilish must be happening, or I wouldn't have run like the others."

Hastings tried another two witnesses after that. One was Friar Fryer and the other was Cecily's father. One of them hadn't been at the castle last night and hadn't seen anything, and the other had been at the castle last night and hadn't seen anything either. Hastings removed a sable-lined bonnet from his head and brushed the fabric in a contemplative manner. The investigation into Roussell's villainy didn't seem to be getting anywhere.

"Let's return to the beadle's testimony," Hastings decided after returning the bonnet to his head. "Something about mists and enormous devils fighting each other? It sounds incredible but that is no argument against it. People would never run from devilry if it was anything ordinary. Can anyone here corroborate what the beadle said?"

The butler from Boston got to his feet once more and bowed again.

"I can corroborate some of it. I was in the priory too. I didn't see any devils. What I saw was a mist, and that was something like the beadle says: a reddish kind of mist, growing and spreading over the castle, until suddenly it vanished."

"A reddish mist," the beadle affirmed. "Yet it looked to me like devils fighting."

"Maybe it was your reddish bonnet you saw," said the blacksmith, "puffed up with your own importance, you reddish mist of a beadle."

"Not another peep from you, Blacksmith," Hastings warned him, "or you will not only find yourself in a cell, but that woman next to you will be locked in there with you."

Smith folded his arms and sealed his lips.

"Now if you ask me what caused that mist," the butler continued, "I am no expert, but maybe it was something natural, and maybe it wasn't. Or maybe it was both, being one of those secrets in nature known only to men of deep learning."

"Continue" said the Lord Chamberlain.

"The answer to your investigations could be in here," the butler added while stooping to fetch something from his cloak, and then he straightened again as he pulled out a bundle of tattered papers. "This is a manuscript on alchemy that I recently chanced on at a Boston fair. It is written in a foreign hand but I can read the preface, since that's in Latin, which I know well enough. It says anyone who learns its secrets will find ways to make some things disappear, and other things appear in their place, and all this happens in the presence of something called—*Red Tincture*? That gets me to thinking, maybe that was the red mist we saw, and maybe alchemy had something to do with Roussell's disappearance."

Hastings rubbed his chin thoughtfully for a few moments then glanced at Lord Grey, who sat shaking his head disapprovingly.

"Hmph this fellow has already tried interesting me in his manuscript hmmm."

"You *are* the country's leading expert on alchemy," Hastings reminded him.

The butler handed the manuscript to Grey with a deep bow, and Grey thumbed through it in the gruff, contemptuous manner of a cynic.

"Smwa, it's mostly Arabic, fwt, but that's no proof that it is genuine, hmm."

"The Latin part of it says most alchemists can't get Red Tincture to work for them, because they only know thirteen things," said the butler, "but it always works for those who know a fourteenth, which only the manuscript can explain."

"Hmph, he means the thirteen precepts of the thrice-wise Hermes Trismegistus, the father of the alchemical science, hmmm," Grey explained to Hastings. "There is no fourteenth precept."

"The manuscript says there is," the butler insisted, "and so I am thinking, if Roussell found out about it—maybe because he took a peep at my manuscript—he might have vanished himself into thin air, in a red, alchemical kind of mist."

Grey kept thumbing through the pages.

"Is it possible, Lord Grey, considered simply as a theory?" Hastings wondered while drumming his gloved fingers on the arms of the prior's chair. "Can alchemy help a man vanish himself?"

"Hmm alchemy is an ancient science, Lord Hastings, not a conjuror's trick," Grey objected before thrusting the manuscript back into the butler's hands. "Phwa the purpose is to separate out the common elements in things, then unite them again in other forms, hmrwa, but the gest is for quold, look you—quold for gest, gist for quold …"

"The quest is for gold?" Hastings said for him. "So, alchemy is like minting money. Roussell would need a license for that. He doesn't have a license, does he?"

"Fwa, he is no alchemist, pwf."

"Practising alchemy without a license—there could be something there for our lawyers. With your testimony as the country's leading authority, it's a step in the right direction. But first we must find him!"

"Mmmm, you have yet to question the girl ha," was Lord Grey's response, "the one that cried *Devil*, just before Roussell vanished, hmra."

Susanna pulled the hood even further over her face then folded her arms.

"Please show yourself, that girl," said Hastings.

She ignored the request.

"My sister, Susanna Mandeville," Square said on her behalf, hoping to avoid trouble, because there was no governing her bad temper sometimes, once she got started.

"Mandeville?" Hasting wondered. "Mandeville from Southwark? Susanna Mandeville, the daughter of Farthings Mandeville, travelling from Bourne? So, this is her. The king has invited your sister to join him at Baynard Castle, the first Friday in March, for a banquet and some dancing. You are returning home with her for that purpose, I take it. But why does she not show herself?"

"She could be feeling unwell," Square responded as usual.

"Nobody is asking her to strip naked, just show her face."

"She hates being stared at," Square persisted.

"Everyone in His Majesty's company gets stared at. She must show herself to me now or forget all about His Majesty's invitation."

Susanna promptly threw off the hood, a movement that almost extinguished the lamp over her head. She swept a few strands of red hair behind one ear then shrugged and studied her feet, resigning herself to an admiring audience. No woman ever had finer skin or more exquisite features, as if she lived in a higher realm, where sickness, misfortune and poverty could never leave a mark. The room grew brighter in the shadow of her beauty, it seemed to Square, and even Lord Hastings looked impressed.

"Susanna Mandeville, I have heard many people commend your beauty, and just as many condemn your rudeness," he declared. "I can now see what all the fuss is about. Yet what of that! We are here about Tom Roussell's behaviour, not yours. What can you tell me about him? What mischief has he been up to?"

He waited for a response but still she kept silent.

"I am prepared to give you more time," he offered. "Roussell has terrorised entire counties in the past. No doubt he has terrorised you too."

She laughed at this and just then the Red Knight stuck his head in at the door.

"We found him!" he said. "Here in Royston."

"Roussell here in Royston?" Hastings marvelled, his hands gripping the arms of the prior's chair.

"Drunk," added the Red Knight.

"*Drunk?* Are you sure?"

"I know a drunk when I see one, My Lord."

Lord Grey and Lord Hastings exchanged astonished glances. Hastings turned his gaze back to the Red Knight.

"Any men with him?"

"Just one."

"The Beast of Ferrybridge, even with just one man," Hastings muttered fretfully, "if the stories about him are true, that's still—"

"I have him under control," the Red Knight assured him.

"Hmmm, my Red Knight is more than a match for Roussell, drunk or sober, what say you," Lord Grey assured his peer.

"Bring him here then," Hasting decided, "but unarmed and bound! Send for a dozen of my best swordsmen. Make it two dozen! Three dozen, just to be sure. But somebody fetch the prior, and some Holy Water. And a crucifix! Well, well, well, the Beast of Ferrybridge. Under our very noses all this time."

Square wondered if he had the stamina to support such an ordeal as this. The Knight of the Lost Sabaton *drunk*! Last night had been a long night, today had been a long day, and this evening looked as if it might never end. A pilgrim on life's journey, he knew that the search for truth requires fortitude, not merely faith. He steeled himself for whatever shocks might come his way.

A period of tense silence ensued while they waited for the prisoner to be brought in under guard. News of his inebriated state was deeply disappointing. Drunkards and prostitutes were the two great plagues of Southwark, and Square had no patience for either. On the other hand, if true knights had no failings, they would make uninteresting reading. He was prepared to reserve judgement. Meanwhile, armed men began stationing themselves inside the chapter house, in the doorway and in the darkness beyond. Soon a canon arrived with an iron crucifix. He handed it to Hastings who promptly grasped it like a club, resting it on his right knee. Another canon arrived with Holy Water in a sprinkler, looking nervous.

"We can't get the prior out of Arthur's Chapel," he announced humbly. "The windlass broke. I have been told to act for him, should you need help."

Square wondered if this was good news. A windlass could only be needed if the chapel was under construction, or if it was undergoing repairs. He would happily donate his labour to such a project, if only somebody would ask. Meanwhile a dog trotted indoors and began sniffing at everyone's feet. Reaching Susanna, it wagged its tail and sat expectantly, apparently waiting for a treat. She ignored it just as she ignored everyone else. Finally, the Red Knight returned, followed by someone in disgrace, a man dressed somewhat in the fashion of a respectable yeoman, except his clothes looked a bit threadbare, and he shuffled like a beggar, being horribly drunk. His hands were tied behind his back. He was helped along by a man with bandy legs and horns on his helmet: his archer, the one Susanna had dubbed *Bandy-Andy*. The archer left him to stand on his own for a few moments, bowing to the two lords while the prisoner swayed uncertainly.

"That's his friend!" the beady-eyed beadle from Ware announced. "The thief that rode off with the horses and the pile of armour."

The archer gave Roussell a shake to keep him alert.

"Whashup?" the knight wanted to know, gazing with difficulty at the faces around him. "Ah knowa theesh fowk, doa Ah?"

"Lord Hastings, Lord Grey and some of the people we rescued at the manor," Bandy-Andy advised him. "I have just been accused of stealing some horses and some armour."

"Tha shold 'em Oakham, remember," said the knight in a loud whisper.

"Hmmm obviously a lie, what say you," Lord Grey confided in Lord Hastings.

"Whoa shays me lying, orrible bloke theear?" Roussell protested. "Ah'll let 'im know wha's wha, n if he doan't look t imself."

He staggered a half-step towards Lord Grey. The dog left Susanna to join his drunken master, growling at the two peers.

"You are now talking to the Lords Hastings and Grey," the Red Knight reminded the prisoner, forcing him onto his knees before kicking the dog out of the way. "Speak with respect or you'll have me to deal with, Beast of Ferrybridge."

Roussell made no effort to resist. The dog took fright and waited uncertainly at the door. The canon sprinkled Holy Water on the troubled scene and muttered prayers. Hastings continued gripping the crucifix, still ready to ward off evil with the sacred power invested in it, or maybe with a two-handed swipe. It was a dangerous weapon either way. He was older than Square by a decade or more, yet he was fit enough to chase deer with the king and ride with him into battle.

"Tom Roussell!" Hastings intoned, while perched once more on the edge of the prior's chair. "You have been brought here before me today, firstly to answer a complaint made against you, namely, that you have taken property from a manor belonging to His Majesty. How do you answer?"

The Knight of the Lost Sabaton squinted at the two lords.

"Wha's this baht?" he said. "*Compleaint?* But Ashtings and Lord Grey? N sa it is. Bu sho wha, tha ashk me this a' Ah say, wha o a! Is nowt wrong, is it?"

"Where are the horses and the armour you took?" Hastings persisted.

"Ah already seeay, shold a Oakham, some things. Resht sold eear n Royshn, if tha musht knowa. Ten pounds Ah got. But losht it a dice, sa doan't ashk."

"There is ten pounds and two shillings in here," The Red Knight announced, holding up a confiscated leather wallet.

"Mine," Roussell protested, shuffling about on his knees, "n not thine! Or is gift for blacksmith, smithy Smith, Smith. Ah promised im some. Saw im just naw n ecar e is. Tha want ten pounds, smithy Smith, Smith? All thine, if tha wantsh. Bloke as served me well. Gi Smith it n Ah'll be my best behaved, n tha want me be. Ah will."

Hastings considered the matter in silence then nodded to the Red Knight, who shrugged and tossed the purse to the blacksmith. Smith grabbed it eagerly with both hands.

"Roussell!" Hastings continued. "You have just been found in possession of stolen property, or the proceeds thereof, and I am detaining you on suspicion of theft. Moreover, you are charged with a breach of the peace and unlawfully practising alchemy in the town of Huntingdon. What have you to say in your own defence?"

"Alchemy?" Roussell wondered, squinting again. "Alchemy?"

"We have witnesses to that effect, and Lord Grey here is an authority on that subject."

"Oh Lord Grey knowas all abaht it, does e? Yesh e ood, ood e. Lord Change-All imself, t alchemisht. Sem side as me up while Towton, n nettles im, li burr i ish shtockings, a does, cause we knowa whoa t coward is, e is n if Ah says it missen, n it washn't alchemy a did it either. But shoa wha is t me?"

"Did you follow any of that?" Hastings asked his peer.

"Hwoff he mocks me ha."

"Say the word, Lord Grey, and I'll cut the blackguard to pieces," the Red Knight offered, half drawing his sword from its scabbard.

"No, wait!" said a new voice.

It was Susanna: her first words since the scare at Huntingdon. She rose from the bench with almost a leap, her face flushed as bright now as if somebody had practised alchemy on it. Was it possible for her to be even lovelier than ever? She circled the prisoner as if rejoicing in his predicament, yet she also seemed wary of her own predicament—the main witness in something like a public trial—pausing for thought before circling the other way. This was Southwark's Susanna and Aunt Marian's Susanna too, both sides together, her gait around Roussell a lady-like stride and a shrewish swagger. Square was reminded of the pump drill, when it begins to smoke. She was hot.

"Behold the mighty Beast of Ferrybridge!" she said at last, pausing to snap her fingers in his face. "The great champion of the rebel cause! Look where he kneels. See how he grins. He would bite if he could. A collar and chain, and a corner to lie in—that might be better than killing him. Or maybe not."

"Oh tha theear now," he observed, shaking his head to get his hair out of his eyes. "Tha followin me? Ish wha this abaht? Bu Ah found tha aht jusht i time, or Ah be theear still, drowned int river, if Ah adn't got escaped missen aht theear fust."

"Pickled in ale, the coward's refuge."

"Wha's it ta tha?"

"You smashed the Hallelujah Coffin at Stamford. Lord Hastings should add that to the charges. A whole town is my witness."

"Lord Grey smashed it fust," he reminded her in turn. "N Vernons tooa."

"A smart answer!" she noted. "You are not as drunk as you pretend. Now answer me this: what takes you to London?"

"Ah already told tha."

"*A orse*," she scoffed in mimicry of his accent. "You made a joke of it the last time. Well, this is where your joking has landed you. Now answer the question, if you know what is good for you."

"She i' charge 'eear?" he asked Lord Hastings.

"The prisoner must answer all my questions and not choose his own topics," she pleaded with Hastings "or we could be here all night, listening to his lies."

"He has a right to defend himself," said the Lord Chamberlain, "but let's see what you can do."

"Ah dooan't 'av ta answer ta daft women," the fallen knight insisted.

She continued circling the prisoner, pondering her options. Life in Southwark had prepared her for confrontations with those she despised. Usually it was the Winchester Geese, if they dared cross her path with their insulting looks, when she chased after them and beat any that she caught. Sometimes her enemies were the stevedores, whenever they ogled or whistled at her from the safety of their barges.

She usually caught up with them later and treated them to a humiliating tongue-lashing, which they had learned to fear more than any thrashing. Now it was Tom Roussell's turn to endure her fury.

"This pathetic creature!" she told everyone, pointing him out with an accusing finger, the same finger that she used to shame Geese and stevedores. "A drunk and a traitor! Does he deserve our pity or our hatred? The cells or the gallows? We shall soon find out, depending on how he answers."

"She talkin' me?" he wondered.

"You are part of the rebellion in Lincolnshire." she declared. "Admit it!"

"Ah'm i' Lincolnshire?" he scoffed.

"He has been staying with Sir Robert Welles in a castle outside Bourne, along with many other rebels," she advised Lord Hastings. "Let him explain that, if he can."

The accused shook his head and almost laughed, so then Susanna set her foot on his back and pushed, causing him to fall face-first. He lay with his nose pressed against the pavement for some moments, as if thinking things might be better for him that way, before finally rolling onto his side and gradually working himself into a sitting posture, resting back on his heels. There he sat with his head nodding in the manner of somebody about to fall asleep.

"We are waiting for an answer," Lord Hastings prompted him. "Have you been keeping company with Sir Robert Welles? Many suspect him of treason."

"Then Ah un-shuspect im treason, if body question me! Or mayhap, if tha is right, Ah was talkin im aht o it, for all tha knowa. Tha av noa right t hold me li this!"

"Rebels torched the king's manor, and maybe you helped them," Susanna dared to add.

"An wha were tha doin a king's manor?" he scoffed. "Soa appen tha torched it yursen astead o blamin me for t."

"Maybe you think we are still in my aunt's house, and you are not compelled to explain your rebel ways, or the crimes of your Lancastrian friends. You didn't even apologise for the hawk. This is where your insolence and folly have brought you at last. You are on trial for your life. Think carefully before you continue with these lies."

"'T awk attacked the wrong woman when she attacked tha," he conceded.

There were times, in their childhood, when Square used to think of her as England's very own Joan of Arc, especially whenever she chased off the bullies tormenting him. She almost looked the part now. There was proud defiance in her manner, and a muscular strength in the way she stood, as if she thought herself capable of beating any foe, however big, however many. This foe was drunk, tethered and outnumbered, yet he had a formidable reputation that had made even the Lord Chamberlain nervous—but not her.

"What takes you to London?" she asked once more. "A man with your reputation, serving the Earl of Warwick—as if we can't guess! So out with it. Maybe a bit of honesty for once will win you the king's mercy."

"Na Ah see wha this abaht," the prisoner reasoned, then hiccoughed. "Everybody thinks, thinks earl o Warwick n me friends bu tha all wrong, wrong, wrong. Ah min my own business. Bu why is questionin me? Whoa is she question fowk?"

"The earl sent you to London," she told him. "Do you deny it?"

"Ah deny everythin tha say, tha woman busybody."

"He has a document that proves he is lying," she told Lord Hastings.

"It's here," said the Red Knight. "We found it in his things."

He produced the same document that Roussell had handed over at the Stamford gatehouse.

"The letter says he is on business for the earl," the Lord Chamberlain observed after perusing it. "But this is just the kind of document any man of consequence will give a valued servant. It isn't proof of treason."

"Treason pooh," said Roussell. "An me tied up li this. Bu don't elp naw, all this treason everywheear. I fact, Ah dooan't work for earl any more, if Ah dooan't want. It is i ma indenture not ta work, if ah dooan't want. Sa Ah'm goin London naw ta find me another job n naw tha av neya reason ta keep me anymore, is undeniable."

Hastings handed the document back to the Red Knight with one hand, and shouldered the crucifix with the other, looking comfortable again.

"How about working for me?" he offered.

Roussell swayed on his knees a few moments while the words sank in.

"Tha?" he wondered. "Me work for Lord Chamberleean? Neya, neya, Ah jiggered o gret men. Fra naw on, it's mayors or aldermens, Ah be lookin for, whoa wants someone ta min is door for im, is all. A safe, comfble job. Keep thy troubles n kerfuffles ta thee own sen, n tha must knowa, all theea gret ones. Ah'm done wi tha all."

"A cunning liar," said Susanna. "He has been sent to London to start a rebellion, just like he did in Lincolnshire. He is so full of treason I can almost taste it."

"She crazy witch," he pleaded. "Ah should nivva let a kish me. It were t biggesht mishtake my life made. Naw all this appens. S true: She kissed me."

She kissed him?

The possibility almost had a voice of its own, shouting itself in Square's hearing as loudly as a blatant lie, as insistently as the bare truth. He wondered if he had heard Roussell aright. Everyone stared at one another, wondering the same thing. Susanna was more agog than any of them.

"*He* kissed *me!*"

"Neya, neya. Castle were mine. Bu' tha walks winsome by as ta seay, come try me, n sa Ah did."

"He grabbed me when I wasn't thinking!"

"As if she dint wan it mooar than Ah ever did! *She* kissed *me* and tha's t truth. Naw she accuses me of causin trouble, bu she started it. Lasht neet, Huntindon. She did."

Square cupped his head in his hands, trying to keep his thoughts breaking out in confused cries. Had the Knight of the Lost Sabaton grabbed an uninvited kiss, then blamed Susanna for it? Or had Susanna invited it and was she lying? That wasn't like her either.

"This is what last night's devilry comes down to?" Lord Hastings marvelled. "A kiss?"

"A stinkin, rotten kiss," Roussell affirmed. "Her lips are li dead things."

"He is lying," she insisted.

"Lips li dead things!" it was his turn to insist.

She made a rush at him with clenched fists, but the attendants who had kept the blacksmith from Wheaton and from Baxter were even quicker now. Finding her path blocked, she turned and hurriedly knelt at the feet of Lord Hastings.

"Don't listen to him!" she pleaded, grabbing his knees in a desperate appeal. "He is trying to shame me for something he himself did. I would never kiss a rebel. Please!"

The force of her personality could overwhelm even a Lord Chamberlain. He leaned back in his chair, surprised—as men often were—by the speed of her movements, the intensity of her feelings. He brandished the crucifix like a weapon again, or maybe it was a mere reflex, caused by flinching.

"Unhand me," he ordered her.

She released his knees. He smoothed his gown then settled a wary but speculative gaze on her.

"How do you mean—*trying to shame you*? You are from Southwark."

"I am His Majesty's loyal subject."

"The kiss embarrasses you."

"I never meant it to happen," she almost whispered.

He passed the iron crucifix to Lord Grey then reached his hands towards hers. Even priests at confession had trouble earning her trust, and she instinctively withdrew them. However, this was Lord Hastings, the king's right-hand man, and she soon relented, placing her fingers in his.

"Compliance in a woman is a beautiful thing, a more beautiful thing than almost anything I know," he murmured, fondling her wrists.

"Can you keep him quiet?"

"He has powerful connections."

"You haven't heard enough to lock him up?"

"Nothing the lawyers can use with certainty."

"I can testify about his alchemy," she offered. "He was talking about it when we were at Fotheringhay Castle. He knows all about Red Tincture. I'll swear to it!"

"Did you see him using Red Tincture?"

"I don't know what it even looks like," she confessed. "But here!" she added, snatching back one hand then spreading her hair to show a scar on her scalp, next showing another scar on the palm of her hand. "He flew a hawk at me. He attacked me at my aunt's home. You can use that, can't you? It's another breach of the peace, isn't it?"

Hastings spent some moments touching the wounds tenderly.

"It isn't enough," he told her. "I need more."

"More?" she protested, snatching both her hands back. "He is the Beast of Ferrybridge, a danger to His Majesty. You are supposed to be the Lord Chamberlain. How can you sit here, weighing evidence as if it matters? He's guilty."

"You are telling me how to do my job?"

"If you don't know what it is, yes."

"A scold and a shrew," Hastings observed, meanwhile tightening the strings of his cloak, next getting to his feet. "People have warned me about you: a troublemaker through and through. If His Majesty needs protecting from anyone—"

"Forgive me!" she pleaded. "I have spoken out of turn."

She knelt nearer to his feet, reached for his hands and kissed them in submission, first one, then the other, finally bowing her head in abject humility. Square was astonished. Hastings looked to be weighing evidence even now.

"Maybe you will learn obedience in time for the dance," he soon said, prompting her to her feet with a pull on her arms.

"But—" she couldn't help saying as she rose from the floor.

"Hush! Insolence gets you nowhere. But now listen, all you others, and mark my words well! This investigation has raised more questions than can be answered in one night. Roussell will spend time behind bars, that much is certain. Maybe he is a secret alchemist; maybe he is a thief; he has handled stolen property—you are all my witnesses that he gave money to the blacksmith. He could be involved in treason. These matters deserve careful thought; but he *has* disturbed the peace, and not even the earl of Warwick can find lawyers enough to refute it. Now I say this to all of you, so keep listening. No mention of these events must escape these walls. These events involve matters of state, secrets as solemn as our duty to His Majesty, and as private as this woman's sense of wounded pride. Secrecy and privacy! Those privileges are worth defending. So, be sure you keep quiet all that you have seen and heard here this evening, each and every one of you, or my men will come knocking on your doors, hot with questions and ready with irons."

He gave everyone a stern look of prohibition, as if his men were already getting the irons together. Next he led Susanna by the hand as far as the door, where he released her into the care of some servants, with instructions to conduct her to the priory guest house for her night's rest. She turned and beckoned to Matilda. Matilda ignored the signal, still sticking by the blacksmith. Cecily volunteered with a meek wave of one hand and the two cousins were escorted out together. By now, the prisoner was asleep on his heels, despite the dog licking his face. The Red Knight kicked the dog aside once again then dragged Roussell to his feet and thrust him out of doors, destined for a cell somewhere. All the remaining travellers were herded after him with a promise of beds in the priory hospice. When Square paused in the doorway for a glance back, Lord Hastings was once more seated in the prior's chair, playing with the strings of his cloak, smiling to himself.

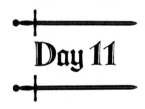

Day 11

Friday 23rd of February

Matilda Keep woke convulsively. She was about to sneeze. She sat upright and tense, struggling for control of her nose. Gradually her will dominated and the would-be sneeze grew quiet, like a mouse when the mistress of the house is awake.

Where was she?

She hadn't slept well last night and she wasn't quite awake even now. There was a thatched roof overhead and lumps of straw all around. A horse snorted somewhere below and a shaft of sunlight moved like water against a wall, innumerable motes swimming in the glare, as if looking for a nose to tickle. Craning her neck, she looked down through the rungs of a ladder and traced the source of light to the morning sun's reflection in a puddle of water, visible through a large hole in a partly demolished wall. Memory unravelled yesterday's movements like a ball of string.

"A dosshouse in Ware," she recalled.

They had reached Ware yesterday afternoon, travelling behind Lord Grey's retinue. The inns had been full already, and the nobleman's household had displaced the guests there, forcing those now former guests to find other lodgings around town, which had left little or no room for travellers still arriving. Friar Fryer was based at the local friary and he had managed to accommodate some of his travelling companions in the small church there. The rest had been sent on to Bethany House, a Franciscan community of lay brothers and sisters, near the centre of town. It too had been overcrowded but extra room had been made for women and children, and meanwhile the men had been directed to a dilapidated house at the rear of the property, used mostly as a henhouse-cum-stables. Matilda could have joined her mistress and the other women on straw pallets in the community hall, if she had been willing, but true love is not easily discouraged and she had preferred stick close to her blacksmith, even though that had meant following him up a ladder to a loft so ramshackle, the gap-riddled floor almost resembled another ladder.

Smith's night had been nearly as restless as hers. His home was at Waltham Abbey, the next town heading south, and she was running out of time to win him over. Her plan had been to surprise him in his sleep but he had vigilantly rebuffed all her attempts, and eventually he had moved to a spot where she couldn't reach him, between Square and Old Will. Sleep must have come to him soon after that and later, while moonlight was creeping in through a hole in the roof, she had sneaked his sword from his baggage and had buried it in her bedding of loose straw, because he was unlikely to ride off without it. Sleep had claimed her sometime later, but not for long. Something had happened next, but what?

She suppressed another sneeze while searching her fatigued memory. She could recall getting woken by a deafening cock crow, in the twilight before dawn, and then overhearing Square arrange with Old Will who should keep first watch over the baggage during an early lunch, promised by the Franciscans. She had offered to stay and do all the watching for them—or did she dream that? No, it can't have been a dream. Square was nobody to dream about, Old Will even less so. She had been willing to forego a meal herself in hopes of getting Smith alone in the loft long enough to make one last effort at seduction.

She was all alone now, except for some hens, perched on exposed joists, and one rooster, eyeing her from her own basket of belongings. The basket had been hauled up yesterday evening with a rope and pulley, and the rooster seemed to know that it couldn't be moved again without a concerted effort. The noise of horses in the yard suggested that other travellers were already loading up their mounts for the day's ride. Meanwhile a hubbub of people in the nearby hall, a clatter of furniture and a whiff of fresh bread, mingled with the odour of a pungent broth, reminded Matilda of what she was missing out on, and what she hoped to get instead.

Smith.

Her eyes turned to the last spot where she had seen him, as far from her as he could get, his bedding a pile of musty old hay no horse could ever eat, but comfortable enough for a mattress, if you could abide the mouldy smell. She could abide almost anything for a man in his prime condition. But where was his baggage? It was only a small bundle of clothes and personal items, usually wrapped in a tattered blanket of russet wool. She could see no sign of it. Maybe he had taken it with him to the hall. Maybe he was preparing to ride off with it. Had the sword gone? She began a frantic search, rummaging through the litter around her bedding for something long and hard. Her fingers soon happened on the sheath and she breathed a sigh of relief. It was a humble sword, appropriate for an impoverished, young blacksmith, but it was all she had of him for now.

"Come and get it, Lover Boy," she said as the image of his handsome face floated before her memory's eye, his shoulders as broad as the Ten Commandments, and just as hard. "If only we can be alone! I might get lucky for once."

She had been unlucky ever since Bourne. Laying siege to a man's heart, when you are not beautiful, requires the steady application of pressure on his weakest points over several days, if not months, but the journey so far had been too short and unsettling for her efforts to bear fruit. Sir Thomas Malory had surprised them all with his treachery, setting her blacksmith's manly heart pulsing with too much excitement for thoughts of romance anytime soon. Later Smith had disappeared with the Beast outside Fotheringhay Castle, and only reappeared after the drama at Huntingdon, where the Beast had frightened everyone by kissing her mistress. Worse still, he had gifted the blacksmith with a lot of money at Royston, enough to fill any young man's head with wild thoughts of his own independence. The blandishments of a widow with money of her own, which she might share with the right man if he gave her some hope, were a waste of breath after that.

Today however the prospects were better. Apart from the chance of surprising him with a morning's dalliance when he came looking for the sword, there was an opportunity to get into some serious flirting with him on the road to Waltham Abbey. His mule couldn't outrun her horse. He couldn't hold out all day against a determined woman, could he? Where devotion fails, desperation succeeds.

Smith was everything to her and yet he wasn't everything that was on her mind. Two other issues had kept her awake during the night: the dance and the kiss. She had known nothing about her mistress's invitation to Baynard Castle until Lord Hastings had mentioned it at Royston. She would never have known about the Huntingdon kiss if the Beast's tongue hadn't wagged drunkenly under questioning. Men were at the heart of both these secrets. When it came to men, what better confidante could Susanna have than her personal maid! Yet Susanna had kept all this to herself.

Matilda was beginning to puzzle over these mysteries once more, while waiting for Smith's return, when the sound of steps reached her ears. Some man was approaching. She made sure the sword was fully hidden in the straw and then she assumed the posture of a woman carelessly asleep, with the hem of her gown hitched high up her thigh. Her legs were her best feature, both her late husbands used to say. The scuffing of boots on the rungs of the ladder soon followed and then came the kind of grunt both her late husbands used to make whenever they found beef lying about, as if mere seeing could never be enough. The next step in her seduction of Smith, all going to plan, would be a slow turning towards him with a beckoning smile. However, he needed no further invitation and lustily hurled himself beside her, landing with a loud *clunk*!

"Ouch!"

He had found the sword.

"You!" Matilda marvelled when she turned towards him.

"Yes, it's me alright," the Beast's archer acknowledged, rubbing a hip with one hand, clutching her bait in the other. "This must be the blacksmith's sword."

The last time she had seen Bandy-Andy was at Royston. His worthless master was supposed to be in a cell there, and this worthless servant should have been locked up with him. What was he doing here? His story, however, was not so important as possession of the blacksmith's sword.

"Give it back!" she said, simultaneously sitting up and making a grab for it.

He held it out of her reach. The rooster on her basket took fright and flew downstairs. Meanwhile the intruder's helmet had fallen off so she made a grab for that instead, thinking to swap it for the sword. He got there first and quickly restored it to his head.

"You are welcome to the rest of me," he told her with a lewd smile.

"I don't want any of you. What are you doing here?"

"Fetching Smith's sword."

"What business is it of yours?"

"Smith has made it my business."

"You have seen him?"

"You would like a report?"

"I would like his sword."

"I shall give you a report instead. He is having a feed in the hall. He feels and looks exhausted. He says it is from lack of sleep, thanks to you, and he has asked me to fetch his sword for him while he considers my offer."

"*Thanks to me*? What are you talking about? And *offer*? what offer?"

"I said I'd fetch his sword for him if I could share a ride with him on his mule."

This reply crowded her mind with more questions than answers. The most obvious question was the one that sprang to her tongue first.

"But you have a horse, don't you?"

"I *had* a horse. That was up until I sold my Squire's horse—that's *Beast of Ferrybridge* to you—at Oakham, and then he sold Malory's horse at Royston, which left him without one, so now he has taken mine instead. I rode our baggage mule yesterday but it is no fun riding with pots, pans and other such gear, so I thought, since Smith owns a mule and not much baggage, and because he owes us a favour in return for the ten pounds the Squire bestowed on him at the priory, I might as well get a ride with him today. A ride would be justice and it beats walking."

Matilda wondered if she was going to sneeze or if her mind was in too much of a whirl for it just yet. Her chance for a tryst with Smith here in the loft had now vanished with this archer's untimely meddling. Bandy-Andy had no right even to be in Ware, or anywhere within twenty miles of here, considering everything that had happened.

"You and your good-for-nothing master are supposed to be locked up!"

"My good-for-nothing master and I spent last night in the manor house here. It belongs to the earl of Warwick. We work for him, so we are welcome at all his houses and inns, all expenses paid: proper beds, a fireplace, and a hearty dinner. It beats all this mouldy straw, broth and holiness you get from the Franciscans."

"How did your master escape?"

"It was like an escape. Just one night behind bars, after kissing your mistress! She would be a fine-looking woman, if her manners weren't so shrill. My tastes are more down-to-earth."

He leaned towards her as if for a kiss and she leaned away as if from a spider.

"You look like a devil in that helmet."

"Everything is devils with you and your mistress."

"So why the horns?"

The projections on either side of his head were crescent in shape, made of highly polished brass that gleamed more brightly than the steel it bifurcated from.

"A hunting trophy!" he explained, removing his helmet again just to show it off better. "They are modelled on the tusks of a wild boar: my first ever kill, when I was still just a boy. Now they help the Squire spot me in a crowd. They are my banner, you could say."

"As if your bandy legs aren't banner enough," she scoffed, "*Bandy-Andy* by name, bandy by nature!"

"*Easy* to my friends," he reminded her, and then she sneezed. "Sneeze again," he urged her. "It puts your legs into spasms."

"Go away!" she objected, covering her legs and pushing him off. "I wish to be alone."

"You wish to be alone with Smith, and he's not coming."

"What is he doing?"

"I already told you: sitting down with the Franciscans for a Lenten feed. Bread and broth this early don't tempt me."

He laid a hand on her ankle and began caressing her shin.

"Get that mangled thing off me!" she objected, slapping at his hand in revulsion, since it was missing a thumb and forefinger.

"I lost them at Towton, near ten years ago," he said as he held the hand up for display, as if it might be another hunting trophy. "That's what comes of using my hand for a shield. I used to be ashamed of it once but not anymore."

"So I see."

"If I tell you a secret—one you must swear to keep from your high-and-mighty mistress—will you grant me a kiss?"

This was an interesting offer. Keeping a secret from her mistress after all the secrets her mistress had been keeping from her would be something like justice, and he wasn't wholly unattractive. He had a pleasant face that seemed always relaxing into a smile, and he was no less muscular than the blacksmith.

"I am not averse to giving favours," she said. "But tell me your secret first and maybe then I will give your offer some thought."

"Prepare yourself for a surprise," he said, sitting cross-legged directly in front of her. "Lord Hastings visited my good-for-nothing master in his Royston cell yesterday morning and discussed terms for his release."

"My mistress will be furious. Nothing less than a hanging would suit her."

"He said he would keep him locked up for alchemy, or whatever else he could think of, unless he signed an indenture agreeing to ..."

"Agreeing to?" she prompted him, since he seemed in no hurry to finish.

"Agreeing to serve the Mandevilles! He is now their sergeant-at-arms."

This was shocking news and Matilda swallowed whatever mouse was tickling her nose.

"Indentured to the Mandevilles!" she gasped. "Their sergeant-at-arms!"

"The Squire was in no mood to hang about so he signed, and here am I, in no mood to hang about either."

He poked his lips at hers and she turned her head, just in time to receive instead a mere peck on the cheek. Even that would have been unwelcome, if she didn't have so much else to think about.

"They used to have a sergeant-at-arms until recently," she reflected. "It's good money for next to nothing: locking doors, putting shutters on windows, keeping petty thieves at bay, and doing errands now and then. Any fool could do it but no, only England's greatest warrior is good enough to lock doors and put up shutters for the high-and-mighty Mandevilles."

"What's in it for Lord Hastings?"

"The indenture doesn't allow my Squire to go anywhere without permission from his new masters, so he's stuck in Southwark until the term of the indenture expires, this time next year. It's a bigger kind of prison cell, and maybe harder to escape."

"My mistress will never agree to it."

"Her brother has already signed."

"Square signed it! With whose permission?"

"Lord Hastings is second only to the king. What more permission do you want? He dangled some bait in front of the dumb trout and the dumb trout swallowed it, hook, line and sinker. But what about a proper kiss? We are fellows, you and I, being servants together in the same household."

"A villain you might be but never my fellow in anything," she answered with a cold sniff. "But go on with your story while I consider if I am insulted by these liberties. What was the bait Square took?"

"There is a chapel in Royston, dedicated to knightly stuff. It's called *Arthur's Chapel*. Your high-and-mighty mistress's holier-than-thou brother wanted to see it, and Hastings said he could, if he put his signature to the indenture. Every man has his price. Now the brother is worried that he has bought himself a heap of trouble with his sister. She isn't to know about the indenture till we are all snug together in Southwark, he says, or we might not get there in one piece."

"She is a worse devil than your Squire, if crossed," Matilda affirmed. "But there is going to be trouble sooner or later. Your Squire couldn't keep his hands off her even in the rain at Huntingdon, let alone under the same roof! She is the last one to be handled like that."

"She is not so unwilling as you."

"I would kiss her paints, even the one she calls *dwale*—the deadliest colour of all—before I suffered to be kissed by a man with only half a hand, and with a pair of horns on his head. But where were *you* when we all got frightened? We never saw you at Huntingdon Castle."

He put his helmet aside, placed the sword next to it then rested on one elbow, as if preparing himself for a long stay.

"Huntingdon Castle is where the Squire said he would wait for me, after we split up at the king's barn. I arrived there before you did, and I was returning from an errand when you went screaming past me. We left Huntingdon soon after that."

"You crossed the bridge? It was gated at one end when *we* got there."

"A few Godmanchester boys were never going to stop the Beast of Ferrybridge. I guess they kept their cowardice to themselves, and that's how people thought we had vanished like devils. Yet all this devilry can't be too bad, if it brings you and me together."

He rested a hand on her knee and she slapped it away.

"I can't abide men always in a hurry!" she objected.

"When is a man not in a hurry?"

"When he is Smith," she reflected with a sigh.

"You are wasting your time. He already has a girl."

"He doesn't have a wife though."

"He's just a boy."

"And *you* are a man? Ha!"

"I'm missing a thumb and forefinger," he conceded as he leaned towards her again, "but I'm not short of anything else that makes a man. Do you catch my drift?"

"I would rather catch slop from a London window."

She was pushing him away again when another voice made itself heard, somewhere below.

"Matilda!"

Startled by her mistress's voice at an awkward moment, she released a stupendous sneeze that unsettled the straw she was sitting in, sending up a cloud of miniscule debris.

"Keep quiet and stay low," she managed to whisper to her unwelcome confidante, all the while sucking back another sneeze.

Matilda regained control of her nose, got to her feet and looked down from the top of the ladder very cautiously, nervous not just about heights but also about being surprised in bad company. As it turned out, her mistress also happened to be in bad company: the Galts.

"Who were you talking to?"

"I was trying to reason with my nose," said Matilda, "but it wasn't listening."

"The Galts have come for Adam's shilling," her mistress explained in turn.

"Two," Adam the Younger reminded her.

Ware was home to the Galts so of course they wanted their money before Susanna could get away. Matilda fished out two bundles of coins—the equivalent of two shillings—from the fat purse she always kept close to her skin, then dropped them from the top of the ladder. Adam's father caught one bundle and his mother the other. They unwrapped them, counted the pieces, tested them with their teeth then led their eldest son off to the nearest alehouse or cockfight, leaving Adam the Younger to attempt a more ceremonial farewell. He was a better son than his parents deserved, just as Susanna didn't deserve the beauty she was born with. It was an enigmatic pairing, and Matilda felt more puzzled than ever, watching them farewell each other.

"Can I see me yet?" he asked, after some embarrassed fidgeting.

"The painting, you mean? I still haven't finished."

"You won't ever finish now."

"Painters see with their hearts more than with their eyes."

"What the eye doesn't see, the courts don't know about," he added.

"That's how thieves talk, Adam. You are better than that."

"Not better enough to come with you though."

"You belong here with your own people."

"The future obeys the rich, my mother always says."

"You have talent, Adam. Believe in it."

"Say it as if you mean it, and everyone believes it."

"You mustn't talk like that."

He wiped his nose with the back of his hand, took a pipe from his tattered cloak, played a screeching note then hurried off. Horses and mules tugged at their tethers, rattled by the noise.

"You should never have encouraged him," Matilda observed from the top of the ladder. "The poor are always poorest of all in thanks."

"Don't *you* start!" the beautiful creature snapped. "Anyway, he got paid."

Just then Matilda heard a man's sneeze somewhere behind her. A few moments later, Bandy-Andy appeared alongside, there being no further reason for him to stay hidden.

"You!" said his master's new mistress

"Yes, it's me alright," he confessed. "Time I got going!"

He thrust Smith's sword through his belt, slid down the ladder and hurried off.

"He was here on an errand for the blacksmith," Matilda explained. "But can you believe this? He tried with me up here in the loft what his master tried with you in Huntingdon."

"You were quiet about it."

"Twice a widow isn't spooked by a kiss."

"*Spooked?*" came the haughty objection. "Roussell was the one that disappeared, not I. But what's his man doing here?"

"Collecting Smith's sword."

"Why isn't he with his master, locked up at Huntingdon?"

"That's what I said too but it turns out they spent last night at the manor house here."

"*Here?*" She stepped closer to the ladder, as if nearer would be better informed. "Roussell is in Ware?"

"Lord Hastings let him go."

"You can't be serious."

Matilda was dying to break the news about the new sergeant-at-arms but checked the impulse. More important than gossip was a maid's duty to teach her mistress a good lesson.

"Would you like to know what else Bandy-Andy told me about the Beast?" she enquired in her archest manner. "Well maybe I will tell you, and maybe I won't. I did promise the villain to keep it secret."

"What are you talking about?"

"Oh yes how forgetful I am! A mistress and her personal maid should tell each other everything, or I would be just a maid like any other, good only for sweeping floors. Yet you never told me about the invitation to the royal dance! I only got to hear about it from Lord Hastings. And you never told me about that kiss! I only got to hear about it from the Beast himself, along with everyone else in the priory. And now you want me to let you in on my own secret about what he is up to? Ha!"

"I have a right to know, after everything that has happened."

"Tell me more about your two secrets—the dance and the kiss—and maybe then I might tell you what I know about the Beast."

"Do you think I am asking for a loan: one of your secrets for two of mine? Well, you already know about the dance and the kiss. So now tell me yours."

"It isn't Christmas."

"I am *this* close to dismissing you!" said the proud shrew, snapping her fingers up at her.

"You don't employ me," Matilda dared to remind her, because she felt relatively safe with the ladder still between them. "Your father does."

"He doesn't know about the loans. It would serve you right if tell him."

"What would you do for money then?"

"Find another banker! I am almost out of patience. You make me ashamed to be a woman."

"Because I am in love with the blacksmith," Matilda guessed.

"Grovelling and fawning and salivating over him the way you always do, and touch, touch, touch, like a cat's paw."

"Oh pardon me for being human."

"You have neglected your duties, spending more time running after him than looking after me. Don't deny it."

"If you were a proper woman, maybe I would have good reason to look after you."

As usual, her mistress was dressed not so much like the daughter of a prosperous merchant as a mere peasant, yet even a peasant knows to cover her hair, whereas hers was as loose as a rose bower. Matilda knew from hard experience that there was nothing she could do to improve the situation. Susanna Mandeville was more like a teenage boy on holidays than a woman intent on marriage and children.

"But I *am* a proper woman," came the scornful reply, as if the beautiful creature didn't know how unwomanly she looked, dressed in that slovenly manner. "Have you forgotten what Lord Hastings said?"

"Something about wounded pride," Matilda recalled.

"So, this is a good time to remind you: not a word to anyone about that kiss, or the Lord Chamberlain's men will be after you, *hot with questions and ready with irons.* And nothing about the dance either, especially not to my father, or *I* will come down on you harder than all the Lord Chamberlain's men, even if they carried all the irons in England."

"Your father already knows all about the dance."

"He doesn't know that I know."

"You are up to something," Matilda guessed.

"It is Papa who is always up to something. I am just trying to get even."

"You are a lot like him."

"Make sure you don't spoil things for me with all your idle gossip."

"Then don't ask me about the Beast!"

A deal seemed to have been struck and further conversation seemed pointless. Meanwhile Lady Lorna was making demands of her own. She had been unsettled by Adam's departing note and now she was threatening to break loose from the rotten post she had been tethered to. Her doting mistress produced a brush from her cloak and began settling her with a thorough grooming, which reminded Matilda that her blacksmith too was about to break loose. It was time to throw herself at him in her most winning manner, so she returned to her basket and began rummaging through it for a light skirt that exposed her legs quite nicely, if she wasn't careful. She was already buckling it on when another male voice made itself heard below.

"We have to talk!"

She looked down through one of the many holes in the floor, just to see who it might be. It was Friar Fryer, looking about him in his usual furtive manner, as if he had heard too many confessions. Matilda never missed an opportunity to eavesdrop, if it could be helped, and she spied on the encounter from the darkest corner of the loft, pausing only to fetch a bodice from her basket.

"Then start talking!" said her mistress, hardly pausing between strokes of the brush. "The sooner you are finished, the sooner you are gone."

"Your rudeness fools others. It never fooled me."

"Maybe I should try harder."

He stared at his feet for a time, as if thinking he should be gone already, or else wondering how best to word whatever he had come to say.

"I am returning to Bourne," he said at last. "What shall I tell your aunt?"

"Returning? What for?"

"The friary warden has learned about my behaviour at the abbey, and he is sending me back to do penance," he explained, meanwhile trying to comb Lady Lorna's mane with his fingers, as if this might win him a more sympathetic hearing. "I'll be blacking the canons' boots and scrubbing their latrines for months."

"Aunt Marian has only just got rid of you."

"I don't mind much. My mission here is almost complete. The silver plate has been returned, and the steward says he'll acquit the Galts at the next session. But that still leaves me wondering what to do about Adam the Younger. He is a nice boy with enough brains and talent to succeed in honest work, if he is helped along. You have felt it too or you wouldn't have taken such an interest in him."

"I wanted to paint him, that's all."

"He needs a good home."

"I'm not his mother!"

"You owe him a good home all the same."

"It's my father's home. I merely live there."

"You will give him a good home, Susanna Mandeville, because it is your duty. It is your duty to the boy you painted, and it is your duty to the woman that painted him."

"My duty to myself? Are you trying your winged voice on *me* now, Friar? Anyway, you know nothing. Now go away."

He continued playing with the mane, like a man who isn't quite done yet.

"What do I tell your aunt when I see her?"

She looked ready to throw the brush at him as a persistent nuisance but relented.

"Tell her we had a safe journey. Say nothing about Malory's treachery, and nothing about Roussell either. There is no reason to upset her. But did you know he is here? The Beast is here in Ware!"

"At the manor house," he affirmed.

"He should be behind bars."

"Your brother doesn't think so."

The brush hung suspended between strokes for a few moments. Matilda knew her mistress well enough to know that she must be sizing up some kind of opportunity, and she wasn't entirely surprised by the cunning words that emerged from that lovely mouth next.

"What's going on, Friar? You have been getting very close to my brother lately. I think you are hearing his confessions. Yet he has been avoiding me for some reason, ever since Royston. Whatever it is, *I* am his best defence. I have a right to be told."

"Shame on you!" he objected. "Confessions are confidential, as you well know, but," he added, gazing around the stable like an experienced conspirator, "I can tell you something about John Smith: a secret of his that might open your eyes to Roussell's true character."

Matilda crept closer to the ladder, the better to eavesdrop.

"Smith was Roussell's servant for a day," her mistress recalled, once more brushing Lady Lorna, "and maybe he learned a few things about Roussell just by eavesdropping, as unreliable servants often do. But what is that to me! Blab on, Friar."

"Pride comes before a fall, and proudest of all are those that never listen with their heart."

"That's aimed at me. I tell you this in return: priests that meddle are the biggest fools of all. My opinion of Roussell is no business of yours. If he ever shows his face around Southwark, and I know where he's lodging, there's a poison of mine that's got his name on it. Wrestle with that fact before you praise him in my hearing."

"You hate Roussell *that* much?"

"He's worse than Malory. Malory's ambitions are as humble as his next victim, but a villain like Roussell—he's a menace to the entire kingdom. I don't understand how the Lord Chamberlain could have let him go."

The friar looked horrified. Square must have confessed to him about the secret indenture, it seemed to Matilda. Her mistress however remained none the wiser about her new sergeant-at-arms, busily brushing Lady Lorna's rump as if it might be the innocent focus of her whole life.

"Listen to me!" the friar pleaded. "Please, please listen to me, in case you do anything you'll regret."

She rested an elbow on Lady Lorna's rump then cupped her chin in the palm of one hand, looking bored even before he could get started. Matilda tried not to breathe in case she broke the spell.

"I won't mention the fact that Roussell saved all our lives at the king's barn," the friar continued, "though that in itself should fill you with shame, if you really intend doing him harm someday."

"Enough already!"

"Just listen a moment while I tell you the blacksmith's secret! It's not about Roussell—not directly. Please hear me out." She looked ready to hurl Lady Lorna's brush at him in spite of this appeal. "We're talking about Smith, remember," he cautioned her. "Draw your own conclusions about Roussell. So, first I say this: I had many talks with Smith when we were in Bourne, and what I learned from him then filled me with deep fear for his future. This was not told me in confession but in ordinary confidence, so my vows don't stop me sharing it with you now."

"A friar who can keep secrets!" she laughed. "I'll give you none of mine."

"Smith has had a hard time. His father died a pauper, cheated out of his business by a lawyer's trick. Smith has been living with his grandfather ever since, learning the blacksmith's trade while paying off the family debts. And then two months ago, after he had made the final payment, he got lucky for once. Someone in Lincolnshire had left him twelve pounds in a will. Smith hurried off to claim it but, when he got there, guess what! He was cheated out of it by another lawyer's trick. Why, he was so angry with everyone, he was near ready to set the whole world on fire, from the lawyer's house in Lincolnshire all the way to Westminster Palace. Yes, his heart had turned rebel! Do you know why he was staying at the abbey? He wasn't afraid of rebels. He was thinking of joining them! But thank the Lord, he has a good heart. That helped me talk him round. Yes, those talks were what brought him back south with us: he is returning to an honest life. And do you think he regrets it now? That ten pounds he got from Roussell makes up for the twelve he lost."

"Thieves are always generous with other people's money," came the surly response.

"Roussell could have kept that money but didn't, and that's the plain truth. But we are not talking about him, so let me tell you instead what a blessing it has been for Smith. That young man has long had his heart set on one girl. Her name is Joanna, and she is the daughter of the Waltham Abbey miller. The miller needs a partner for his business, and he is seeking a husband for Joanna, so he is asking eight pounds, that being the difference between her dowry and a share in the mill. It is a roaring business, built close to where two streams meet—*like Adam and Eve, holding hands in Paradise*: that's how Smith himself describes those streams, as if describing himself and Joanna! I expect them to be married within days. So, you are wrong about somebody I had best not mention by name. If he were the man you despise, would he have brought such innocent joy into this world, gifting two lovers with the money they need, just when they most needed it? Like two streams meeting in Paradise!"

Matilda stifled a sob of dismay.

Day 12

Saturday 24th of February

Susanna stood gazing on London a few miles away, as if it were a painting she had barely started. This far from completion, the world's greatest city was just some preliminary smudges in brown and grey, the foreground an expanse of hills and fields, captured in various shades of green. The gigantic spire of St Paul's hung over the smudges like a brush suspended from an invisible hand, the artist pausing between one bold stroke and the next, as if conscious of the magnitude of the task ahead, and yet she could already recreate the broad outlines of approaching buildings, all the lesser spires of parish churches peering over the crenelated town wall, Aldersgate opening onto street scenes, children haring through crowds in Cheapside, visitors forever gathering outside the debtor's prison in Bread Street, gargoyles leering drunkenly at the wine merchants, meticulously checking the seals on their barrels in Thames Street, the painter moving through all these scenes, looking not just at pictures but stories, which she builds layer on layer, step after painstaking step, from a fugitive scene surprised down London alleys, to a town across the river, becoming at last the familiarity of home, the converted warehouse in the gated lane, a handsome set of stairs leading to the family apartment, then the crowning glory, a loft glassed to catch the sun, offering good light and inspiration for her masterpiece.

"Maybe I can work on Isaac this afternoon," she liked to think, because she longed to get the boy finished and done with, "but not if we are stuck here much longer!"

Weeks of rain had left the main roads into London a quagmire, forcing a detour through Hampstead. It was a scenic, little travelled route over hill and dale, finally grinding to a halt at a gate where some landowners had decided to collect tolls. Lord Grey and his retinue had passed through free of charge, as the great ones always do, but Susanna and her companions, lagging in the rear, had arrived to find the gate closed and padlocked. The toll was twopence for every mount, and sixpence for every packhorse, baggage-mule and ass. It was extortion, in a journey already too full of troubles, and nobody was willing to pay. A messenger had been sent forward to Lord Grey with an appeal for help, and meanwhile Square and Cecily's father had dashed off to a nearby manor house, hoping to reason with the owner. They had yet to return, and the toll collector had remained intransigent. Susanna had grown bored waiting, so she had taken Lady Lorna aside to browse weeds along a boundary wall, at last pausing to imagine the distant metropolis as a work in progress. Next she reflected on the journey that had brought them here.

"What a journey this has been!" she confided in her pet. "Twenty miles a day since we left Bourne, on roads crowded with refugees and trouble-makers, if we can call them *roads*—*tracks* rather, or *bogs*. We both know how you hate getting your feet wet, but have you refused even a single puddle? No. Nothing has discouraged us, Lady Lorna. We are an example that everyone would do well to follow, always going about our business, in spite of everything. That was until we came up against these extortionist bumpkins with their padlock and key. We should be paid for our efforts, not tolled. My gowns are filthy, my thighs raw, my butt numb from all these days in the saddle—not that I am blaming Mary of Reading. She is a lovely horse."

The mare was waiting patiently in the care of Old Will, nearer the gate. If Susanna felt in the smallest way sorry that the journey was coming to an end, it was for the mare's sake. She would soon be back in her Smithfield stable, and some unknown rider would hire her tomorrow, as if she were just any other horse. But other regrets soon crowded her out of Susanna's thoughts.

"Which was worse?" she recalled with a shudder. "Getting robbed by Square's storyteller or getting rescued by his Knight of the Lost

Sabaton! And that Kilsby-like kiss. I feel sick just thinking about it. Lord Hastings commanded everyone to keep quiet, but can't you hear it, Lady Lorna: all the gossip linking me with a notorious rebel? And—*lips like dead things?* A rebel would say that. Everyone will believe it of a spinster, as if I'm single, not out of choice, but on account of bad breath or something. If that lie ever gets out, I'll die of shame. It is certain to get out, now that Roussell is at large again."

Why hadn't Lord Hastings kept him under lock and key? Even if some clever lawyers for the earl of Warwick had sued for his release, surely there was still a dungeon in a remote castle somewhere, where a public menace could be held in secret for many years, until finally emerging with blinking eyes, and lips like dead things, long after the world had forgotten him. Maybe there had been some good reason for his release, too deep and abstruse to be shared with her. Maybe Roussell had been telling the truth and he actually was riding to London in search of honest work. A veteran rebel was surely looking for trouble. Maybe it had found him first. Maybe he was dead in a ditch somewhere.

"Good riddance to bad rubbish!" she couldn't help thinking.

She hadn't set eyes on him since their confrontation in the chapter house at Royston. She had seen his archer a couple of times, most recently yesterday afternoon, just outside Waltham Abbey, home of the blacksmith. Smith had ridden past her in a hurry, goading his mule to a quick trot while singing festive hymns, elated to be coming home to his sweetheart ten pounds richer, and Bandy-Andy had been perched on the rump, contributing a lusty vibrato. The Beast must have been somewhere nearby. Later that evening, Matilda had snuck into Smith's yard and had peered through a chink in one shutter, like a lovesick fairy. She had returned with an infuriating report: Roussell and his man had been seen carousing with Smith and his grandfather, all illuminated by a wax candle. It was a decent cottage, apparently, and no doubt the two rebels had slept well. That gift of ten pounds was hardly an act of selfless kindness. The Lancastrian diehard had bought himself Smith's gratitude and thus somewhere comfortable to lodge anytime he passed that way, possibly even a hideout in case of trouble.

Susanna and Matilda had not slept well. Their host had been an old acquaintance of Farthings: an impoverished boat builder with six children, including two infants that had bawled in unison all night. At least it had been warm, the tiny apartment hugging everyone like a dirty blanket. Susanna had been so bone-weary from her travels, she could have slept even through the wails of the infants, had they not been punctuated by Matilda's broken-hearted sobs over her lost blacksmith, and maybe she could have slept through that too had it not been for an unfortunate discovery made while unpacking their things: a gaping crack in the top, righthand corner of Isaac's portrait. The damage could be repaired later, or at least hidden, yet it was a painful reminder that a woman's greatest hopes and ambitions can be thwarted by the silliest mishaps, and it had filled Susanna with such despair for her future, she had felt as if Matilda sobbed for them both.

Her patience for the wretched maid was wearing thin this afternoon. Susanna had once seen a sketch of the Plague on its way to London, a ghastly skeleton riding a nag as bony and terrible as a living grave, so dismal a visitor, even the flowers seemed to be wilting as it passed. Matilda reminded her of the Plague even now, her hired horse listlessly browsing the muddy track near the gate, while she hardly cared if the gate opened or not, because nothing could change the fact that she had lost Smith, the latest love of her life.

"There is no better antidote to love than Matilda," Susanna confided in Lady Lorna. "Feast your eyes on the sorry spectacle and learn from her folly."

Life in Southwark could be tough but it had been a good school for Susanna, teaching her to be independent. She could never take men seriously after seeing love traded in the streets like a bad cough. Only a very special man could tempt her. Meanwhile she was a free spirit, her own woman, a great artist in the making, someone in whom the breath of life arose so powerfully, she could put life into any surface, summoning from wood, paper or plaster not just the figments of her imagination, but characters and presences that often seemed more real than life itself. Yet even a great painter can never turn her heart against love in a world as fine as the one seen from Hampstead today.

London wasn't everything. This far outside the city walls, it hardly seemed anything at all, a mere smudge dwarfed by charming vistas on every side, where hills and slopes and rolling fields lay framed between stands of trees, the eye drawn to the nooks and crannies of a teeming countryside, everything in sympathy with everything else, such as the wren perched warbling amid delicate sprays of a leafless bush, while listening clouds opened in an enormous smile, rewarding its music with a shaft of sunlight. The sunlight moved and rolled along the ground like a wagon, illuminating violets and primroses along the wood's edge, the alphabet of Spring, even as a new-born lamb tottered and gambolled by its mother, drunk on milk. How could any woman not warm to the intensity of life, the thrill of some future love as great as all this? Meanwhile, somewhere beyond the distant ridges, the mighty Thames could be imagined smoothly rolling through its ancient valley, summoning her thoughts back to the city, His Majesty's castle by the river, every bend of the silvery water a portion of the happiness that must be hers, if only she could merge her life with his.

Merge *her* life with his? The ideal man should merge *his* life with hers! Could there be room in their lives for both him and her? Could she be both a lover and a painter?

"I am like you," she confessed to the river, its presence surmised from an indentation in the far hills, possibly the very stretch of water joining her home in Southwark to his palace at Westminster: "an impulsive yet languid creature, rolling and turning amid the banks where I belong, my future somewhere else, maybe only imagined. But can a man's commanding arms around me really drive me onwards, or is it my own talent? No man could steal me from a life of painting. No man but Edward Plantagenet. *My* Edward."

Lady Lorna moved off a few yards.

"No indeed, Lady Lorna, such words are not meant for ears like yours. His Majesty is a married man. It is wrong to lure men from their wives. Yet who is his wife? An Ah-Ha, a woman not one whit better than a merchant's daughter. And yet he is England's king. England needs all his attention. There is no room for me. Yet what is England? There is no England, just muddy roads, toll collectors, haughty lords, villains, and a world of endless strife. My love for Edward is a Heaven above all this. My love! My Edward."

She leant against the boundary wall as if it might be the king's manly chest, and gazed across the distant treetops as if into his majestic eyes, until Lady Lorna summoned her attention back to the here and now with a half-bray. She was trying to reach some thistles over the wall but the lips kept coming short.

"Well, it's just a dance I'm invited to," Susanna reflected as she plucked the weeds for her darling. "Nothing might come of it. Nothing will come of it if I don't learn some steps."

She wondered where she might learn some steps, and then it occurred to her that her father would certainly arrange some lessons. Farthings had two hopes for the dance at Baynard Castle, she was sure of that. The first was that she would behave and dance so beautifully in front of the whole court, she would end up winning him a rich and influential son-in-law. Failing that, he must be hoping that she wouldn't behave so badly as to drag her whole family into an abyss of humiliation and shame. What wouldn't he give to ensure co-operation! She was in a powerful position. Was she up to the challenge, and would she make the right choice?

"Either I must turn the world's greatest man into my lover, and rule his heart like a queen," she told herself, "or I must find my way to Utrecht and paint even better than the Dutch. A lover or a painter! It has to be one or the other. But which? Am I a woman first, or a painter?"

Some riders were coming across the gated field, led by the messenger that had gone with an appeal to Lord Grey. In the middle of the troop, rode the precocious lecher, Edward the Bedward, his pink face peeping from the cavalcade like a hopeful penis. Susanna wished he had some other name than *Edward*, the same name as her king. She reflected on the wife of the London goldsmith, discovered by Farthings in His Majesty's bed. She couldn't bear to end up like that, a mere conquest for public display, just another woman.

The extravagance of the riders' vestments and the clink of their appurtenances convinced the toll collectors that further attempts at extortion were useless, and the gate opened even before the hooves came to a halt. Meanwhile a gate began opening in Susanna's mind, and another gate began closing. The free spirit from Southwark buried her head in her hood, determined not to get noticed, all alone with her decision.

"I am a painter first, a woman second."

Tom Roussell had never been inside the walls of London until now. It reminded him a bit of York, which he had visited several times over the years, but this was even bigger. He had never liked York and he liked London even less. He was accustomed to seeing the world from castle battlements, with a clear view beyond the roofs and walls of the neighbouring village or town, far into the countryside, where everything is green with life, and everything happens with the steady, slow rhythm of the ploughshare and the scythe. This was nothing like that. Hamlets and villages crowded the outskirts like too many children, and it was even more crowded inside the walls. He didn't feel like a Londoner but at least he could talk like one. He had learned the king's English while still a page at Skipton Castle, well enough to converse easily with important men, or so he thought. The locals soon proved him wrong: he was tone deaf.

"Watch where you're going, you idiot!"

"I'm new here," he pleaded while lending a steadying hand to a stranger he had almost knocked off his feet—this was in the crowd bustling through Newgate.

"A Yorkshireman!"

"Is it that obvious?"

"Listen to yourself."

"We speak the same tongue."

"I hear you better than you see me."

Tom reminded himself that he had come here to find his brother, not bandy words with a smartarse town dweller.

"I'm looking for an Italian," he advised him.

"Lombard Street, straight ahead. It's all Italians there."

"Doing what?"

"Good question."

Reaching Lombard Street was no simple matter, however, not even from Newgate, it was so difficult finding a path through the mass of people always gettting in the way. Everyone seemed to be in a hurry to do something somewhere else in London. Resistance also came from behind: Easy dragging his feet. Neither of them had wanted to come to London, especially with England now on the brink of a new rebellion, but Easy's reluctance was getting to be downright discouraging. Tom understood how he felt. It would have been a whole lot safer for them in the north, where there were always friends to hide among if things went from bad to worse, whereas here surprises lurked around every corner and, whichever way you turned, you were more likely to lose your way than lose your pursuers.

"Guess what!" he told Easy as they forced their way through the bustling crowd in Cheapside— maybe some humour would help lighten his mood. "London reminds me of the Lincolnshire fens."

"Where you've sworn never to set foot again," Easy recalled.

"There is nothing in the distance here, nothing I can see beyond buildings and crowds, crowds and buildings; and in the fens–"

"We couldn't see anything in the distance there either."

"Just miles and miles of fens wherever we turned to look! And waterways, waterways choking in endless marsh and more marsh. Here it is all streets and lanes that get choked in this damned crowd."

"We're drowning in people."

"Big cities are no place to live."

"Let's go home."

"After we find Peter."

It was in the fens that Tom had first heard about Peter's return to England. That part of the world discourages visits even more than London: a rotting wilderness of rank mists and ranker pools, where inhuman things creep, crawl, float and flap in pursuit of the next meal, a slithering eel or a dead seagull, arriving on floods and abandoned by tides. Tom would never have risked a journey there had Kilsby and Denby the Dasher not organised it for him. Even then he would never have gone but for a message from an old comrade—*Midge Mason*, an ex-Lancastrian turned bandit and smuggler—requesting a meeting on a matter so secret, it couldn't be trusted to a third party. Tom had ignored the message for months, until finally running out of excuses. Midge's headquarters turned out to be much as he had imagined them: a barge at the end of a jetty, deep in a reed-choked lake. A trained warrior knows how to probe armour with a stiletto, feeling for a chink, and Tom could sense the water testing the hull for just such a chink. That hadn't been all that had set his nerves on edge. The fateful conversation still echoed in his hearing, even above the noise of London streets.

"Peter! Are you sure?"

"It was him alright: a clumsy fool that fancies himself cleverer than others. Full of himself, about covers it."

"He isn't the only clumsy fool in the world."

"He is the only clumsy fool that looks like him."

"Back from Paris, without a word to me?"

"We fetched him off a Portuguese tub at high tide, under clear stars, early last summer. He was pretending to be someone else, saying nothing except a lot of Italian gibberish. We landed him at King's Lynn, and there he took ship for London. All the while I'm thinking to myself, this Italian imposter is Peter Roussell, that daft-aft scholar-brother of Tom's that hardly knows where he is even at the best of times. So, I'm thinking, what's this idiot doing back here? All we ever get off that tub are spies. Drink?"

"Not if I can help it."

"You look as though you could do with one. Cheers!"

"But how did he look?"

"Like I said—the same idiot as ever."

Peter had been their mother's pride and joy, and Tom had promised, on her death bed, that he would always look after him. Not staying in Lincolnshire felt like a betrayal of old friends but not searching for Peter would have been betraying her.

"Keep up!"

"I'm trying," Easy pleaded after getting trapped between somebody shouldering a yoke of buckets, and a team of liveried servants sharing a pie with each other, "but we must watch where we're going, Squire, and even where we're not going, because in a city this big, trouble comes from all directions at once. It can creep up behind, or drop from above, or rush out on either side and, in short, there is no battlefield more crowded than London."

"Did you have to bring *that* along?"

Easy's horned helmet was attracting an intrigued following of small boys. All the rest of their armour and weapons had been left with their horse, mule and baggage in a stable at Smithfield, just outside the city. The stable was charging sixpence a day, including insurance against theft, but it was worth the price, since it was easier scouting quietly around town as just another two drifters, seeking a future for themselves in the world's greatest metropolis, rather than as armed retainers of the formidable earl of Warwick, looking for an Italian.

"I do my best thinking in this helmet, Squire."

"Don't think, just use your eyes."

"Or you and I will end up looking for each other," Easy conceded. "But remind me how your brother looks."

It was six years since either of them had last seen Peter but certain things were hard to forget.

"He's twenty-three now. According to Midge, he hasn't changed. So, we're looking for the usual blue eyes, sandy hair, middling height, and daft-arsed manner he had the last time we saw him."

"*Daft-arsed* is a big target, Squire. Can you narrow it down?"

"He often stands with his head tilted to one side," Tom recalled, "like he's discovered something that doesn't quite add up."

"Like *this*, you mean?"

Easy stood in a doorway, where there was less traffic, and demonstrated the tilted head of a hanged man.

"That's an image I don't need," Tom objected.

"Never you mind, Squire! If anyone gets hanged thanks to your brother, it'll be you, not him."

"He spells *five yards* faster than he can run them," Tom recalled next, "but his walk is the thing I remember best. He has a strange way of shuffling his feet like a ... like *this*."

Tom couldn't think of an analogy so he demonstrated the movement instead.

"Like he is in leg irons?"

"Stop imagining the worst!"

"It *is* your brother we are looking for, isn't it?"

"The dog is more help than you," Tom protested, because at least Wakefield was searching the street, even if it was only for unusual smells. "I have heard nothing but complaints from you ever since we set out for London."

"If your brother wanted us to find him, he would have written you a great, big letter advising us of the fact."

"He almost never writes," Tom countered, meanwhile looking up and down the street for a glimpse of shuffling feet (impossible to find in such a crowd) or the tilted head of a hanged man (impossible to get out of his thoughts, now that Easy had put it there); "and I don't care if he wants to be found or not. He is going back to his studies in Paris, even if I have to haul him aboard the nearest ship as ballast."

"Ballast is all he is good for."

"*I* will look for him," Tom decided. "*You* go find us some lodgings. Make it somewhere in the city walls, and keep it cheap."

"Why cheap?"

"Because all we've got is the ten pounds I took back off Smith this morning. Getting Peter safe out of London could end up costing us all that and more."

"The earl of Warwick owns half of London. We could stay at any one of his fine establishments and even get paid for it."

"We are not here on the earl's business!" Tom snapped, because they had already gone over this.

"Kilsby thinks we are."

"If the earl's business is setting London ablaze, stirring up mayhem, starting riots, all with my brother's help, as Kilsby thinks, then obviously Kilsby isn't thinking straight. Besides, we already tried being Warwick's men on the way south, and all it got us was a lot of hassles. Warwick almost has more enemies than friends this year."

"But if we stay at one of his places, we can return the money you took off Smith."

"*We* need the money. He just wants to get married."

This was something else Tom and Easy had already argued about. Smith was a good man, and it was a shame to disappoint him, but that ten pounds was the only money they could get their hands on in a hurry.

"Lord Hastings could end up arresting you for theft a second time, if Smith lodges a complaint."

"I was arrested for disturbing the peace mostly," Tom reminded him, "and I simply took back from Smith what was already mine."

"It was Malory's first," Easy reminded him in turn, "and someone else's before that. All you did by taking it back off Smith was turn a good friend into an enemy."

"I was drunk when I gave him that money."

"You weren't *that* drunk."

"Look here, Easy!" Tom snapped, turning to confront his critic, even if it forced other pedestrians to walk around them. "We needed that ten pounds, and our only hope of keeping it out of the hands of the beadle, the butler and Lord Hastings was giving it to someone honourable enough to give it back. Now just lighten up, for God's sake, and stop with the nagging."

They continued moving along the street.

"You chose the right man, Squire," Easy resumed. "Anyone else would have refused to return the money, after you had made a gift of it, but no, not Smith: he up and threw it in your face, like it was dirt. That lad has principles. But if you had asked for the money back *before* we had stayed at his house, instead of this morning, maybe he wouldn't have taken it so badly."

"I'll get the money back to him someday."

"Why not today? You indentured yourself to the Mandevilles, so let's stay with them. It's the same pay as for the earl: two shillings a day, plus free board."

"The indenture was the Lord Chamberlain's idea, not mine. I don't want to be anywhere he knows to come looking, and I mean to get Peter out of London long before the Mandevilles even notice I'm missing."

"The maid fancies me."

"Her mistress hates me. Now go and get us a place of our own."

Easy went off to look for cheap lodgings, and Tom continued looking for Peter, which meant first finding Lombard Street. Lombard Street ended up finding him first, since he was in it before he knew it. It emerged where Cheapside forked three ways, and Tom merely followed the right-hand fork, which soon began to be crowded with foreigners, many with darkish skin that spoke of sunny days, dark eyes that spoke of outlandish mysteries, and exotic clothes that smelt of strange appetites. The fanciest of the foreigners loitered with notebooks and clattering abacuses under the wide eaves of multi-storied buildings, reminding Tom of the only thing he knew for sure about Italians: they understood money. A nation of merchant bankers, they knew better than anyone else how to calculate exchange rates and securities, where best to invest and how best to disguise usury, prohibited by the Church and outlawed by the Crown. Meanwhile carts still lurched and rattled along the street, children played chasing games, slops descended from windows in sudden showers, and pigs plundered mud for scraps, just as they did pretty much in the rest of the city. Only daft-arsed scholars were hard to find. Tom peered into the darkness of a narrow lane where shadows moved suspiciously. One of them emerged smiling, face as white as a ghost's, lips as red as blood, baring one of her breasts as a sample of her other wares. Tom waved her away and continued the search, always assessing everyone as if it might be his brother in disguise, always getting assessed in return, as if he might be another customer in need of a loan or a good time. It had been years since he had replenished his wardrobe and he wasn't in the earl's livery now. His ordinary clothes were those of respectable man a bit down on his luck, because most of his earnings in the last six years had been paid back to the earl, in exchange for the letters of credit funding Peter's education abroad.

"I should be with my friends in Lincolnshire," he told himself as he moved along the street, searching every Italian for signs of Peter, meanwhile trying not to invite curiosity in return. "I'll throttle the little fool when I find him."

Day 13

Sunday 25th of February

Farthings was already on his way home from a night with his mistress, a widow in London, when he was greeted at the Southwark wharf by some Winchester Geese.

"Your Princess is back."

"And the Saint."

"Yesterday evening, just before curfew."

"Poor Farthings."

He had wanted his daughter home and he had been expecting her to return soon. Now the reality of it caused his heart to skip a beat, so that he almost stumbled and fell off the wharf. The Geese steadied him and helped him some of the way to his house in the gated lane behind the church. It was usual for him to feel nervous whenever she returned from one of her periodic banishments to Bourne but this time the stakes were greater than just his peace of mind. He stood to lose everything. The carpentry business was in ruins and the wine business had dried up. The king's invitation could resurrect his hopes or it could put the final nail in his mercantile coffin. Everything depended on her.

Worrying over her behaviour on his way between wharf and home had become routine over the years. Now it all came back to him, a history of problems weighing ever more heavily on his mind with every step he took.

She hadn't always been difficult, as far as he knew. Her mother had never complained about her, but it was thirteen years since her death—one of the few casualties of the Plague that year—and things had never been the same after that. Farthings had mourned for a decent period before bringing home a mistress, with whom Susanna had quarrelled even before the woman had finished unpacking. He had responded to this challenge with as much forbearance as a father can manage, transferring his mistress to a London apartment, but by then Susanna had already developed a habit of picking fights, not just with their own household but with the neighbours as well. She needed training in manners. According to his landlord, the bishop, the best way for a girl to learn the art of respectability is to serve in a great household as a lady's maid, so Farthings had sent her then to Lorna Blakeney, the wife of a wealthy wool magnate in the Cotswolds. It had seemed like a shrewd move since Susanna was already remarkably pretty at twelve, and the only heir to the Blakeney fortune was a fourteen-year-old boy. The boy had met expectations, falling in love as quickly as any other gauche adolescent, but she had come home in disgrace within a few months, after forcing him to eat his grandfather's Latin essay on the Blakeney family history. She had deserved a thrashing but Farthings had failed to complete it, the girl fighting back like a wild thing. Her first banishment to Bourne had happened soon after that.

Luckily her aunt was a strong-willed woman and Susanna had returned the better for it. Farthings had given the girl a dainty, white mule as a pet, just to show that all was forgiven. She had named it Lady Lorna Blakeney, just to show that it wasn't. It was too much a runt to be any good for real work—otherwise Farthings would have had little reason to give it to her—and when one of their carpenters had tried loading it with timbers, on the grounds that it was just a mule, she had called the man a dog and had beaten him with a stick, on the grounds that Lady Lorna was actually a donkey. She had been a donkey ever since.

His next step in providing her with a future had been to betroth her to a German chandler in the Hanseatic quarter of London, a man of great wealth and impressive physical stature. Germans were unpopular but so was Susanna, so it had seemed like the ideal match. Unfortunately, his eyes were such a pale shade of blue that Susanna had insisted he must be blind. The betrothal had ended suddenly at a dinner in the German's honour when she had upended a bowl of cream on his head, saying that it matched the colour of his eyes. That had earned her a second banishment to Bourne.

The next betrothal had been to William Walden, a good match until she had done what no sensible girl would do, allowing the boy's cousin to lure her to his private apartment. It was too painful even now for Farthings to think about as he walked homewards. Opening the gate of his lane, he slammed it behind him, as if shutting out a nightmare. That rape had led to her third visit to Bourne. It was at her own request but Farthings saw it as punishing her. She had brought secret feelings of disgrace into a household that could skate over such feelings quite well without her.

The next candidate for her hand in marriage had been a bookseller, visiting from Bruges. He had some talent for painting, which should have disposed Susanna in his favour, and he had some of the German's advantages, as far as Farthings was concerned: marriage would get her out of the country, not just out of his hair. However, Susanna had taken an immediate dislike to his brushwork ("It stinks like your breath!") and that had been the end of that episode. There had been no visit to Bourne on that occasion: Farthings hadn't liked him either.

A ship's captain had been next in the line of prospective sons-in-law. His absences at sea had allowed Susanna to ignore him for a year. When at last he had bobbed into view, he had demanded a kiss, and she had instructed him to close his eyes, before pressing the heel of her shoe to his lips, with the advice that there was more of that to come if he wanted it. He had taken the hint, returned to sea and they hadn't heard from him since. That had earned Susanna her fourth stay with her aunt.

Spicer had been the last candidate and the worst mistake. Farthings had not only lost a prospective son-in-law this time but also much of the business that had come to depend on the little creep's remarkable skills. As if that weren't bad enough, the bishop was now threatening to review all their mutual arrangements, including waived tolls, amnesties from fines, and other lurks that had allowed Farthings to undercut his rivals. Now those lurks could end up being as elusive as Spicer.

Farthings seemed to be running out of good luck but what is luck? Luck is a cart loaded as high as a weather vane: a careless push can set the whole thing toppling down, or a timely pull can help keep it all upright. His luck would stay good if Susanna didn't push. It would improve a lot if she helped pull. The king's personal invitation to a dance was an enormous opportunity. It could end up being the crowning glory of the Mandeville fortunes, or it could crush them forever, depending on whether she pushed or pulled.

Royalty usually gets what royalty wants, especially royalty like Edward Plantagenet. The dashing prince had taken England and its crown by storm, and he took women by storm too, if they were willing. Most were. Susanna had always admired him in spite of his sexual escapades, dismissing them as mere gossip. The last time they had danced, he had been too busy teaching her the steps to teach her other games, apart from a brief kiss. Next time he might go further, and how would she react then? Would she allow herself to be wooed for once? She was no less a beauty than the goldsmith's wife, and a royal affair could be at least as good as an arranged marriage, considered simply as a financial opportunity. Unfortunately, she hadn't taken kindly to any of the other arrangements Farthings had made for her, and those had been quite respectable. What if she poured cream on His Majesty's head, or stuffed a Latin essay into his mouth, or kissed him with her shoe? But that was not the immediate problem. The immediate problem was just getting her to attend the dance. She must attend if Farthings was to keep faith with Lord Hastings and His Majesty. And yet she would never co-operate if she knew how much it mattered to her long-suffering father. She could be really vindictive sometimes.

He arrived home knowing that the greatest battle of his life was about to begin. It would need all his personal resources of courage, audacity, diplomacy and cunning to ensure her co-operation, and he must adapt to meet the challenges when and as they arose. His nerves however began to fail the moment he entered the hall. He was shocked by the quietness and stillness of the place. It was Sunday, he reminded himself, but it had looked like Sunday here ever since he had sent for Susanna. In one corner was a rood screen that Spicer was supposed to be working on, now just a neglected pile of wood. On one side of the doorway stood a river boat, still minus half its planks. Perhaps the situation was best summed up in the bishop's Noah scene, high and dry on a bench on the other side. The Ark and the animals were finished but Noah and his family were still just a pile of oak blocks. The world of Farthings Mandeville seemed to have been overwhelmed by a rising tide of bad luck.

"Terrumber!" he said to himself, that being the dirtiest word in his vocabulary: it was the name of a hated rival in an adjoining Southwark manor, to whom Spicer and Lister had gone immediately after resigning from this household, and to whom others of his men had since drifted, so that Will Terrumber, and not Farthings Mandeville, was now the merchant best able to supply Southwark's carpentry needs.

"Terrumber!" he cursed again, for his staff had also been his bodyguard and now there was no-one to protect the household if Terrumber and his gang of thieves ever got over the manor walls, or if customers of the Winchester Geese ever went on a rampage, as they did on occasions. The bishop's men were little help in times like those, being like a tortoise, slow to move about and quick to withdraw into the bishop's palace, their shell.

Farthings rested a hand on the Ark, wishing he were small enough to get inside. It was too big to throw so he picked up a cow instead and threw that. Spite lent the throw both force and accuracy, skittling the oak blocks reserved for Noah and his family so that they fell with a crash like thunder, the noise reverberating ominously throughout the otherwise quiet house. Renewed silence was followed by soft footsteps coming down the stairs.

"Papa?" came a voice he knew well. "Is that you?"

"Yes, Red!" he said as he advanced to the foot of the stairs to receive her, for a merchant knows how to look confident even when he feels his fortunes are sinking. "How was your journey?"

She was slovenly in her appearance as usual and, as usual, she looked lovely anyway. Her hair was as uncombed as a fire. Her feet were bare, her toes as shapely as her fingers, and just as blue: it was ferociously cold this morning. She wore no makeup. Her flush was her own. She had wrapped herself in nothing more than a threadbare cloak, a plain smock and an ugly skirt, and maybe her breasts were as blue as her other appendages. She could be colder than any winter when she chose. He embraced her with genuine affection briefly, in spite of all the trouble between them, and she accepted his attention as fastidiously as a cat.

"Let's not talk about me," she offered. "Tell me all about yourself, poor Papa! Cook says most of the men have left. Spicer and Lister too. How will you ever manage without them?"

Sympathy was a rare thing coming from Susanna. A carpenter works with the grain.

"I am ruined financially," he declared, now allowing himself to look like a subject worthy of compassion. "Spicer left when he heard you were coming back, then the others, one by one. I have no idea how we are to pay the bills, Susanna. We shall soon be going to bed hungry every night, and waking next morning to nothing but stale bread and watery ale!"

"A bit like having Lent early."

"You are getting more and more like your aunt," he observed, for she had spent enough time with his sister-in-law to have grown accustomed to privations. "How is the good woman?"

"Good as always. But you look terrible. You must have been worrying yourself sick."

"It is a relief to have you home, Red. I don't mind hardship if we are all in it together. What is family for if not to comfort each other in hard times? It might even be good for us, learning how to pull together for once. One family, one destiny! It is time we started acting like it, don't you think?"

He emphasised the point with a kiss on her forehead.

"Sounds good!" she offered. "What do you want me to do?"

"It would help if you could be a bit more sociable for once. Winning friends is not a science. It is all about inventing or creating reasons to like people. I can't think why you were never good at it, My Girl, you being so interested in art, paintings and all that. You just have to make the effort. Spicer for example: was it necessary to terrorise him? He has many good qualities, and he was important to my businesses."

"You think I am the answer to all your problems," she concluded.

"You are the cause of them," he conceded, meanwhile wondering how best to mention the invitation to the dance: two weeks spent wracking his brains hadn't clarified the matter.

"Then you must pack me off to Utrecht. Once I am out of the picture, everything will fix itself. Spicer will come back, so will Lister and the others. You'll see!"

This was a delicate moment. He could never send her to Utrecht. The promise that he might do it someday was just about the only hold he still had on her.

"Well of course I would like to send you to Utrecht," he pleaded as he made towards the kitchen, anywhere being somewhere to run while he regathered his nerve.

"Utrecht is why you summoned me home, isn't it?" she said on his heels. "That is what Square told me."

"Things have got even worse since then, and I simply can't afford to send you abroad just now."

"How can you afford not to, if I am the cause of all your problems?"

The kitchen was separated from the main hall by a brick wall and it was ruled by a great fireplace, where Cook was busy even now preparing lunch. Oysters were frying in a pan that salivated with wine, a fish stew was steaming fragrantly next to them, and the oven breathed over everything the wholesome influence of fresh bread. A well-stocked table was the last privilege Farthings would ever surrender, even if it mocked his salutary warnings about impending poverty. He took a seat by the hearth and began warming his hands near the flames. His reunion with Susanna had started badly: she had somehow got him begging for sympathy like a weakling, when he needed to bargain with her from a position of strength. It was time to change direction.

"But how was your journey? You still haven't told me."

"I am already looking forward to the next one: Utrecht!"

"You must be exhausted though," he liked to think.

"You know me better than that."

"You get your stamina from me, My Girl."

Cook went off to borrow some saffron from a neighbour, leaving Susanna to stir the stew in her absence. Her mood suddenly changed.

"Papa, something awful happened on the way home," she said once they were alone together. "It is best you hear it from me first."

"I'm listening."

"It wasn't Square's fault."

"That blithering idiot—what has he done now?"

Her loyalty to her brother was another of his holds on her. He had forced her into many concessions over the years, thanks to Square, and she would never have agreed to meet any of her prospective husbands if Farthings hadn't first forgiven him for something.

"Why must you always insult him!" she protested as usual.

"I'll stop insulting him when he starts behaving like a man."

"One family, one destiny," she reminded him.

"What did he do this time?"

"It is more your fault than his. You should have come north yourself, or at least helped him with his preparations."

"Surely I can trust him to get something right for once. But tell me what happened."

"The men he took to Bourne tried to rob and kill us."

"Terrumber! I hope he didn't pay Malory in advance."

"Of course, the money is important to you."

"You are much more important, Susanna," he assured her, "but you obviously survived, and we need every penny we can get our hands on. But let me hear the rest of it."

"You shouldn't joke like that."

"I never joke about money."

"You are such a pig sometimes."

"You are keeping me in suspense."

"From gallows if I could."

"One family!" it was his turn to remind her.

She bit her lip and stirred the stew some more, like someone deciding whether or not to continue with her story. Farthings resisted the temptation to apologise for being a pig.

"Malory lured us to a barn," she resumed at last. "It was one of His Majesty's manors, not far from Bourne. Everything had been torched and trashed by rebels but the barn was still standing. Malory was going to lock us inside and anything could have happened then. They intended setting fire to it with us still in there, I think. We found a lot of torches and rags, smothered in pitch and grease. But Square was incredibly brave. He and Cecily's father—the Nortons were with us—"

"James Norton! He would be helpful in a situation like that."

"There was also a blacksmith from Waltham Abbey, and he was helpful too. We three refused to surrender our weapons. That was until Square offered up his own life in a trade for ours. Malory's thugs put a knife to his throat."

"The poor boy. Is he alright?"

"He will be if you don't make him feel bad about everything."

"What happened next?"

She had begun playing with the stew in a listless manner, as if it needed an extra ingredient and she couldn't think what it might be.

"This man showed up," she said suddenly, as if complaining: "Tom Roussell. Everyone thinks he saved us."

"You think differently," he observed.

"Perhaps you have heard of him by another name: *Beast of Ferry-bridge*? A good name for a Lancastrian thug! His rebel friends have been sneaking about Lincolnshire, invading respectable homes, terrorising innocent travellers, stealing, murdering, arson—that's more his style than rescuing victims. He was headed for London. I am certain he was using us for his own advantage somehow."

"Is that what James Norton thinks?"

"Oh, you know Cecily's father! He's grateful for Cecily's sake. Square is infatuated: another knight in shining armour."

"Naturally you dislike a rebel."

"Roussell's politics aren't the only reason, Papa. He flew a hawk at me. I still have these scars."

She left the stew to show him some scabs on her palm and scalp.

"My poor child! A hawk did this?"

"Roussell pretended it was an accident."

"You think it wasn't?"

"He is friends with Kilsby. Kilsby is alive."

Farthings wondered if he was waking from a dream or slipping into a nightmare. Kilsby had drowned at sea on a ship bound for Calais two years ago. It had been one of those enormous ships belonging to the Wool Staple, and it had gone down with all hands, leaving London abuzz with the astonishing news for weeks afterwards. Kilsby's name had been read out at St Paul's Cross along with all the other poor souls. The loss of so many lives was a tragedy but Kilsby's death was a godsend: finding a decent husband for Susanna was difficult enough already without *him* snooping about, looking to cause trouble.

"Kilsby! *Alive?* It was him you saw, not someone else?"

"It was him alright."

"But where?"

"In Marian's house. As I said, his friend flew a hawk at me. Kilsby used it as an excuse to get inside the door, as if they had come to apologise. They are both the earl of Warwick's men, both rebels. Kilsby smirked and leered and spoke in riddles, all to let me know he was alive and I was on his mind again."

"I know what's on his mind! He'll wait till I've found you a respectable husband, when his silence must be bought, and then he'll demand more and more and, if I don't pay, he'll spread rumours about your lack of virtue, and the Waldens will back him up again. If only your behaviour was above suspicion, Susanna, he would have nothing to work with!"

"If only I were like other girls?"

"Or like your brother. Now that's an idea!" he said, grabbing her hands to inspect the palms again. He reached for the scabs on her forehead next. "Can you bleed from the feet?"

"What? What are you talking about?"

"The Holy Stigmata! Christ bled from his palms, head and feet. Some saints are said to bleed like that even to this day. Your brother gets called a saint, and he doesn't have your angelic looks, let alone wounds like these. It's a bold plan, but why not! People believe anything, given a chance. You just have to keep the wounds open and I'll do the rest. A rumour is all we need, a miracle, a sign appearing magically, a handful of witnesses. Who will listen to Kilsby and the Waldens after that!" She gave him a look that helped him see how preposterous her sainthood would be. He wondered if he was losing his mind along with his businesses. "Damn Kilsby!" he cried in despair. "Yet I have only myself to blame. I should have protected you from him," he couldn't help saying, years of anguish and frustration welling up inside him. "But how does a man protect a daughter like you? I have given up trying. You never do what is best for you. You are your own worst enemy—and mine. Spicer left as soon as he heard you were coming back, then the others. Soon I will be in breach of all my contracts with the bishop, and the Thames watermen won't trust me again, if that boat in the hall doesn't get finished. Business is about trust and trust is all about delivery on time. I am a ruined man—thanks to my daughter. So here I sit dreaming up miracles, as if you could ever be mistaken for a woman above reproach, because I am at the end of my tether. Kilsby back from the dead! That's all I need."

Susanna walked about the kitchen, her head cocked, listening.

"Do you hear it, Papa: the silence out in the hall?"

"It's quiet," he acknowledged, "even for a Sunday."

"It sounds peaceful."

"Like a grave."

"A grave?" she repeated before suddenly laughing in his face. "If it was yours, I'd *dance* on it."

She skipped around his chair and spread her skirt between her hands, so that the speed of her movements fanned the chimney flames. Her unkindness was like a knife to his heart but they had been through recriminations many times before, and her choice of words on this occasion gave him an idea.

"Speaking of dancing," he observed as she circled him again, "here is some news you'll be interested in: I have been hiring the hall out to a dance instructor. You'll see some lessons today."

"Such a clever Papa!" she observed, her improvised gyrations coming to a sudden stop by the pot of stew. "Always finding new ways to make money."

"It isn't much—there are better venues for dancing—but every little helps. Maybe you would like to join the fun."

"Why would *I* want to learn dancing?" she said, sampling the stew on the end of a wooden spoon.

"You took dancing lessons from the king once," he reminded her. "Maybe next time you can give him a lesson."

"The king? That was a while ago. But *next time*?"

"There is always a next time," was the coy response he managed to come out with.

She would certainly use the royal invitation as a stick to beat him with, if she had the leisure to wield it, and he was now resolved to keep it secret till the very day itself. The stew wasn't entirely to her taste, judging by the wry face she made. She put the spoon back, grabbed a basket of dried herbs from the pantry, then stepped into a pair of shoes by the back door.

"Time for Lady Lorna!" she said as she went out.

Farthings resisted the temptation to call her back. Leaving home without an escort, dressed like a peasant, was not the behaviour of a woman that hopes for a respectable marriage any time soon, but Southwark had always been home to free spirits of every sort, and Liberty Manor was the freest ward in it. Their landlord, the bishop, never discouraged her visits. Lady Lorna was allowed to lodge in his palace stables for free, probably because he enjoyed the unguarded spectacle Susanna always made, visiting her pet with little treats. Still, it grieved her poor father, thinking of his beautiful daughter getting about the manor like some hapless waif.

Farthings left his chair, picked up the spoon Susanna had put down and sampled the stew. It needed more salt. Meanwhile he reflected on the conversation they had just had, wondering if that too could have done with more salt. He had never quite recovered from a weak start, and yet it could have been worse. At least he had introduced her to the idea of another dance with the king someday, and he had also got her thinking she might not be going to Utrecht. She hadn't lost her temper so far. The foundations for success had been laid, and he still had a few days left to build on them. However, Kilsby's return from a watery grave was deeply disturbing, and it was hard for Farthings to escape the feeling, as he headed from the kitchen for the hall, that his overall position was worse now than when he had alighted at the wharf.

Someone else was now in the hall: Old Will, gathering up the timber skittled by the cow. His ancient face was pale as always, like a moon baffled by everything it sees, or doesn't see. Farthings wondered if he should question him about the eventful journey home. He decided against it—the old man spoke only in hand signs these days, and his arms were currently full—so he gave him a pat on the back as welcome home then continued the two stories up to the loft, where a large array of glass windows did much to dispel the house's present aura of an abandoned warehouse. Glass was insanely expensive anywhere let alone in rented premises, but some of the cost had been recovered when this space had functioned as a scriptorium, and later, after the death of his drunken painter, Farthings had taken some pride in sunning himself in just about the only solarium this side of the river. He had almost forgotten it was usually Susanna's favourite room too until he observed a new painting propped against a wall. It showed a blank-faced figure with an armful of firewood. Farthings was reminded of Old Will carrying an armful of oak, except the dimensions were those of a boy. He resisted the temptation to be curious about it. Susanna's interest in art had always been an unwelcome mystery. It would never find her a good husband.

Sunlight is the best place for cutting through dark subjects, and Farthings soaked up a little warmth while he pondered the implications of Susanna's distressing news about Kilsby—actually old news with a new twist. A ship had sunk with the loss of almost two hundred lives, and Kilsby, who should have been the only one on board to have drowned, now seemed instead to be the only one who had survived. Where was God? There surely was a Devil, and Kilsby must have made a pact with him: a few more years of life in return for all the misery he could yet inflict on others, the Mandevilles especially. Nevertheless, sunlit glass feels warm to the touch, even on cold mornings, and Kilsby's survival could simply be a case of bad luck. Luck always changes for those who hang on long enough. Kilsby might die again. The wine shipments might flow again. Those were the lessons to be found in the window this morning.

Latticed with lead, the opaque glass gleamed like a hundred blinded eyes, yet they included a casement that opened on a great view: verdant countryside to the south, Southwark's manors to the east and, if you leaned out far enough, you could pick out the inns lining the approaches to the bridge and—leaning out still further—the Thames northwards, between the cathedral-like church of St Mary O'Rie this side of the river, and the massive Tower of London on the far side, maybe the busiest stretch of water anywhere in the world, where barges and ships followed the tide upstream and downstream, and a flotilla of rowboats ferried passengers hither and thither from one bank to the other. Farthings opened the casement now and took in the great spectacle with a sigh of pleasure, as if dipping into a gigantic cake. Nearer to home, he could glimpse the comings and goings of neighbours, some abroad on errands, others putting in a brief appearance at their own windows and doors, busy about domestic routines. Most conspicuous of all was someone lightly stepping along the top of a boundary wall, basket in hand, next clambering onto the roof of a shed and finally descending into the bishop's garden via a great leap and squirrel-like jumps through the branches of a stately ash tree. It was one of Susanna's mysterious routes around the manor, explored as a child and never surrendered.

She wasn't his only child in the window this morning. He glimpsed Square in the distance, threading the lanes homewards from church. He was easy to recognise even this far off, thanks to his unique choice of covering: a monk's habit, dyed green. He usually wore it Saturdays and Sundays, when he could set aside his work as a carpenter long enough to imagine himself a priest instead. Nobody could accuse him of impersonating the religious orders—grey Franciscans, black Augustinians, brown Dominicans and white Carthusians—but green couldn't hide the fact that he would gladly have joined them by now, if only Farthings would let him. His son's faith was too intense even for many churchmen, his piety too idiosyncratic. He attended at least two church services every day, as if God hadn't got enough of him the first time, and his *amens* provoked sniggers even in the chancel. If piety could be bought and sold by the pound, such a son might be an asset. Farthings had often wished the boy could change sex with his sister, because then he would have two children he could be proud of, or at least not ashamed of: a bold son and an obedient daughter.

Square's footsteps, always faltering and ponderous, were soon heard on the steps from the ground floor to the next floor, then from that floor to the loft, like a penitent monk mounting to Heaven in a series of prayers. Farthings set his heart against a warm welcome.

"This painting is new," he said while waving a disparaging hand at the faceless boy, the moment his green son entered the room. "Where does she get the money to pay for all this nonsense? Who is it supposed to be, anyway, and what's he meant to be doing?"

"Isaac, the son of Abraham, gathering firewood for a sacrifice," Square answered as he approached respectfully. "I don't know," he added, apparently in response to the first question.

"Abraham tried sacrificing his son to God," Farthings recalled. "I wish I were Abraham. I'd remind God that I too have a son, whom I would be just as happy to consign to the blaze, along with all his sister's paintings. Sir Thomas Malory, you nincompoop? Your sister has just told me."

"He deceived others besides me," Square reasoned when Farthings turned to confront him.

"Where is the three pounds I gave you? I want it back."

Square handed him a roll of paper instead.

"It's an indenture, witnessed and sealed by Lord Hastings," he explained. "The other signatures are mine and Tom Roussell's: our new sergeant-at-arms. It is for a term of one year. I have just shown it to the bishop's steward as a matter of courtesy, since Roussell will be living here."

"New sergeant-at-arms?" Farthings wondered as he opened the roll. "Witnessed and sealed by Lord Hastings?"

"I signed it on your behalf."

Square was not important enough for his signature to be endorsed by Lord Hastings yet the signature and seal looked authentic.

"Two shillings a day plus free board!" Farthings gasped in horror the moment his eyes alighted on the salient details—Lister only got sixpence a day and paid back fourpence of it in daily board. "Who negotiated this!"

"It is the same deal he gets from the Earl of Warwick."

"Do I look like the earl of Warwick? But who is Tom Roussell? Wait a moment. Isn't that the man that attacked your sister with a hawk? The one she calls *Beast of Ferrybridge*? He is friends with Kilsby, isn't he? That's what she said. She said nothing about any indenture."

"I didn't know how to tell her. Roussell is not the varlet she mistakes him for."

"*You* are a better judge of character?"

"I was wrong about Sir Thomas Malory."

"Malory tried to kill you," Farthings affirmed. "What stopped him?"

"The Knight of the Lost Sabaton," Square explained, or seemed to explain.

"*Knight of the Lost* ..."

"*Sabaton*. He was wearing only one when I first saw him."

"You mean Roussell?"

"*Roussell* is a name for any ordinary man. Sometimes, though, a man is his mission, a mission reserved for him by higher powers, and then Roussell is the Knight of the Lost Sabaton, a force for good in this world."

"What are you blabbering about!" Farthings protested. "Explain *this*," he insisted, slapping the indenture with his fingers.

"Lord Hastings drew it up, in consultation with Roussell. I merely signed it."

"I never gave you permission to sign any indentures, did I?" Farthings couldn't help protesting. "Is it any wonder that Malory almost killed you! And here is my reward for putting my faith in you: an indenture with a man I never met, who could be no better than Malory, or Kilsby either, for all I know! But why is Lord Hastings doing this to me? What's going on?"

"She kissed him," Square revealed. "Or he kissed her: Susanna and the Knight of the Lost Sabaton. They kissed."

This news was as astonishing as Kilsby's return from the dead. Farthings felt for a chair and gradually sat down.

"*They?*" he marvelled. "You mean *he*."

"He says *she* started it. She denies it. They argued over it in front of Lord Hastings, and he ordered everyone to keep the story quiet. Then I signed the indenture, and he said you had a right to know."

"I still don't know! They kissed? But how could it happen?"

"It happened at Huntingdon. I don't know why. There were many reasons against it. It caused a public disturbance, which became an investigation at Royston priory, which is how Lord Hastings got involved."

"But what is *your* part in this?"

"Have you heard of *Arthur's Chapel?* It is where King Arthur's sword is kept: Excalibur! There have long been rumours about it at the

Tabard, yet nobody in the Friday Club knew where to find it, until I overheard Lord Hastings mention it at the Royston priory. He arranged for me to see it next day, but only if I signed the indenture. So, I signed it. And there I found myself at last, all alone, yet not alone, in a place so sacred, only Arthur's knights and their ladies may enter there. I became as one of them, enclosed in a great circle of chivalry, all as bright as angels, waiting shoulder to shoulder, rank on rank: Camelot! That kiss and that indenture made it possible."

Square's head was buried in the shadows of his hood yet his eyes were bright with the windows' reflections, as if haunted by the experience he had just recounted. Farthings had often heard stories of secret societies, such as the Hospitallers and Knights Templar, and even some guilds were known to be involved in arcane rituals. He wondered if Square had fallen in with one of those. Truly something strange must have happened, because Square ordinarily never acted on his own initiative, and now he was making decisions for the whole family. It was hard to know what it all amounted to. Whenever in doubt, however, a good merchant returns to basic principles: two shillings a day, plus free board, was more than they could afford. He wasn't legally bound by his son's signature, as far as he knew. On the other hand, it would be folly to challenge anything Lord Hastings had put his name to. Farthings resolved to approach the great man for an explanation as soon as possible. Meanwhile he had a new sergeant-at-arms to deal with.

"Where is he now, this Tom Roussell?"

"Somewhere in London. He will make himself known to you at the right time, after Susanna has settled in. That isn't in the indenture. It was a spoken agreement between us."

"*Right time?*" Farthings wondered. "*Settled in?* What does that mean?"

"The knight didn't ask so I expect he knows."

"Even I don't know what it means. A week from now? A month? But let that go. Keep your sister in the dark about this indenture, same as with the dance. I will tell her when I see fit. But you haven't told her, have you—about the dance? Let her remain in the dark about that too. Meanwhile see what you can do with Noah and his family. The bishop wants them finished by the ides of March, remember."

"I'm no good working with curved shapes," Square reminded him. "Try to be a little less stiff."

Square went back down to the hall to try his hand at carving the patriarch and his family. Farthings brooded some more over the indenture, meanwhile soaking up some more of the sunlight. Life didn't feel brighter in the sun with the indenture hanging over him. It was only a roll of paper but it weighed like a mass of lead on the precarious load of other things already on his mind. What was Lord Hastings up to?

Still baffled, he went downstairs to add the indenture to the documents stored in his office. He had barely reached the first floor, however, when he had another strange encounter: Matilda, looking dishevelled and desperate as she emerged from the room that she shared with Susanna. Farthings had been paying her fourpence a day as Susanna's personal maid, plus an extra twopence a day to nag her into marriage and to spy on her for him. He had yet to see any useful return for the additional twopence but it now occurred to him that she could at least explain the kiss and the new painting in the loft. Susanna's monthly allowance had been cancelled, so where was she getting the money to continue her fool hobby, and could she really have kissed anybody, let alone a friend of Kilsby? Yet Matilda's appearance needed an explanation first.

"Are you alright, Matilda?" he enquired. "What's wrong?"

"I hate men."

She swayed before him like another precarious load of things on his mind.

"I noticed a new painting upstairs. Your mistress painted it?"

"My mistress distresses me."

"You are drunk?"

"I have been looking into this keyhole," she affirmed, holding an empty jug up to her eye, "and there is nothing in it, nothing, nothing, nothing. What is a woman? I ask you, Goodman Farthings. Is she not queen of her own heart? And whoever breaks that heart—is he not a traitor? Mmm? So, Smith and Beast are both together in it. Both traitors. Off with their heads!"

She demonstrated her meaning with a great sweep of the jug.

"Smith and the Beast? You mean Tom Roussell, the Beast of Ferrybridge? But *Smith?*"

"The blacksmith from Waltham Abbey, that traitor: John Smith."

"Both traitors?"

"Ten pounds. The Beast gave it to him. And what shall Smith, the Waltham Abbey blacksmith, be doing with ten pounds? And their home shall be two millstreams, like Adam and Eve holding hands in Paradise. Ha! And then I hear him say Smith wants to join rebels and set all England aflame. As if he hasn't done enough harm already."

"A plan to start fires? Try to think carefully. Does the blacksmith have anything to do with a man named Kilsby? Kilsby is friends with the Beast."

"Yes, Kilsby, the mystery man. Who is he?"

"Is *he* in the plot to start fires?"

"They're all in it together. All men are the same."

"Witnesses?"

"Only a widow in love," she said as she turned back to her room.

She nudged the door with one foot and it slowly swung shut between them.

Day 14

Tuesday 27th of February

Tom spent his first three nights in London in a rented room in Cripplegate, four floors up a groaning staircase, in a building only held up by prayers and by adjoining buildings. Last thing every night and first thing every morning, the nearby church set the high apartment rocking eerily to vibrations of its bell. There was only one bed, which he shared with his roommates, Easy and Wakefield, yet the warmth of their combined bodies barely held out against the besieging chill of the night sky, thick on the shingled roof not far above their heads.

The apartment offered no excuse for late rising and they had returned to the streets early every morning, looking for Peter almost before the sparrows could start chirping, or the bell could start the building shaking. The season of Spring was upon them, and people weren't so rugged up, or so huddled indoors, that a man couldn't find his own brother in the streets, if he wanted to be found. Tom had already seen enough of London to find Peter several times over, and he had walked enough of London even to be found by Peter several times over. Maybe the fool had recognised Tom and was now hiding from the one person in London that had his best interests at heart: some sensible advice, a good thrashing and a berth on the first ship out of England. Tom was feeling increasingly desperate. So, at noon on this, his fourth day in London, he decided it was time for a change of plans. If he couldn't find Peter, he must at least find someone else to do it for him.

A suitable confidante, a stranger with no qualms about helping strangers, someone whose loyalty is for sale but who will honour his commitments—such a man is a needle in a haystack. A quick search means taking a risk. Where better for risk-taking than England's financial centre, the hub of its Italian community, Lombard Street! Tom had already spent many hours there scouting, walking casually, watching and listening, sizing up words and faces, till at last he thought he could distinguish the honest bargain from the sly deal, the frank rebuff from the sneaking hope, the pat on the shoulder from the stab in the back, in short, the characters of the men making the deals. He had made his choice by late afternoon: a clerk-cum-tout in the retinue of a proud Florentine. He sent Easy and Wakefield to search Cheapside and the Strand, and then he followed his man to a tavern, where he introduced himself with a bundle of coins spread on the table. The Italian sat back and stared at them a while, like a fox that discovers rabbits right outside its den.

"There is a second pound on the heels of that," Tom added while taking his seat across the table, "if you are interested."

"A Yorky."

"Well spotted."

The clerk took a sip of red wine.

"Your name, *Signore?*"

"Don't ask. I'm looking for a young man: an Englishman disguising himself as an Italian. Can you help me?"

"His-a name?"

"Same as before."

"He-a family yours, this *Signor* Don't Ask, *Signor* Don't Ask?"

Tom favoured the joke with a smile, and secretly wondered if the fellow was a little too sharp to be trusted. Good English—good enough to identify Tom's accent—indicated a long-time resident who understood London at least as well as he understood an abacus. A cynical twinkle in his eye advertised a citizen of the world that any other man of the world could do business with, if he trod carefully.

"The fellow I am looking for will be using an Italian name," Tom offered, meanwhile leaning a little closer. "I have to find him quicksmart so no more jokes. Speed and discretion! Can you help or do I take my banking somewhere else?"

The Italian prodded the coins with a meditative finger.
"*Finge di essere Italiano, dici?*" he asked. "He act-a *un Italiano?*"
"Let's just say a jealous husband is involved."
"*Un coraggioso ragazzo!*" came the smiling response.
"He is about your height, but younger—twenty-three years old—blue eyes, sandy hair, a scholar—and clumsy."
"*Clumsy* not-a Italiano, *Signore.*"
"He speaks fluent Latin and French. I don't know how good his Italian is."
"Italian Yorky? Not-a good."
"I didn't say where he came from. That is not to say he isn't from there. He is smart with languages. You might not even notice an accent, supposing he had one."
"I will-a notice, *Signor* Don't Ask, as soon as snap-a my fingers in Englishman's face!" he declared, snapping his fingers in Tom's face. "Only you English make-a the clumsy."
"You will help me then?"
"He not Lombard Street. I look around. Give-a me three days."
"What about now?"
"Not so sure. You pay-a second pound-a now."
"Another ten shillings now, the rest later," Tom offered, throwing half another packet on the table.
The Italian swept the money into a purse.
"Antonio Della Bosca, Tabard Inn, Southwark. He help-a now maybe."
Alarm bells began ringing in Tom's head. His indenture with the Mandevilles had listed their address as *Liberty Manor, Southwark.* Was that anywhere near the Tabard Inn? What if he ran into one of them? What if he ran into *her?* It was an unlikely chance, but so was running into her at Huntingdon. Moreover, London and Southwark were separated by the Thames, as big a river as Tom had ever seen. He couldn't imagine himself crossing it, not even to find his own brother, and yet the time for such squeamishness was long past.
"*Antonio-della Something,* you said? I'm not good with names."
"Antonio Della Bosca—teach-a dancing," his informant explained. "If Signor Don't Ask act-a like *un Italiano,* he learn-a move *con finezza e passione.* Start-a noon bells."

"It's already past noon."

"Della Bosca, you find him. But take-a care, *Signore*: if he help-a you and you forget-a me, *i miei compagni* find-a you. *Hai capito?*"

"Discretion never forgets," Tom warned him in return.

Impatience had cost him an extra ten shillings in advance. It was a shame to waste it loitering in a tavern, so he left the Italian to his wine and headed for the bridge, hoping to speak with Anthony-Della-What-ever before dark. The nearer he got to the water's edge, however, the less ready he felt. He could glimpse the river's enormity between wa-terfront buildings, as if it had already overstepped its banks and was now residing in the city. Anxiety rose in his muscles like the hairs on the back of his neck. The bridge, when it finally stood before him—he had always avoided it till now—was an even more amazing and trou-bling spectacle than the wide water under it. It was its own town, a crowded road encased in towering buildings and shops from one shore to the other, teeming with people, carts, packhorses and everything else you wouldn't normally associate with a river, all suspended above the water like bubbles about to burst.

He paused at the entry to the bridge, as if before the jaws of Hell, and closed his eyes, trying hard to recall a life that extended beyond this moment and its terrors. Courage was still wanting, so he did what every soldier does in his darkest hours: he reached for his lucky-charms. He began with the toes inside his left boot, where he had cut off the end of his stocking, as a reminder of the shoe he had lost the day he had almost drowned. It was always a bad sign if he couldn't feel where the wool ended and bare leather started, and that was the sign he got now, the toes too cold to feel anything. Next he reached into his cloak and tunic for the amulet of pebbles he always kept around his neck. It was as cold as his toes, as if they were underwater still. There was then only one other thing to do. The first company he had served in, and which still commanded his loyalty, was Lord Clifford's bodyguard, the Flower of Craven. They were the lifeblood of the Lancastrian cause, always the first to enter the field of battle and always the last to abandon it, because they had a special place, a state of mind, where exhausted bodies could draw strength against overwhelming odds, even when every other company broke ranks and fled: the *Heart*. It was a place so deep in the life of the men, so dark, there was usually no thought or feeling in it, only a wakeful silence, like the silence of a forest in the hour before dawn. He tried to go there now. The trees stood hard against his entry, refusing to admit the coward he knew himself to be. He was still trying to reach the assurance of its embrace, slowly bringing his breath down to the speed of the faintest breeze, when the crowd of pedestrians gathering behind him shouted at him to get moving or else get out of the way.

He got out of the way.

Crossing wasn't within his abilities today, so he resolved to attempt it first thing tomorrow. Meanwhile it occurred to him that he needed a disguise, in case he ran into his supposed employers. He headed for Cheapside and bought a stylish pair of ready-made boots that he had noticed two days ago. Next he stopped at Threadneedle Street and put in an order for a handsome cloak, to be collected in the morning. Nobody who had ever met Tom Roussell in today's old boots and threadbare coat would recognise the well-dressed man-about-town crossing the Thames tomorrow.

Day 15

Wednesday 28th of February

Tom woke late in the morning, shaken up by the neighbouring bell. The sun by then was already reaching through a gap in the shutters, fingering his new boots. He had a high opinion of his new boots and a dread of thieves, especially here in London, so he put them on quickly, feeling strangely protective of the handsome leather, the neat stitching, the sleek design. He had often felt that way about refurbished armour but never till now about boots. He tiptoed to the door, letting Wakefield and Easy get some more sleep. His old cloak also stayed behind and he soon regretted it. The weather down in the streets was dank and freezing cold, wood-smoke and mist groping doorways as blindly as beggars. So it was just as well that his new cloak was ready when he called in at the tailor's shop, the polished fabric nicely matching his new boots.

The murk outdoors favoured concealment rather than discovery, but it was already beginning to clear in a light breeze, so he stopped at a haberdashery to trade his old bonnet in for a handsome new one, as an additional disguise. All these purchases cost a lot of money, even with a trade-in. His only regret was that it had been the blacksmith's money. Still, it was hard to feel guilty while looking good. He had a right to look good. A warrior who has spent years scraping and stinting, always denying himself luxuries so he can send money to his two brothers, one a drunkard overseeing the maintenance of a crumbling estate, the other a clever fool neglecting his education in Paris; a warrior moreover who has given loyal service all his life to a cause that had put him at the losing end of too many battles; who too often finds himself vilified and misunderstood—wasn't he entitled to lavish a bit of money on himself for once?

Among the infinite variety of goods in the haberdasher's shop was a set of stage props for pageant plays, including false beards for biblical kings and prophets. He wouldn't look so good in one of those since he wasn't an Old Testament king or prophet, and nobody except foreigners, lunatics, ships' crews and two rebel noblemen sported facial hair in today's England. Nevertheless, the better his disguise, the better his chance of catching Peter by surprise, or not being surprised by the Mandevilles, and he hired one for a halfpenny. The haberdasher tied it on for him before he left the shop, concealing the strings in the locks of his hair and under the new bonnet. The itchiness of the whiskers almost helped him forget the immensity of the river he was about to cross, and meanwhile his new bonnet, boots and cloak empowered him with fresh confidence, so that he strode towards the bridge without hesitation.

He might have continued striding from one side of the river to the other if the traffic hadn't got in his way. London Bridge was a seething, self-hindering mass of humanity, flowing confusedly through a tunnel of built-up homes and overhanging shops, where the Thames had turned itself into the city, or the city had turned itself into the Thames. Nobody moved as Nature intended. Everyone nudged everyone else, heads bobbing in only two directions, with the outgoing tide and the incoming tide, as far as the eye could see. There were occasional gaps in the walls either side, where idlers milled about in pedestrian bays, taking in the fresh breeze coming off the river, but fresh air didn't tempt him. He looked neither to the left nor to the right, and meanwhile he tried not to think about the water, a great tangle of murky currents moving irresistibly somewhere beneath his new boots. Eventually he came to a gatehouse at the far side, the parapet flocked about by pigeons, amid them heads stuck on pikes, thoughtfully preserved in a coat of pitch but obviously human in spite of that. One he knew from reports must be the head of William Wallace, dead almost two hundred years. Oddly enough, he felt more fellowship with that ferocious Scot than with all the Englishmen swarming around him. Scotland was

nearer his boyhood home than was London, and Wallace was as high
and dry as a man can ever get on London Bridge.

Many inns lined the main street through Southwark, and among
the first he came upon was the Tabard. According to yesterday's informant, the dancing started at noon. That was still a little way off, so
Tom sat with a jug of ale on a bench in the gravelled courtyard, and
waited. His whiskers felt blatantly false but nobody appeared to notice.
The inn's patrons were mostly travellers toasting the beginning or end
of their adventures. Occasionally peddlers tried interesting him in foot
balm, some passing touts gave directions to brothels and cock fights,
and the inn-keeper asked if he wanted another drink. He replied to
them all with a few words in a foreign kind of accent, appropriate to
his beard—he had once served with a Swiss mercenary of German
extraction—and nobody seemed suspicious. Meanwhile he kept a
careful eye out for the tilted head and awkward shuffle of a scholar
that could spell *five yards* faster than run them, and who couldn't find
his own arse in the dark, not even if you guided his hand to the spot.
No amount of dancing practice could have corrected that.

The dregs of another beer were swilling around the bottom of his
jug when the noon bells finally rang out across town, and there was
still no sign of a dance. He asked a stable hand.

"Not here anymore," came the reply from under a mare's chin.
"Try the manor across the road—Farthings' house."

"Farthings, *mein guter Kerl?*"

"That's all I know."

Farthings was an unusual name but families are often named after
their trades, and money seemed to be the main trade in this part of
the world, so Tom nodded his thanks then crossed the street to a manorial gatehouse. A porter was too busy chasing a mouse to answer
questions, and Tom didn't actually need directions, simply following
the sounds of a pipe and drum till he reached another gate, this one
opening onto a lane between two rows of substantial buildings. The
buildings had the dimensions and look of old warehouses, recently
prettied out front with a variety of veneers, painted signs and mock
porches: ostentatious additions that reminded Tom of his false whiskers. Pathways along the sides had been blocked with brick fireplaces

and chimneys, the hallmarks of luxury. Music came from the biggest house, standing almost as tall as the Cripplegate tower he had been staying in, but much sturdier in construction. He had spent most of his life studying fortresses and manor houses, analysing their strengths and weaknesses before advising owners how to improve things, and he couldn't help pondering this one. The wall around the manor and the gate at the end of the lane were quite inadequate, and yet this house had no protection of its own. The original entry seemed to have been the size of a castle drawbridge, but it had been bricked up and replaced by an ordinary pair of double doors, not reinforced oak but flimsy timber anyone could drive an axe through. There was no parapet and there were no arrow slits, nowhere for defenders to shoot missiles or pour boiling oil from. A few men with hammers could bring down the whole facade without any hindrance at all.

The music came to a sudden stop, an opportune moment for Tom to knock on one of the doors, where a sign indicated the home of a merchant-cum-carpenter. Tom made sure his whiskers were still secure, rehearsed a few more words of his Swiss accent, and was just about to rap on wood when somebody yanked one of the doors open, clutching one eye, and hurried off down the lane. There was so much smoke and soot in and around London, you could be blinded by it some days, and here the atmosphere smelt of sawdust as well, so maybe that was the fellow's problem. Tom gave it little thought: the door was open and he ventured in.

The doorway confronted him with a surprising hall. Pillars as big as tree trunks supported the distant roof, about ten yards off an earthen floor. A circuit of walkways gave access to high, windows on either side, otherwise out of reach from the floor. The hinged shutters had been pulled back and sparrows twittered along the window ledges, flew between the walkways and perched on the beams bracing the pillars. A high wall stretched up to the roof, dividing the hall from what must be private apartments beyond. A balcony, which was part of the walkway, was reached by a handsome set of stairs, and thence another, steeper flight of stairs led to a balcony high among the rafters. This struck Tom as a significant feature. A single archer could command the entire hall from the first balcony, retreating then to the upper balcony, if that became necessary. It was an unusual home but it had potential.

He remained not far inside the doorway while his gaze settled on some more details. The lower balcony was suspended over a dais, he realised, and the dais was furnished with a long table and chairs on one side. Evidently Farthings and his family were accustomed to dine in the manner of nobility, while lesser members of the household must make do with benches and trestle tables at ground level. There was a trestle table beside the doorway, featuring a display of wooden carvings: a miniature herd of different animals, standing two by two. A model of the Ark, high and dry at the end of the table, left no doubt what the carvings signified. Tom reached for his amulet of river pebbles, taking comfort in the docility of their smoothness. If any festival in the Church calendar deserved to be rubbed out, in his opinion, it was the commemoration of the Flood, a time when he usually did all he could to avoid looking on anything deeper than a jug. Fortunately, most parishes didn't begin commemorations until the ides of March, still some weeks away.

On the other side of the door was a pair of trestles supporting not a table but the remains of a boat, with only half its planks still attached. How did it get here? Tom's mind filled with visions of the Thames breaking its banks, smashing the boat against buildings and finally wafting the wreckage through the open doorway, until it came to rest here on the receding tide. On further reflection, however, it occurred to him that the boat was probably half-built, the work of carpenters, rather than half destroyed, the relic of a flood.

A flash of metal in the corner beyond Noah's Ark, and a sudden noise of smashing and cutting, drew Tom's hand instinctively to the hilt of his sword. His fingers closed on vacant air, and then he remembered that his weapons were stored with his armour in the Smithfield stable. Luckily it turned out to be a false alarm. It was just some carpenter astride a block of wood, squaring it with an adze. There was nobody else in the hall but Tom could hear an approaching noise of gossip and the shuffle of numerous footsteps, moments before a small crowd emerged through a doorway beside the dais, males and females, flamboyantly dressed in the padded shoulders and elaborate head-dresses of the well-to-do. Some were drinking from cups, which they rested on the dais before everyone stepped towards the centre of the hall, where the space between pillars was greatest. A drummer and a piper appeared next, draining their cups in big gulps, and then came a fat man and a lean man, talking loudly in Italian. Tom half stepped behind a post, surveying the scene while deciding what to do next.

Music started with a clap of the lean Italian's hands, and then the fat Italian shouted something like *basic dancer*! Everyone formed a dance circle. At first it looked like any ordinary dance on a village green, but without the singing or the fun, and then something mysterious happened: the dancers began breaking into separate couples, male and female, performing elaborate routines in each other's company, before reforming the circle again. Apparently, it was some kind of mating ritual. Tom had seen many shocking things on the battlefield but this was scandalous enough to seem shocking too, though the only casualty was public decency. Still, it looked like it might be fun after all. It soon ended without any real mating occurring and then the fat Italian shouted something like *salt hello*! This turned out to be a faster dance, requiring more practice and fewer clothes. Elaborate headdresses and padded shoulders were discarded next to the cups on the dais. The ring of dancers grew smaller, some couples moving aside to rehearse steps on their own. One of the Italians demonstrated steps with the grace and strength of a stag hurrying through a forest, black curls and mustachios skipping around his dark face according to an exotic rhythm all their own. The other man was just as nimble at times, though encumbered with a big paunch. Some of their students moved as awkwardly as daft-arsed scholars but none of them looked like Peter. There was however a girl that Tom seemed to remember from somewhere recently. The details only came back to him when she almost tripped over her own feet, and the lean Italian caught her in time to prevent a fall. Tom had first seen her at the royal manor, outside Stamford, where Sir Thomas Malory's criminal antics had caused her to faint into some other man's arms. She was a pampered creature yet she had a connection with Susanna Mandeville, didn't she?

Tom resisted the urge to beat a quick retreat. Susanna Mandeville was a difficult woman, but dancing was hardly her style, and he couldn't see her anywhere. His mission was to find the dance teacher recommended to him by yesterday's Italian clerk, and this was no time for nervousness, he decided, so he waited for the lean Italian to come within reach—he was demonstrating a skipping move for a couple of pimply adolescents – then shot out an arm and pulled him behind the post, away from prying eyes.

"*Hier:* Anthony-Somebody?" he demanded to know in his Swiss accent, detaining the young man by the elbow. "*Ist das* your name, *mein guter Kerl?*"

"Signor Antonio Della Bosca!" came the correction after a bewildered stare. "*Il maestro di danza.* Him-a there!"

The Italian pointed to his paunchy colleague. The paunch suggested a likely informant—a worldly man with big bills to pay—so Tom let the lean one go, focussing on the new target. Something about the fat man soon made Tom suspicious: he wasn't obviously Italian. Most Italians are dark-haired, but this one's hair was sandy, the same colour as Peter's. Maybe the paunch was padding. Tom drew nearer for a better look. Meanwhile *il maestro* kept himself inside the ring of dancers, as if it were a moat, and he always seemed to be turning away as Tom patrolled around the edges. As soon as the music stopped, Tom advanced through the broken ranks, grabbed the imposter by the shoulder and turned him like a pig on a spit in need of roasting. But the face that spun to meet him was middle-aged.

"*Ah un altro uomo!* You join-a dance, *Signore?*"

"*Wir* talken," Tom said as he dragged him by the arm to a less crowded space in the hall.

"*Sì?*" the dance master queried.

"*Ich looken* for *Englander*—Englishman disguised as Italian. *Verstehen?*"

Anthony-Whatever responded to this with a blank look until Tom prompted him with a coin, held lightly between thumb and forefinger. The Italian swooped on it with a broad smile then deposited it inside his jacket. "*Ehi!*" he called to his darker assistant. "*Hai visto qualche inglese fingendo di essere italiano?*"

"*Sì, la stanza è piena di loro,*" the assistant called back, much to Anthony-Whatever's amusement.

"What did he say?" Tom wondered

"Pietro say *sì*, room-a full fake *Italiani*. But I think-a some more and now you join-a *la danza*."

"*Ich* must *finden* him *schnell*," Tom insisted as he brushed off the fat Italian's hands, the fingers soft yet urgent as they palpated his arm, pressuring him to dance.

The music started again and the circle formed once more. Tom meant to keep aloof but Antony-Whatever was too quick for him.

"*Ehi Bella Ragazza*! Look-a here! *Un bell' uomo*! *Bravo e forte*!"

"If he gropes me, he'll get what the other got," said Bella-Whatever, just now emerging from the same doorway that the others had used earlier, minus a partner.

Tom could hardly believe his eyes. There was no mistaking the extraordinary beauty of her face and figure, the negligent simplicity of her dress and grooming: Susanna Mandeville. Her copper hair floated like liquid fire, the current jumping or flowing around her in expectation of more trouble. Tom's beard seemed hardly big enough to hide behind.

"Your name-a, *Caro Amico*?" the dance master enquired.

Tom ignored the question. The sight of the ruined boat, the proximity of Noah's Ark, fresh memories of the mighty river Thames, and now the immediate presence of the woman he had kissed in the rain at Huntingdon, water dribbling from her lips, all combined to trap him in the tidal current of a recurring nightmare, as if somehow he might drown even here.

"This-a Susanna," Anthony-Whatever persevered. "You dance-a together, *Signore*?"

There comes a moment in every disaster when retreating and standing firm seem equally desperate. Generally, it is best to hang on, otherwise the retreat turns into a rout. Tom steeled himself. One of his hands was joined to one of hers and then the instructor bound them to the new circle, linking their free hands with other hands on either side. The Italians introduced some new steps to the same music as before. Everyone danced in the stiff and awkward manner of daft-arsed scholars, and Tom followed their example, because it was wise to be cautious in this setting. The others risked colliding with each other and with the wooden pillars stationed around them, but Tom risked even more: he risked getting recognised.

"What's wrong with *you?*" Susanna Mandeville soon wanted to know. "Are you all limbs and no joints?"

This seemed unfair but he decided not to reply, in case she detected his northern tones under the Swiss accent. Besides, the dance didn't allow much talking. She soon skipped into the centre of the circle without waiting for an answer. There all the women joined hands briefly to make a smaller circle, turning slowly to the left as the men skipped around to the right. Tom went with the flow, stopping when the others did, moving again when they did, hoping for a new partner as the women skipped back out to re-join them, but he soon found himself with her again.

"Where did you get that beard?" she wanted to know this time. "A pageant play?"

He hoped she was joking. He circled around her, as the other men did with their partners, and all the while he kept wondering if she had seen through his disguise. Her hostility suggested maybe she had and yet she didn't seem quite hostile enough. Soon male and female were required to stand side by side, each with one hand on the partner's waist, stepping together in a tight circle. This moment proved to be particularly difficult for Tom.

"Don't try anything," she warned him, brandishing a fist in his face as his hands rested on her hips. "You wouldn't be the first today."

He found this strangely reassuring. Evidently it wasn't just him. Nevertheless, it was a relief to join the other men in the centre of the ring, just to get away from her for a while, turning slowly to his right as she edged with the women to his left. Again his hopes for a new partner were dashed and he found himself stranded in the middle, with nobody else he could turn to but her. He held up his hands to disclaim any intention of groping her. She was the last woman in the world he wanted to grope after that unsettling kiss at Huntingdon Castle.

Once the music stopped, paunchy Antony-Whatever shouted something like *Salt-hello-furious-oh* and then he and his limber assistant demonstrated some more steps, the younger man taking the vigorous male role, the maestro winning laughter as the caricature of a woman. The students rehearsed the steps as separate couples, their inexperience making jokes of them all. The Italians were quick to offer help to the least able but they seemed in no hurry to help Tom and his belligerent partner, though he was new to all these moves and needed more help than most. Eventually she decided to help him herself.

"Left foot, you idiot!" she explained. "You are meant to lead with the left. Do you have whiskers in your ears? Can you breathe through that sheep's arse? *Left*, I said. Like this!"

She demonstrated his steps for him and he watched fascinated. Many of the dancers had shed cloaks and surcoats by this time, but she was the only woman whose kirtle might look well on a peasant, stripped down for the harvest. Even when she stood still, the flowing lines of her figure were a dance all on their own. Meanwhile he was getting uncomfortably hot. His cloak was a stifling nuisance, the bonnet felt like a lid on a cooking pot, and he was perspiring heavily under the beard. Still, he dared not divest himself of his disguise and, anyway, he had often experienced worse conditions in the heat of battle, stewing inside a suit of armour.

"What are you staring at!" she objected next. "I finished showing you the steps. Now you do them."

Her rudeness was confronting but it was against his nature to walk away from a confrontation. He began applying himself to the task and soon mastered the steps. It was no harder than combat drill, a simple set of routines repeated until they became second nature. He was just beginning to feel satisfied with these manoeuvres, in spite of the oppressive heat, when the two instructors decided to demonstrate yet another set of moves, this time more difficult than anything so far. The assistant enacted a vigorous routine for the men, culminating in a great clap of the hands overhead as he leapt high into the centre of the hall, landing again in a brief crouch, all done with a robust fervour designed to impress the ladies. Antony-Whatever meanwhile demonstrated a set of pert moves for the women, with angular thrusts of the hips and sultry turns of the head, all done with the temperamental posturing of a tease or a flirt. The students happily re-formed the circle to try out the new moves themselves. The pipe and drum beat out a frenetic rhythm and kept it going even when the dancing stopped, as it often did with many a laugh and good-natured smile, all the dancers being tolerant of their own and each other's mistakes—all except Susanna High-and-Mighty Mandeville, who couldn't be nice to anyone, especially any man that dared to be in her vicinity.

Her taunting looks and jibes were aimed at Tom most of all, but if the intention was to discourage him, she had miscalculated. He felt driven to greater discipline, fluency and vigour. His discipline, fluency and vigour in turn seemed only to provoke her to ever more taunting looks and jibes. The two instructors applauded and pointed them out as an example for others to follow, after which Tom couldn't help trying even harder, while she matched him step for step, an equal in nerve and athleticism. Some of the other couples hoped to rival them, the dance becoming ever more impassioned. It was as if Tom had come to the surface of a wild river, swimming confidently, wanting to get out but wanting to stay in, stroking with the current as it swept him he knew not where. Something had to give way and eventually something did. He was leaping into the centre of the circle with a prodigious bound and a resounding clap of his hands, when the strings of his beard snapped and it dropped onto the floor like a dead cat. Immediately he reached for it with the right hand, but someone else almost slipped on it, propelling it sideways. He reached for it again, now with his left, but this time a shoe came crashing down on his fingers. Tom glimpsed his thumb and little finger poking out from under fawn leather, handsomely bound with red laces, while his other fingers lay trapped beneath the heel. Pain soon blinded him to everything. All disguise was forgotten.

"You!" his dancing partner gasped as he rose from the floor. "Papa!" she shouted up at the stairs, as if an intruder had got into her home. "Papa!"

The music and the dancing by this time had already stopped. A rotund figure emerged onto the balcony overhead and began coming noisily downstairs, demanding to know what could be troubling *My Girl*. He was beaten to the scene of action by a carpenter carrying an adze, handled absent-mindedly as a tool rather than a weapon. Tom recognised him as the one he had seen earlier, bending to the task of hewing wood. Now that he could see his face, he discovered that it was the brother he had signed the indenture with in Royston. The brother recognised Tom too.

"Knight of the Lost Sabaton!" he cried, almost dropping the adze in a fit of admiration.

"The Beast of Ferrybridge!" the sister corrected him, snatching the adze from his grasp.

"This is Tom Roussell?" her father wondered, arriving on the scene.

"The rebel!" she affirmed, lifting the adze high over her head.

Tom's reflexes prepared for a quick step inside the arc of the downward blow, if it ever came. However, her stance was defensive, and he stood firm, nursing his aching fingers in the midst of an astonished hall. It was time to exercise his battle-tested resourcefulness, and the old instinct for survival didn't let him down.

"Tom Roussell, reporting for duty!" he said, saluting first her brother then her father with a snappy, military-style nod of the head.

"He is our new sergeant-at-arms," the brother informed her.

"Don't blame me," said the father, stepping out of her reach. "They worked it out between themselves—without my knowledge."

"Lord Hastings came up with the idea," added the brother. "But who better to guard our home than England's foremost knight!"

"*Sergeant-at-arms?*" she wondered, almost dropping the adze in her amazement. "*This* man? But he was someone else a moment ago—and look there: his beard!"

She prodded the bundle on the floor with the toe of her shoe.

"I was testing your defences," Tom advised everyone, still perspiring from his virile exertions and still in pain, but increasingly determined not to show it. "Many a castle falls to subterfuge. Consider yourselves captured!"

A bold smile was his only disguise now. His dance partner looked outraged.

"Leave him to me," he heard her Papa advise her. "But continue with the dancing, Everyone! This man and I have business upstairs."

The pipe and drum sputtered back to life. The dancers formed into a circle again but only for gossip this time. The new sergeant-at-arms retrieved his beard from the floor and followed his employer upstairs, watched by many pairs of eyes.

Tom was led into a small room where writing materials and some strong boxes indicated a place of business. The father closed the door then sat himself at the table in a high-back chair, next to an open window. He waved his guest to a humbler chair opposite. Tom removed his cloak with his good hand before taking his seat.

"So, you're Tom Roussell," said *Papa*, leaning back in his chair for a longer look.

"And you must be John Mandeville."

"Farthings," came the correction. "Give me a farthing and I'll stretch it into a pound. Ask me for a pound and I'll give you back your farthing. I'm careful with money about covers it."

"Otherwise they would call you *Pounds.*"

Tom wrapped his aching hand carefully in his false whiskers. He had broken fingers in the past and he recognised the symptoms now: excruciating pain, dark swelling, and loss of mobility.

"You keep nursing your left hand," Farthings observed.

"Somebody jumped on it just now."

"My daughter?"

"No, it was a man's shoe," Tom recalled, wincing at the memory. "Fawn leather, red laces. I had dropped this thing," he added, indicating the beard, "and I was reaching for it when it happened."

"Count yourself lucky. If it had been her, she would have kicked you in the head while you were still down. Can I give you anything to ease the pain?"

"A physician might help."

"Can you afford that?"

"I'm indentured to the earl of Warwick. Injuries in his service are all paid for by him."

"I'm not the earl," said his new employer, gazing out the window. "How about a strong drink instead?"

"It wouldn't hurt."

"Choose!" Farthings offered with a glance back over his shoulder, indicating a shelf where there were three miniature kegs, each decorated with a different figure. One looked to be somebody emptying a bucket of water, another was a thing with claws, and the third appeared to be two fish chasing each other's tail.

"Signs of the zodiac?" Tom wondered.

"The water signs," Farthings affirmed. "Pisces holds water,

Aquarius wine and Cancer cider. You look as if you could do with the cider."

Tom had already had enough of water signs this morning but his throat was parched dry, and he was desperate for refreshment, so he merely shrugged his indifference. Farthings got to his feet, ladled the crab's contents into a beaker then passed it across the table.

"Brewed from scrab apples," Tom mused while warily sniffing the contents. "But you Londoners keep calling them *crabs*. Hence the water sign."

"Actually, it's supposed to be my son. My daughter is Pisces, and I'm Aquarius. She painted them as a child, and I always keep drinks in them. That one there," he added, pointing to a miniature keg on the table, decorated with an archer, "is her mother. She passed away some years ago. I keep sweetmeats in hers. So, what do you think?"

"Pisces suits her."

"The cider."

"Not bad."

"The kegs were made here, when I employed a cooper, a long time ago. My main business is carpentry. Sometimes I repair boats for the Thames watermen, but most of my work is for my landlord, the bishop of Winchester."

"Hence Noah and the Ark downstairs?"

"Yes, he wants something special to commemorate the Flood this year. The Ides of March! Plenty of time yet, you might think, but not so: most of my carpenters left around the time I sent for my daughter. We'll be lucky to finish by Christmas at this rate. So, what do you think of her?"

"This is an unusual house," Tom observed, preferring to change the subject.

"The basic structure is ancient," said the merchant, stepping aside far enough to clap an appreciative hand on a support post, "but sturdy and strong! They used to service the fishing fleet here, when there was an inlet just outside. They made and repaired nets, sails, masts and so on. It was a warehouse after that. Now it's my workshop and home. So, what do you think?"

"It's a good enough house."

"You know what I mean. You kissed her."

This was an issue Tom hadn't planned on addressing today or ever again. He began to feel irritated. His new employer still hadn't sat down after filling the beaker with cider, and there was something inquisitorial about this line of questioning, even if his manner was convivial.

"*I* kissed *her*? Is that what she is saying?"

"I heard about it from my son. Nobody else is talking, least of all her."

"I'm happy to forget it, if she is."

"A bit late for chivalry."

"Listen!" Tom snapped, leaning forward angrily. "*She* kissed *me*."

"Yet she wanted to brain you with an adze just now."

"Yes, and you can add that to all the other outrages I have suffered at her hands: a slap in her aunt's house, a lot of silly accusations in Royston, time spent in a cell there, an indenture I don't want, and now broken fingers!" he complained, nodding at the beard "She might as well have jumped on them herself. I rescued her from a hawk once, and then from a gang of cut-throats, and this is how she pays me back!"

"*I* am the one paying," was the retort: "two shillings a day plus free board."

Mandeville filled a beaker from Aquarius and sat down with it. He took a sip, then smacked his lips and smiled. He didn't look anything like the daughter, apart maybe from the blue eyes. His jawline was solid like her brother's, but his face had a more amiable cast than either of them. It was the look of somebody habitually satisfied with life, even despite whatever worries had etched permanent furrows in his brow.

"Some jobs aren't worth the trouble at any price," Tom couldn't help saying.

"You speak with a strong accent," Papa observed, as if nobody had ever mentioned it before.

"Dooa Ah?" Tom fired back with the full Wharfdale brogue.

"You don't notice? It's like garlic then, and yet she didn't notice either—not at first."

"I didn't speak to her."

"Who are you meant to be?"

"A Swiss pikeman," Tom explained, once again signifying the bearded hand as his witness, "*mein guter Kerl.*"

"Sounds German. She doesn't like Germans."

"Does she like anyone?"

"She admires the king."

Tom bit back a pointed comment about a pretender's right to rule, and then something else occurred to him.

"A man left here, clutching his eye, when I arrived," he recalled. "I thought maybe it was a bit of soot or something, but—"

"The third one in two days. Usually she is quicker with her tongue than with her fists, but something has been troubling her lately. She won't say what. The Italians are already threatening to take their dance lessons elsewhere, if things don't improve soon. Any ideas what the problem might be?"

"You are asking me? Maybe she doesn't like dancing."

"Or men taking liberties."

"We're back to that are we?" Tom complained. "Didn't I just say I rescued her? Has she told you? Herself, her brother and their whole party! They had got themselves into trouble, big trouble, just outside Bourne. Their guide, Sir Thomas Malory—he was going to rob them and anything could have happened after that, if I hadn't come along when I did."

"My son's fault: he hired him. I have made enquiries since then, and it turns out Malory is leading a charmed life. He is a knight, otherwise he would have been hung long before now. My son thinks you are a lot like him: another knight in shining armour! She thinks you aren't much better. I can see her point. Malory has friends among the Lincolnshire rebels, and so do you, don't you?"

"I am not responsible for everything the comrades get up to."

"I could say the same about my children. But what do you think of her?"

"You keep asking that question."

"You keep avoiding it."

"What do *you* think of her?"

"Sometimes I think I am the only man she respects—apart from the king."

"Does that make you feel lonely?"

"Unique."

One of Papa's knuckles began playing a rhythm on the window sill, keeping time with the music and the dull thump of feet just now resuming downstairs, audible even through the closed door. It coincided with the pain throbbing in Tom's hand. Farthings shot him a sympathetic glance, mingled with curiosity.

"Tell me something about yourself."

"What have you heard?"

"People call you *Beast of Ferrybridge*. You are indentured to the earl of Warwick. Before that, you were with Lord Clifford's bodyguard, the *Flower of Craven*. Pretty name, hard men! I heard they were the biggest thorn in the Yorkist side."

"You heard right."

"His Majesty trod them into the mud at Towton," he dared to say even without blinking. "You are the only survivor."

Being the only survivor had long been a millstone around Tom's neck. He had got used to it, more or less, because, like all the other stories about him, it wasn't quite true. The Flower of Craven were dead and gone but they had roots: families, friends, servants and old auxiliaries who always provided sympathy and support—men like Easy. Besides, the Heart lived on, always gathering the living with the dead.

"*Mud* is a poor name for ground so dearly bought."

"I have offended you?"

"Not you," Tom replied after a resentful sip from his beaker: "just your words."

"So, what brings you to this part of the world?" Farthings prompted him next.

"I nearly came here with the '61 Lancastrians," Tom explained, remembering what it was to be in a dangerous mood. "You Londoners wouldn't open the gates for us, maybe because we plundered some towns along the way. But here I am in spite of everything: a '61 Lancastrian, at large in the great city at last!"

He drained his beaker then shot his host a plundering, pillaging kind of smile, the sort that might be expected of a '61 Lancastrian.

"Then I did offend you," Farthings observed.

"The Flower of Craven were good men—the best."

"Then I apologise."

He looked as if he meant it, so Tom shrugged his forgiveness.

"But you are wrong, you know," Farthings continued. "This isn't London. This is Southwark. If you '61 Lancastrians had crossed the river, we would have welcomed you with open arms—provided you paid, of course. All the best entertainments are within easy reach. I can direct you to them. Or, if you are more into making money than spending it, I could put in a good word for you with the right people, in Southwark, in London, even Westminster. The king himself takes an interest in my affairs. Look upon me as an opportunity. You should be paying *me* two shillings a day."

"It's my usual wage."

"What do I get in return?"

"What the indenture says."

"My last sergeant-at-arms did the same kind of work, running errands, watching doors and windows, stuff like that. Sometimes he had to scare off thieves and drunkards. Simple work, basic wage."

"The indenture wasn't my idea."

"It wasn't my idea either," said Farthings, leaning back in his chair while savouring another mouthful of wine.

This was too good an opportunity to miss.

"How about you don't pay me and I don't come back?" Tom offered.

"Lord Hastings brought us together."

"I won't tell him if you don't."

Farthings gazed at the rafters as if pondering an apple whose ripeness he wasn't sure about.

"He locked you up at Royston for kissing my daughter," he continued. "That's what led to the indenture, I was told."

"I was arrested for disturbing the peace."

"Same thing. You signed the indenture to get free. Agreed?"

"I'm willing to apologise instead, if it helps."

"The indenture says nothing about that kiss."

"It would look silly if it did."

"It has got me puzzled. Give me a piece of timber and I look for the grain. Show me a coat and I look for the seam. I have looked at that indenture long and hard and I can't find trace of grain or seam. Where does it lead us? What holds it together? Lord Hastings is no fool. He has got something planned. I'll ask him about it when I see him tomorrow. He is a busy man, just back from the Midlands, but I think he'll see me. As I said, even the king takes an interest in my affairs. But maybe you can fill me in first. Why did *you* sign the indenture?"

Tom had signed the document without ever meaning to honour it, as a mere opportunity to get out of prison. If forced to hazard a guess, he could say it was meant to keep him off the battlefield, in a nice, cosy job that paid absurdly well for next to no work.

"I don't know," he said instead.

"Let me tell you what *I* think," Farthings volunteered. "You are here to scare people."

"I get along with people just fine, given the chance."

"Don't be so modest. You scared me just now with all that talk about the '61 Lancastrians. Lord Hastings must have given you names of people he wants seen to."

Tom replied with the only name he could think of: none. Farthings leaned forward.

"Well, I'll give you a name," he said or whispered: "*Will Terrumber.*"

"Never heard of him."

"He is a rival of mine."

"A vendetta? Forget it."

"I am not asking you to kill anyone, just frighten people a bit; a few bruises, some scratches, nothing fatal. Where is the harm in that?"

"I fight honest battles."

"Come, come, you are not the only man-at-arms here. I train with the Southwark militia every month. So does Terrumber. Accidents happen when men go about in arms together. Let's not pretend they don't."

"They happen all the time," Tom affirmed, "with militias."

"My previous sergeant-at-arms watched my back for me. I expect you to do the same. I'm vulnerable now, more than ever. Terrumber will be sizing up his opportunities. He has no principles. An accident will happen to me if it doesn't happen to him first."

"There is nothing in the indenture about helping with vendettas or serving in any militia."

"You are a lawyer as well as a warrior?" Farthings scoffed.

Tom treated this as a rhetorical question. Farthings finished off his beaker of wine, took the lid off the keg on the table and pulled out a dish of liquorice. He popped a piece into his mouth then gestured to Tom to help himself. Tom could drink cider in any company but he was more particular when it came to treats like liquorice. He ignored the offer. The dancing had stopped again by this time. Soon the only sound was the sound of liquorice being sucked off the merchant's teeth. Tom tried forgetting how much his broken fingers hurt, until the dancing resumed once more, the tramp of feet reverberating up through the floor and into his chair, then working along the arms, finally dancing with the pain as it throbbed in his fingers.

"This is what really worries me about your indenture," Farthings announced, sitting forward again in the manner of someone who is getting down to important business at last: "the issue of loyalty! I expect loyalty and I give it back, whenever it is deserved. Yet there is a limit to it. Everything in moderation! So, I am thinking, if you came to London and Southwark, looking for work, you have now put aside your old loyalties. Would that be right?"

"Everything in moderation."

"Yet you are still indentured to the earl of Warwick. That's a conflict of loyalties, it seems to me."

"Two masters? It could be."

"I am not into politics. People interest me, politics don't. I have nothing against the earl. I feel only respect. However, I am loyal to the throne and whoever sits on it. That isn't always the case with your earl, is it. So now I am wondering, if there is more trouble between the king and the earl, whose side are you on, and where does that leave me?"

"Difficult question."

Farthings picked his teeth with a thumbnail.

"But now we come to the next issue: your associates. My daughter says that you spent some time at Grimsthorpe Castle, near Bourne. You were a guest of Sir Robert Welles, the leader of the Lincolnshire rebels. There was someone else there—*Bernard Kilsby*? Have I got the name right?"

"*Bertram*," said Tom. "He is indentured to the earl of Warwick. What about him?"

"He is a friend of yours?"

"A colleague."

"Do you trust him?"

"He has an eye to his own advantage," was all Tom was willing to say just yet.

"There is nothing wrong with that," Farthings conceded. "A man must have an eye to his own advantage, or he won't know which side he is on."

"I got the impression, when I was in Bourne, that he has some kind of issue with your daughter."

"Everyone has issues with my daughter."

"But there is something about him in particular?"

"His is a name I have heard mentioned in relation to a certain matter," Farthings explained vaguely.

"Nobody much likes him," Tom then volunteered, because Kilsby wasn't important enough to keep quiet about. "He keeps himself to himself pretty much. He talks like a wit but nobody laughs at his jokes. All very deep and mysterious. I get on with him because I have to, that's all."

"Nobody could be friends with the man you have just described."

Farthings had more reason than most to dislike Kilsby, though he didn't know it yet. Kilsby had talked Sir Robert Welles into releasing Malory and his gang from their cells at Grimsthorpe Castle, along with all their horses, armour, weapons and supplies. No doubt it was part of his mad scheme to start a rebellion in London—much like the plan foisted on Tom—but it was doomed to fail and had nearly cost the merchant a son and daughter. Tom had only learned about the story-teller's release after noticing his magnificent horse was no longer in the stables, and he had heard enough about his drunken men to have no illusions about their gallantry, or about the safety of anyone in their care. That was why he had followed them from Bourne, intervening just in time to stop an outrage at the king's barn. Kilsby was an idiot when he wasn't brilliant. However, he had released Tom from Middleham Castle six years ago, so it would be poor gratitude to find fault with him now just because he had been too generous releasing someone else.

Farthings refilled both their beakers from the crab, returned Tom's then took a deep draught from his own.

"It's time we were frank with each other," he said. "I have been holding back till now because, well, some things are not easy to talk over with a stranger. But maybe we can be friends, you and I."

"It's not a bad cider," Tom acknowledged.

"This place is usually busy with a dozen carpenters. They all left when I advised them that Susanna was coming home. I told you that already, I think. What I didn't say was why they all left. They left on account of her."

"I am not the only man she has threatened with an adze?"

"She doesn't need an adze. Ask your predecessor. He was a tough veteran of the French wars but that didn't help. You have no idea what you are up against. Your military skills are no use here, not against her. She is quick with her fists but it's her tongue a man like you should fear most. She is clever. She knows how to hurt people. She is going to make your life here a nightmare."

"Thanks for the warning."

"But if we are friends, you and I, maybe I can help."

"Yes?"

"Her big dream is to be an artist in Utrecht. That's a Dutch city. It is going to cost me a lot of money, shipping her off and setting her up as an independent woman. I can't afford it—not if I am paying you two shillings a day. But suppose I pay you a fifth of that. The amount I save in wages would then be enough to keep her in Utrecht a long, long time."

Tom gave him a look that said he had stared into the face of Hell too many times to be bullied out of his entitlements by the antics of a mere girl and her manipulative father.

"Perhaps you mean to kiss her again," Farthings supposed.

"I'd sooner kiss you."

"Yet you danced with her just now."

"I was testing the household defences," Tom reminded him.

"Hers, you mean. First a sneaking kiss, then a sneaking dance—what comes next? I am not paying you two shillings a day plus free board so you can sneak into my daughter's bed and ravish her whenever the fancy takes you."

"If ravishing your daughter was part of the deal, I'd want *six* shillings a day," Tom assured him, "plus free board."

Farthings grimaced as if a smile were a glove he could hardly get himself into.

"You want my daughter. Admit it."

"I really don't."

"You expect me to believe that?"

"How can I explain it to you? Nobody eats red meat on Fridays or during Lent, right?"

"Not publicly."

"Have you ever sat at a rich man's table, and they served what looks like a juicy steak, or a casserole with lamb in it? Then you bite into it, and it turns out to be fish."

"A good cook can disguise the taste of most things, but fish is difficult."

"Her kiss is like that."

Farthings finished his cider then fetched himself another drink from the crab. This time he nursed the beaker as if it were a headache.

"I don't know what to do with her," he confessed with a sigh that seemed to work its way up from his toes. "We love each other, make no mistake. She is still My Girl, and I am still her Papa. But somehow everything went wrong when her mother died. *Susanna* isn't her real name. We christened her *Sarah*, but she always has to get her own way, and so she came up with her own name. We have been calling her *Susanna* ever since. Once she gets something into her head, it sticks, and then we must all do as she says or she never gives us a moment's peace. I would beat some sense into her if I could, but she hits back. She knows by instinct where and when a man is most vulnerable."

"The only man she respects, eh?" Tom scoffed as he unwrapped the false whiskers to inspect his fingers—they were now black and he couldn't move them at all.

"Are you married, Tom?"

"Why do you ask?"

"Just curious."

This was followed by a colossal crash of timber. The music came to a sudden stop. Farthings threw open the door and rushed out to investigate. Tom grabbed his cloak and followed. The cause was clearly visible from the top of the stairs. Somebody had crashed into the Thames river boat and now lay in the wreckage. Pisces was standing over him, calling him a clumsy oaf that should teach himself to dance before daring to instruct others. Tom wondered if the clumsy oaf might be Peter but a more careful look revealed Anthony Whatever's assistant. Farthings hurried downstairs to restore order. Tom headed straight for the open door without pausing for goodbyes, putting as much distance as quickly as he could between himself, Pisces, the Crab, Aquarius, Noah, the Ark and the river boat in the hall.

"Are you married, Tom?" he recalled as he hurried from the gated lane. "I am never going back into those waters."

Day 16

Thursday 1st of March

Lord Hastings exchanged bored looks with members of the public then sat with his head thrown back, gazing at the ceiling of the Star Chamber, because its colourful and orderly depiction of the heavens was more interesting than the current session of His Majesty's Council. The Council had met to discuss the recent troubles in Lincolnshire but the clerks had finally overwhelmed curiosity with too many reports and too much written testimony, all read out in tones as flat as ink. One of the councilors occasionally amused himself with audible recitals of Latin poetry, a small volume open before him. Another was visibly asleep. Even His Majesty struggled with drowsiness, occasionally nodding and shaking his head as if affirming or rejecting some point the clerks were making. It was only towards the end of the morning's proceedings that things livened up, when one of the two principal witnesses was at last summoned to appear: Sir Thomas *Rubies* Burgh, the Constable of Lincoln Castle.

His entry into the chamber was dramatic. The main doorway was thronged with spectators, and they were still making way for him when suddenly he appeared elsewhere, through a wall that opened mysteriously: a secret door! Even here, officials needed to clear a path for him, a surprised crowd of nobles, knights, prelates and other illustrious guests stepping aside amid a great buzz of curiosity and wonderment, while others craned their necks and stood on tiptoes as if for a glimpse of a visiting potentate, an ambassador or papal legate. He cut a lonely and forlorn figure in spite of all that, being divested of the jewels he usually sported but still clinging to his pride. He had been driven from office, home and county by malcontents and ruffians, supporters of Lord Welles and his cohort, and he was here to obtain justice, or maybe to avoid it. He bowed humbly to the king then began his speech boldly.

"I am to blame for all Lincolnshire's problems, Your Majesty! Yes, I am to blame. It is all my fault. At least that is what your enemies are telling you. My private ambitions have stirred up local resentments, they say. My greed has provoked a feud with Lord Welles, they say. Lord Welles is merely defending his own interests, they say. They are lying. Lincolnshire's problems are a repeat of last year's rebellion. Have people forgotten? The battle was, and the battle still is, between today's England, which rewards true merit (the England that I stand for,) and yesterday's England, which looks only to the past, mired in nepotism and corruption (the England that Lord Welles embodies so shamelessly!) I call on His Majesty to intervene in this dispute, not just for my sake but for the sake of England. It is time we were all rescued from this persistent mischief."

These were fighting words. Hastings forgot about the ceiling. The faces around him were no longer blank, eyes were no longer struggling to stay open. Everyone was on the edge of their seat or up on their toes, bursting to hear more, bursting to comment. The uproar was considerable, and the king himself had to call for silence before Rubies could continue.

The Lincolnshire inquiry had been scheduled to take place two weeks ago but Lord Welles, the other principal witness, had refused to attend, citing fears of treachery. Subsequent negotiations had failed to draw him from the Abbey, his sanctuary, and the king had finally lost patience this morning, ordering the Council to proceed without him. Even some of the regular councillors had not shown up, unable to attend at short notice, and these included the traitor's most powerful ally, the earl of Warwick. Their absence had been made good by the inclusion of some hastily summoned deputies and, just to prove that no skulduggery was intended, the doors had been opened to the Westminster public, crowding the chamber with

as fine an assembly as could be gathered in a single morning. Some
of the nobles were buffoons, some of the knights were unchivalrous,
and not all the prelates were pious, but everyone looked splendid in
ermine and velvet, English wool and Flemish workmanship, silver
buckles and trinkets of gold. It was a spectacle as impressive as the
heavens painted on the ceiling, and now at last Rubies was treating
them all to entertainment worthy of the occasion.

"Wealth, power and influence are prizes to be won through natural
talent and hard work," he said at the end of his testimony, reiterating
his main theme; "they are no longer the fawning servants of a few,
ancient, over-proud families."

"Bravo!" cried Hastings, banging his fist on the Council table, for
he had helped write the speech and he was ready to defend it in the
verbal skirmishing that was certain to follow.

His rapturous applause was echoed by other *Sons of Towton*: gentry
who had prospered under King Edward since his victory at the Battle
of Towton a decade ago. Representatives of the old nobility, however,
gazed discontentedly, like oaks wrinkling their leaves at a cold wind.
Their ranks had been decimated by endless feuds and wars, and their
only spokesman in today's Council was the king's younger brother, the
duke of Clarence, seated next to Hastings. He had been a key figure in
last year's rebellion, not on His Majesty's side but against him. *Claptrap
Clarence* was the traitor's title among the Sons of Towton.

"*Over-proud?*" Claptrap wondered, smiling as he rose from his place
at the table, the better to be admired by all. "Did I just hear the Constable of Lincoln Castle say *over-proud families?* What he means by that,
I dare say, are the noblest of England's nobles: those of us that were
born to our titles, and who are justly proud of our long heritage of
illustrious achievements."

The oaks rustled happily. Clarence was in his element here and he
looked set to grow in confidence, if somebody didn't clip his branches
soon. Rubies was no match for this swaggering adversary, so Hastings
got to his feet, smiling with wry pleasure. An upstart Son of Towton
he might be, but he was also the Lord Chamberlain, the king's right-
hand man and closest friend. Even a duke is fair game, if it is done
with aplomb.

"*Noblest?*" he wondered, repaying Clarence's quibbling tit-for-tat. "Did we just hear the duke say *noblest of England's nobles?* By that, I dare say, he means himself."

"Am I not of the same blood as my brother, the king?" came the haughty reply.

"Yet we must distinguish carefully between His Majesty and you, in case we end up mistaking you for our king."

This jibe was well received by the Sons of Towton.

"An amusing argument," Clarence acknowledged with an ironic nod at the titterers in the audience. "But perhaps Lord Hastings and his friends are always so besotted with good luck and newfound riches that they never heard of Magna Carta, the contract between an English king and his nobles. My brother is one of us, the first among equals, our spokesman. Kings come and kings go, but England endures, thanks to our fellow nobles and our Magna Carta."

The oaks, thus prompted, swelled in the full bloom of their pride, all equal to His Majesty in their own opinion, which of course made the treacherous duke their great champion, if they were silly enough to be guided by him.

"Of course my friends and I have heard of Magna Carta," Hastings retorted, "but has Magna Carta heard of you?"

"What do you mean by that?"

"You mentioned it just now as if it might be a personal friend of yours."

"Our frivolous Lord Chamberlain chooses to make light of these troubled times," the duke lamented for the sympathy of his friends.

"The king's brother hopes to profit from these troubled times," Hastings countered on behalf of everyone else.

"It is not the king you mistake me for now but yourself," said the duke, turning to frown on Hastings, "for who has profited from these times more than you?"

"Whereas your greed has caused you to fall further than anyone else," Hastings fired back: "once the king's admired brother, now the earl of Warwick's son-in-law!"

The duke had married Warwick's daughter in defiance of the king's wishes, just seven months ago. That act of disobedience had fanned last year's rebellion at a delicate time, when His Majesty was in the north with only a small force. Caught napping by a wedding party turned war party, its leaders in cahoots with rebels, he had been taken captive and imprisoned in the earl's stronghold, Middleham Castle. It was no secret that Warwick had meant to put Clarence on the throne, but a worsening breakdown in public order had soon forced him to release Edward, the only man with the charisma needed to keep England together.

"I am proud to be the Earl of Warwick's son-in-law," the duke now told the assembly, before turning back to Hastings. "Are you ashamed to be his brother-in-law?"

Hastings had married the earl's sister when Warwick was still loyal to the king. Here was an opportunity to set the record straight.

"His brother-in-law, I might be, his creature I am not."

The Sons of Towton applauded.

"*Creature?*" Clarence objected. "Is that aimed at me? Am *I* on trial here?"

Here was an opportunity for His Majesty to restore order, and Hastings welcomed it. Anything that enhanced His Majesty's authority enhanced his own, and everything His Majesty did was unpretentious, aligning him with the Sons of Towton rather than with the duke and the old nobility.

"Nobody is on trial here," the king assured everyone. "We are simply inquiring into the Lincolnshire troubles. I urge my brother to relax a little, and maybe my Lord Chamberlain might try avoiding the appearance of levity."

His Majesty was seated on a platform high enough to look regal, yet low enough to seem accessible to all, with Councillors on his right, a bench of clerks and lawyers on his left. Not for the first time, Hastings found himself marvelling at the contrast with Claptrap. They could have passed for identical twins, both kings among men: exceptionally tall, well-built, clever and extraordinarily handsome. His Majesty however seemed in cheerful command of every situation. Claptrap usually managed to look like the king suffering indigestion.

"But this *is* a trial, Your Majesty," one of the Council dared to say.

It was a bold comment and all eyes turned to the man responsible, now rising from his seat at the table. Hastings sat down, his thunder stolen for now, but Clarence remained defiantly on his feet. The new speaker was Viscount Bourchier, better known to the king's friends as *Silk*, because he had recently draped his head in the silk underwear of the king's latest mistress, Jane Shore. Ordinarily it was his father sitting at the Council table, being a capable administrator, but he had been unable to arrive on time, so Silk had volunteered to sit in for him. It was clear, however, that he was actually here on behalf of the queen's family. His wife, Anne Woodville, was standing behind him, whispering in his ear, when she wasn't trying to avoid the peacock feather that hung drooping from his velvet hat. The extravagant feather pointed like the tail of a weather vane, putting her downwind every time he turned towards the king.

"Who is on a trial here?" the king demanded to know.

"England," said Silk, as prompted by his wife.

The chamber buzzed with murmurs of surprise and annoyance.

"Which law has England broken?" said the king, now repressing a smile.

"None, Your Majesty," Silk replied, pausing for Anne Woodville's whispers, "but others have (what was that, My Dear?)—others have broken so many laws with impunity (*such* impunity, you say?) with such impunity—England might as well be (what was that?)"

"The friend of criminals!" she repeated, loud enough to be heard by half the room.

"Others have broken so many laws with such impunity that England might as well be the friend of criminals," he loyally repeated for the whole chamber to hear. "The queen's own father and one of her brothers were murdered (*murdered*? Should we say that, My Dear, in public?)"

"Murdered by the same traitors causing us problems again this year!" Anne Woodville added, her excitement lifting her voice to a high pitch.

The queen's family was a byword for over-ambition even among the Sons of Towton, and here was an unfortunate demonstration of their influence. The beheading of the queen's father and one of her brothers had actually vindicated last year's rebellion in the eyes of many, and it had protected the earl of Warwick's good standing in the wider community, since the executions were done on his orders.

Clarence had emerged from the rebellion without any credit, as the would-be king who had betrayed his own brother, but another tilt at the Woodvilles wouldn't do his reputation any harm, and he jumped at this chance.

"*Murdered*, says Anne Woodville!" he scoffed without so much as a glance at the woman in question. "It had been hoped that the execution of her father and brother would serve as a salutary warning to others not to get above themselves, but maybe that was hoping too much."

"Murdered!" she insisted, screwing up her face like a handful of mud she would throw at him if she could.

"The Woodvilles have married themselves off to just about everyone with a title," Clarence reminded the chamber. "Such a multitudinous family, raised suddenly to such heights—is it any wonder that two of them fell from their lofty perches and plummeted to an early death?"

This was greeted by nods among both gentry and nobles alike, but it was not appreciated by the Woodvilles' greatest supporter.

"My wife's family is not on trial here any more than you are," the king told his brother. "We are simply here to learn about this year's trouble in Lincolnshire, as I already explained. So, let's put old grievances aside for now, and show each other some respect. The doors are open and England is watching!"

"I love and honour my brother, the king," said Clarence with a respectful nod of his head, "but the meddling of the queen's family cannot be dismissed as easily as we all might wish. They have married into titles they have no right to. Even our seventy-years-old aunt, the Duchess of Norfolk, ended up marrying one of them, and that particular Woodville was just twenty years old! I am not sure which was lower: his station in life or his age."

It was a stale joke and it had never amused the king. He was exceptionally fond of their aunt, and the young man had already paid for his presumption with the loss of his head.

"You have said enough on that score also, Brother," the king responded with a frown. "Now let's all focus on the business in hand. The main issue to emerge looks like this: either Lord Welles is engaged in a private feud with the Constable of Lincoln Castle, or he is leading a rebellion against my government. We should all keep our minds on that question. A feud can be settled through discussion. A rebellion must be put down. Now, we have just heard a speech by Sir Thomas Burgh, summarising events as he sees them. So, now it is the turn of Lord Welles, if we are to get both sides of the story. Has he arrived yet?" Whispers were exchanged through the doorway and then one of the officials shook his head. "He seems determined not to co-operate," the king lamented.

"Lord Welles stands here!" said Clarence, brandishing a roll of paper. "These are his words, and they merely need the lend of a voice. I am happy to supply it in the interests of a fair hearing."

"We refuse to hear the words of a subject while he continues to disobey us," the king objected.

"Yet others are absent, and have we not heard people speak for them?" Claptrap reminded everyone, shooting a contemptuous glance at Silk and Anne Woodville.

At this moment there could be heard, ever more distinctly, the mellifluous sound of Latin verses, rising in volume till they were clearly audible to everyone in the chamber. The Councillor next to Silk had been reciting from a book of Latin poetry earlier in the proceedings, usually softly and to himself, but he had now resumed the reading more loudly, as if to drown out Clarence's voice. It was John Tiptoft, the earl of Worcester. A nobleman by birth but a Son of Towton by preference, he was one of England's greatest scholars and also one of its ablest administrators. To the king's friends, he was *Read-a-lot*, because he never went anywhere without a book. Everyone else usually styled him *Book*, because he never forgot anything, especially not grievances.

"Even the words of a dead Roman can get heard in this place," the king's brother observed, "and yet Lord Welles is condemned to silence?"

It was a clever jibe. The oaks murmured their sympathy.

"I wish you were a dead Roman," Read-a-lot muttered in between more Latin verses.

"Did anyone else hear that?" Clarence wondered—it was only audible to those at the Council table. "Tell everyone what you just said!"

"Do we need a translation?" Hastings interposed.

"That Councillor cares more for books than he cares for people," Clarence advised the assembly, pointing a denouncing finger at

Read-a-lot. "He just said he wishes that I were dead."

"You misunderstood him," Hastings objected. "He merely meant that a traitor like Welles would sound better in the words of a dead Roman, rather than in the English of His Majesty's own brother."

"Shall we try that then?" said the duke, unrolling the speech. "I shall read it in English and someone can translate it into Latin for me."

Clarence would have read it then and there but Read-a-lot forestalled him, jumping to his feet and immediately treating the assembly to yet more Latin poetry, the mellifluous and resounding phrases outshining the stars they reverberated among. Few understood the words but that hardly diminished their charm. The beauty of Read-a-lot's Latinity was famed as far as Italy, where it had once moved the Pope to tears of joy. As Deputy of Ireland, he had recently moved the Irish to tears of despair, thanks to the cruelty of his administration. Everyone respected his brilliant mind but nobody much liked him as a man, not even Hastings, his closest ally.

"Listen to that heartless scholar!" Clarence urged the assembly. "There he stands, mouthing the words of some Roman long since dead and gone, while here stand I, a duke of this realm, clutching the words of an English peer pleading for his life, unable to get a hearing."

It was a poignant gesture, or it would have been if he had been standing in a church pulpit, safe from contradiction. Here in the Star Chamber, it invited a sharp response.

"*You* the king's brother?" Read-a-lot jeered, leaving a Latin sentence hanging in the air. "God's mercy! I mistook you for Lord Welles. They are his words you are holding, aren't they? Or maybe you are here as your father-in-law, the earl of Warwick. A mouthpiece for traitors either way. For we cannot say you have always acted like His Majesty's brother."

These witty words, delivered with snarling ill-humour, were almost a declaration of war. Hastings was glad they hadn't come from his own mouth yet he still joined the other Sons of Towton in applauding them. Clarence, who had strong grounds to demand a retraction, even an apology, chose to be histrionic instead.

"If you are referring to last year's troubles, then what treason did Welles, Warwick or I commit? Those of us who bear the king's true interests at heart are under the truest obligation to liberate him from the clutches of false and deceiving friends."

"Truly true nonsense," Read-a-lot concluded.

Another titter of laughter rippled among the Sons of Towton. The King silenced their merriment with a look of disappointment. Some oaks murmured support for the duke. His Majesty silenced them too, with a deprecating smile. Tact was his greatest gift, always ready when he needed it, and yet it was backed by his sheer physical presence. He had won the crown on the battlefield with slashing sword and thumping mace.

"We shall listen to Read-a lot's musical Latin some other day, and to Lord Welles' testimony when he reads it himself," he decreed. "Till then, both the noble Councillors can resume their seats. Meanwhile what do *you* say? You have earned a reputation as one of England's wisest heads."

This was addressed to the Councillor nearest the throne, a bishop whose impartial advice had been welcomed by both Lancastrian and Yorkist regimes. He had opened today's session with a public prayer and he was still wearing his bishop's miter and pallium. Now he slowly rose to his feet before leaning on his bishop's staff.

"I find that it is often helpful in circumstances such as these, Your Majesty, if people would just accept appearances rather than dispute facts," he announced. "So, let us all try agreeing with one side and say that the Lincolnshire troubles *look* like a rebellion. Let us also try agreeing with the other side, saying that these troubles *look* like a private feud. That would be a good place to begin a meaningful dialogue."

"We are Councillors, not theologians," Read-a-lot scoffed. "We need a decisive judgement about facts, not endless quibbling about appearances."

"But these troubles are nothing new," the bishop pleaded, "nor are they confined to Lincolnshire. I note, for example, the recent quarrel between some Derbyshire households, the Greys and Vernons. Too often such private feuds harm our nation just as if they were rebellions, and too often rebellions are tolerated just as if they were private feuds. We act against neither in the appropriate way, because we fear mistaking each for the other."

"Then what do you suggest?" asked the king.

"Wouldn't it be in everyone's best interests if we had just one army for the entire kingdom, Your Majesty? Instead we have many private armies at the service of many great men, such that, whenever one of these great men sallies forth, nobody knows if he is settling a feud, starting a rebellion, or merely taking a tour of his estates. Fixing this problem, fixes everything."

This was an old argument and Hastings couldn't allow it to go unchallenged. His own cohort now amounted to one of the largest armies in the country.

"So long as people oppose an increase in taxes, private armies will have to do," he reminded everyone, half getting to his feet. "We are here to protect the laws, not make new ones."

He sat again amid general applause.

"Well there are existing laws that could be better enforced," the bishop persisted cautiously. "Private armies always look rebellious so long as they keep wearing their masters' personal liveries. We already have laws against this fashion. Why not enforce those laws, if that would bring peace to His Majesty's troubled and divided land?"

"With all due respects to the bishop," said Silk, his peacock feather sweeping a furious arc, "the soonest way to start trouble with otherwise respectable men is tell them you don't like the way they are dressed— and we could always say the same about you. This isn't a damned cathedral. It is the Star Chamber."

"I have an idea!" said Read-a-lot, closing his book with a resounding thump. "Let's pass a law requiring everyone to obey the laws, since we already have enough of those!"

"You may laugh at your jokes as much as you please," retorted the duke, once more brandishing his roll of paper, "but some of us are serious men. So, I will grant that the bishop is half right. The Lincolnshire unrest *looks* like another private feud. That is because it is another private feud. It is not a rebellion. That is the very point Lord Welles himself makes in his speech here, which I shall now read in spite of all these disruptions."

"No, Brother!" the king decreed. "I am postponing this inquiry till after lunch. If Lord Welles hasn't appeared by then, this Council will continue its deliberations in private. I can't get fairer than that. So here ends this public session for this morning. Now let's all get something to eat."

Hastings was proud of his king and he followed him from the Star Chamber with a deep sense of satisfaction, tempered by a sense of relief. Opening the doors to the public had seemed like a bad idea to almost everyone—it had risked exposing divisions within His Majesty's Council, which might further undermine people's confidence in his government—but Hastings had come up with the idea, His Majesty had insisted on going through with it, and now they had both vindicated themselves with commanding performances. Nobody in England could reach out to all sides better than His Majesty. He loved life, because he was larger than life, and inevitably he would breathe life into the country's flagging fortunes, so long as Englishmen remained loyal. Hastings was his loyal lieutenant, his Lord Chamberlain, his friend and his advisor, and it showed now in the admiring gazes that greeted them both as they passed through the crowds on their way to White Hall. Good reports of today's business would soon gallop throughout the kingdom, eventually reaching everyone that mattered: there were irreconcilable differences in the realm, and trouble was looming, but His Majesty was the master of every occasion, with the assistance of clever friends like the Lord Chamberlain.

Now they had other business to attend to: lunch. This was never an interruption to His Majesty's business. His preferred business was dining and having sex. The sex was usually private but the meals were ritual occasions, featuring the best cuisine, the best music and the best company England could supply, usually paid for by the guests and always requiring careful planning. A chamberlain, and even a Lord Chamberlain, should try to memorise such an event well in advance, both the menu and the guest list, and Hastings was able to brief the king fully on their way from the Star Chamber. This was no easy feat. Menus he had no trouble remembering, because they follow a natural order, founded on the stomach's tolerances, and the pleasures of the palate, but names are as difficult as people, demanding attention at any time for any reason. They always need a special effort and he never started the day without a written list of names near to hand, from which to refresh his memory at spare moments.

What and who would be today's highlights? He needed no list for these.

The highlight of today's menu was a ship modelled in marzipan, actually a fountain from which gushed a sample of wine plundered from five French ships, recently captured in a daring raid on the mouth of the Seine. The highlight among the guests was the man responsible for the raid, the notorious sea-rogue, Guy Loveday. His name was a nice summary of his character. Loveday, according to all the women that felt free to offer an opinion, was simply the handsomest man in England. According to their husbands, he was England's foremost plunderer of the nation's marriages. In fact, His Majesty was more swashbuckling in that regard, though most husbands kept quiet about it, and yet Loveday was at a disadvantage, spending much of his time at sea. Loveday, in short, was a man after His Majesty's own heart, and they had split the French booty between them. Some of it was paying for today's meal. They would probably share some women tonight but, when Hastings summoned one of his clerks to bring him the guest list for the banquet, there were no women on it. Maybe that was just as well. Guy's ways with women were known to be a little too free and spontaneous for a formal occasion. Hastings sent word for some of the palace maids to make themselves available later.

The absence of women made for a duller spectacle but at least it got rid of Anne Woodville, a right-royal pain in the neck, thus opening the way for an uninhibited spirit of camaraderie, all men together, toasting their own and each other's successes. Loveday sat on the king's right, Hastings on the king's left, amid a jolly assembly of knights and magnates, leaders of men, and men of action. Sampling the very best fare in England and the best wines from France, Hastings accounted himself rich in everything that makes life worth living—everything for the moment but women, and that would be fixed this evening—all thanks to his friendship with Edward Plantagenet, the bravest and best natured man that had ever lived! He touched on this theme in successive toasts throughout the afternoon, beginning with the first course and continuing up to the fifth, when he had trouble getting out of his chair. Dessert was on its way, and he was wondering if he was about to be sick, when he was told someone had arrived with important information: a Southwark merchant, Farthings Mandeville. The name hardly rang a bell in the Lord Chamberlain's memory in his present state—it wasn't worth interrupting the banquet for—until suddenly he connected it with the name of the daughter, Susanna Mandeville, whose face, figure and manner he could never forget since first setting eyes on her at Royston. A private talk in the open air was just what he needed to sober up for the evening session of the Council, he then decided, so he met her father outside Whitehall, near the Chapel of St Mary Undercroft.

"I have here an indenture that my son signed on my behalf in Royston, engaging Tom Roussell for a year at two shillings a day plus free board, with your signature witnessing it," Farthings explained after a bow so deep, it looked like he was planting peas in the gravelled path.

"I remember," Hastings assured him. "But speak on."

"Once again, my humble apologies if I have interrupted ..."

The chanting of monks in the nearby chapel fused with the hubbub of diners in the hall, lending the words of the Southwark merchant an exotic quality, like a homely pudding swimming in a subtle and complex sauce. Hastings resisted the temptation to smile. Keeping the mind working when inebriated was a challenge a Lord Chamberlain should always be ready for.

"No need to apologise!" he told the merchant, resting a patronly hand on his shoulder. "I am happy to take a friendly interest. But we must get to the point, Farthings, or we shall forget how this conversation started. The point is not to be underestimated."

Farthings mouthed something more in time to the heavenly music, as if he might be sampling the dessert in the hall, so that Hastings once again felt a need to repress the smile that was never far from his lips whenever at court, in case he appeared flippant. The merchant seemed to be expressing some kind of regret or reluctance about the indenture with Roussell—not surprising, considering Roussell's reputation. Hastings however had invested considerable hope in that indenture. It was time to be firm. The marzipan ship was still fresh in his memory and that gave him an idea.

"Smuggling French wine is a crime, you understand," he advised Mandeville.

"My Lord?"

"He who reneges gets reneged on in return: England's great unwritten law. Let that be your thinking when thinking about that indenture with Roussell."

"Your Lordship!" Farthings begged, bowing for extra consideration, as if a Lord Chamberlain doesn't have enough people bowing to him all day. "I am most anxious to please you, but—"

"There are no *buts*, Mandeville. There is *will*, *shall* and *must*."

It wasn't like a friend of His Majesty to be this peremptory with loyal subjects, however, and Hastings quietly reminded himself to be more magnanimous. He waited till Mandeville completed some more grovelling then once more rested a patronly hand on his shoulder.

"Now listen," he urged the merchant. "I say this as a friend, so listen. England relies on you. This fellow Roussell is a great catch. We must keep him ours. Or we must keep him out of trouble. We must keep an eye on him. That is your role from now on. You are his keeper. I should have told you sooner, but affairs of state have distracted me. So do this for England. Or do it for yourself. Just do it."

"But what is this about, and why me?"

"Why not you?"

"Many reasons, My Lord."

"You are refusing? Get to the point, Mandeville. I am a busy man."

"I don't know where he is. He didn't report for work till yesterday afternoon, and then he made it clear he intended not coming back. He didn't stay long. He sneaked away—no farewells, no explanations, no apologies. I haven't seen him at all this morning. He has gone."

This was worrying news.

"Where is he now?"

"I don't know. He won't be easy to find. He showed up yesterday in a fake beard. Even my daughter didn't recognise him."

Hastings turned to the bevvy of clerks that followed him everywhere.

"Go and tell Read-a-lot what you just heard."

One of his men hurried off with the message, and meanwhile Hastings comforted himself with the knowledge that Read-a-lot had spies everywhere. If Roussell was in hiding, they would find him soon enough. Mandeville however wasn't satisfied.

"Roussell is in breach of his indenture, isn't he?" he pleaded. "Isn't that grounds to have him locked up? And there is something else. I am not sure if it is relevant or not. It concerns a blacksmith from Waltham Abbey, named *John Smith*. He received ten pounds from Roussell when they were at Royston. You were there, I was told."

"Yes, stolen property," Hastings recalled. "What of it?"

"Ten pounds is a lot of money for Roussell to be generous with, don't you think? And there is a woman in my service, who thinks she overheard a plot being hatched, a campaign of arson, involving Roussell and Smith. She was in an emotional state when she mentioned it to me, and she has since changed her story, but maybe she spoke the truth the first time. Maybe that ten pounds was meant to help the rebels."

"Smith, Waltham Abbey," Hastings said over his shoulder.

One of his clerks duly made a note.

"It is almost certain that the plot was instigated by a man named *Bertram Kilsby*," Farthings added. "He works for the earl of Warwick. You would know him for a villain if you ever met him. His eyes—my daughter calls them *pond-weed green*. His talk is all slyness too. Will your clerk make a note of him as well?"

Kilsby was a name Hastings already knew from reports. The colour of his eyes hardly mattered but it seemed important to Farthings for some reason.

"Kilsby's eyes and pond weed," he said over his shoulder, just to keep the merchant happy. "But speaking of your daughter, Mandeville, she is coming to the dance tomorrow?"

"That's something else I came to see you about, My Lord," the merchant answered with another deep bow. "This business with Roussell has shaken her. She is not ready for social engagements just now. I am sorry to disappoint you. I had even brought some Italians to the house to teach her some steps. They have refused to come back today, her behavior being so difficult. I fear she will be just as bad at Baynard Castle tomorrow. She may even refuse to attend."

"She was alright with dancing when I mentioned it at Royston."

The indenture dropped from Mandeville's fingers.

"You mentioned it to her, My Lord?" he asked after stooping to retrieve the document. "The banquet and dance? She knows about His Majesty's invitation?"

"Is that a problem?"

"A girl like that should be introduced to these things carefully."

"Now listen, Farthings!" said Hastings, jabbing a finger at his chest so as to drive his point home. "It is too late to try wriggling out of agreements now. Your daughter has always been difficult. Everyone knows it. The Shrew of Southwark! But what is that to me? I am used to difficulties. I solve difficulties. It is all about watching and learning. I observed some signs at Royston. She was damned unpleasant and rude at first, yes even to me. Then Roussell showed up. Suddenly she was all as helpful as helpful can be. But there it is: human nature in a nutshell! The best way to make friends is scare them with enemies. It works with the French. It works with the Burgundians. It even works with the Germans. It will work with her too. Roussell is your answer. The sooner we find him and send him back to her, the sooner she will make herself more agreeable."

"As I said, he has gone missing."

Hastings began to think Farthings might actually be the kind of man that lets everyone down.

"Your co-operation is all I expect," he said in a disapproving tone.

"But how can I afford him?" Farthings pleaded. "Two shillings a day plus free board is too much. The Spanish olives haven't arrived. The London vintners have seen to that. The king must favour my petition or I am ruined."

"Damn it, Farthings, you worry too much!"

"The deepest apologies, My Lord!"

"Come, come, we are friends," Hastings reminded him, even wrapping an arm around his shoulders, as a last chance for him to come good. "The girl must learn obedience. If not Roussell, maybe someone else. Just get her to the dance. Then I'll steer you towards some Italian friends with deep pockets. Or don't you understand? The king is the most generous of men, if we keep him happy. That's the key to your future success. You'll see!"

They parted, Farthings to wherever he was going, Hastings to dessert. He arrived back in time for an exotic, cream concoction, followed by a final toast between the king and the sea rogue, bringing a warm end to festivities. It was time then for a return to more serious business: the evening session of His Majesty's Council.

Serious business?

As was often the case with His Majesty, the evening venue for the Council turned out not to be the Star Chamber but wherever they happened to end up in his private apartments at Westminster Palace. On this occasion it was his librarium, because he was reluctant to let go of Guy Loveday and he meant to show the rogue a book on navigation, recently bought with some of the proceeds from the river Seine adventure. The room was small enough to be lit by the few candles they had brought with them and, briefly, by a large glass window, some of whose panes were so translucent you could make out the shadow of the Jewel Tower, gradually fading in the evening light. Dwarfing the room, and even the king himself, was an enormous, exquisitely carved lectern, actually a pulpit destined for a cathedral somewhere, as soon as one could be built for it. Carpenters had widened the doorway just so it could be brought in, resulting in a magnificent pair of doors that wouldn't look out of place at the end of a cathedral nave. Such surprises were the least surprising thing about His Majesty's extraordinary life, so nobody questioned any of these improvements. A greater surprise awaited them once the doors closed behind them. Guy Loveday had smuggled in one of the palace maids and, far from being interested in the king's book, he was already doing some navigating of his own, up in the pulpit, where the buxom creature was propping herself against the wood panelling of the breastwork, ready for him to drop anchor. Any other king might have been irked by these distractions but not Hastings' good friend, Edward Plantagenet, and even the librarium's lack of chairs didn't bother him. He rested his heroic frame on the floor, softened only by a rug, then stood a candle on a nearby shelf, inviting Council to join him. This they all did, each according to his own ability, wherever a pile of books, a shelf or a wooden chest offered an extempore seat or back rest.

"Lord Welles has chosen not to explain himself, and now we must proceed without him," said the king. "Any ideas about what to do?"

Most of the Councillors were now soused and bloated after the banquet but that was often a good state to be in when considering decisions that could affect the lives of thousands, even millions, because only the most salient details stayed in the memory or penetrated the fog of contentment, resulting in fewer digressions and quibbles.

"The question now is what to do," added Hastings, lying flat on his back, the better to conserve his energy. "So that's our focus for this evening."

"Is it a feud or a rebellion?" the bishop wanted to know, making room for himself on a chest by moving books from the lid to a nearby shelf. "What is His Majesty's decision?"

"Both," said the king, "on your own advice, Bishop. Lincolnshire seems one thing to some, and something else to others. We should respond in an even-handed kind of way, is what I am saying, I think."

"That would make us look confused," said Read-a-lot, standing by a bookshelf with the new book on navigation open beside him.

Malice never rests and he was as sober as ever, turning pages without quite turning his back on the other Councilors, because he had an extraordinary ability to attend to several tasks simultaneously. He could always be relied on to get straight to the point, whatever he was doing.

"So what's your verdict?" Hastings prompted him.

"Respond with force!" came the response, while another page was turned. "The rebels caught us napping last year. Not this year. We send commissions of array to the counties tonight ... this map of the Thames is well drawn. The beginnings of a decent force can be assembled in London within three days ... the shoals are clearly marked. We leave Sunday, gathering more strength as we head north. We arrive in Lincolnshire mid-month then crush the rebels once and for all ... but the tidal range is exaggerated, I think."

"What does a scholar know of statecraft!" scoffed the king's brother—envy never rests either, and he too was as sober as ever, standing with his back against one of the closed doors. "Is all England to suffer a disturbance of the magnitude our bookish peer now proposes, just to deal with a private feud in a single Midlands county?"

"I don't mean to disturb *all* England," Read-a-lot fired back. "You and your master, the earl of Warwick, can stay home. That will do much to reduce the magnitude of the disturbance, and the size of the threat."

"You are determined to make an enemy of me," Clarence observed.

"We are all good men," the king insisted, his eyelids springing open after a brief flirtation with sleep. "So, my brother and Warwick are welcome to march north with us, if that is what we end up doing. But if my brother is right, and it's wrong to create unnecessary fuss, then Read-a-lot is also right, for the same reason, and maybe they should stay home. But now I am beginning to sound like the bishop, agreeing with everyone. What does our swashbuckling Cupid say?"

Loveday replied from the pulpit with a wave of his free hand, the other hand busy out of sight. The maid was now completely out of sight too but she could be heard mouthing something.

"Such eloquence," Clarence commented sourly. "Let's retire to a brothel somewhere, if this is what good government amounts to."

"You underestimate the wisdom of our common instincts," the king advised him with a chuckle. "Guy is making a strong argument, that our first business is to mind our pleasures. Which gets me to think-ing: instead of heading north with overwhelming force, how about a pleasurable journey with a few good friends, intent on a good time? Meanwhile we get a good feel for the lie of the land. Am I right, Guy?"

Loveday was now too distracted to respond.

"*A pleasurable journey*, Your Majesty?" said the bishop, using his miter to shield his eyes from the lewd pulpit, though there was little to see now except the smile spreading across Loveday's face. "We are approaching Lent, when your kingdom will be busy fasting and reflecting somberly on Our Lord's death and resurrection. And wasn't it an unguarded moment, in another period of crisis, that led to your capture and imprisonment last year?"

"The queen won't like it either," said Silk, his peacock feather tickling the bishop's nose as he turned to address His Majesty: Silk was a creature of the Woodvilles even without his wife behind him.

"I hear you," His Majesty offered, now lying flat on his back, his head pillowed in the palms of his hands, "but maybe I should explain myself a bit more. I am thinking of a small group of friends, partying our way northwards, at towns and manors along the way, treating the Lincolnshire troubles as just another private feud, but ready to expand into a great army at short notice, if and when it turns out a rebellion. The good people in Lincolnshire won't object. We don't want to alarm them. An even-handed approach, Bishop! In some ways, it is your own idea as much as mine. And it is not all pleasure. It will be a working party."

The king's plan didn't immediately strike Hastings as a great idea. However, he had too much faith in his friend to doubt either his wisdom or his luck: he was still king after a decade of rebellion, treachery and turmoil.

"We could call it the *Friendship Tour*," he suggested.

"A good name," the king affirmed.

"I am not opposed to this idea," said Clarence, smiling at last. "A large army will alienate the north. A small group of friends will invite trust."

"I disagree," said the bishop. "There is, I earnestly believe, a perception among people at all levels, high and low, civil and religious, that Your Majesty is not as serious in your responsibilities as you should be. This Friendship Tour will alienate your friends here in the south, especially during Lent."

"It seems His Majesty can't win," said Hastings, propping himself on one elbow. "If we take a big army to Lincolnshire, we alienate the north. If we take a small group of friends, we alienate the south."

"Lent is no time for war or pleasure, but which do we prefer?" His Majesty concluded with a smile. "And it is *my* kingdom after all. So, a Friendship Tour it is!"

"May I suggest you be in no hurry to set out?" Clarence added. "I might yet achieve peace through my own negotiations, given a few more days."

"Did you achieve peace with your marriage last year?" Read-a-lot scoffed, turning a page as irritably as a ship's captain on the wrong side of a falling tide. "There is no time to waste! His Majesty must send out letters of array tomorrow, commanding our friends to prepare for war, and we must set out this Sunday. We won't be overtaken by events this year—not if *I* can help it."

"Good advice!" said the king, because Read-a-lot was too brilliant a man to be left feeling unappreciated, even though His Majesty preferred more diplomatic counsels. "But we might delay our departure, if my brother can come up with something definite by Sunday. Meanwhile, My Lord Chamberlain, we must begin our own preparations for the Friendship Tour. Nothing smooths ruffled feathers sooner than wine, women and song, in my experience—in moderation, of course."

Hastings sat up, feeling suddenly alert and ready for serious business.

"I will send word north tonight for friendship at all our stops."

"Beauty is as rare as gold and not all those stops are blessed with riches," His Majesty added. "Beauty with stamina enough for a long campaign is rarerest of all. We need to take along Amazons with the looks of Venus. My Jane Shore will suit, I am certain of that. Who else?"

"Elizabeth Oldhall," offered Hastings, since she was the king's mistress prior to Shore, and the king's friends were now due to take their turns on her.

"Oldhall is getting a bit past it, isn't she?"

"Physically she is up for anything," Hastings insisted.

"We need a third," the king decided, "as a kind of spare. How about the Mandeville girl? You have been raving about her since you got back from the Midlands."

"Susanna Mandeville, the daughter of a Southwark merchant," Hastings advised the rest of the Council, or those who were still awake. "Her father recently fetched her from Lincolnshire for tomorrow's do at Baynard Castle."

"The Shrew of Southwark!" Silk recalled. "My wife will oppose her going."

"The girl is difficult," Hastings conceded, "but all she needs is a touch of magic."

He waved an imaginary wand.

"Describe her to us," the king urged him.

"I'm not a poet," Hastings pleaded, "but if I were, I would say that a rose is lovelier for its thorns, if only we can get around them, and then I'd liken her to the dew, when it is couched on a rose petal, perfectly rounded, because not wanting to be touched, yet ready to cling to the glove that caresses her, like an exquisite kiss."

Hastings paused while dwelling on the face and figure he had seen at Royston, then he woke with a start, remembering the recent news.

"Is there a problem?" the king observed.

"I just had an interview with her father. I might have lost the magic."

"He means Tom Roussell," Read-a-lot interpreted for him, since Hastings had been briefing him on recent developments. "Better known to most people as *Beast of Ferrybridge*."

The effect was magical even here. Those Councillors who were still awake became suddenly more wakeful, and those who had been asleep began to stir. Even the king was moved, though far from ignorant about some of these matters He shifted his posture from semi-recumbent on one elbow to sitting upright. Only Guy Loveday seemed oblivious, resting exhausted on the breastwork of the pulpit.

"Let's not fuss over reputations," Hastings pleaded on behalf of his Lancastrian legend. "Roussell is older and wiser these days, and he has come south for a quieter life."

"Hastings indentured him to the shrew's family, and now the villain has disappeared," Read-a-lot added, turning another page: "A young man's trick! And *wiser*? More cunning maybe. He is dangerous still."

"The indenture comes with a penalty clause," Hastings assured everyone. "If he won't comply, we simply lock him away till he does."

"We have to find him first," Read-a-lot reminded everyone.

"Roussell could be useful," was the king's considered judgement. "His opinions carry weight among the rebels. Can we invite him on the Friendship Tour?"

"Spoken like a true king," Hastings observed.

There was a loud *thump*, Read-a-lot closing his book as if they had all struck a reef.

"Have you both gone mad!" he said. "A man like that in our own ranks?"

"He has disappeared, you said," the king recalled, "and maybe we are getting ahead of ourselves. But the Lord Chamberlain's poetry has won me over. So, those three then: Shore, Oldhall and Mandeville."

"Your Majesty, at this time of year, loose women like those …" the bishop tried pleading.

"Amazons and ambassadors, My Dear Bishop! When better for charming women who can fight a bit than now, heading north into a feud that looks like a rebellion?"

"You can invite them during the dancing tomorrow," Hastings advised him, "if they all show up."

"Your Majesty!" said Silk, once again tickling the bishop's nose. "If those Amazons and ambassadors are going on tour with you, somebody must oversee them on the queen's behalf."

"You and your wife are welcome to take charge of them," the king replied as Guy Loveday finally slid from view. "You see, Cousins and Friends: business and pleasure are made for each other. Otherwise we'd soon lose our appetite for both."

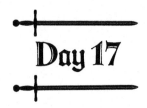

Day 17

Friday 2nd of March

Susanna awoke to the faint glow of daylight in her bedroom window, a translucent sheet of cheesecloth stretched across a wooden frame. Glass would have been nicer but cheesecloth had two advantages: her father could afford it and she could paint on it. The silhouette of a butterfly usually spread its wings there, one of her own creations, but the light was too feeble for it just yet.

It was unlike her to be awake this soon, the morning's chill so oppressive, her face felt icy. The nausea of a restless night still haunted her and she sank deeper into the covers, wondering what had disturbed her usual routine. Two bells across the river soon provided the answer, tolling six o'clock in unison. How well she knew those bells! They were always the first to ring the hours, guided by mechanical clocks. One belonged to the townhall, the other to His Majesty's London fortress, Baynard Castle, the venue for today's banquet and dance.

"This is the day!" she recalled.

Excitement had kept her awake much of the night and it revived now to the swelling sound of church bells, all following the lead of the townhall and castle: a torrent of chimes, cascading along both banks of the Thames. She almost jumped out of bed, ready to dance to their haphazard refrain, but the real dance wasn't scheduled until noon, so she stayed under her blankets and reminded herself that these early morning bells merely roused people to their first prayers and the first business of the day. Were this the dead of winter, the church bells wouldn't stir until His Majesty's bell struck eight, because the world obeys two different times: the unvarying rhythm of the mechanical clock, kept by punctilious men like His Majesty and merchants like Farthings, and the shifting rhythm of the seasons, observed by churches and their pious flocks. Susanna too obeyed two different times. In Bourne, she always rose with her aunt, in obedience to church bells. In Southwark, she was neither pious nor punctilious, only stirring from bed when she felt like it, usually well after sunrise, sometimes not till noon. Today she felt a bit like her aunt's respectable niece, awake with the birds, but also a bit like her father's wilful daughter, loitering in bed in a great metropolis. Most of all, she felt like her butterfly, about to spread her wings.

"Just a short trip across the river decides the rest of my life," she reflected as she lay in bed, staring at the dark ceiling. "Today a dance in London, tomorrow—where shall I awake? In his bed, or this one? A woman first or a painter? Up the Thames to Westminster or down the Thames to Utrecht? Today's dance points the way."

These reflections were interrupted by an enormous snore from the other side of the bed: Matilda. Here was another reason why Susanna hadn't slept well. It was not the snoring that had kept her awake so much as all the preliminary sobbing and moaning. The wretched creature was still broken-hearted over the Waltham Abbey blacksmith, because he was marrying another woman. Susanna almost despised her for it, yet also pitied her, because the tears were a reminder of her own predicament: the king too was married to another woman.

Another woman?

An army of servants, courtiers and guards waited on that other woman's every wish. Worse still, she belonged to the most ambitious and ruthless family in the land, the Ah-Ha Woodvilles. They would never tolerate a serious rival for the king's affections, and neither would Susanna. Her bright hopes were edged with danger. She recalled the decision she had already reached at the Hampstead tollgate.

"I am a painter first," she told herself once more, "a woman second."

Her plans to reach Utrecht were already well advanced. She had now mastered enough dance routines to keep step with His Majesty later today, yet she had also behaved badly enough during lessons to give her father nightmares. If everything continued according to plan,

Farthings would promise her Utrecht this morning, as the price for her co-operation this afternoon, in case she behaved at Baynard Castle the way she had behaved at home.

Her shrewish antics had peaked two days ago, after one of her dance partners had squeezed her left buttock in the kitchen while taking refreshments. He had already groped several women in dances before then, but he was a loyal customer of Signor Della Bosca, who merely winked at his liberties, so she had finally taken justice into her own hands, poking the creep in the eye with a sharp left. Then, as chance would have it, the Beast had replaced him soon afterwards, looking as hairy as a dealer in Russian furs. She had almost brained him with an adze, after his whiskers had fallen off, and she had finally taken her fury out on Della Bosca's assistant, pushing him into a boat after the clumsy idiot had trodden on her foot. The two Italians had quit shortly after that, citing her behaviour as intolerable, and they hadn't show up at all yesterday. The loss of a day's lessons was unfortunate—she had yet to master some of the more difficult dances—yet at least she had given her father timely proof of her powers as the Shrew of Southwark, if he still needed any. The Beast hadn't shown up yesterday either and that was the best proof of all.

Or had she gone too far? Her father had yet to inform her of the king's invitation. Maybe he hoped to spring it on her at the last moment, but what if he didn't feel up to the challenge? Keeping the dance from her could be a cowardly way of keeping her from the dance. She would never do anything to offend His Majesty, of course, but Farthings wasn't to know that. He still had no inkling that her shrewish manners guarded a woman's heart. His own motives were easy to fathom most days. A merchant operating outside the protection of the London guilds can only thrive with the help of friends in high places, and he could ill afford to inflict on them an abusive and violent daughter. That threat had long discouraged him from opening the door to an endless stream of well-heeled fiancés. However, he couldn't really keep her hidden today of all days, could he? Ignoring an invitation from the king might look disloyal, even rebellious. Farthings could be thinking he risked ruin and disgrace whether he took her to the dance or not.

The pressure had obviously got to him yesterday. He had returned home in a bad temper after some errand across the river, and when she had asked him what the matter was, he had shunned her with a scornful look. He had then locked himself in his office, emerging only once all night, shouting for Cook to bring him a meal. Maybe the non-appearance of the Italians had put him in a foul mood—they had been one of his few, remaining sources of income till then—yet the non-appearance of the Beast had saved him more in wages than he had lost in the hire of the hall, and he should have been feeling happy with her in total. There could only be one reason for his unpleasantness, as far as she could make out: he was fretting over today's dance. That could be a good thing, if he capitulated to her demands later this morning, but what if he never mentioned the dance at all, or even refused to take her?

Yes, maybe she had been too shrewish lately even by her own standards, but it wasn't entirely her fault. A pinched buttock merits a poke in the eye, doesn't it? The two Italians weren't above reproach either. Some of their former students had once come to the house complaining about missing jewellery, and Signor Della Bosca was seen loitering in the pantry the very afternoon a pie had gone missing: he was quicker with his hands than he was with his feet. His leaner compatriot was so clumsy at times, he couldn't possibly be a thief, yet why was he masquerading as a dance instructor? A more patient woman than Susanna would have felt justified pushing him into the boat, after he had trodden on her toe. And how could she *not* have threatened the Beast of Ferrybridge with an adze, once he had dared show his face, or not show it, here in her own home of all places! The new sergeant-at-arms! It was intolerable. All these rogues had got what they deserved or could consider themselves lucky if they hadn't.

She was impatient to get the day started, eager to see how it would all end. Another snore from Matilda, however, reminded her that it was still too early. It was important to seem her usual self, a woman in no particular hurry, so she continued loitering in bed until finally her butterfly began to emerge, sometime after His Majesty's bell rang seven, when at last she threw off the blankets and jumped to her feet.

It was still early by her usual standards but it was best not to be too predictable.

She always started her days with a visit to Lady Lorna, now lodged in the bishop's stables. Her preferred route was also a highway for the neighbourhood cats, meandering along boundary walls and over some roofs, climbing down a tree then springing across the raised beds of the bishop's herbarium, finally leaping onto the boardwalk that supported his lordly toes to the stalls of his beloved thoroughbreds. It was best managed in a light smock, hardy skirt and nimble slippers, if you didn't mind the intense cold this time of year. Today however was not the right time to be taking such risks, either with her limbs or her reputation, so she dressed for Southwark's muddy lanes, in a thick gown, thick cloak, thick stockings and wooden pattens. The pattens made a terrific din as she left the room, then grew silent as she paused outside her father's office, listening. There was no noise inside. It was unlocked and she peered in. He wasn't there. Her pattens resumed their clatter as she came down the stairs, otherwise the house was deathly quiet. She soon found her father with her brother in the kitchen, both seated at a table by the fire, both turning to investigate the heavy footsteps, this part of the house being paved.

"You're up early," Farthings observed. "Going anywhere special?"

"Utrecht would be nice," she reminded him.

He ignored this.

Friday is the one day of the week when Christians must fast until noon but Farthings was addicted to breakfasts, and Cook had long been in the habit of indulging him with private treats, such as fluffy, white bread with a piquant topping of toasted oysters, chased down with a spicey claret. The only meal on the table this morning, however, was a quarter loaf of stale bread, accompanied by an ale so musty, it smelt like bilge water from a North Sea hulk. Farthings obviously hadn't touched any of it: it was just for Susanna's sake. He was brooding over some accounts, a large volume of notes, records and receipts that she had long come to know as the *Almshouse Book*. Its proper place was upstairs in his office but he liked to make a great show of frowning over it now and then, whenever he wanted everyone to think they were living beyond their means. Everything pointed to a lecture. Susanna decided to keep him in suspense, so she proceeded to the pantry to fetch the morning's treat for Lady Lorna. However, the pantry door was locked. This early in the morning, it was never locked. Susanna tried again. It was definitely locked. It was a bit late for such precautions—Signor Della Bosca no longer worked here—but when Susanna asked for the key, Cook responded with an awkward shake of the head. The good woman would never defy Susanna except under instructions from Farthings. The battle for Susanna's future had already started, she realised, and she returned to the table, ready to get on with it.

"Why so glum, Papa?" she asked as she sat opposite him—the sooner they got the lecture out of the way, the sooner they could get down to the morning's real business.

"Ask your brother about Noah."

Square was sitting with a timber manikin on his lap, about the size of a small child. Susanna recognised it as the biblical patriarch he had been working on for some days.

"I slipped with the chisel," he revealed, "and broke his nose off."

"Can you fix it?" she asked. This was not the sort of conversation she wanted to be having just now but it was important to seem relaxed.

"If I were Spicer, yes—he would simply piece in a new nose—but it's fiddly work and this oak is knotty. It's easier starting all over again."

"Except he has already spoiled all the spare wood," Farthings continued for him, "so now he must cut off Noah's head and replace it with timber we were keeping for one of his sons, which leaves that son headless or very short. But that's a small loss! Noah doesn't need a son if his son is as useless as mine. A carpenter ten years, and he wastes wood like a fool apprentice! Yet so pious, maybe he thinks we can eat his prayers. I should throw him out into the street for all the good he is."

Bullying Square was a favourite trick that had worked for Farthings many times before. She wasn't going to fall for it this time. Square would just have to look after himself for once. She yawned and stretched in the manner of someone who has nothing to do all day but come up with pleasant ways to spend it.

"Life is a holiday for some people," Farthing observed with a grimace, "but never for long, My Girl. It's time you came to your senses, while you still have time. Wealth doesn't fall from the sky like rain.

It doesn't grow like flowers. People only get wealth when there are men to work for them—not men like your brother, but real men that know what they are about. Do you think I can snap my fingers and all Southwark's mice will turn into Spicers, begging for work? He left on account of you, Susanna. Spicer left on account of you. So did Lister. So did all the others. They all left when they heard you were coming home. And now, just yesterday, it was the turn of the Italians! Look at these accounts. Our income has dried up, our debts keep flooding in. We are destined for the almshouse, and it is all thanks to *you*, so maybe we should start learning to live like it."

She casually filled her father's mug with some bilge water, then lifted it to her nose like a woman that cares so little for luxury, she could drink almost anything.

"Is that why you are keeping the pantry locked?" she said over the rim.

"It's practise for poverty. Today Lady Lorna misses out on her treats. Soon we'll have to sell her. I'll throw your brother out into the street before then, but he's frugal and he won't buy her much time. Then it will be your turn and mine, without a roof to keep dry under, or a fire to keep warm beside. Yes, life for us Mandevilles is going to get hard and harder, all thanks to you, Susanna, because you never can be nice to anyone, not even to save your own family. So it's time you changed for the better, or get used to doing without."

"I can always stay with Aunt Marian."

He nodded. He closed the Almshouse Book. He crossed his arms and chewed one of his fingernails, deep in thought. Susanna silently wondered what he would try next. So far, it was just the usual threats and warnings.

"I talked with Lord Hastings yesterday," he soon revealed.

This startled her. Southwark merchants ordinarily don't move in the same circles as Lord Chamberlains. Susanna's mind reeled trying to take in the staggeringly few topics that could have come up for discussion. One popped into her head, well suited to the theme of the Almshouse Book.

"The king has rejected your petition?"

"No, we hardly mentioned that. Something else."

"Yes?"

"Can't you guess?"

"I'm not a mind reader."

"It concerns you personally."

He gave her a knowing smile, as if he suspected her of being coy.

"You talked about the price of herrings," she offered with a shrug.

"Tom Roussell."

"Tom Roussell?"

"We talked about his future here."

"He doesn't have a future here

"He frightens you?"

"Don't be silly. *I* frighten *him*."

"More than he frightens you?"

"He is the one that keeps disappearing. He disappeared from here two days ago. He disappeared from Huntingdon before that. He disappeared from the king's castle at Fotheringhay. He disappeared from Aunt Marian's backyard first of all. I know because I was there each time. He's not coming back to this house any more than Spicer is."

"Hastings has got men out looking for him. They'll be bringing him here as soon as they find him."

This was shocking news.

"But why? What business is it of his! What's going on?"

"It's politics, My Girl. One good turn deserves another, and sometimes the great ones do a bad turn first, because undoing it looks like a good turn afterwards. The indenture with Roussell was the bad turn: two shillings a day, plus free board, will ruin us. But if we give Hastings something he really wants, he'll offload Roussell onto some other poor wretch."

"But what could he possibly want from us?"

"How much are you willing to give? Better still: how much does Roussell frighten you? There is your answer."

This was a challenging revelation. She broke off a chunk from the stale loaf and knocked it against the table several times, listening to how inedible it sounded, while wondering where the Lord Chamberlain's bad turn was headed. Roussell had a way of sneaking up on her that was disconcerting, even more disconcerting than his habit of suddenly disappearing. He would have many opportunities for sneaking up on her if they were living under the same roof. But if she ever reached Utrecht, he would be a distant memory, and if she ever shared the king's bed, his name would soon appear on a warrant for his arrest, on whatever charge she could come up with.

"Roussell has more to fear from me than I have to fear from him," she insisted.

Farthings drummed his fingers on the Almshouse Book, like a man counting beads on an abacus.

"Susanna," he said after a few moments, "there is to be a banquet and dance at Baynard Castle this afternoon. You and I have been invited. The king wants to dance with you, and I have already said Yes on your behalf. I hope you don't mind."

Now at last they had come to the moment she had been anticipating for so many days! She dunked her chunk of bread into her mug, softening it long enough to keep her father in more suspense.

"Did you hear me, Susanna?"

"A dance with the king this afternoon? Why didn't you tell me sooner?"

"I wasn't sure how to."

"I have already danced with him once before."

"A second time would hurt?"

She bit into the uninviting sop of bread as proof of her invulnerability.

"Papa, I honour him as our rightful king. That doesn't mean I have to dance with him all the time, does it?"

"It would please Lord Hastings. One good turn deserves another, remember."

"I'd sooner kick that idiot in the shins."

"The Lord Chamberlain? You can't be serious."

She wondered how best to respond to this: it was important not to frighten Farthings too much, just enough. In the end, she kept quiet. It was enough for Farthings.

"Roussell might not frighten you, Susanna, but he frightens me," he came out with next, obviously begging for mercy now, as he always did when everything else failed. "I want you to come with me to the dance. I want you to partner the king. I expect you to be on your best behaviour. It's not asking much. Yet you are not like other girls—I appreciate that fact—and maybe you need a special reason. So, what do you want?"

The time for subtlety was over.

"You already know what I want."

"You want to paint like the Dutch. Well, come with me to Baynard Castle today, be on your best behaviour, and I will send you to live with your uncle in Utrecht."

"That's a promise?"

"A solemn promise!"

"You would never break a solemn promise."

"Otherwise you would never forgive me," he affirmed.

"Then you won't mind putting it in writing. I want a proper contract."

He stared at her.

"You are my daughter, not my client."

"You always look after your clients. Now I want to be treated like one."

"What other daughter has a written contract with her own father?"

"What other daughter has you for a father?"

"A contract with my own daughter? I never heard such a thing. What would my enemies say? No, never, impossible, it doesn't happen!" He banged a fist on the table. She shrugged in reply. He soon started counting more beads on his imaginary abacus, trying to calculate some way out of his quandary. There was only one way out of course. "Just suppose I consider this absurd idea for a moment—what are your terms?"

She had already decided these and it was a relief to voice them at last.

"I will accompany you to the dance, and I'll behave just like the simpering, brainless daughter you have always wanted. Yes, I will be utterly charming. I will dress pleasantly, speak pleasantly, move pleasantly, and smile pleasantly, whether or not anyone deserves it. Nobody will have any good cause to complain about me, certainly not the king. I might even appear flirtatious at times. But that's all I can promise."

"That's good enough for me. And in return you can live with your uncle for a year, if he is willing to pay your bills—as soon as we can find a ship for you. Agreed?"

"My needs are modest," she assured him, otherwise he was certain to reject her demands, "but not *that* modest. I must leave for Utrecht within three months, not a day later; and you must let me live there for a period no less than three years, on a yearly income of six pounds, with no requirement to get married. All this must be agreed to in front of witnesses, and entrusted to the bishop's scrivener, even before we cross the river, or the deal is off."

He looked scandalised.

"*Six pounds every year for three years? No requirement to get married?*"

"Look on the bright side, Papa: I'm saving you the cost of a dowry."

"Your beauty is your dowry."

"I have made you a generous offer."

"Can a daughter of mine stoop so low?"

"You're right. Make it eight pounds."

"Terrumber!" he cried, banging both fists on the table. "Five pounds or eight pounds, one pound or only one penny, you'll never get it out of this merchant, you lying sneak. You have known about the dance for days. Lord Hastings told you when you were at Royston. Don't deny it. He mentioned it to me yesterday. Yet you come downstairs pretending it is all news to you this morning, so you can ambush me in this undaughterly manner! You have been thinking up this contract in secret for days, all the while expecting me to sign up to it in a single morning! Fie on you, you treacherous creature."

Susanna began to feel angry too. If anyone had been played for a fool this morning, surely it was her.

"Was the dance supposed to be a secret?" she retorted. "So, who is the treacherous creature now, you lying sneak!"

"I knew what tricks you would get up to, you vixen."

"Give me Utrecht, Papa or I will give you hell."

"Listen to her!" he complained to Square, whose humble face was now a mixture of horror and shame. "But I am ahead of you, Susanna, and here is something else you should know. I heard it from Lord Hastings yesterday. He already knows what sort of monster you are. The Shrew of Southwark! So, don't go to the dance. You have already embarrassed this family as much as you can. I have nothing more to fear."

"Maybe I will go to the dance, just to prove you wrong."

"I forbid you to go."

"I don't need your permission to behave badly. By the time I am finished there, the Mandeville name will be forever mud."

"This for a daughter who blackmails her own father!" he shouted, grabbing the bread from her fingers and throwing it in her face.

It almost hit her in the eye.

"This for a father who throws food at his own daughter!" she answered, lashing out with one foot.

She had forgotten she was wearing pattens. The wood struck his shin with the force of a mallet, and he winced, almost wept. He clutched his leg to throttle the pain, and meanwhile Square got to his feet with Noah, because he always left the room when things got this ugly.

"Square!" Farthings pleaded. "Tell her she must obey me. The Ten Commandments say to honour her father. I am her father. I'll even go to church with you—every day for the rest of my life! But only if she comes to the dance and behaves herself."

This was outrageous. Farthings went to church like most people, for the occasional wedding, baptism and funeral, otherwise just once a week, because it was expected of everyone and it was good for business. Deals were sometimes discussed in whispers during the liturgy, and contracts were often ratified at the church door. He would never go to church every day if he could help it. There weren't enough deals.

"He's lying," Susanna cautioned her brother, just in case he was *that* naive.

"A liar or a prophet?" Square murmured, once again sitting down with Noah. "What if a man says something, never meaning it to come true, but it happens anyway?"

"What are you talking about?"

Square rocked to-and-fro with Noah on his knee, working up to some kind of declaration, then he stopped and fixed Susanna with a steady gaze.

"This is not the first time that godliness has visited him," he revealed. "The day that he asked me to fetch you from Bourne—he had just found the goldsmith's wife in the king's bed—I thought I couldn't possibly bring you back here, not for a dance with *that* man, king or not. But then he said something so pious, I knew I had to obey him."

Farthings stopped cradling his shin.

"I did?"

"Don't you remember?" Square urged him. "You said: *the king will turn saint before Susanna turns whore.* Your own words!"

"He had no right to talk like that," she objected.

"But what if it is true?" Square pleaded, reaching around Noah to take one of her hands in his, as if her hand were a pump drill, rising and falling, rising and falling under his vacillating pressure. "What if the king really does turn saint for your sake?"

"You don't know what you are saying."

"I know he is the worst lecher ever to wear a crown," he assured her, "yet stranger things have happened. Just think about it. Kilsby turned up alive in our aunt's house, when he was supposed to be dead! Sir Thomas Malory was supposed to protect us. The world's greatest exponent of knightly chivalry! Instead he tried to rob and kill us. The Beast of Ferrybridge was supposed to be a villain. Instead, he turns into the Knight of the Lost Sabaton, and rides to our rescue! Then, just when he lost his way, got drunk and was arrested for disturbing the peace, when I might have despaired of this world, and lost faith in chivalry, the Lord Chamberlain makes him our sergeant-at-arms. And so it came about that I found myself in Arthur's Chapel, where such things were revealed to me, such joy and radiance, I can't, can't …"

His face had become bright with wonder, as if recollecting a miracle. Whether or not there actually was such a chapel, or he had just imagined it, Susanna couldn't be sure. This much she did know: there was no time for this nonsense today of all days.

"Square, all these surprises have now got you imagining too much," she reasoned with him. "How could I possibly turn His Majesty into a saint?"

"You don't know? It's an old story. There is no dragon, however terrible, no wilderness, however desolate, no enemy, however numerous, that a true knight won't dare face in his quest for a lady's love. Then what if that knight is a wicked king, and you are the lady? He makes up his mind to seduce you, yet you rebuff him and rebuff him again and again. The strength of your virtue, the beauty of your person—all this is too much for him. He falls to his knees. He begs for mercy. You remind him of his duty. You tell him that he rules by the will of his people. You command him to rise a new man. He rises a true king, yes, a saint even. All his men rise with him. All England rises with him, a nation ready for heroic deeds, all under the spell of a warrior maid. Such things happened in France with Joan of Arc. Why not England today?"

He was squeezing her fingers in a transport of joy, living the story that he was imagining. She wanted to believe his story too, if only for his sake, if only for the moment. Farthings looked desperate to believe it as well, if only she would go to the dance and behave herself.

"Square," she felt compelled to say, meanwhile trying not to laugh at the absurdity of it all, "Joan of Arc was burned at the stake."

"That can never happen to you," he assured her, "not while our sergeant-at-arms is the Knight of the Lost Sabaton. A true hero shall stand by you, to be your shield and your sword, and nothing can stop you then, if only you believe! This vision came to me in Arthur's Chapel."

Just then an involuntary snort of laughter burst from her, and the spell was broken. Square's hand flew from hers as if his drill had snapped in pieces. Farthings was himself again.

"You nincompoop!" he snapped, almost frothing at the mouth. "I knew I shouldn't have looked to you for help. You can't even get Noah's nose right, and now you are making England great again? My daughter, the Shrew of Southwark, now our very own Joan of Arc! Our sergeant-at-arms, the Beast of Ferrybridge, now the Knight of the Lost Sabaton. All thanks to King Arthur. Wish me up a hoard of gold and silver while you are at it! You will both end up in the almshouse. How is that for a prophecy! Now get out of my kitchen. Get out of my sight, the pair of you, you idle fools!"

This was not how Susanna had imagined her morning turning out, but it wasn't over yet. Her defiance, combined with Square's foolery, had put their father in one of his sudden rages, utterly beyond reason, yet those never lasted long. He would accept her demands, if only she gave him more time. Time was short, with noon fast approaching, but she had done as much as she could for now. Cook was passing the table with a basket of eggs, so Susanna jumped up and grabbed one. Farthings ducked, in case she meant to throw it at him, but she merely cradled it in her palm and followed her brother and Noah out into the hall. There Square picked up a saw and began cutting off the patriarch's disfigured head, every movement heavy with melancholy. She took herself slowly upstairs to the loft.

The loft.

What would she ever do without it? It was her nearest thing to a private chapel, her first resort in times of hope, her final refuge in despair. She was on a knife's edge now, her entire life hanging by a thread. She needed to be alone with her fears, her hopes, in the comforting light of the great window, yet someone else was already up there, waiting: Isaac. He confronted her as she opened the door, a boy leaning against the glass, his face as blank as ever. She had tried finishing him every day since returning home from Bourne, but Adam the Younger had already faded from memory and she could no longer recapture that special look. A crack in one corner hadn't helped her confidence, but that could be patched over later, if only she could get started again.

"What do I do now?" she asked the boy while resting the egg next to her paint box. "Your father and mine—what do they care! I'm a painter first, a woman second, his property never. You fulfilled your destiny. How do I fulfil mine?"

Isaac kept his secret, whatever it was.

"There is hope for me yet," she reminded herself. "Papa can't hold out much longer. He will agree to my terms."

Isaac looked doubtful.

"There is a chance he might not give in by noon," she conceded. "I could go to the dance on my own. But what then?"

She broke the egg, pierced the yolk sack and released the golden contents into a small dish, gathering little gleams of hope from the sticky life at her fingertips. She added a drop of vinegar and mixed some powders in it, creating a dark base for the features of Isaac's face. But as soon as she applied it to the brush, she began wondering where to start and how the boy should look or even why it was important to get him finished. The paint dried on the bristles before she could use it. Again and again she tried to create his face and each time nothing happened. She stood in front of him for what seemed like hours, struggling with her emotions, striving to seem as blank as he was, so that nobody who interrupted her here would ever guess the turmoil she was in. Morning dragged on towards noon as her hopes tottered on the brink of failure, and all the while she longed for the sound of footsteps on the stairs, her father coming to apologise, to plead, to surrender to her terms. When at last the footsteps came, they were Matilda's.

"There is a man here to see you!" she announced, breathlessly clinging to the door. "The handsomest man I ever did set eyes on. Guy Loveday. I have heard stories of a sea captain of that name with those maddening looks. It must be him."

He must really be worth a good look if Matilda had come to the loft for his sake: she was afraid of the stairs, being almost a ladder for steepness. Susanna ventured onto the little balcony, far enough to espy a well-dressed, well-made figure waiting with Farthings in the hall below.

"What does he want?"

"Your father didn't say."

Susanna stepped out of her pattens and made her way quietly down to the next balcony, gliding then to her bedroom. She put on some slippers and a respectable cloak, submitting next to a bit of hair brushing from Matilda before calmly descending the hall stairs. The visitor was indeed ridiculously handsome, as if conjured up by Matilda in a dream, the ultimate fantasy lover, male sexuality served piping hot in shapely hose, a pert doublet, exuberant cloak and natty bonnet. He also happened to be very charming, bowing deeply with a great doffing of his hat before smiling again as he straightened on her arrival at ground level. She barely resisted the urge to throw one of her slippers at him.

"Yes?" she asked curtly.

"This is Guy Loveday, a friend of the king," said Farthings on his behalf. "I sent word to the Lord Chamberlain that we wouldn't be coming to the dance. The Lord Chamberlain must have spoken to His Majesty, because His Majesty has sent us Loveday, as our personal escort."

Everything about Loveday, including his name, seemed dangerous. He was about her own age, his hair a wealth of auburn curls, his face a volatile mix of pride and shamelessness, eyes smouldering reflections of desire, mouth loitering with a burglar's intent, nose heroic, chin cloven like a devil's hoof, throat reaching into his manly garments with a promise of more bare skin to come, if she dared follow him, and a red welt under his Adam's apple—a battle scar? If he had been the king, she would have gone with him anywhere. Instead, she remained true to her original purpose.

"Utrecht, Papa."

Loveday mimed a heart-broken appeal. Her resolve turned to curiosity instead.

"Why doesn't he speak?" she wondered.

"It is a mercy he doesn't," said Matilda, who had followed her downstairs and now stood eavesdropping on the bottom step. "If he sounded as well as he looks——"

"Go back upstairs and await my displeasure!" Susanna told her.

Matilda retreated upstairs and meanwhile Farthings unrolled a parchment for Susanna to peruse, revealing exquisitely formed letters that resembled a work of art more than just a page of writing. She had never learned to read but she could make out the letters forming Edward's name at the bottom, with Roman numerals signifying that he was the fourth king of that name, underscored by a seal that must surely be the mirror of his personal signet ring.

"An invitation in the king's own hand," Farthings explained. "It says that he desires the pleasure of your company at Baynard Castle, for dances, feasting, mirth and good times. A bold undertaking for a Friday! How unlike the previous king! This is not just an invitation, Susanna. This is a test of loyalty."

She could see her brother in one corner of the hall, pacing about in fervent prayer, hands clasped under his chin. Meanwhile one of Loveday's attendants stepped forward with some fabric neatly folded over the forearms. The sea rogue knelt on the floor at Susanna's feet, took command of the fabric and held it out to her, his head bowed.

"It is a gift from His Majesty, the invitation says," Farthings commented after another glance at the parchment. "A gown made from silk, all the way from the Far East. The needlework is Flemish, I think, the design Italian. The best workmanship and materials in all the world! I reckon it between ten and twenty pounds. Our money problems are solved already."

It felt unreal, the fabric so delicate, it touched her hands as softly as eyelashes, yet the style of the gown and its embroidery were an enigma, hidden by the folds. She could hardly wait to try it on.

"I cannot accept," she said, fingering the gift as lovingly as if it were hers already.

"You must accept," Farthings whispered. "His Majesty won't be denied."

Loveday began an irresistible mime, begging her to come. Some of the mime needed an interpreter and Farthings obliged.

"He has brought a royal galley for us," he revealed. "It is tied up outside the bishop's palace, ready to take us to the castle. Red, My Girl—Susanna—you can't say No, not now."

"Even so … even so," she stammered, the momentousness of a royal invitation beginning to dawn on her. "I don't think I can go, unless … I might go. No, I will go. Wait."

She carried the gown up the stairs, forcing herself not to hurry. Matilda stood waiting for her in their bedroom, eager to study the gift. They removed the cheesecloth shutter and studied the workmanship in full sunlight. The fashion and embroidery were striking, the garment divided diagonally between black and white, a golden sun marking the right breast, a silver moon the left. Shimmering peacocks sported under the sun, grey owls drifted under the moon. It was a masterpiece and it turned out a good fit, the fabric stretching to accommodate Susanna's finely muscled limbs and broad shoulders. The sleeves came a little short but that was easily hidden with some quick needlework and a bit of lace. All that was needed then was a matching cloak, a head-dress and a pair of shoes.

"I have nothing to go with this gown," Susanna lamented. "Nothing so beautiful."

"Trust me!"

Matilda opened both her own clothes chest and Susanna's then plunged her arms into the folded fabrics like a washerwoman at two tubs, pulling out different colours and designs until settling on the one cloak that matched perfectly. It was one of Matilda's own cloaks, the exotic threads reflecting the eyes of the peacock tails. Next, she judged between competing head-dresses, finally choosing yet another of her own things, though something she rarely wore: a simple velvet cap, a gossamer-thin veil hovering around it as lightly as a mist. Finally, she brought out Susanna's shoes—her own were too big—and agonised over which pair complemented the gown's bold contrast of black and white. Suddenly a moment of genius took hold of the wily maid and she made a new pair of shoes, comprising one white shoe and one black, each a different design but all the more striking for the boldness of the contrast. Susanna accepted all her selections. Matilda was an artist in these matters.

Grooming came next. Matilda brushed the coppery locks as if polishing an icon in the temple of Love, then applied the makeup as if it were a sacrament. A small but costly mirror of Venetian glass, held at arm's length, allowed Susanna to keep an eye on progress, Matilda turning the face into a haunting moon of white powder, slowly restoring the best details to a clearer copy of themselves, gradually making the brow and nose a shade more distinct, the cheeks a pinch redder, the eyelashes a touch more lustrous, the mouth—the mouth, she said, was already a red rose: nothing should be added to it. The modest cap and transparent veil were the final addition, a coy covering that complemented rather than concealed the beauty confronting Susanna in her little mirror.

"If only I were the mirror!" gasped Matilda from beside the faithful glass. "We would astonish each other."

Guy Loveday looked astonished too. He led the way to the wharf backwards. The royal galley offered Susanna a chance to be astonished in turn, a gilt frame purposely made for people to look beautiful in, rowers waiting in glittering brocade, oars held upright in manly salute. Even Farthings seemed handsome in this setting, reclining amid purple cushions like a middle-aged Cupid, albeit with a wounded shin, a smudge of blood from his kitchen injury gradually staining his straw-coloured hose. Meanwhile Loveday looked so handsome, Susanna could hardly bring herself to look at him. He must have been born to this setting, with eyes brooding over unfathomable depths, and a lascivious smile flashing around his lips as obscenely as a fish's tail.

Approaching midstream, the royal galley was joined by a flotilla of other boats emerging from between the pylons of London Bridge, all slowly converging on the castle upstream. The passengers were all in their best finery, carried as delicately as if they were eggs in an artist's fingers, all part of a great picture now painting itself in Susanna's presence: lords and ladies, rich merchants and their courtesans, dowagers and their sycophants, Italian financiers, their wives and laughing daughters, English bishops and their mysterious concubines, plus a swarm of local celebrities, foreign dignitaries and a host of others.

"Such a pretty splash if they all fell in!" Susanna couldn't help observing.

"People like those don't fall in," Farthings observed.

"Not at this hour," she conceded. "His Majesty chose the right moment."

The river was often much higher on one side of the bridge than the other, its tidal surges choked off by massive pylons, regularly producing a torrent between them, where water angrily spilled down to its natural level. The currents near the bridge were sometimes strong enough to snatch boats even from their moorings, finally spitting the fragments out into the calmer waters below. Upstream and downstream however were in perfect balance just now, the Thames bridging the pylons with a calm surface, a golden opportunity for its children to display themselves in all their stately brilliance. A daughter of the river, sensitive to its moods from the moment she was first cradled by its banks, Susanna sensed its rhythms bearing her in particular towards a day and night of triumph, a woman first, a painter second.

*"**Tom Roussell**, the great champion of the Lancastrian cause, put out of action by a couple of broken fingers!"*

313

Easy was carefully wrapping a bandage around Tom's left hand, taunting him for idleness, and Tom was trying hard not to wince or look embarrassed. Both men were accustomed to injuries and they had suffered worse breaks to their bones than this. Easy had even lost some of his fingers. All that Tom really needed was to rest his hand for a few weeks. Hence the bandage. His idleness was harder to explain and he hadn't even made the effort.

"I was tired, that's all," he now pleaded.

"But will you be going out today?" Easy persisted, completing the bandage with an elegant knot. "The sooner we find your brother, the sooner we are gone."

"Don't forget the buttons."

"Then you *are* going out!" Easy concluded while buttoning Tom's jacket for him. "Anywhere must be better than this ruinous pigeon loft."

Pigeons could get in through a hole in the eaves, and sometimes flapped about the room in a fit of alarm, whenever Wakefield barked at them, as he often did, but Easy was quite mistaken. Worse, far worse that the loft was a warehouse that had once served the fishing fleet, and which was now home to Cancer, Aquarius and Pisces, not to mention Noah. It was all Tom's worst nightmares, the horror of water, rolled into one spot, within spitting distance of the mighty Thames. And as if that weren't bad enough, Farthings was clearly desperate to find a husband for his troublesome daughter, and she was beautiful enough to tempt a man, even in spite of his better instincts. Fortunately, however, nobody could send Tom back there if they couldn't find him. On the other hand, he couldn't find Peter if he didn't go out looking. Easy had done all the searching yesterday and nothing had come of it.

"Where first?" Easy asked as they headed down the creaking stairwell.

"Lombard Street. Maybe my Italian informant has earned his second pound."

Lombard Street however turned out to be mysteriously quiet this morning, both ends visible through a thin crowd of Englishmen.

"Is it a holiday?" Easy wondered.

"A holiday for Italians," Tom guessed, since there wasn't a glimpse of one anywhere, not even under the eaves or in the doorways, places where the bankers and their shifty clerks usually touted for business.

"Finding your brother has just got a whole lot simpler," Easy observed. "Now we only have to find *all* the Italians."

The mystery was soon solved by a town crier, shouting above the lowing of a cattle pen and the crowing of a poultry yard, where Lombard Street converges with Cornhill and Threadneedle Streets.

"*Hear ye, hear ye, hear ye!*" he cried after a great ring of his handbell. "His Majesty, our glorious King Edward, lunches today with London's Italian community, at Baynard Castle, with dances as main entertainment, promoting peace, prosperity and trust between all good men and true, all at no cost to the burghers of this great city!"

"That's a party I wouldn't mind gate-crashing," Tom responded with a laugh, because bravado is always good in the mornings. "All we need is a battering ram and a few hundred friends of our own."

"Do you think Peter is at the castle?"

"I hope not."

"*Hear ye, hear ye, hear ye!*" the crier continued after another ring of his handbell. "His Majesty, our glorious King Edward, leads a Friendship Tour Lincolnshire-way, departing this Sunday, with Lord Hastings and other worthies, promoting a peaceful Lent for all good men and true, all at no cost to the burghers of this great city!"

Here was a new mystery.

"A *Friendship Tour?*" Easy wondered. "What do you make of it, Squire?"

"Good men and true won't object, if it's for real."

"You think it could be a trap?"

"A trap for someone."

This was followed by a growl, Tom's dog alerting them to an approaching threat.

"But what comes here?" Easy wondered next.

"Maybe the king read our minds."

Men-at-arms, bearing swords, pikes and longbows were advancing down Lombard Street and others were rushing to block off Cheapside.

"Look there!" said Easy, pointing out an archer among them, easily recognised by his habit of walking sometimes in a crouch, sometimes high on his toes, as if stalking deer over a hedge, or defending a parapet. Most people in a position to know had long nominated him the greatest archer in all England, certainly the most accurate: Jack *Murderer* Shaft. Easy considered himself a rival: "The arrogant prick couldn't face me alone."

"Easy, Easy," said Tom. "No trouble today, if you please."

The archers stopped short to take aim and a single man came forward, swaggering on foot as if he were twelve feet tall. Tom recognised this man too, partly thanks to the swagger but mainly on account of the coat he wore over a padded jacket: a red hand on a white background. The red hand seemed to reach towards Tom with every step that brought them closer together. The last time they had met was inside a cell on a cold night in Royston, where he had given Tom a parting kick in return for all his insolence towards Lord Grey. Tom's unbroken fingers reached instinctively for his only weapon, a common knife.

"Easy, Squire," said Easy. "You are just a legend these days."

"Says who?"

"The flab around your belly."

"It doesn't show."

"You are no match for this man and you know it."

The Red Knight's skills in combat, demonstrated so publicly at Fotheringhay Castle, were too shocking to be kept quiet, and Tom had mentioned them to Easy over more than one jug of ale. Comparisons made him feel soft and prematurely aged. He let go of his knife without further prompting.

"We meet again," said the Red Knight, arriving close enough to rub noses.

"I'm sorry—have we met before?"

"Are you blind, Beast of Ferrybridge?"

"Either that or you're blocking my view."

"I'll give you more room if you are ready to fight me, you coward."

"You were sent here as an errand boy, so quit the chatter and let's hear it."

"The pleasure of your company is earnestly solicited at Baynard Castle!" came the response, with a mocking bow.

"You are being ironic now."

"Only because you won't fight."

"I don't have a sword."

"Would you like the lend of one?"

This was an invitation best ignored.

"Easy and I were just deciding whether or not we might join the king for some dancing. Are you and I to be partners?"

"Lose the knife," the Red Knight shot back. "You won't be needing it."

"Now you are getting personal," Tom objected, resting a proprietorial hand on the hilt of the item in question, more a kitchen utensil than a weapon. "I wasn't aware that Lord Grey had any authority here in London. Who sent you?"

"Heraldry is another of your weaknesses, or are you really blind?"

Thus invited, Tom looked past the Red Knight and eyed the liveries of his comrades. Murderer had now lowered his bow, directing some pikes to guard an alley, which exposed his coat of arms. Skilled archers were always in high demand, and Murderer had often changed his coat, going wherever pay was best. Today's version featured a blue sash, enclosing the tell-tale cross of St George: the Order of the Garter. Evidently his latest paymaster was somebody close to the king, or close enough to throw his weight around even here in London. There could be no wriggling out of this encounter.

"Let me guess," said Tom: "Murderer is in command here, and you merely volunteered to be an arsehole."

"Knife!" the red arsehole insisted, holding out his human hand.

Tom passed the knife to Easy, who then surrendered it on his behalf. The Red Knight tried not to look peeved but he was one of those pricks that can't helping resenting even minor insults.

"Why do you still work for this has-been?" he asked Easy.

"He's not so bad once you get to know him," came the lame reply.

"Get all the rest of his gear and head for the Mandeville house in Southwark. This has-been comes with me."

Tom nodded his reluctant assent. Easy took Wakefield by the collar and set off with him to collect their belongings, with a small detachment of guards in attendance. The Red Knight headed off in another direction, and Tom followed on his heels, surrounded by the rest of the troop, mostly youngsters looking nervous. Someone must have told them old stories about the Beast of Ferrybridge. Meanwhile Murderer loitered in the rear, ready as ever to release an arrow. The Red Knight was right about one thing: Tom had never been one for all the finer points of heraldry, or he would have known from the intricate devices on the coats around him which Knight of the Garter had sent for him. He asked one of the youngsters.

"Read-a-lot," came the tense answer.

This wasn't a name that Tom was familiar with but he had no doubts about who was meant. In Lancastrian circles, the eminent thug was more widely known as *Book*, because he never went anywhere without one in his hand, if it wasn't too heavy, otherwise it followed him on a portable lectern, strapped to the back of a servant. Other names for him (polite ones) were John Tiptoft, earl of Worcester, and sometimes *Monster of Ireland*. A nobleman by birth, a brute by choice and a scholar by training, he had a cruel streak as long as the Thames, Humber and Irish Sea put together. Tom tried not to feel or show the knot of dismay tightening in his throat. His archer, his dog and his property were on their way to the Mandeville house but that was no guarantee he would join them soon or even in one piece.

Baynard Castle lay in a westerly part of the city, next to the river, whose water could be glimpsed through the gated arch at the end of an adjacent street. The castle wall was part of London's riverside defences, but it was still separated from the city by walls all its own, if you could find them in the jumble of neighbouring houses and lanes. The original castle, built by the Normans, had first seen daylight as a partner to the Tower of London, further downstream, the city being caught in the middle, like a prisoner splayed between fetters. London still shrank from the Tower but it had now intruded on Baynard Castle, tall buildings nudging the ancient parapets and even peering into arrow slits. Tom could imagine neighbours on either side leaning out from their embrasures and windows to borrow an egg or a cup of flour, yet the crenelated gatehouse was still patrolled by helmets, halberds and bows, reminders of a deeper truth: London wasn't all good neighbours. Today the approaches happened to be crowded with the horses, litters and servants of His Majesty's guests, waiting for their masters to have done with fun, so they could go back home to Lombard Street, or wherever else they had come from. There were also some wagons, loaded with folded tents, possibly preparations for the so-called *Friendship Tour*.

Tom followed the Red Knight into the northern gatehouse, where a porter treated him to an indiscreet search for weapons. Murderer took some stairs, probably to the parapet—a good vantage point for shooting guests who outstay their welcome—and then the Red Knight led Tom into the courtyard. Here carpenters were busy, erecting a scaffold at one end. It looked ominously like an execution was about to take place. The Red Knight however pointed out a door at the other end, at the foot of a tower.

"Two friends of yours are waiting at the top," he said. "Time matters even for you has-beens, so tarry not, Beast of Ferrybridge."

The braggart smirked unpleasantly before swaggering across the courtyard and disappearing into a laneway, followed by Tom's entire escort. There was something mysterious about all this. The Beast of Ferrybridge wasn't so tame these days that his enemies should leave him unguarded, especially not here in the king's London residence. However, it was best to do as directed, so he made for the tower door, then carefully proceeded up some steep stairs, past storerooms, dormitories and guardrooms, all the while keeping his back to the wall as much as possible, because a man could be murdered here and nobody would be any wiser. As it turned out, the Red Knight had spoken the truth. Two friends really were waiting for Tom, and time really did matter here. The ancient tower had been converted into a clock tower, with ropes, pulleys and massive weights dangling through a hole in an upper floor, through which Tom observed two men tinkering with an elaborate mechanism of cogs, wheels and capstans. He recognised them immediately.

Not all Lancastrians who had gone over to the Yorkist side were villains or craven opportunists—they were not all like Lord Grey, the Red Knight's master. Some were honourable men whose chivalry and good sense always entitled them to respect, whatever side they were on, and that included these two. One, formerly a Lancastrian provisioner, was now the chaplain at Baynard Castle, and he had always been skilled in mechanical devices, especially clocks. The other, a fearless knight and talented administrator, was now so trusted by the York-ists, he had been made captain of the King's Own Company, based upstream at Westminster. Technically they were more like enemies than friends but Tom was as happy to see them as if they were his friends still. They were happy to see him too but there was little time for greetings. They stuck their fingers in their ears and urged him to do likewise, whereupon a sudden movement in the mechanism caused a capstan to turn, a weight to descend, ropes to creak and pulleys to groan, followed almost immediately by a terrific clanging from a bell two floors overhead. It was the worst time for broken fingers, and Tom only managed to plug one ear, while he counted the chimes for twelve o'clock.

Susanna had often imagined herself arriving by boat at His Majesty's London residence. The reality, seen up close, took her by surprise. Massive walls rose from the river in the manner of a forbidding cliff, demanding to know what business such a common, insignificant woman could ever have with them. Her confidence wavered like the ripples plashing against the stones. She had never made love to a man before, not a real man. A bit of half-hearted kissing and fondling from Witless William, her rape by Bertram Kilsby, and the sneaking kiss the Beast had snatched from her at Huntingdon were no preparation for the king of England. Yet here she was, the woman who would be his mistress, as bold as daylight.

Her gilded galley nosed past the castle's commercial wharf, then past His Majesty's private wharf, before arriving at the public wharf, where all the other guests were alighting. Here a bevy of obsequi-ous pages greeted everyone as they stepped ashore, and here the sea rogue, Guy Loveday, left with a wry shrug, the royal galley bearing him away on other errands, still looking as if his heart might break. It was a fetching mime, lips pouting with a pleasurable kind of pain, aching to be kissed. Susanna was glad to be rid of him. She wanted to give all her attention to the king, whenever he should appear. She expected him to greet her personally now that she had got this far, and she was disappointed that he didn't. His officious minions did all the courtesies on his behalf, minus his regal grace and manly presence of course. A steward at the riverside gatehouse ticked her name off a list as if she were a shipment of apples, assigning her and Farthings to a table named *Unicorn*, said to be the name of a ward in Florence. Her appearance caused a stir wherever she went but otherwise she was treated no better than any other guest. You would never know that His Majesty had sent for her especially and that her gown, peeping from under a shimmering cloak, was his personal gift.

They were ushered through the riverside gatehouse and into what must once have been the castle bailey, now more like a London ward, crowded with buildings and fissured with lanes. A minstrel entertained them briefly along the main street, gliding from one visitor to another, until they reached a massive barbican, where they joined a throng pooling outside another gate. Here they waited a short time until the arrival of noon, heralded by the castle bell striking an ominous twelve times—an absurd number of hours, it had always seemed to Susanna, since the eight hours rung by Church towers give plenty of time for monks to chant, the faithful to reflect on their lives in prayer, and painters to paint at their leisure. The barbican mercifully shielded her ears from the repeated din, and she was wondering if mechanical clocks have bell-ringers, and how they manage to survive the uproar, when the gates opened and a merry flurry of pages in carnival masks and parti-coloured pantaloons came cascading down a flight of steps, summoning everyone into their separate groups. *Unicorn* was the first to be led in. Now Susanna began to feel privileged above all others, as the hubbub of the crowd outside grew distant and the architecture grew softer, stone walls yielding to gilded furnishings, exquisite tapestries and timber panels as warm as a suntan. She felt as if she had slipped a hand inside His Majesty's armour.

The sensation of intimacy didn't last long. The great hall wasn't ready yet for a banquet, servants still on ladders, garlanding walls with paper flowers, still laying carpets of rushes over damp stones, still scrubbing

benches and tables. Unicorn continued damp even while guests, mostly
Italians, seated themselves. Susann didn't mind Italians in moderation, or
at least not as much as she minded a damp bench. She admired them as
painters of course, almost the equal of the Dutch, if not better (opinions
under St Sebastian's window varied), yet she shared an English mistrust
of them, as a race of bankers. These ones were true to type. They used
hand gestures to support their broken English as eloquently as if they
were painting portraits, but frequently reverted to unfathomable Italian,
in the manner of bankers secretly calculating profit margins. Farthings
discussed business with them as if it were the menu. Susanna tried ignoring everyone and everything but the occasion itself, and meanwhile
the middle of the hall gradually filled with knights, baronets and their
ladies, and then the front of the hall filled with even more important
dignitaries, lords of the Church and lords of the realm, their ladies and
stewards, loyal gamekeepers and pet monkeys, as ever more servants
came and went in preparation for the start of the banquet, assembling
basins, towels and ewers on side-tables, everything ripening.

A sudden flourish of trumpets! Everyone arose from their seats in
expectation of a great arrival.

Yes, His Majesty! He appeared, as usual, in the distance, glimpsed
through a forest of heads and shoulders, yet he still cut an imposing
figure, as tall as a siege tower, as colourful as a city fair, smiling as
imperiously as a man born to rule, as sincerely as a true friend. There
really was no such thing as distance with this man. He could touch
her heart from anywhere. Ascending the royal dais and situating himself on the other side of a canopied table, he waved a bold welcome
to the entire hall. He sat. Everyone else sat, or dropped, breathless
with admiration. It was only then that Susanna noticed, like a guilty
secret, a small woman sitting next to His Majesty: the Ah-Ha creature
herself, a woman trying hard to be a queen, a queen trying hard to
be a woman. What did the king see in her? She looked pretty from a
distance, even beautiful once perhaps, but something in her manner
evoked a woman who is weary of everything, herself most of all. At
least it appeared that way from the back of the hall.

The master of ceremonies strode to the front of the dais: Lord
Hastings. He looked more impressive than when Susanna had seen

him in the chapter house at the Royston priory. Here he was dressed for office, his Lord Chamberlain's robe bearded with lace and draped in magisterial chains, while he banged his mace on the floor as if he thought himself every inch a true lord, whereas Susanna knew him to be the idiot that had released the Beast from custody and, worse still, who had inserted the arch-Lancastrian into her household, as sergeant-at-arms. Never the less he obtained the assembly's respectful silence and then thanked everyone for coming. He especially thanked the king's Italian friends because, he said, they were paying for everything. Dancing, he added, was an Italian forte, and the English guests would be paying in blisters and aching sinews. The jest was rewarded with some undeserved laughter. Susanna barely found the patience to listen, until he began spelling out the important details: there were to be eight dances only, with four scheduled for the end of the first course, timed for one o'clock, and another four at the end of the second, timed for two o'clock. There would be no dancing after the third course, he added, because everyone by then would be too fat or too tired even to lift a finger, let alone a foot. He paused for more laughter. He said and did some other things of a more ceremonial nature, while servants passed through the hall bearing finger-bowls of rose water and towels scented with lavender.

Susanna and Farthings washed and dried their hands, ready for the first course. This was the happy half of Friday, when strict abstinence ends and only birds, cloven-footed animals and dairy foods are excluded from the menu. A king's kitchen can make a banquet out of anything, and anything out of almost anything else, so that every dish is spiced with curiosity, if not downright scandal. It all arrived like a Mediterranean Spring, with a vegetable concoction impersonating braised kidneys, neatly presented in baskets of dried fruits, jostled by dishes of robust olives, trays of bread rolls stuffed with the likeness of scrambled eggs (the eggs were said by a servant to be almond paste coloured with saffron), cups of almond milk with islands of strawberry wafers, and more than Susanna could look at let alone sample, climaxing at her table in pickled pears and fried mushrooms, sprinkled with parsley and thyme, all housed under a raspberry-topped pastry shell, representing what looked like a woman's breast but which was said to be the dome of a Florentine cathedral. Everything was washed down with a red wine while sweet music floated from the gallery.

The remnants of the enormous first course began to be carried off to the scullery, the second course began to be assembled on side-tables, and Susanna was thinking she had already eaten too much, when Lord Hastings appeared on the dais once more, this time proposing a series of toasts, first to the king, then to some Italian dignitaries, and finally to jolly Bacchus, the Roman hero of wine and dancing, because, he said, it was fast approaching the hour for the first round of dances. The courtyard was ready for frivolity and all that was needed now, he solemnly declared, was a signal from the heavens, whereupon he cupped a hand around one ear, listening for the signal, and almost immediately the castle bell struck one. People applauded, as if he might be a magician or a wit, but Susanna folded her arms in protest—a magician he might be, a wit never, or the Beast would have remained locked up—until the moment the stewards began motioning everyone towards the main doorway, when she was among the first on her feet, unable to resist a growing sense of excitement.

There were supposed to be four dances after each course, she recalled, and she had yet to be told when her turn would come. She could feel her heart about to burst, hoping yet almost fearing to be the king's first partner—a few days' dancing lessons no longer seemed sufficient—but still she reached the doorway almost before anyone else, Farthings close on her heels. Outside was a courtyard she hadn't seen till now, its gatehouse accessed from the city, and she paused on the stairs to take in the view. Attendants, in a variety of liveries, were loitering around the edges of the yard, waiting to be of service to their betters; meanwhile labourers were spreading sand over the cobbles and, nearer the stairs, maids were garlanding a large, wooden platform.

"A dais for the king and his partners to dance on!" Farthings observed. "A great day for us Mandevilles."

They were soon pressured off the steps by people arriving behind them, and then it no longer seemed such a great day to Susanna. The pushy crowd, the lack of recognition (as if she were just another guest), the lack of information, the last-minute preparations by castle staff, the feeling that her own preparations had been too few and too rushed—everything reminded her of a poorly made sketch, unworthy of the work it was preparation for. Meanwhile guests continued to issue from the hall, and stewards kept ushering Susanna and Farthings ever deeper into the yard, ever further from the dancing platform, until they found themselves standing with a crowd of servants, waiting on their masters' beck and call. Most were Italians, their liveries not so loud as the English version, except in full sunlight, when they blushed in extravagant detail. One of them Susanna already knew too well: Signor Antonio Della Bosca.

"What is *he* doing here?" she remonstrated with her father.

"Where better for a dance instructor?"

"*Thief*, you mean."

"If the king loses his crown, we'll know where to look. But let the man earn a living. He still owes me for the hire of the hall."

Antonio's assistant, Pietro, also came into view.

"And what is *he* doing here?"

"Good question!"

Pietro was skipping around a piece of furniture—a tall candle on a wooden stand, its three feet carved in the likeness of a lion's paws—clockwise in the robust manner of a cocky male, anticlockwise in the mincing steps of a coquettish female.

"He has found his ideal partner," Susanna observed. "They both have wooden feet. How did such a clumsy man ever come to be a dance instructor?"

"It is a world of imposters," said Farthings. "I don't think he's Italian."

"I don't either. Why the disguise, do you think?"

"For dance instructors and bankers, it pays to be Italian."

"The moustache isn't Italian."

"He is part Catalonian, I was told."

The last guests to issue from the hall were some of the greatest nobles and magnates of the realm, requiring lots of space to be admired in. Stewards ushered everyone else still further and further back, until Susanna found herself standing among labourers who had been spreading sand just moments ago. As soon as the stewards withdrew, she pressed forward again, shouldering aside first her equals, then some of her social betters, while Farthings came behind, apologising for her as they went. They soon reached a point where further advancement would be unwise, coming at the expense of people too important to upset, without any compensating improvement in the view, and there Susanna stopped, unsure if she liked the view or not.

His Majesty was emerging from the hall, leading his little queen down the steps as if she were an obedient spaniel out for a recreational walk, and then he led her up the steps to the dance platform, where they both paused for the polite notice of the assembly. There they were soon joined by a handful of other couples—English nobles and leading lights of the Italian community—all smiling, all pleased to be seen in each other's company, until the dance started, when they all became very solemn. It was a tedious affair, accompanied by two shawms and a drone, harmonised at a slow tempo, the steps so simple, Susanna had learned them in a single day. It was a *bassadanza*, a stately dance if done with feeling, now just a dull parade for a drab queen, the Ah-Ha mistaking her every move for an object of universal wonder. When it came her own turn to dance with His Majesty, Susanna knew she could do it with more life than *that*.

After another dance, as tedious as the first, the queen finally quit the platform. It was a breath of fresh air for the king and he was suddenly in a jovial mood, shouting to all his guests below to make spaces for themselves on the cobbles, if they wanted to share in the fun of the *saltarello furioso*. It was one of the most challenging dances of all and yet a section of the crowd promptly formed into circles, so that Susanna and Farthings were once more forced out to the edges. By the time she had again thrust and angled her way towards a satisfactory view of her perfect man, he had been joined on the platform by some new couples, and a solitary creature of extraordinary beauty, blonde ringlets framing a flawless face. Only an unmarried woman—one as bold as Susanna—would dare show as much hair as this.

"Who is *she*?" Susanna wondered.

"Elizabeth Shore," Farthings explained.

"The one you saw in the king's bed," Susanna recalled with horror. "But she's married. She has a nerve, parading herself in public like this!"

"The king calls her *Jane*, I have been told."

"Why *Jane?*"

"She shares *Elizabeth* with the queen."

"But why so much hair?"

"Italian wives are not so prudish about displaying theirs, and she shows hers in their honour, I think."

"She should be at home with her husband, darning his underwear!" Susanna complained, giving vent to the aunt within her. "It's shameful."

The king was enjoying himself in the woman's company even now. Susanna had been performing this form of saltarello with the Beast when his beard had fallen off but there was no such awkwardness about His Majesty. He leapt into the air with a glad cry, clapped his hands and landed again on the platform with marvellous grace, highlighted by the resounding thud of his regal physique impacting on wooden boards. The goldsmith's wife sprang into his arms with a merry twitter, circled him provocatively, simpered at his elbow and generally flaunted herself like one of the Bishop of Winchester's Geese, and yet no Goose ever looked or moved quite like *Jane.* There was something altogether desperate about the woman's antics, Susanna soon decided. When it came her own turn to dance with His Majesty, she knew she could do it with more dignity than *that.*

Meanwhile Susanna was under scrutiny herself. Lord Hastings was staring at her from the top of the hall steps, and he proved it by smiling and nodding to her when she chanced to look in his direction. Next, he descended into the crowd, his retinue clearing a path for him. The last time they had met, in the Royston priory, she had thrown herself at his feet, begging for the Beast to be kept behind bars, and all she had got in return was fondling from his sticky fingers, grandiose promises and a sergeant-at-arms a thousand times more odious than Lister with the blisters. The fact that that bad turn was preparation for a good turn, if Hastings could get his way somehow, hardly improved her opinion of him. She could feel her hackles rising with every step he took towards them.

"Here beauty awaits partnering!" he announced after she gave him a token bow of respect. "I'm your first dance, when this one ends."

"My daughter will be delighted and honoured," Farthings replied, making a deeper bow than she had ever seen him make to anyone before.

He was always trying to match her with the wrong man, and this seemed to be the latest example.

"I came here to dance with the king," she reminded them both.

"I scheduled that dance," said Lord Hastings, pausing for a hiccough, "for two o'clock, after the second course."

"Like a wonderful dessert," Farthings dared to add.

"*Dessert?*" she objected. "How about the bowl of cream the German got?"

It was a private joke but the alarm in the look that Farthings shot her next was not lost on the Lord Chamberlain.

"Is there a problem?"

"This is something like the trouble I mentioned yesterday," Farthings babbled.

"Ah yesterday! But tell me, Farthings: any sign of Roussell yet? A Will o' the Wisp, that Beast of Ferrybridge. But he shall be found, found and returned to your watch and care, the soonest it can be managed."

"He should never have been released from his cell in Royston," Susanna couldn't help complaining.

This elicited a monstrous grin.

"You are safe here with me," he assured her.

"This wouldn't be the first dance he has sneaked into!" she countered. "He managed it at our house in a fake beard."

"A fake beard!" came the reply, Hastings peering about with a preposterously contrived look of concern. "There aren't many beards in England, fake or not, but we must keep our eyes out for it, in case it harbours that notorious rebel, the Beast of Ferrybridge."

"Are you drunk?" she marvelled.

Farthings grimaced apologetically.

"I deeply regret this insolence," he pleaded after a desperate glance at her. "I was planning to send her to Utrecht, but not now—not if she continues like this."

"Utrecht?"

"She likes to paint. The Dutch are masters at that sort of thing."

"Maybe she would dance with me if I were Dutch," Hastings observed with a haughty look. "But I am merely the Lord Chamberlain of England."

He bestowed an ironic bow on her then turned and headed back to the hall, looking very much like a peeved courtier intending to remove an insolent guest from His Majesty's list of dances. Susanna began to experience regret almost immediately. Why couldn't she be nice to an impertinent man at least once in her life, when so much was at stake! How much had her annoyance cost her this time?

The saltarello ended, another saltarello started, and still she was just a spectator, cooling her heels on the sand and cobbles while the goldsmith's wife practised more of her false charms on His Majesty. Susanna hated gazing on the spectacle but not as much as she hated thinking about her rudeness to the Lord Chamberlain just now, in case it spelt the end of her hopes. Eventually the music stopped, bringing this set of dances to a merciful end, whereupon everyone returned indoors for the next course. Susanna was such a mixture of emotions, she hardly knew where she was going, merely following the crowd. By the time she was fully conscious of her surroundings again, she was already seated back at Unicorn, next to her father, surrounded by the usual Italians, everyone greedily dipping knives and spoons into new dishes. She tasted nothing but the bitterness of remorse, too deafened by memories of her snide comments to Lord Hastings, and by his parting words of scorn, even to hear the music playing in the gallery, let alone the idle chatter of her fellow guests. If only she could go back in time, back to the courtyard, she could undo the damage to her hopes with just a smile for once and a few polite words, but what chance of that! She was more likely to regurgitate the first course, churning uneasily in her anxious stomach.

Time seemed to lose meaning, every moment measured by one awful realisation—she had come a hundred miles to dance with the king, and had spent ten years dreaming of a royal romance, only to ruin her chances within an hour of her wishes coming true—until a strange sensation began taking shape in her vicinity, an awareness of herself that many others shared, all eyes turning towards her. The unreality of her predicament rose to something big and uncanny, as Lord Hastings materialised at her elbow, offering her his hand once more.

"I'll take you to the king now, if you will permit me."

He looked sober. His fingers looked sober too. She rose to the proffered hand as if it were the king's own, this unexpected chance to redeem herself dawning on her with the insistence of a beating heart, the thrill of the moment heightening all her senses, even as every face turned to follow her progress along the hall, from the back of the room, where the least important guests sat, to the front, where the nobles and magnates had dined in magnificence and where the king now waited, eyes trained steadily on her alone. He was a dream. Would she wake before she reached him? He stood a full foot higher than Susanna, on long, shapely legs handsomely enclosed in coloured stockings. His barrel-sized chest seemed inflated as much by virility as by a voluminous cloak, the fabric a forest of shimmering threads, while his eyes twinkled with uncomplicated joy. She bowed of course. His magnificence deserved no less. He amazed her then with a kiss on the cheek, a touch as silky as the gown that was his gift. It was hard to believe that such manliness could be so tender and yet he was unquestionably real. He had been the last dignitary to venture from the hall for the previous set of dances, accompanied by his queen, and now he was the first to venture out, accompanied by Susanna. The courtyard appeared almost empty again, except now everything looked ready and utterly perfect.

"Our second dance!" he observed as they emerged into the sunlight together, the noise of a large crowd following them.

"Second dance?" she wondered, hardly able to comprehend the enormity of the moment.

"You were Maid Marian last time," he reminded her.

"No, I haven't forgotten that. The greatest day of my life!"

"Today will beat it."

"Nothing in my whole life could ever beat this," she couldn't help saying, her voice sounding strangely gauche.

"It means a lot to me too," he graciously declared. "I rushed this dance forward a quarter of an hour, I was so looking forward to seeing you again."

"I don't know what to say."

She had always known his company would lift her to new heights of happiness, and she actually felt larger in his presence, yet somehow less substantial, a creature as trite and bloated as a dandelion puff.

They were approaching the royal platform, where they would soon dance together, and she felt almost ready to float away.

"You are something of a mystery," he observed as they paused at the bottom of the steps, where some pages relieved them of their cloaks "I had heard that you can be unpleasant."

"I was rude to Lord Hastings a while ago," she recalled with horror. "I didn't mean to be!"

"Hastings was testing you out," he replied with a chuckle. "It is others that have warned me against you."

"People have no right to talk about me."

"*Brawling shrew?*"

"If sometimes I offend people," she humbly confessed, because a woman must be honest with her ideal man, or she wouldn't deserve him, "it is only because I want everything to be perfect, and sometimes, disappointment gets the better of me."

"I know what you mean," he responded with a smile. "I want things to be perfect too, but would you like to hear my remedy for a short temper? I just try to enjoy myself, whatever the situation might be, and then I don't mind things so much."

This was so frank, so perceptive, so charming, yet so surprising, she felt a sudden urge to kneel before him.

"Your Majesty!" she said, hitching up their gown in readiness for a genuflection. "Nature has made you the happiest and most regal of men."

He checked her impulse with a steadying hand on one of her elbows, keeping her on her feet.

"Just between you and me, *Edward* is fine," he advised her, still smiling. "Now I want you to give me all your attention, because I have an important request."

"I am all yours."

"Sometimes a man has to be forward, even if he is a king—especially a king—or events and duties get between him and his pleasures, so pardon me if all this sounds a bit sudden."

"Yes?"

"My friends and I are leaving this Sunday—the Friendship Tour. The criers have been announcing it all morning, and maybe you have heard? The plan is to travel into Lincolnshire, treating ourselves to a good time while making new friends along the way. You have just come back from that part of the world, I have been told."

"It's swarming with rebels," she warned him. "You must promise me not to expose yourself to danger, Your Majesty or I don't know how England can survive!"

"The queen's sister is coming too, so it is quite within a woman's abilities, if she doesn't mind roughing it a bit."

"You are asking *me* to come?" she marvelled.

The thought of days, weeks, maybe months in the company of her ideal man daunted her almost as much as the prospect of all the food yet to be served up at the banquet, another full course, including yet more dessert.

"Your father will come too," he offered, as if that might make things easier.

"Does he have to?"

"It's court protocol," he explained, and then he took both her hands in his. "Lord Hastings is giving him the news even now. It won't change my plans any. You and I shall have many opportunities to be alone. How seriously do you take Lent?"

"Not as seriously as my aunt. Lent started for her over a week ago."

"Six weeks from this Wednesday to Palm Sunday is long enough for most of us, and too long for a king. There is no such thing as abstinence when there is no such thing as rest. I go to the battlefield and I go to bed whenever I must, whatever the season. Are you ready for that kind of schedule?"

"I'm ready for anything!"

"The calendar that interests me most is written in the heavens," he added. "We are approaching the spring equinox now. When better for man and woman than the equinox, the nights as long as the days! I chose your gown with that thought in mind. You shall be my dawn and my sunset whenever you step in or out of it."

"Your Majesty!" she gasped, overjoyed to be wanted but alarmed too, because she could hear the crowd descending the steps towards them—close enough for their conversation to be overheard. "You mustn't say such things—not here."

"That matters to you?"

"You are the king of England," she reminded him. "Of course it matters."

"Hastings says you are ambitious to be a painter," he said, suddenly pulling her to him. "You will need a patron. Every painter must have a patron. Why not a king?"

"Oh my God," she marvelled, gripping his arms tightly and almost dancing already. "Oh yes, yes!"

"But now let's attend to the moment," he laughed as they prepared to ascend the platform together. "It's the *piva agitata*, one of my favourites."

"The *piva agitata*!" she gasped in dismay, for that style of dance was the most complex of all, the tempo too varied to be mastered in the few days she had been a student of Signor Della Bosca. "I can manage a saltarello."

His Majesty's face was a picture of polite disappointment.

"Never mind," he soon said, giving her hand a reassuring squeeze. "The final two dances are both saltarellos. You shall be mine then. So, I will be keeping the best till last!"

With that neat compliment, he left her and plunged into the crowd gathering around them. He soon emerged hand in hand with another woman, leading her up to the platform in Susanna's place, a ravishing brunette this time.

"Elizabeth Oldhall, the wife of a Smithfield saddler," said Farthings, suddenly appearing at Susanna's elbow.

"Another *Elizabeth*?" Susanna wondered with disdain. "Does she have a special title, like *Jane*? I can think of several that would suit."

"Just Elizabeth, as far as I know. She is another one on her way out, I have heard. But My Girl, My Girl, Lord Hastings has just told me: a Friendship Tour. Friends of the king! What friends we shall make, eh."

Oldhall was tall and elegant in a willowy kind of way, and oh so beautiful. Worse still, she could dance! She negotiated the piva agitata with ease, twice in a row in fact, a complicated series of rapid and slow moves executed with the energy of a squirrel hunting nuts, now stalking, now leaping, now mincing, now arching her back as if for a flirtatious scratch. Susanna bit her lip. When it came her own turn to dance with His Majesty, she knew she could never do it with as much style and vivacity as *that*. However, she took comfort from His Majesty's parting words: he was keeping the best till last. Naturally he was a man of his word. As soon as the music stopped again, he abandoned Oldhall like an old pastime and advanced on Susanna with enthusiasm.

"Now for the best," he reminded her.

Then it was Susanna's turn to be led onto the royal platform, the latest target for gossips and admirers in the crowd below, the loudest of them a plump, middle-aged man, bragging in a loud voice for all to hear, saying that he was her father and that she had been the prettiest child in all Southwark, now the most beautiful woman in all England.

"She takes after her mother's family for looks!" he shouted, glad to be heard everywhere. "God bless my dear wife. Yet Susanna takes her character from me: a will of iron and the heart of a lion! Those rebels in Lincolnshire don't scare us."

Susanna and the king were soon joined by a half dozen of his closest friends and their ladies, all standing in a charmed circle, smiling each to each and all to all. The two Elizabeths were there: Elizabeth Oldhall with Lord Hastings, and Elizabeth *Jane* Shore with a handsome baron. The third Elizabeth in that neighbourhood—Edward's drab but pretty wife—stood watching from the hall steps, a languid figure, crowded out of the dance by her namesakes and by a girl from Southwark. Susanna almost felt sorry for her, but not really, not while the only man that mattered in this world was all her very own, his left hand in her right, and the promise of his patronage still ringing in her ears. The painter from Southwark was destined for greatness and the world too seemed to know it, because the castle bell chose this very moment to strike two o'clock—once for His Majesty and once for her, or so it seemed. It was a new age, not just a new hour, and it was accompanied by the right music, strings and pipes conjuring up a happy, confident melody. Life would always be like this, Susanna reflected: a glorious dance for the beautiful and the strong, while sunlight reached over the high walls, flooding everything with surprising radiance.

The first steps were still being taken when there came a bewildering sound of angry cries, a stir becoming a tumult somewhere at the end of the yard. A trumpet sounded a frenetic alarm and the dance music stopped like a horse gone suddenly lame. The king's manly face grew dark and thunderous. Had rebels got inside the walls, and was the castle under attack? He took a mighty leap over the guard rail onto the cobbles below, bounding straight towards the centre of the disturbance. Susanna marvelled at his athleticism, his power and grace, his courage and daring, and she would have jumped after him had she been wearing a common skirt. Instead, she hurried down the steps. She couldn't bear to lose him now, no matter what dangers awaited her, and she wasn't alone, because two women left the platform with her, matching her stride for stride along the length of the courtyard, hot on His Majesty's heels: his previous mistresses, Oldhall and Shore.

Tom and his two friends chatted about old times, as if still living them, while they examined and tested the king's clock. It was currently losing about a fifth of an hour every day, and the castle chaplain was looking for ways to improve it. First, he realigned the small weights governing the *clink-clunk* of a swinging arm that he called a *foliot*, and meanwhile the three men reminisced about the Lancastrian victory at Wakefield. Next Tom helped make some adjustments to the rigging of the larger weights, and inspected ropes for chafing, while they all reflected on the Yorkist victory at Towton. Eventually the chaplain decided that many factors must be behind the lost time, all associated with the clock's age, which could only be improved by replacing the entire works. The three men all admitted to feeling a bit old too, thanks to their various injuries, yet Tom's friends could talk more confidently about the future than he could, since they had put themselves on the winning side.

The reunion was no accident of course. Tom had no doubt that they were under orders to draw him into the Yorkist camp, and where better than here, discussing past, present and future while they tinkered with a clock! Tom knew the clock to be a child of the growing city, its commerce and its industry. Its brother was the cannon, spawned in foundries. His loyalties however went back further than that, rooted in the rhythms of the countryside, and villages sheltering under the protection of castle walls. The bells of his childhood gave voice to the seasons, rung by monks, sending the faithful to the fields in the morning, and welcoming them home to the fold in the evening. Yet what warrior in this day and age, priding himself on his trade, can fail to admire the workings of a machine, an army of cogs and weights, ropes and pulleys, each moving in its own manner and at its own pace, yet all in unison! It was magic to watch, even if it lost one fifth of an hour every day.

Promotion, titles and wealth came quickly under King Edward's banners, his two friends said, provided a man has the necessary talent, as well as the wisdom to learn from his mistakes. Tom was England's greatest warrior but even he had made mistakes. Had he learned from them? It was a tempting offer. He envied them, he said in reply, and he respected their right to choose their own masters. He hoped they respected his right too: he could never shift his allegiance to the Yorkist king, not even to please good men like themselves. Neutrality was the most he could manage.

The bell struck one o'clock and soon music and the hubbub of a large crowd could be heard even above the ticking of the foliot. A window overlooked the courtyard, and Tom observed a lot of movement, people spinning in rough circles, like inefficient cogs. The king and his guests were dancing in the Italian style, said the captain of the Westminster barracks, and the chaplain said another round of dances was scheduled for two o'clock. Not long afterwards, Tom and his friends parted without hard feelings. The chaplain went off to the town hall, to inspect the clock there, and the captain invited Tom to share a hearty lunch with him in his barracks at Westminster. Tom declined the offer on the grounds that he was feeling tired. In fact, Baynard Castle was the best place to find an Italian today, and that's why he stayed.

He loitered in the courtyard for some time, waiting for the crowd to return for the next round of dances. There was a muffled uproar from one end of the yard, where a large doorway stood invitingly open: a banquet must be in progress in the castle hall. It was tempting to take a peep inside but the approach was guarded by the scaffold Tom had already seen earlier, erected near the foot of the stairs. Too many old friends and allies had been executed for him to feel comfortable in its shadow, even though it was now garlanded with cheerful flowers, and people had been dancing on it not all that long ago. Meanwhile he wasn't actually alone. Some individuals passed by at various times—mature men absorbed in their own affairs, and boys running errands—and dozens more lounged, leaned and squatted along the walls of the courtyard: servants and labourers, waiting to make themselves useful. Some played dice, their livery and sing-song chatter typically Italian. None of them looked like Peter yet Tom did recognise one of them. It was the informant he had been looking for this morning, the shifty-eyed clerk he had already invested more than a pound in, here wreathed in smiles while accepting winnings from some unlucky compatriots. This was not the time or place to resume their secretive acquaintance, so Tom cocked his bonnet over one eye and continued patrolling the yard as if waiting for further instructions or an escort out.

The courtyard looked like the remnant of a much larger bailey. The original dimensions were indicated by a crenelated wall, glimpsed between the roofs of intervening buildings: what was once a proper castle was now a city ward. People and orders must often get lost here, Tom reflected, and maybe that was why he had been left to wander at will, unsupervised. On the other hand, Murderer was still hanging about the gatehouse parapet. Tom recognised him by the unique way his head bobbed between the merlons, an archer habitually ready for an opportunistic shot. Murderer could slot an arrow through the smallest chink in a man's armour, even from a hundred yards. He would have no trouble skewering Tom through his new bonnet, new cloak and new pair of boots, even if the gatehouse had been in Smithfield, outside the city walls. Tom was tempted to leave while he still could. Then again, he wasn't doing anything wrong. If the king's men were planning to kill him, they would have already done it by now.

The shifty-eyed clerk and his friends were not the only Italians playing dice. Other groups were squatting and loitering around games in an alcove between the gatehouse and the clocktower. They were unusually quiet for gamblers, especially for Italians. A poor fit for their elegant livery! Tom approached for a better look and they grew ever quieter, finally becoming silent. White cubes lay unclaimed in their midst or rolled unnoticed from disinterested hands while he passed by. They were large-boned men, their necks brawny, their faces battle-hardened: an all too English look these days. A gleam of metal indicated one man's furtive attempt to conceal a weapon. Tom pretended not to notice and moved on as if enjoying an afternoon stroll. He hadn't found Peter but he had stumbled onto something just as alarming: Peter wasn't the only Englishman in London disguised as an Italian! But whose side were these imposters on, why were they here, and did they have anything to do with his brother? It was a riddle Tom had little time to ponder. A festive gathering soon emerged from the hall, cascading down the stairs and gradually flooding across the yard towards him. He was soon surrounded by more Italians than he believed possible in an English setting. One of them had to be Peter, surely, but their numbers baffled him, just as a massed flock of ducks might baffle a hawk, presenting too many targets all at once. Nothing jumped out at him, nothing rang a bell. Soon a buzz of shawms, the shrill peep of a recorder, a blaring of bagpipes and the banging of a drum summoned his gaze back to the scaffold, where a ring of people in sumptuous attire now frolicked and gyrated above the heads of the crowd. Their moves were accompanied by an immense noise of clattering wood, the sound of feet landing heavily on timber boards

Tom had the strangest experience at that moment. The world no longer kept a single time, and he was no longer in a single place. He was here and now, at Baynard Castle, but he was also somewhere far away, amid the thunder of hooves and the clash of arms, a charge coming hot on the heels of a cacophonous shower of arrows, cavalry wreaking havoc on broken ranks of infantry. Head and shoulders above all the other riders then, and all the other dancers today, galloped, spun and surged an imposing figure, relishing the confusion. A shock of recognition leapt across the years like a madman with an axe: Edward Plantagenet, the Yorkist prince! A king now.

Almost a decade had passed since the catastrophe at Towton, when Tom had chased after him from one scene of carnage and mayhem to another, burning to avenge the deaths of Lord Clifford and the Flower of Craven, but always, always coming short. He was closer to the imposter now than he had ever got then. The big Plantagenet was born to a charmed life and here he looked it, some gorgeous creature flaunting herself at his side, as fickle as victory, as coquettish as England itself. Nearby gossips identified her as Elizabeth Oldhall, the wife of a Smithfield saddler. Tom began thinking how he wouldn't mind throwing a leg over Oldhall himself, if only he could kill her partner. Meanwhile the crowd around him started dancing too, wherever they could create space enough to strut their stuff, hundreds of people talking over each other, over the music, over the noise of each other's feet, shuffling and jumping in rough unison, people skipping in rings or practising steps in small groups, some applauding or just watching, waiting their turn. A few rehearsed steps under the watchful eye of an Italian instructor, a portly figure that Tom recognised from the Mandeville house: Signor Anthony-Whatever-His-Name-Was. He was demonstrating mincing steps to a knot of bejewelled ladies, cordoned off from the crowd like jewels themselves.

The music stopped long enough for the Yorkist king to bow in happy acknowledgement of almost universal applause, and then he nodded a command to the musicians gathered on the hall stairs, when everything started again, a dance much like the one before, with Oldhall hurling herself at her partner as if she were the English crown and he were a king indeed. The crowd resumed its own interpretation of the moves, and Tom resumed the search for a wavering pair of clumsy feet, and a head cocked in scholarly thought. Still nothing jumped out at him.

When next the music stopped, the usurping monarch descended into the crowd, taking Oldhall with him. A rider dismounted is a rider in trouble. Tom checked the urge to go after him. Something else was happening in his own vicinity, the crowd opening up and making way for—what? Rapid attempts by people to get out of the way, and looks of consternation, indicated something big approaching, maybe a great man and his retinue, or the Red Knight and his troop of guards. No, it was an Italian, an Italian with a moustache, dancing with a candle and its stand, showing off his skills to anybody that cared to notice, amusing a few bystanders, annoying others. Something more than just the buffoon's antics and moustache caught Tom's attention: his shoes. He had seen the fawn leather and red laces once before. Nowhere is out of bounds for revenge. Tom moved quickly to intercept him, using his good right hand to grab the culprit by the shoulder, meanwhile keeping the injured left in reserve, if the rascal should put up a fight.

"Try dancing with a man instead!"

The Italian took fright and struggled to break free, exactly like someone with a guilty secret. There was no need for the left hand, any more than if Tom had caught hold of a mere boy: the rascal lacked even the instincts let alone the training necessary for combat. Tom shifted his grip from the shoulder down to the wrist, squeezing sinew and bone until the wretch released his wooden partner.

"*Mi scusi, ma ho altre cose da fare,*" the Italian pleaded, still trying to wriggle free

"Men look each other in the eyes when they talk," Tom objected, tightening his grip on the wrist. "It is you, isn't it!"

"*Non ho idea di cosa si sta parlando.*"

"You are the bastard that trod on my fingers. I recognise your shoes."

The Italian gave up struggling. It was only then that he looked directly at Tom, whereupon Tom experienced another, even greater shock of recognition.

"You!"

"*Sì, il mio nome è Pietro—Pietro Russicelli. Dobbiamo ballare.*"

"Pietro Russicelli?"

The name sounded strangely familiar but everything else had changed—except the eyes. They were still blue and Tom could still look through them, deep into the soul that Peter had never learned to keep hidden, an open book.

"What the hell are you up to?" Tom couldn't help wondering aloud.

"I might ask the same question," came the whispered reply. "*Ma dobbiamo ballare!*"

Peter grabbed the broken fingers of Tom's left hand, in the manner of a dance instructor about to demonstrate some steps. Tom experienced another shock, this time of pain. Peter apologised in Italian—it sounded like an apology—then stepped to the other side and took Tom by the good hand. Tom was in no mood for dancing, especially now that his broken fingers throbbed with a new sense of outrage, yet there was clearly a need for it here: dancing was camouflage and many pairs of eyes were trained on them. They stepped to one side together, then to the other side, next forward and then backward, ending with a quarter turn, when they faced each other again.

"What the hell are you doing here!" Tom insisted in a whisper through gritted teeth.

"*Ora un passo a sinistra!*"

They repeated the previous moves but in the opposite direction, an opportunity for Tom to get some bearings on the situation, while the crowd around them returned to its own interests, watching other dancers, practising steps, applauding, gossiping.

Tom's friend Midge had told him, in the fens, that Peter looked the same as ever. Naturally Tom had been expecting a mawkish scholar of youthful aspect. This was a different Peter. He had lost his boyish face in a lustrous black moustache, his academic pallor in a swarthy tan, his absent-minded clumsiness in the strut and swagger of a young man who fancies his chances in life. Maybe he wasn't clumsy anymore.

"You trod on my hand," Tom reminded him. "At the Mandeville house."

"You stuck it under my foot."

"Two fingers were broken!"

"Hence the bandage."

"What are you up to?"

"You're too late to stop me, Tom, now that I am this close."

"Close enough to throttle you, you idiot!"

"To *him*," Peter explained.

He nodded in the direction of the scaffold, where the king was returning with a new partner, a smaller woman than Oldhall but highly visible, wrapped in a gown divided between day and night, her figure voluptuous in its curves yet firm in its sinuous strength—another shock of recognition! It was her, Pisces Mandeville. What was *she* doing here? Tom turned his horrified attention back to his brother, concentrating on matters in hand.

"The king?" he asked under the cover of the music, just now re-commencing for the next dance.

"Is that what you call him now?" Peter scoffed. "*King?*"

"What are you up to?"

"You think you are the only hero in our family?"

"You have friends—here in the castle?"

"Justice needs no friends."

"This can't be happening."

"The moment he comes within range, his death is certain."

Self-confidence had always been one of Peter's worst faults. His cleverness had long since reduced this complex world to a simple set of propositions, dividing everything between good and evil, Lancastrian and Yorkist, courage and cowardice, without any grey areas in between, all demonstrated in arguments that only Peter and Aristotle could understand. That was how he had once ended up a raw recruit at Bamburgh Castle, loaded with ideals and devoid of experience, just days before it fell to the Yorkist cannons, six years ago. He would have had a brutal awakening to the realities of war then, if Tom hadn't first bundled him into a ship headed for France, with a smack across one ear and a serving of sensible advice in the other: *get a good education and stick to the kind of battles you were made for.* Now here he was in the lion's den, eager for death or glory, as if he had learned nothing. Tom was living his worst nightmare.

"Are you carrying a weapon?"

"*Ora guarda come ballo intorno a te!*" said Peter, skipping around Tom, as he had done with the candle earlier. "*Ora è il tuo turno per farlo!*"

It was Tom's turn to skip around Peter. He executed the move in good order, just as Peter had shown, so that nobody watching them dancing together would suspect anything was amiss. Military discipline had never been more important than now.

"How?" Tom asked when he stopped alongside him again. "How will you kill him?"

"The candlestand, of course."

The alleged weapon still stood where they had left it, looking utterly innocuous. Tom breathed a sigh of relief. It was hardly proof of murderous intent.

"Are you going to set fire to him?" he asked.

"Obviously not. I would have to light it first."

"Hit him on the head with it?"

"You were a hero once," Peter scoffed in his turn. "Now you are just a legend. They are all saying that about you, the exiles in France."

"How will you kill him?" Tom persisted. "How?"

"Watch and learn," came the reply, Peter stepping towards the candlestand.

"Listen to me!" cried Tom, pulling him back by the arm. "Somewhere around here is the most dangerous swordsman in the world today. Up there on the parapet, the deadliest archer. Add a company of thugs, looking to play dice with our skulls, and an entire castle of Yorkists just itching for trouble, plus the king himself, no slouch when it comes to a fight, and surely even you can understand: you are only a danger to him if he dies laughing."

"Then let him die laughing."

The bell overhead tolled as ominously as Fate, iron clapper striking iron cheek once.

"Your mind is made up?"

"Nothing can stop me now."

"Not even this?"

The bell tolled a second time and Tom threw a punch with his good hand. He didn't give it all he had but it was enough to send his brother sprawling across the cobbles. The reaction was as immediate as a trap springing shut. A dancer nearby threw off his fancy cloak, dagger at the ready, and more arrived an instant later, including the fake Italians that had been playing dice, some looking ready to gamble with bare knuckles, others staking their claims with flashing swords. Everyone else recoiled, shouted, protested, screamed. A trumpet sounded an alarm, the music silent at last. Peter was quickly manhandled back onto his feet, struggling with a burly guard at each arm. Another two grabbed Tom but he knew better than to resist. They had been caught in some kind of ambush but caught doing—what exactly?

The king arrived with a mighty bound, impatient for action, an alarmed and irate look in his eyes.

"What goes on here!" he demanded to know. "What goes on! This is my castle, all these people my guests! Who are *these* two?"

"Traitor!" Peter shouted.

"He means me!" Tom was quick to assure everyone. "I'm his brother and I punched him just now."

"Search them for weapons!"

"This is a fine way to treat guests!" Tom protested as he began to be searched, the guards pulling him this way and that, as if he might be a bread roll in need of tearing apart. "I was invited here! Ask the men that brought me. Jack Murderer Shaft was one, up there on the parapet. There are no weapons on my brother either. He is here as a dance instructor—a danger only to his partners! Look at my hand, if you don't believe me: he trod on it. That's why I punched him just now."

He managed to free his bandaged hand, displaying it to the anxious and outraged crowd that gaped at them from all sides. The guards grabbed the hand again, and it was then that he noticed a woman pushing her way through the king's other friends. The recognition was mutual.

"*You!*" she gasped, her black and white gown matching her wild stare, as if she were bursting apart with contradictions. "And this is your—*brother*, you said?"

Here was too good an opportunity to miss.

"Yes, brothers," Tom affirmed, eager to get their story sorted early, before anyone could think to separate them. "Tom and Peter Roussell! Peter is a scholar. He left England six years ago, studying in Paris for a career in the Church. Now he wants to be a dance instructor instead, the idiot. I chanced to hear about it up north, so I came to London looking for him. He has been hiding from me ever since, the sneak, but he is going back to his studies in Paris, with another black eye if he gives me any more trouble. There is nothing sinister about any of this."

"Tom Roussell!" the king marvelled, since they had never got this close before.

"The rebel!" the woman affirmed. "The brother has been in my house, pretending to be Italian. *This* one showed up there the other day in a fake beard. Everyone be on your guard! They are a threat to your safety, Your Majesty. I am certain of it."

Nothing excites a crowd to violence sooner than a woman with a shrill complaint, in Tom's experience, and he acted quickly to put this one in her place.

"We are a threat?" he scoffed. "To each other, maybe, but not the king. Where are our weapons? Go home and keep your sauce for your pies, you fool woman!"

"I saw a candlestand somewhere," she persisted. "The brother was carrying it. It must be a weapon of some kind, Your Majesty. Find it, someone!"

The Red Knight now appeared, pushing his way forward with the would-be murder weapon in his grasp, right on cue. Fortunately, the improbable weapon looked less deadly than ever. The candle had fractured in the melee and it was only held together by the long wick, so that it hung drooping in a shamefaced manner. However, saboteurs, spies and assassins are about as popular in a castle as heresy in a church pulpit, and men have got lynched on less evidence, once suspicions have been aroused.

"A candle is her witness!" Tom responded with a bold laugh. "And who is she to speak out of turn? *Susanna Mandeville*! Remember that name, and watch out for her, every man in her vicinity. She ambushed me once with a kiss at Huntingdon. Ask people there, if you don't believe me. Luckily, I got free. I'd sooner kiss a dead fish. Yes, she kisses like a dead fish and now she'll do anything to shut me up, in case you others learn from my mistake."

This silenced her for a moment but it didn't keep her in her place. She flew at him with both hands, clawing at him as if to tear out his tongue. His arms were pinned by guards and he managed to step back far enough to draw them in like shutters, but somehow she still found an opening and swung a right fist that caught him on the point of the chin, so that his head turned sharply. He was astonished to see darkness for a dizzying moment, a sure sign that she had come within a whisker of knocking him out. She would have thrown another punch if the king himself hadn't restrained her. His men grinned at her temerity, and the king almost laughed, until someone else pushed through the crowd, arriving breathless. It was Book. He wasn't carrying any literature with him on this occasion but Tom still recognised him by another notorious trait: Book's head was as far from his heart as the human neck can manage, giving him the air of a stoat.

"Separate them!" cried the stoat between deep breaths, panting from his hurry to arrive.

"I've got her," the king assured him.

"The brothers!" Book explained. "Separate them, Your Majesty, before they stitch their stories together. There is treason afoot. We must get to the bottom of it."

"We are guests here!" Tom protested, determined not to be separated from Peter. "I punched my own brother, that's all—you think I did that as part of some stupid plot? I was invited here. My brother was invited too. This is no way to treat guests."

It was an important point of protocol.

"Your Majesty, both these men are *my* responsibility," pleaded Book. "They have been under my surveillance this whole time."

"Were they invited here?" the king demanded to know.

"I arranged for them both to be here, Your Majesty, because I knew they would try something, and it was my intention to catch them red-handed in the attempt."

"Congratulations!" Tom scoffed. "You caught us in a brotherly quarrel. Is that a crime?"

"They are our guests till I learn otherwise," the king decreed. "Release them."

"No, Your Majesty!" Pisces pleaded. "For your own safety, no!"

"These men are our enemies and they must be kept restrained!" Book added, appealing to the crowd. "They are a danger to His Majesty's life and a threat to the security of this kingdom. Everyone, prepare yourselves for action! Expect trouble. *All'erta! All'erta!*"

This was loudly supported on all sides until the king silenced everyone with a wave of his huge hand. Then he pulled Susanna Mandeville even closer to his side, commanding her in particular to keep quiet. He waited for his prisoners to be released from the clutches of the guards, all the while giving Tom a frank look of appraisal from head to toe. Tom repaid the favour. The Plantagenet was a giant, well over six feet high, hard work for the men that must bury him, maybe not so hard for any man that was born to kill him. Tom was the Beast still, perhaps a little flabby around the middle, a bit soft after years of giving orders rather than obeying them, but definitely a match for His Highness. The man himself soon acknowledged as much.

"This is Tom Roussell, the Beast of Ferrybridge!" he informed the crowd around them. "Let me tell you a few things about this man before anyone else tries anything. Settle all of you now, and hear me out!"

The big imposter waited for some more protests to subside, then discouraged further outcries with a forbidding glare. The Mandeville woman still wanted to argue but he silenced her with another squeeze of her waist, followed by a shake of his head. She rested a protective hand on his chest, and fixed Tom with a hateful look. Tom's hackles rose still more. Her king shot a smile at him before addressing the crowd again.

"Tom Roussell made his name at the river Aire ten years ago, standing alone against the best and finest that an entire county could muster!" he shouted for all to hear. "The crossing was at Ferrybridge. He was all that stood in their way. That's right! One man against three hundred, a third dead inside half an hour. The rest fled. I heard it from good witnesses or I'd never have believed it. So many deaths are an everlasting regret! Yet it was an act of heroism. By an enemy? I have many friends who were his comrades once. Shall we punish those friends now just because they fought on the wrong side then?"

"It is wrong to lose," Tom couldn't help saying.

"His archer did most of the real fighting for him on that occasion and on every other occasion since," the Book informed everyone. "He's a fairy tale more than a legend."

"A warrior is entitled to a rest sometimes," Tom countered.

"Try joking with William Wallace, once I stick your head next to his," Book hissed.

"Lighten up, Read-a-lot," the king urged him. "Today the man is guilty of causing a disturbance, that's all."

"You must not acquit him of treason without proper enquiry," the learned stoat objected.

The king ignored this, turned back to Tom and smiled yet again as if they might actually be friends, meanwhile still keeping an arm around Susanna Mandeville's waist, a gesture that struck Tom as somehow the act of an irreconcilable foe.

"I saw you in the fighting at Towton, not long after your heroism at Ferrybridge," the imposter remarked pleasantly, the Mandeville woman still looking daggers. "My bodyguard had heard reports and they kept me posted on all your movements."

"I was trying to kill you," Tom couldn't help remembering. "A long time ago."

"Then last year, it was you that escorted me to Middleham Castle, wasn't it?"

"Yes, your prison. Someone had to do it."

Guarding the royal prisoner might have been one of Tom's proudest moments, if he had captured him in battle, but the imposter had been betrayed by his own brother, the duke of Clarence, and had surrendered to the earl of Warwick without a fight. It had been a shameful episode in the history of the kingdom, and Tom had wanted no part of it, but the earl had trusted him and nobody else to keep the royal prize safe from Lancastrians and Yorkists alike, and Tom had accepted it as his duty.

"I glimpsed you several times while I was the earl's guest," the big phoney continued, "but you kept your distance. You should have introduced yourself to me, and maybe we could have been friends even then."

"Is it my fault I never liked you?"

"He can't hide his hatred even now," observed Book.

"He would be less dangerous if he did hide it?" the king fired back.

"He would be less dangerous if he were dead," Book insisted.

"I don't kill guests," came the oh-so regal reply.

"Your Majesty, you must listen to your friends!" said Pisces, still resting a hand on *Her* Majesty's king-sized chest. "This man is a danger to you. I have a bad feeling about this. He must be kept locked away, for your own safety."

"These matters need more scrutiny," he conceded. "Everyone else back to the hall for the next course! I'll be there shortly. Guards, stay ready."

The crowd headed reluctantly back to the great hall, under the watchful command of stewards, and meanwhile Peter and Tom were separated and encircled by a grim troop of hard-faced heavies. Tom waved his encouragement in a gap between their belligerent faces but Peter didn't respond, too busy nursing the eye Tom had punched. Meanwhile the king went and stood with Pisces, tête-à-tête by the scaffold, and Book hurried into the hall, probably to hunt out some thumb screws. The Red Knight stood guard over Peter's candlestand, examining it as suspiciously as a dog sniffing a tree. Hospitality in His Majesty's home was already strained near to breaking point and a battle seemed to be looming. Tom had learned from the Flower of Craven that there was always one place where a man could regain strength, determination and composure, no matter how desperate things might look: the Heart. He closed his eyes and went there now.

Tom trod the darkened path that wound through the tall sentinels of the forest, guardians of the river Wharfe, towards a rocky enclosure, the almost-cave where Lord Clifford had schooled his men in the right character, all gathered by the waterfall, the river's finest stream descending lighter than rain, purified by the elemental spirits of fire and air. Here their company had always assembled, the living and the dead, in shadows that moved, amid rocks that dreamed, under a sun that warmed the green canopy of the Flower's living cathedral, remembering, listening, drawing strength from each other for the future. They had long expected Tom to trade blows with the Yorkist king, and now he had exchanged words instead, yet there was no murmur against him, just a rustle of departed friends opening their ranks to receive him once more. Here he stood and grew, moment by moment, gathering courage from stillness.

Tom was shaken from the Heart by a stir around him. Pisces was headed back to the great hall, escorted by a page, and the king was now in conference with a courtier that Tom had last seen at Royston: Lord Hastings. At the other end of the yard, some royal flunkies were in earnest conversation with the Red Knight, and one of them soon glided to the king with a report of some kind. Hastings himself went to speak with the Red Knight then returned to the king for a quick conference, next retraced his steps and loudly ordered everyone to follow the Red Knight, whereupon the lout with the red hand grabbed Peter's wooden dancing partner and swaggered off towards the bailey buildings, Hastings on his heels. The guards prompted the prisoners to get moving too and soon they were all trooping down a lane, past stables, an inn, stores and houses, around some workshops and into a yard, where stood the remains of what must once have been a church. It was missing all but one of its stained glass windows, scorch marks on the stonework indicating a recent fire, and the roof had been patched with new shingles. The Red Knight was the first to enter, followed by Hastings, Peter and some guards. When it came his own turn, Tom paused at the blackened doorway, his surprise deepening as he looked in. The church was now a scriptorium, a score of scribes penning whatever letters, reports, records or accounts a king and his officials need preserved and copied. The kingdom's business was in no better shape than the building, but at least the high, open windows offered good light to work by.

A row of desks, alternating with candles—each like the one Peter had danced with—extended along the only aisle, and a smiling Lord Hastings waited for Tom next to the one nearest the door. Both men had seen enough of each other at Royston for Tom not to be fooled by the smile, and for Hastings not to be in awe of the legend.

"Be smart and you'll get out of this alive," Hasting whispered.

"Alive wouldn't hurt," Tom conceded. "Why here?"

"It's where your brother got this candle," Hastings explained, indicating the item in question, sagging next to the first desk. "Read-a-lot thinks he has found evidence of treason. It is all bluff."

"You are telling me this because …"

"I made you the Mandeville's sergeant-at-arms for a reason. The girl is overly proud. Train her."

Just in case there was any doubt about his meaning, he laid a hand on Peter's candlestand then carefully straightened the flagging wax, so that it stood erect. The moment he let it go, the candle sagged again, as if ashamed of the meaning put on it. Tom was astonished. Men-at-arms are sometimes given indecent orders but the Flower of Craven had always kept their missions simple, too simple for orders like this. However, he needed friends, so he nodded his understanding of the message and left Hastings to mistake it for his assent, before continuing further inside.

Peter had been given some freedom to move and he was now haunting the middle of the nave, the least damaged part of the building, where multi-coloured light poured through the only unbroken window. The window was a magnificent example of the glazier's art, depicting someone at a writing desk, quill in hand. Tom supposed it must be a holy scribe, probably Moses writing the Ten Commandments, but it turned out to be a famous poet, the name inscribed in black letters on a scroll of white glass: *Geoffrey Chaucer*. Tom had vague memories of studying him as a schoolboy but now he was more interested in his shadow, because Peter was standing in it. The fake Italian changed colours as he shifted this way and that, a patchwork of red, green and yellow. He reminded Tom of a fugitive deer, brought to bay in autumnal woods, when its hues change with the changing light, filtered through green, red and yellow leaves. The punched eye was already swollen and looked alarmingly red, sometimes black, depending which colours were added to it. Tom stepped closer, hoping for some meaningful kind of exchange.

"Stay calm, say little," he whispered, giving Peter's shoulder a comforting squeeze with the fingers of his good hand.

Peter shrugged him off, still sulking over his bruised eye and his spoiled plans for heroic martyrdom, before guards hurried between them, anxious to stop them sharing their stories or planning their escape. Tom continued his stroll along the nave, out from Chaucer's shadow and into the broad daylight streaming through the other windows. Sunlight quivered in the feathered pens of the scribes busy in the adjacent aisle while he kept an eye out for some kind of make-shift weapon or escape route, in case things progressed from bad to worse. The candlestands between desks could prove useful in an emergency, wielded as clubs or missiles, but it seemed wisest to ignore them for now. The windows looked inviting, if someone could fly like a bird, otherwise the sills were too high. Something like a chancel survived at the far end, fenced off by a grille. Tom wondered whether or not it would give access to a door but his approach was quickly blocked by the Red Knight, standing with his thumbs in his belt, sneering. A strange babbling behind the thug's back suggested that he was guarding more than just a gate, and Tom managed to snatch glimpses of something mysterious happening in the aisle. The noise was coming from a desk, where two scribes sat with a man of high status, his satin sleeves terminating in ermine: Lord Grey! One of the scribes was uttering an outlandish language completely unknown to Tom, and the other was talking Latin, but Lord Grey spoke only in English, mangled as usual. At first glance, it looked like a chance meeting of verbal misfits, but then a second glance revealed a tattered manuscript, open at an extraordinary diagram, depicting a human figure, half man, half woman, encircled by a dragon swallowing its own tail. It reminded Tom of some weird illustrations he had once found in a book on alchemy, as a young page at Skipton Castle, and he guessed the manuscript must have something to do with Grey's obsession with that arcane subject. Further curiosity was barred by the Red Knight, once more moving to obstruct his view, so Tom turned aside to browse some literature on an adjacent shelf. This was mostly disappointing stuff, a pile of official documents, good only for keeping clerks in salaried employment, yet there were also a few books for amusement and instruction, made out in multiple copies, probably as gifts for the king's friends. Tom was still perusing titles when Book suddenly appeared at his elbow, like a stoat in a rabbit warren.

"I think your stay in London is going to be almost as long as," he said, pausing to run a finger along some leather spines, "William Wallace's."

"His pickled head has made a big impression on you," Tom observed, "but I'm not even dead yet."

"Soon," Book vowed.

The learned stoat dragged out a volume with *Cicero* branded on the cover in big letters, opened it on one of the lecterns guarding the archways of the aisle and stood reading silently. Two can play that game. Tom chanced on a volume he was familiar with from his schoolboy days—*De Arte Venandi cum Avibus: The Art of Hunting with Birds*—and he set it open on the lectern next to Book's. He was carefully leafing through the pages, searching for something his rusty Latin could manage, when the king came striding through the door, grabbed himself a chair and carried it as far as Lord Hastings, now seated at the edge of Chaucer's shadow. There the Yorkist pretender sat like a man in complete control of his surroundings, removing his bonnet, shaking out his locks and draping one leg over an armrest. The room stooped to a collective bow. Tom couldn't bring himself to share the obeisance, and neither could Peter. Fortunately, nobody seemed to notice their disrespect. Peter was still camouflaged by stained glass, and Tom was already bowing over his book for a closer look at some troublesome words. The scribes were all ushered outside and the king's attention soon rested on Lord Grey.

"Is that you, Lord Grey?"

The nobleman rose from his studies and again bowed to his monarch

"Lord Grey has recently made a great discovery," Hastings said for him.

"Hmm, wah, fwt, a treatise on the precepts of Hermes Trismegistus, mmm, written by Avicenna!" the nobleman explained. "Well fwt, Arabic most of it huh but the Latin says, hmmm, there is a fourteenth precept, uh, which was never before suspected by masters of the alchemical science, what say you."

"Here in my scriptorium?"

"Hmmph, a butler from Boston found it, fwah! He hardly knew the value of it. Five pounds he wanted for it eh. Huh I would have paid ten times as much, if he had asked, hmmm. Wah the secret discovery of Avicenna, a fourteenth precept! In Arabic. So I brought it here, look you, for getting into Latin and English pfwt. Lord Hastings translated the arrange … arranged the trans … arranged the translation for me hmrwa. A great discovery!"

"Our coffers will soon be brimming with alchemical gold!" the king observed with a smile for Hastings—the sort of smile Tom might have shared with a lieutenant if one of their men had reported for duty with a woman in his baggage. "But I have many guests and duties awaiting me, so let's get on with it. Read-a-lot! You have something to say, don't you?"

Book turned a page with relish, as if flaying a victim.

"The Roussell brothers are in London to assassinate Your Majesty and destroy your government," he announced without even lifting his eyes from Cicero. "They are in league with the rebels in Lincolnshire and with the exiles in France, in a plot that involves them personally in murder and arson. I already have all the proof I need."

"In that book?" Tom wondered. "Cicero is your witness?"

"Such jokes are often a sign of guilt," he advised the king.

"I once heard that you can read poetry, sing psalms and sip soup all at the same time," Tom persisted. "So why can't I tell jokes and be serious at the same time?"

He turned a page of *De Arte Venandi cum Avibus*, demonstrating blithe indifference to the specious trial Book was trying to arrange.

"He is mocking us," Book observed.

"I couldn't quite cut through his northern accent," said the Yorkist king, casually smoothing out a wrinkle in his hose. "Guests should be careful not to abuse our hospitality. On the other hand, these men are our guests and not our prisoners."

"Your Majesty, I cannot serve you as you deserve if my hands are kept tied," Book pleaded.

"I will permit some pressure," said the big monarch after looking thoughtful for a while.

"So, Tom Roussell, let's start with you," said Book, savagely turning another leaf of Cicero. "Why did you come to London, if not to commit treason?"

"I explained my reasons outside, didn't I? I had heard my brother was here. The sluggard is supposed to be in Paris, studying for a career in the Church. I came here to find him and send him back."

"That isn't what you told Lord Hastings in Royston. You told him that you were looking for employment in a quiet household."

"That too."

"Lord Hastings subsequently helped you to an indenture with a Southwark merchant, Farthings Mandeville, all of a week ago. Yet you didn't report for work until the day before yesterday. Why was that?"

"I see!" Tom scoffed. "You are going to say I was busy with some kind of treasonable plot, and that's why I didn't show up. A fine imagination you have! The Mandeville son told me not to start work for a while, on account of his sister being cranky over that kiss I mentioned earlier. So, I waited a few days. That is all there is to it."

"You didn't report for work yesterday either."

"My fingers got broken. I'm allowed at least one day off for injuries, aren't I?"

"You said your brother trod on them, and that's why you punched him."

"He trod on them in the Mandeville house the day I reported for work."

"Yet you punched him only today."

"He was disguised as an Italian then too and I only now found out it was him."

"*Disguised*," Book noted, as if it might be the rare conjugation of a Latin verb, or important evidence of treason. "Why is your brother disguised as an Italian?"

"He was hiding from me, because he knew I'd send him back to his studies in Paris."

"Yet you didn't recognise him when he trod on your hand?"

"I did say he was disguised, didn't I?"

"Didn't *he* recognise *you*?"

"I was wearing a beard from a pageant play when I was visiting the Mandevilles. I did it to test their powers of observation. The fact that my brother and I both happened to be in their house the same day, both in disguise—that is something of a strange co-incidence, I grant you. But it was the Mandevilles' doing as much as ours. They invited Peter to teach dancing and they indentured me to be their sergeant-at-arms. You don't suppose they are in on our treasonable plot, do you? They must be, if coincidences are proof of guilt."

"He should have been a lawyer," quipped Lord Hastings.

"Only because he makes such a poor witness," said Book. "He is obviously lying. I shall return to him later."

He signalled for somebody at the door to approach: Signor Anthony-Whatever. The portly dance instructor paused in front of the king, giving him a bow as ornamental as one of those Venetian carnivals people often talk about, then he turned on Peter and engaged him in a heated argument in Italian. It quickly resulted in some colourful pushing and shoving in Chaucer's shadow, and ended with their hands in each other's hair, both pulling like washerwomen fighting over a scarf. Some guards separated them. The real Italian made a rude gesture with a finger inches from Peter's face then spun on his irate heels and left.

"What was that about?" asked the king.

"This young man's Italian is very poor," said Book, waving a dismissive hand at Peter. "Signor Antonio Della Bosca only hired him on the understanding that Englishmen wouldn't notice. Now that he is clearly English, he has dismissed him from his service and is refusing to pay him his wages."

"Nobody would know I was English if my brother hadn't told everyone," Peter objected, one hand cupping the eye Tom had punched. "Therefore, Della Bosca has no case against me. I am entitled to my wages,"

"The brother has a logical turn of mind," Hastings observed.

Peter had been a fierce debater as a student at Bolton Abbey, proving anything from the existence of God to the identity of the classmate who had once stolen his inkwell. He was in a much more dangerous forum now but evidently its horrible potential had yet to dawn on him fully. Book was ready to educate him.

"Here I have Signor Della Bosca's written testimony," said the learned stoat, taking a document out of his cloak and waving it about for all to see, "wherein he states that Peter Roussell consorted with manifest traitors abroad and with suspicious types here in England and, moreover, that he attempted to draw Della Bosca himself into his perfidious schemes. Proof of treason!"

"Della Bosca is a liar and a cheat," Peter objected. "Ask the Mandevilles about a missing pie and some jewels he took from students. Proof of a weak case!"

"*A liar and a cheat?*" Book queried. "Is that why you worked for him?"

"It's an imperfect world," Peter answered with a shrug.

It was a shrewd response. Tom turned another leaf, satisfied that they were doing alright for the moment.

"Tell me something about yourself," the king invited the champion debater. "And somebody get a physician for his eye."

"What is there to say?" Peter answered as a guard hurried off for a doctor.

"Why not admit to being a traitor?" Book interposed. "Or are you a coward as well as a sneak?"

"A coward and a sneak?" Peter responded with disdain. "You may banish your enemies from a faithless kingdom. You cannot banish old loyalties from a faithful heart."

This was impressive rhetoric but it sounded much like an admission of treason. Tom gently lifted *De Arte Venandi cum Avibus* with both hands, assessing its weight: it might yet make a useful missile.

"I admire loyalty," the king declared. "A kingdom cannot survive without it."

"Sometimes loyalty is proof of treason, Your Majesty," added Book. "So, Pietro Russicelli! Tell the king what you have been doing in France."

"Why don't *you* tell him, if you know so much," Peter sneered.

"Proud and stubborn," Book observed, "just like all Lancastrian hotheads. In fact, you have spent the past six years in Lorraine, in the company of the false queen, Margaret of Anjou, and her scheming band of exiles."

"Actually, I have spent all that time in Paris, studying for a career in the Church."

"You were never in Paris."

"Don't be absurd," Tom protested. "I have been paying for his education in Paris, every year for six years now. Ask the Earl of Warwick. He arranged the letters of credit."

"His letters were always redirected to Lorraine, to the very chateau your brother has been sharing with the traitors," Book insisted. "Do you think I have no spies of my own?"

This had a horrible ring of truth. Chaucer was painting Peter green, red and yellow, yet he still managed to look as guilty as the day Tom had surprised him behind the alder copse at home, sneaking a drink from one of Ebbtide George's flagons of wine.

"What did you do with the funds I sent?" Tom demanded to know.

"Some of the exiles are scholars," Peter explained lamely. "Honestly Tom, they are the best teachers in the world. Your money was well spent."

"They include some of the best legal minds this country has ever produced," the king acknowledged with a smile.

"My brother is *my* responsibility, Your Majesty," Tom pleaded, even managing an obsequious bow, because the situation was now desperate enough to require it. "He has betrayed me, not you, and I'll deal with it at the appropriate time."

"I also have a younger brother: the duke of Clarence," the king offered with a chuckle. "He is now the earl of Warwick's son-in-law. I never gave him permission for that either. These indiscretions are only a problem if they keep happening."

"They do keep happening," said Book. "Peter Roussell removed a candlestand from here earlier today. There are too many witnesses for him to deny it. The only question is why he took it."

"I used it to demonstrate some dance steps," Peter explained. "Nobody said I couldn't."

"Let's hear what Lord Grey has to say."

All eyes turned towards Lord Grey. He looked surprised to be called upon for evidence, until the Red Knight whispered something to him, when his face brightened with a look of fiendish delight. Testimony usually carries more weight with a nobleman's authority behind it, and Tom guessed it was going to be weak.

"Huh, the candlestand turns into a dagger hmmm," Grey declared, the Red Knight nodding in affirmation. "Hrwa he was going to stab you with it, Your Majesty. Italians one moment, devils the next, these Roussells. Born traitors both, fwt."

The allegation was even weaker than Tom had expected

"A dagger?" he scoffed, bestowing an ironic glance on the nearest candlestand. "Lord Grey thinks he can turn anything into gold, so maybe he can demonstrate some of his skills as an alchemist by turning this stand here into a dagger."

"He has to turn himself into an alchemist first," Peter added with a scornful laugh. "Didn't we all hear him just now, bragging about his precious manuscript and its fourteen precepts? He spent five pounds on it, he said. Five pounds! Anyone can get copies of that same manuscript in France for nothing. It's a blatant forgery. I know because someone tried selling one to Margaret of Anjou and the exiles in Lorraine, but they were too smart to fall for it. Some alchemist! Some witness!"

Grey responded to this information with a shocked look, then a furious glare, his eyes growing as bloodshot as a wolf turned inside out. The Red Knight rested a hand on his shoulder.

"Let me deal with this, My Lord," he offered, whereupon he strode past Tom, past Peter, past Hastings and the king, all the way to the desk nearest the door, where he grabbed Peter's wooden dancing partner and then returned with it to the king's side, declaring: "This is the stand the accused took from here. Now behold a dagger, Your Majesty!"

He pulled the candle from its brass holder and tossed it aside. Then, after some concentrated effort to loosen an iron collar, he pulled the candlestick from its wooden base. It emerged with a wicked point, glittering with the deadly intent of a stiletto. Tom was shocked. Hastings looked shocked. The king looked shocked. Even Peter looked shocked, except in his case it was the look of someone shocked to have been caught lying yet again.

"A trick I learned from a Neapolitan," said the Red Knight, inserting the candlestick back into the end of the stand, then tightening the collar. "Neapolitans will use anything for a weapon, and this kind of stand is common. It is the very sort of thing a trained assassin looks for, once he gets inside the gate."

"What further proof do we need?" said Book. "Margaret of Anjou's father is the king of Naples. Peter Roussell was trained by Neapolitan agents, at her behest, then sent here as an assassin—yours, Your Majesty. Hang him."

"This is ridiculous," Tom protested. "We just saw my brother wrestling with that tub of lard, the real Italian, Anthony Della-Something. I'd back a mere candle to beat the pair of them any day. The Red Knight himself struggled to get it free. My scholarly brother couldn't manage it even if he tried for a month!"

An important moment had been reached. The king removed his leg from the armrest of his chair and set both feet on the floor, readying himself for action.

"I am beginning to suspect treason," he warned the guards, whereupon they all began pressing towards the centre of the room.

"Treason?" Peter scoffed as he retreated further into the poet's shadow, till the way was blocked by a desk. "I could crush you all under the weight of this scriptorium, Archimedes says, if only I had a lever long enough to move it, or I could burn you all in the flames of a mighty fire, if I had the mind of a necromancer. I could even try turning you all into gold, if I were Lord Grey, which thank God I am not. But *could* doesn't mean *would*, and *would* doesn't mean *will*. You can't prove anything like that, except your own stupidity."

"A lecture in law," Book jeered. "Why did you come to London if not to assassinate the king?"

"To practise my Italian," Peter retorted, as if humour might rescue the situation. "Didn't you say it was poor?"

"Unable to forget a grievance," Book observed. "Such men are always dangerous."

"Peter is *my* problem!" Tom implored the king. "If he does anything after this that you judge to be in any way treasonable, let *my* life be forfeit."

"A traitor's pledge," jeered Book, resting an elbow on his Cicero. "So, I return to you, Beast of Ferrybridge. You were at the king's manor, outside Stamford, around the time it was torched. You took some horses from there. What did you do with them?"

"Those horses didn't belong to the king, as I already told Lord Hastings at Royston. Most of them were inferior mounts, brought up from London."

"You are evading the question. What did you do with those horses?"

"I sold one of them at Royston. My man sold the others at Oakham."

"Liar. Your man took the others into Lincolnshire, to supply the rebels with mounts. Sir Robert Welles has them now."

Even inferior horses can win battles, if they carry the right men to the right place at the right time. Evidently Book had a good informant.

"Yes, I sent them to Sir Robert Welles," Tom now decided to admit, "but it was nothing to do with any so-called rebellion. I was just repaying him for an old debt, that's all."

"Yet you have been telling people that they were sold at Oakham."

"Sir Robert isn't popular here in the south, so naturally I avoided mentioning him. Why would I want to turn people against me? Is lying for one's own convenience a crime?"

"We all tell lies when it suits us," Hastings agreed.

"Have you brought up the prisoner?" Book asked a guard just then appearing at the door. "Bring him in."

A man was brought into the room under guard and in chains. He bowed to the king then stood with an air of sullen defiance, looking every inch like a felon after a rough encounter with the Law. His hair was dishevelled, his face puffy and blear-eyed, his clothes torn. Tom recognised him in spite of that. It was Smith, the Waltham Abbey blacksmith.

"This man has been accused of conspiring with rebels to set England ablaze," Book explained, "as part of a campaign of arson instigated and financed by our so-called guest, Tom Roussell."

"Ridiculous," Tom protested.

"You make a ridiculous guest," Book conceded with a hiss for a laugh, "but did you give him the money or did you not?"

"I gave him ten pounds but——"

"A lot of money," Book noted.

"I was drunk at the time. I got it back from Smith after I sobered up."

"And God forgive you, for I won't!" Smith snarled, rattling his chains. "I have been interrogated, chained, beaten, pushed around and denied sleep ever since yesterday, all on account of you and that accursed ten pounds, which I never even got to keep."

"Where is the ten pounds now?" Book asked Tom while turning another page of Cicero.

Tom stifled the dismay he felt on Smith's behalf, concentrating on just answering the question.

"I have already spent some of it——on rent, on purchases like this cloak, these boots and bonnet, and some other trifles."

"Is the blacksmith your friend?"

"Just someone I met, that's all."

"Then let's hear what else the blacksmith has to say," said Book, looking up from his *Cicero* to encourage Smith. "Would you call this traitor from the north a friend of yours?"

"He is no friend of mine," said Smith.

"Would you say he is capable of treason?"

"He is capable of anything!" the blacksmith declared, emphasising his words with another shake of his chains.

"Now let us review the allegations," said Book, once more leaning on his dead Roman as if they were bosom friends. "It is said that Roussell gave you ten pounds to start fires throughout England, as a signal for rebellion. I think you refused to be part of this treacherous scheme, and that is why he took the money back. He even threatened to kill you, if you didn't keep quiet. Will you swear to all this on oath, or do you need more time to think?"

"This is all rubbish!" Tom protested.

The blacksmith looked as if he might be about to pull an iron from the fire, saving himself at Tom's expense, but instead he hung his head in stubborn silence, every inch a witness that won't connive in a lawyer's tricks. Tom thanked his lucky stars for honest men.

"Silence is no proof of a conspiracy," Hastings commented.

"Let the blacksmith go," the king decided.

"I don't need him now that I have the brother to work on," Book conceded.

"On what charge am I to be held?" Peter demanded to know. "You haven't come anywhere close to proving your case yet."

"Your moustache is un-English," came the arrogant reply. "That will do for a start."

The chains were removed from Smith, and he fired one last, accusing look at Tom.

"The next time you pass through Waltham Abbey," he said, rubbing his chaffed wrists, "keep going."

He left a free man. Tom would have breathed a sigh of relief on behalf of the blacksmith if Book's threat to start working on Peter weren't still ringing in his ears. It was time to take the bull by the horns. Their friends in France might have persuaded Peter that he was an assassin but Tom knew his brother better—better even than Peter knew himself. Now everyone must be made to see the truth, so Tom left his lectern, grabbed his brother by the scruff of the neck, dragged him from the coloured shadows into the daylight streaming through a missing window, then bewildered him with a flurry of rapid strikes, cuffs, prods and slaps about the face, which Peter resisted with comic ineptitude.

"Apologise to His Majesty!" Tom demanded.

"I'm sorry, I'm sorry!" Peter blabbed, a hero in theory only.

"Bow to His Majesty!" Tom added, forcing his head down between his knees, as easy as layering a yew branch.

Peter made the humiliating bow to their hated enemy then threw himself on the nearest desk, weeping inconsolably. Tom almost felt sorry for him.

"He is harmless," he told the king. "I stake my life on it."

The king pondered the matter for a few moments.

"Agreed," he soon said.

He rose from his chair and led Hastings and Book to the doorway for a private conference. Tom returned to the book on hawks, confident that his timely intervention had saved the day. The conference soon ended. Only Hastings and Book returned.

"You have heard about the Friendship Tour?" Hastings asked Tom. "It will be our last attempt at peace with your friends in Lincolnshire. Farthings Mandeville and his daughter have accepted an invitation to come with us, so you must come too."

Tom avoided saying anything, meanwhile admiring the diagram of a goshawk.

"You are indentured to serve them," Hastings prompted him, "and you have some training to do—remember?"

"I am also indentured to serve the Earl of Warwick."

"He could be coming as well."

"I would rather hear that from the man himself."

"These brothers need more persuading," said Book.

"*I* will come," Tom then offered.

"Both of you will come," Hastings insisted. "I will see to it that you are both well looked after."

"I also will keep an eye on them," said Book, returning Cicero to the shelves.

"Mmm my Red Knight will help too hmmm," said Lord Grey. "You hear that, Red Knight, ha? You will keep a watch on these Roussells, hmmm."

The Red Knight approached Tom's lectern, peered at his book then turned to the title page.

"*The Art of Hunting with Birds,*" he observed, translating from the Latin. "Anything in there about hunting Beasts of Ferrybridge, Tom? I'll write that chapter myself. Yes, My Lord, it will be my pleasure."

He closed the book.

Not the End

Now read

MIRRORED SWORD PART TWO:

THE TOUR

Printed in Great Britain
by Amazon

73229729R00214